The Sooner

S.G. Alan

authorHOUSE®

Cover illustration by Tania Scheyvaerts

AuthorHouse™ UK Ltd.
500 Avebury Boulevard
Central Milton Keynes, MK9 2BE
www.authorhouse.co.uk
Phone: 08001974150

First published by AuthorHouse 11/12/2010.

ISBN: 978-1-4520-2404-2 (sc)
ISBN: 978-1-4520-2405-9 (e)

This book is printed on acid-free paper.

Preface

Pal:

Now here's the thing. I've been thinking for some time now that I'd like to tell you about what happened back then…what really happened I should say. You know it's all very well pretending that I'm completely deficient and Zerrin, although she's always prosing on about truth and honesty and such, says I should just keep a lid on it but it's so bursting to come out. The fact is I'm not just this quiet, ordinary person who walks about in varying degrees of saeness like everyone else. I've seen things, I know things. Amazing, cool stuff that if you knew it you'd think I was some kind of hero or something. Well I suppose Jak was the hero really but I did some pretty neat activities too and I'm a bit fed up with hiding my light under a bushel if you know what I mean. So look… this is the deal…you tell me what you know, I mean what the Monitor and the witnesses told you …all that you saw on Channel One and then I'll tell you the rest.

Go on…go ahead I'm listening.

"Chapter 1: The Monitor"

Jak doesn't know that I am watching him. That I see what he sees. That I know how he feels. Sometimes I know exactly what he is thinking.

Day 1042 from tagging.

Today Jak is singing.

"I Remember yesterday, when I didn't have no bills to pay." He shouts out the lyrics to a Moinxe rock song as he dances his way around the kitchen. The Blang is the latest dance craze to hit the Unicamp. Jak is trying to perfect an intricate vault and his manoeuvers are interspersed with attempts at preparing his breakfast. Progress is necessarily slow and Jak feels sure he'll be late for training.

"Who gives a flying wapwer?" Jak yells. "Life is short. The Zenans beat the Torags 2.4 to 5.9 and I'm as cool as a Nepha in my gleamers."

He shimmies to the elevator, inventing a new side buzz on the way. Impressed with himself, he consigns this move to memory.

I can tell he is entirely happy, without a care in the world.

But today is the day it all starts, which is why I have begun here.

"STEN!" He shouts above the Moinxe beat, "you'll never make president of the Crimmer Council if you sleep in your hammock 'til midday."

His friendship with Sten Tor is the reason I watch Jak.

Jak casts an appraising glance around the untidy room. He picks up a sock and, rolling it into a projectile, hurls it through the open door of the utility in the simple belief that he is inaugurating a cleanup project.

Jak writes a note to Sten and sticks it on the side of a jam pot. An overflow of preserve holds it in place. It reads thus:-

A preparatory clearing of the throat is heard at this point. and the narrator stops.

"I have the… er note here."

"Then read it."

"It says… begging your pardon…. 'Listen, you lazy, mutant, zephwart; kindly clean this novahole of a neosphere up, before my Dad gets back at five. I've left you some breakfast in…' The rest of that passage is obliterated by preserving syrup, though we did find the remains smoldering in the oven…. ."

“Yes thank you for that,” responds the administrator, sarcasm and not, at this stage, boredom making his voice heavy, “kindly proceed with the reading of the note.”

“Er.... Yes it says...er...,‘ I’ve borrowed your gleamers. Trust you don’t mind. If Senya calls tell her I’ll meet her at the Spinning Bauble at seven. Dang!’ .... Begging your pardon.....,‘ No, tell her I can’t meet her ‘cos my Dad ’s coming back tonight. On second thoughts don’t bother. I’ll call her later. See you, Jak.”

“Thank you Stabbard. The narrator may continue.”

Jak, silent, watching and listening, shifts uncomfortably in his seat. What a complete idiot he used to be just three short months ago.

At 3.20 Jak calls home to say he will be late because his carboconductor is cracked and he is taking it to Unim’s pad to fix it. He hears the crackle that signals the neosphere is offline but I can tell he is not worried, he merely thinks he has overlooked paying the bill, it often happens. He dismisses it from his mind and heads off for Unim’s pad.

At 4.65 he arrives at the neosphere. I can tell he is puzzled when he sees Sten’s corroded speed on the pad. His wonder increases when, upon entering the ‘sphere he notices that Sten’s usually vain attempts at attaining order are less successful than ever. He surveys the confusion and feels vaguely irritated then he notes with a start that his father’s favorite picture by Milsen has peanut butter smarmed across it.

"Prott!" He shouts loudly. "Where the heck are you Sten?" As his friend fails to emerge from the silent interior of the neosphere, Jak proceeds to deflect the debris of four weeks unsupervised revelry into the scubbies.

He discovers Sten at 5.33.

Jak finds his friend's lanky form lying full length in the store.

A bubble of saliva drools at the corner of his mouth and his eyes are wide open. Staring. 'Lifeless, like the windows of an empty room,' Jak thinks.

"Sten?" He whispers hoarsely.

I can tell he is extremely distressed. At first he thinks Sten is dead but when he leans over his face he feels living breath on his cheek.

Jak exhales.

For 5.3 seconds Jak crouches immobile over his friend unable to think coherently then he runs through the pad to take the mobile from his dhinabeam and calls the emergency services.

The adjutant smiles disinterestedly from the screen.

After what seems to be an endless time answering frustrating questions, first from the adjutant then the doctor, he finally feels like he's getting somewhere when Dr Frayne frowns after he repeats that his friend has not been taking drugs or any toxant. The doctor looks up and Jak sees his face for the first time.

"Your friend; is he or has he ever been a detainee?"

Jak is taken aback, "No!" he responds blankly. The doctor sighs and reaches again for his pen. During this interchange Jak has navigated his way back to the store.

Sten's body is still prone; there is no change. He holds the mobile to Sten's face.

"Look he's dying isn't he?" Jak's voice is a bleak whisper yet the doctor's interest seems to revive as he glances up at Sten's face on the screen.

"Is there a mark behind his right ear?" He asks. Jak inspects the area.

"Yes, yes there is."

"Let me see it."

Jak holds the mobile close to Sten's ear.

"Mmm...," remarks the doctor, "and you say he's not a prisoner. He looks like he's been erased though."

"Erased? What are you talking about? Can you just tell me if he's going to be alright?"

"Oh yes." The doctor is calm, soothing, but then his brow creases again, something nagging him. "Look son, I think you should call the precinct. I'll come out immediately with a van. Don't worry; your friend is going to be fine. Now what's....,"

Jak hears the explosion that emanates from beneath the 'sphere an instant before he loses balance. His head comes into painful contact with the central support beam, the mobile spins from his grasp. The innumerable miscellaneous items that he had so recently consigned to the scubbies spew across the 'sphere as it lists drunkenly. Then almost immediately the scene changes gear. The flight of the moving objects is arrested and they begin to float lazily. Simultaneously the lights flicker out. The ensuing darkness is relieved only by the ambient glow of a single pilot light.

The 'sphere shudders as a second, less powerful blast, breaks the unnatural silence. Jak, petrified against the center beam, not really comprehending the significance of what is happening, sees the neighbouring 'sphere which is 500 metres away gradually slide from view. The neosphere is disengaged, slowly spinning its way listlessly into space! For one mind-folding, horror-filled moment, Jak thinks of the void out there, but then he remembers the grid above, its protective web spanning the darkness, waiting to receive the escaping globe.

I can tell at this particular time that Jak still thinks the recent sequence of events is unconnected. That the disengagement of the 'sphere is some kind of accident. That Sten's incapacity is an attack of ill health of some kind, that the disconnection of the interbeam is an oversight.

He launches himself, with his feet, off the support and floats through the open plan quarters. In one of the kitchen drawers he feels sure there is a mobile light. He is right; he takes a cell from his wallet and slots it in. As he switches it on another beam from outside dissects the darkness. At this stage Jak believes that those outside must be the sector patrol. It doesn't strike him that the rescue is far too precipitous.

Jak pulls himself to the viewing station and peers out into the darkness. He does not see the expected patrol vehicle. He cranes his neck to see past the supports, nothing. He is puzzled but not yet suspicious.

Jak pulls himself up the elevator to his sleeper. His covers, levitating, ghostly figures, obscure the way. He hesitates afraid of being stranded in the middle of the sleeper without leverage. Then under the hammock he sees his puller boots, and there is the Jetpak suit and helmet, oscillating gently. Donning them is a little tricky but it is the sort of thing every Keltian youth has done often. He has a sudden clear memory of himself and Sten playing zoobstars beneath the grid. I see it very clearly and it chokes Jak up a little as he thinks of Sten as he is now, still as death.

His confidence is somewhat restored by the memory of their nephalike escapades however. He manoeuvers himself into the gravity aids. Once switched on they allow him to move about almost normally. He glances up through the centre skylight to the security rendered by the grid. There it is. He can see it glinting like a fine silver gauze in the distance. A tiny space is blacked out. The fear, suddenly, is back like an icy splinter piercing his momentary bubble of bravado. A tiny space in the grid is blacked out? Why? Tendrils of an improbable yet ghastly suspicion begin to probe Jak's unreceptive consciousness. He gazes up at the tear. Yes, from this far away it is tiny but Jak knows that inevitably it will be just big enough for the 'sphere to pass through, to be lost forever in the endless space beyond. Jak's hands are clammy and cold beads of perspiration stand out on his brow. Will the Patrol arrive before the 'sphere reaches the breach? He remembers the lights he had seen, was that the patrol? How come they had appeared so soon? Why had they not hailed him immediately? Why has he heard no sirens? Jak begins to believe that something is wrong. He pulls himself together and goes down to the store to search for the mobile. He finds it floating amid some terrza balls, but when he attempts to call the precinct he finds the frequency jammed. His uneasiness intensifies. He hurries as fast as he can in his puller boots down to the pad, but the airlock is secured. Jak is confident he can by-pass the emergency seal and prize the door open. The outer door will then be free but he feels wary. If he is able to accomplish this, will safety, death or capture await him as he emerges from the 'sphere? Is it possible that he will be called upon to outpace those on the outside? He peers cautiously out of the viewer beside the airlock. There is someone out there. Who is it? Why aren't they helping? It seems to Jak that they are just silently watching. The concept chills him. In the darkness he can just determine the lines of two Kreydek 5000s. He knows that each sports ten five hundred cell jetters. His own twelve hundred are puny in comparison. Jak closes his eyes. Imperceptibly he has become aware that an escape is necessary.

He thinks of the severed umbilical. There is a maintenance hatch to the inside but he will undoubtedly be spotted if he tries to exit there and anyway in the unlikely event that he is able to manage it unnoticed his Jet-pak will never last long enough to reach the surface. He would be left floating out there until his air supply ran out, unthinkable. All the while Jak is conscious of his ascent, of time passing inexorably and as yet he has accomplished nothing. Sten remains still as death in the store, deprived of essential medical attention. The enemy, whoever they may be, are still waiting, their predatory eyes watching for any sign of escape. The 'sphere is heading straight for outer space, it's career unchecked and he is doing nothing. His impuissance makes his head reel..., and then the light of inspiration dawns. Jak sets to work. First he brings Sten's dhinaspeed down to the maintenance hatch. It is an old incapacious model, very slender and will just about scrape through. He plots a nonexistent course onto the computer, then propels the inert Sten up to the pad and installs him into his own dhinaspeed. From his sleeper he collects a variety of electrotools and sets about bypassing the seal in the airlock. This accomplished he searches for a wrench in the rear of the pad and upon finding the desired item he wedges it between the two sliding doors of the airlock. He looks out of a porthole, the grid is frighteningly close now; he feels the time slipping like a tangible thing away from him. Back at the maintenance hatch Jak pauses for a moment checking over his plot, questioning himself, willing his scheme to work despite the unavoidable perforations in its structure. The biggest problem is that the decoy might slip away undetected. Jak imagines the mortification of manufacturing the perfect escape and then being left behind, but he can hardly leave Sten and they cannot both squeeze into the miniscule speed. Perhaps he could send Sten off to escape through the maintenance hatch? Immediately he pictures himself watching the sinister black kreydeks chasing the vulnerable little speed and then the fireball as it is blown to bits by their imagined weaponry. He shudders. Rather they both go together than that. Taking a deep breath he unlatches the drawbar of the hatch and guides the speed into the chamber. It is too long! Jak disengages the jetters and takes them through separately. Finally he has the entire speed reassembled in the shaft. Jak opens the flange and the jetters ignite. With its beams blazing, the speed emerges from the umbilical.

Jak can't wait around and see the outcome of his ruse; he must make his move. Various cables, SLN components and other combustibles are alight in the shaft due to the confined ignition of the jetters, but Jak has no alternative other than to make his way as quickly as possible back to the chamber. The flames lick hungrily at his crelton jetpak suit. As the temperature rises Jak wonders feverishly whether there is sufficient detroxinide gas in the umbilical to trigger an explosion. The time it takes him to reach the chamber seems interminable to but is actually only a few seconds. The scorched material of his suit is searing his skin. He feels it fusing to his forearm but the urgency of returning to the pad makes his physical distress diminish to inconsequence. He feels instinctively that this will be his only chance for survival, the only chance for both Sten and himself.

Back in the pad, finding leverage against a vertical support, he forces the airlock open with the wrench he has previously lodged between the doors. By the time the outer hatches have commenced their automatic release Jak is ensconced beside Sten in his dhinaspeed, flange fully open, jetters droning expectantly, cell counter pulsating.

The first thing Jak notices through the expanding aperture is the grid. The 'sphere is already passing through the severed cables. Instantly Jak throws the switch and the dhinaspeed swoops beneath the oncoming capillary of the grid. They are so close Jak can see the iridescent cell structure within the outer membrane, but what of the enemy? They are nowhere in sight. Jak exults. His scheme has worked. The 'sphere eclipses his view but as it slips through into outer space he can see three rapidly moving points of light away in the distance. Yes it has worked. He can hardly credit it. He gives a shout of elation and his voice sounds deep and strong in the confined space of the speed.

It is this, the sound of Jak's exultant call, which fills the auditorium as the administrator switches off the narrator.

"Proceedings will commence tomorrow at midday." He intones. There is a general stir in the hall but the sound of Jak's shout lingers still. It is the sound that is heard on the early evening news across the network.

Jak hears it and groans. His case is just the kind of thing to attract public interest. He imagines what the days ahead will be like. Hell, absolute hell. All his personal thoughts and actions going out live to the twelve nations. Indignation at the Monitor and the

Crimmer Council surges up as it has done time and time again since his lawyer revealed he'd been tagged. It was bizarre watching yourself from the perspective of the Monitor tag, hearing your thoughts and actions discussed, looking into your mind. It could really mess with your head… but it was fascinating. If it weren't for her he wouldn't have minded so much. He could even have found it in himself to enjoy it. Jak groans again as he thinks of her once more.

Chapter 2: Krey Remembers

I heard the shout whilst reposing in my chambers. Although my screen was on I had not been following the news item. But when I heard Jak Dane's shout something akin to recognition alerted my senses. I had not known that he had been tagged. Cynically, I suppose, I was not surprised. Of course I should have known, I should have been informed. However the incompetence of others is something I have come to expect.

I remember that day, when Disman came into the office, his face portending doom, and informed me that the boy had somehow eluded them. I transferred my gaze to him and appraised his countenance for a protracted moment. It suited my purpose to keep him waiting in this way. Disman raised his hand, I believe with the intention of relieving a restriction caused by the seeming tightening of his collar but let it fall without accomplishing this feat. The chill sweat was on his brow. The room was utterly silent except for the stilted breathing of Disman. At last I spoke.

"Are you afraid of me Disman?" I asked. I waited while he groped in his mind for the correct response and finally said nothing. I laughed, a faint, sibilant, mocking laugh I suspect.

"Ah, how I do despise you Disman." Eventually Disman cleared his throat in preparation for speech. "You may leave us," I ordered quickly, I did not want to listen to his feeble excuses, "I will attend to this matter myself."

Relieved Disman obeyed with alacrity. As he departed, Felice entered. She was dressed solely in black as usual, other than a silver demicloak hanging in soft folds from her shoulders. She showed me a smiling face of dusky beauty. I looked at her for a moment appreciatively as she lowered herself gracefully into a chair.

"Ah Felice, my dear." I noticed a subtle inflection in my voice and it interested me. "I trust you have efficacious tidings?"

She nodded disdainfully. "The doctor was pathetic. It was facile."

"You never fail to show your ascendancy over your contemporaries." I approved.

"What of the boy?" She enquired as she peeled off a pair of long, black gloves.

"Disman's capabilities are not as satisfactory as yours my dear, he allowed the boy to outwit him."

"How astonishing." her expressive brows were raised and a sarcastic smile hovered about her lips.

"It is regrettable. Now if you will excuse me I have some messages to transmit, your brief visit was as delightful as ever."

Her lips drooped petulantly but she rose to leave. "Does Straiff know you have Verdor's son on the loose?" She questioned, spitefully. I stared at her coldly and vouchsafed no reply. Eventually her defiant eyes faltered before my scrutiny and she departed without another word.

When they were gone I remember feeling strangely unsettled. I took my mascots from the locked drawer of my desk and commenced tapping the crystals together, not of course in any agitation but gently very slowly very deliberately with an exact intermission between each tap. This action always calms me and allows me to compose my thoughts. Individually transfixed in the spherules of phoris crystal are two morphis spiders. They are not large but they are beautiful, the deadliest creatures this side of the Tor Star. It amuses me to have them as mascots, others may find them unnerving and my love for them perhaps a trifle morbid, but what care I? I aquired them on my first visit to Census in a torrent forest on the west side of the Great Veltor Lakes. They were on the corpse of my faithful guide Trem. The female had injected her venom below his eye and was in the process of spinning a webbed cocoon for her young while the male stood guard. I admired them greatly at that time and now I can caress and admire them whenever I feel the need. I like to watch my long white fingers turning the gems and the iridescence of the turquoise blaze as it catches the light. Yes I remember feeling much better almost as soon as I held them in my hands.

Ah. How sweet it is to write ones memoirs. If I continue I may complete these details before the end of the trial. I could then release them if I am called as a witness and still be able to purchase that tract of land and build my Coleatan Chateau.

Chapter 3:
Gathering Storm

Jak enters the city dome via the north portal. His destination is Casualty. With Sten slouched beside him he plots a ground course. After the exhilaration of escape I can tell he has now returned to frantic concern for his friend. As he travels he wracks his brain for some solution, some reason for the bewildering and terrifying events that have accosted he and Sten that day. Had Sten got himself involved in something? This question is frequently asked and then rejected. To Jak's troubled mind there does not seem to be an explanation. He pulls up before the casualty building. His mind fully occupied with recent events, he fails at first to notice the patrol guards grouped around the entrance. He is about to call out for assistance when he hears a female guard mention Doctor Frayne's name. He looks up, suddenly alert.

The guard is attempting to comfort a distraught young ensign. The girls face is wet with tears. Intuitive warning bells start to ring in the back of Jak's mind. He hears his own name mentioned and his stomach tightens. Why do the Securitor have his name?

"We should be receiving a picture of the boy any minute," announces another guard, "he's only eighteen and listed as stable." He shakes his head sadly. "Seems he's stolen a phial of cantrotonic acid and other medications so maybe that's why he did it."

"You can't believe anyone would do that, let alone a kid," replies his companion. "I hope they erase him, its less than he deserves."

"Should be put down I reckon, never be any good to anyone." Someone else says disgustedly. At that moment a senior Securitor emerges from the foyer.

"Well the doctor's dead," he says flatly, "I pity whoever has to tell his wife." This is greeted by a fresh burst of weeping from the ensign. Jak staggers back against the speed, the doctor dead! His mind reels. The voices of the patrol guards, raised in aggressive comment, begin to recede as he almost slides into unconsciousness. The realization that he is again on the verge of being captured pushes back the encroaching darkness. Jak stumbles to his side of the speed. It is fortunate indeed that the guards are otherwise occupied or they must surely notice his erratic movements and his ashen face.

Here the transmission is paused. The administrator looks enquiringly at Stabbard who clears his throat.

"Er… yes your honor we have the police report and photographs."

"Have them posted and I must solemnly advise all voters to read the police report with care."

Transmission is resumed.

Jak takes his place in the speed and manoeuvers his way out of the Dhinapark slowly and as inconspicuously as possible. It isn't until he is travelling along the outer south flight path that his mind begins to clear. The Portals, he knows, are the only way out of the city. To enter or exit you must be cleared by the PLA monitor. By now his PLA must be on every computer in the city. It seems to him he is inextricably trapped, yet he must exit the city. Here there is no one to turn to for help, for advice or for medical assistance and capture is only a matter of hours away. An overwhelming sense of longing for his father engulfs him. Verdor, infallible, indomitable; he would know what to do. Jak longs to unburden the weight of this day onto his shoulders.

The south portal looms ahead and Jak slows to a stop before the monitor. With a fearful heart he lifts Sten's limp hand and places the palm against the screen. He prays that Sten's PLA has not also been released. He waits tensely as Sten's details flicker across the screen;

STEN TOR: PRETANOX FATHER CALCY: PRETANOX DECEASED MOTHER MARSA: PRETANOX DECEASED YEARS 18 MONTHS 4 DAYS 28 BLOOD TYPE 0074H VACCINATIONS 47B 24S 53T 459Y 77S 51C 92R CARRIER NONE TERRITORY CELLARVILLE QUARTERS 17 PERTOR BUILDINGS TACE VEIW CELLARVILLE HEIGHT 6.2

WEIGHT 10.3 TAKEN 7.13.24 HAIR LORTON BROWN EYES VERTICE GREEN

DISTINGUISHING MARKS SMALL SCAR ABOVE RIGHT EYEBROW GRADES B17-4 E4-2 L9-2 S1-1 H1-1 C4-7 LISTING STABLE BRACKET 1200 NOMINATED ENTRY NOMINATOR VERDOR DANE EXIT PASS GRANTED

As this final caption appears Jak expels his pent up breath slowly and the portal sighs open.

It is 7.36 when the dhinaspeed enters the gravity free outer territories. In the north a hazy dawn is breaking. The rock formations make long shadows in the dust. Jake gazes round at the bleak prospect. The inferior living standard is instantly discernible. In comparison to the sterile salubrity of the city, the outer territories are unwholesome, dilapidated, subtopia. In the distance a cluster of viridescent forest domes supply the city and the individual habitations of Cellarville with air. The network of taupe pipelines bringing in air and water stand out in stark, unattractive relief against the dry ochre of the rock and dust of this planet, Ecracon 3. In the middle distance Jak sees the disordered, unplanned, landscape of Cellarville, considered aesthetically unacceptable by the Keltian planning department, it is camouflaged by a gigantic mirage hologram. As Jak approaches Cellarville through the industrial buildings of the outer territory, the news screen among the advertisements at the base of the hologram catches his eye. The face of Doctor Frayne appears and causes his already tense body to tighten. Instead of passing through into Cellarville he pulls up beside the screen and tunes into the broadcast on his speed radio.

The Administrator asks Stabbard to play the appropriate archive.

"…Doctor Delon Frayne. He was found brutally murdered in his office at the casualty buildings in Keltian City North. Securitor Patrols are searching for Keltian, Jak Dane and Pretanox, Sten Tor for questioning. Both men are aged eighteen. It is believed they have in their possession a phial of cantrotonic acid and needle guns. They are not to be approached under any circumstances but if seen, members of the public are urged to call the precinct on this emergency number 47-26-42. Earlier this morning Dane and Tor carried out an arson attack on the Dane family home, Neosphere 17. The luxury 'sphere was found adrift in the Stratos passage, by a Straiff supply ship. It is believed that Verdor Dane was inside the 'sphere. Deliberate fratricide is suspected. The 'sphere has been towed to the precinct holdings for forensic tests. Meanwhile Doctor Frayne's widow, Seli, and their two children have been taken to Compassion to be treated for shock. Could anyone with any information please contact the precinct? Here is that number again 47-26-42.

Teri Tex the famous Yosha rock star has been accused of…."

Jack switches of the radio and there is silence. Images flash across his mind, images of Verdor his father, of Sten lying on the storeroom floor, of Doctor Frayne, the hostile faces of the securitor guards and lastly the haunted, lost eyes of Seli Frayne as he had seen them on the news. Jak does something then that he hasn't done since he was a little boy, he cries and the tears flow between his fingers as he buries his face in his hands.

Eric Tor has the dubious reputation of having a PLA warning of 7 listed against him. He lives in Clancy, Cellarville, runs several disreputable dance clubs, an illegal gambling circuit, a string of black-market interspace pirate stores and any number of small illicit enterprises. No respectable citizen would have any dealings with him, but Jak feels he is no longer respectable. Eric Tor is Sten's brother and the only person Jak can think of to turn to. Jak looks back at Keltian City. The myriad facets of the main dome catching the light of the rising sun make it look like a giant jewel lying in the desert. Clusters of neospheres rise up like numerous antennas probing the stratos. One large 'sphere, isolated from the rest, revolves endlessly. It's gentle oscillations making it glitter in the sunlight. The Spinning Bauble. He has spent many evenings there with Tess, Senya or just the lads. Hanging out, dancing. Jak realises suddenly that in one night he has lost something irretrievable, something carefree. He turns away from viewing the city, looks quickly at Sten and feels ashamed of the shallowness of his thoughts. The woman Seli Frayne, the doctor, Sten, they have lost much, much more. Shadows of guilt flitter across his mind. Incomprehensibly, he feels the weight of blame settle on his shoulders. Why is he to blame? He doesn't know but the feeling sticks. He knows without a doubt that the doctor's death was a result of his call.

"What is happening?" He calls aloud as he rubs his throbbing temples distractedly. Then with a last lingering look at the city, Jak turns and enters Cellarville.

The town is still asleep, which is perhaps just as well. Most Cellarville inhabitants are either Pretanox or Kersa with a smattering of Sitrians, Plytens and Temmans. They are mostly labourers, working in the mines and subterranean pumping factories. Relations between the Keltians and the other races are not easy. Many Keltians view the outer territory dwellers not only as poorer but also as inferior. The other races are not allowed to live in Keltian city. Many of the Pretanox and Kersa lift envious, covetous eyes to the city, to the wealth and comfort within. Jak has lived with racial tension all his life, it has been part of Ecrecon 3 culture ever since the Keltian mining core discovered this planet rich in forisvex and tobault and colonized the place ninety-four years ago. Due to a careful upbringing Jak is what is known as a new generation equalite. Jak is more aware than most youngsters of the potential problems for a Keltian entering Cellarville; that's why he is glad the town is asleep. Jak cruises a ground course through the quiet streets, amongst the jumble of homes, drinking halls, dance clubs, eating houses and shops all anchored by various means to the planet surface. Ahead a rubbish ship silently eradicates the atmosphere of floating debris. A sleepy night patrolman strolls along the boardwalk in his puller boots, a 457 lazer slung over his shoulder. An inebriated reveler sleeps off his excesses, floating under a shop awning. The patrolman pulls him down with his grappling hook. Jak watches him tow the sleeping figure away then travels across the slumbering town. The buildings gradually deteriorate into the slums of downtown Cellarville. Ahead is a tunnel, its opening sealed by an airlock and above a sign reads "Welcome to Clancy." Jak's resolve begins to falter a little, how can he, Jak, erstwhile respectable Keltian, perpetrate an entry into this subterranean den of iniquity? The outer door begins to open accommodatingly and Jak yields to the invitation. Immediately he realises his mistake and cursing his gullibility, he tries to reverse but already the doors are too far closed. He just succeeds in obliterating the rear end of his speed and smashing his skull against the side panel. The broken, burning speed slews off at an acute angle. Groggily he watches six dark figures, mounted on what appear to be high-celled peltervors, converging on him. In the harsh, artificial lights of the fume filled airlock they look like demons emerging from the smoke of the abyss, the red danger beacons flashing behind them and the fire alarms blaring. Jak brings his speed around and with desperate intention, collides with two of the peltavors. Sparks fly and one figure lays motionless. The other picks himself up. Jak's speed cannons off into the wall. The impact rents his vehicle in two. Jak is thrown clear and lands heavily on his side. He can see Sten, still strapped into the front half of the speed, his arm twisted at a grotesque angle. He is shaking his head, slowly, from side to side. His eyes are open but no pain registers in them. Half stunned Jak rises to his feet. Before him are the remaining peltavors. The unseated figure advances on him with a weapon raised, Jak doesn't wait for him to use it. On the floor beside him is the disengaged door of his dhinaspeed. He lifts his crude weapon in an instant and with a bellow rushes at the surprised assailant. He swings the door wide and belts him in the chest, the man reels backwards. Jak lunges round following the momentum of his swing and dislodges another from his peltavor. The unexpected violence of his attack has caught them off guard but not for long. Jak feels his brain explode with pain as someone strikes his unprotected head from behind. His legs seem to liquidate beneath him and he sinks slowly to the ground. As his eyes mist over he sees their faces hanging threateningly over him. It is in fact a merciful relief when blackness comes, smothering fear and pain like a thick blanket.

Chapter 4:
Eric Tor

All too soon Jak is struggling through the waves of oblivion. He is brought back to consiousness through the sound of gentle laughter. He opens his heavy lids to look into a pair of merry green eyes. The man is looking at him with mingled admiration and amusement on his face. Jak only really notices the amusement. Anger wells up like a flood.

"Get off me!" he yells, or at least he intends to yell, however the man bows his shaggy head forward to catch his whispered words. Shaggy Head lets out a shout of appreciative laughter. Jak winces as his jangled nerves protest against this raucous sound.

"Sorry lad," he apologizes, "you must have a pelter of a headache, Dace! But you're a game little Nepha. Who'd have thought a curly, towheaded, innocent looking kid like you would have practically done in one of my guys and put out of commission two more, the fools."

Jak feels puzzled, the stranger before him does not seem to emanate an hostile presence. The effort to untangle the problem is too much and Jak begins to slide away but a lingering sense of danger tugs at him and he feels he must not rest. He struggles to open his eyes.

"Who are you?" He questions with an effort.

"Eric Tor at your service."

A wave of relief floods Jak's mind.

"Sten?" he asks.

"Don't you worry Sten's going to be fine."

Jak feels a certain amount of release, and allows himself to sink into oblivion.

It is now noon of the following day. Jak wakes. He is alone. He props himself up on one elbow. His head throbs a little, he feels a bit like he's been pushed through a food mixer but other than that he knows he's O.K. He glances around the room with interest. It is spacious and sparsely yet expensively furnished. The sheets covering the bed he is laying upon are made of costly natural silk. An extravagant centre light illuminates some fine sculptured art forms. Jak can't be sure but he thinks the glittering teardrops are made of phoris crystal. He decides to explore the possibility of this and sits up on the bed. The movement makes his head spin and he is trying to hold that errant member in place when the door opens and a scantily clad, generously curved female enters the room. She poses for a moment in the doorway to allow his astonished gaze to dwell on her luscious beauty.

"I'm your nurse!" She explains in a deep, husky voice that makes the statement sound strangely suggestive.

"Hi!" he responds, nervously.

"My name is Leela and you're Jak Dane." She comes close, tossing her waist length reddish brown curls, and places a long red fingernail on his chest.

"I've heard you're very brave." She continues breathlessly. Jak feels a little breathless himself and thinks that much more nursing like this and he'll be a nervous wreck.

There is a general snigger rippling across the auditorium. The narrator pauses. Jak looks sheepish. He catches Zerrin's scornful eye. The administrator calls for order and the narrative is resumed.

"Now, now, Leela, stop your teasing." Eric Tor's resonant voice is heard from the doorway. He comes striding into the room and slaps her pert behind jovially.

"So you've met my little woman." He gives a delighted chuckle. "Aah she's a good girl."

Jak seriously doubts the veracity of this statement however he clears his throat and gives a tentative smile. She winks an improbably long lashed eye at Jak then turns to her man who kisses her soundly on her luscious red lips before sending her about her business.

Whatever that might be!

"What a sexy woman!" Eric says with a gusty sigh. Jak nods his agreement and they watch her as she walks with undulating grace out of the room.

"Now my boy," he turns abruptly to Jak "let's hear your story."

Jak stares at Eric for a long while without uttering a word. He feels feverish and there is a fearful reluctance to evoke the recent past. He passes his fingers through his hair in agitation and winces as he comes into contact with the livid welt on his scalp.

Painfully he raises himself off the bed and begins a slow pacing of the room, making an effort to get to grips with himself. He can tell Eric is quietly watching his troubled face; giving him time. Finally he says encouragingly,

"Come lad if you tell me what's happened I'll likely be able to help you."

Jak comes to a halt before Eric and stands gnawing at his lip. A worried crease furrows his brow.

"I think they've killed my father!" he blurts out at last. There are no tears just this bald statement but Jak is pretty choked. His face works convulsively as, ignoring his battered frame, he flings himself into a vacant seat and tries to hide his emotion with a hand to his forehead.

"No lad, you don't know that." Jak can tell Eric feels his attempts at comfort are clumsy.

Jak drops his hand and leaning forward in his chair, stares dejectedly at the floor.

"Have you seen the news? Have you heard what they're saying about me?" he whispers.

"Aye I've heard it. But why don't you tell me what happened."

There is a lengthy silence, then Jak starts to pour out the whole, disjointed, implausible story and with it he pours out a good deal of his frustrated thoughts, his incomprehension of what is happening, the fear that now and then engulfs him, the self imposed guilt over the doctor, his pessimistic conclusions about his father and his overwhelming worry about Sten. When he has concluded his recital he feels emotionally and physically drained. Eric, who has listened attentively without interruption throughout does not proceed to interrogate him as he had half expected but persuades him to take a sleeping draught and instructs him to rest.

"Don't you worry lad we'll sort this thing out," he places a heavy hand on Jak's shoulder. "first thing is to find out why your interbeam was tampered with I'll see if I can recover the recordings and see if there are any messages that will help unravel this web."

Jak nods, grateful to leave things in Eric's capable hands. Eric gives his shoulder a squeeze and then leaves him to sleep.

Chapter 5:
Krey Is Displeased

As I watch Jak Dane's young innocent face, battle scarred but restful, I remember with a twist of annoyance what happened two days later when I made my next move. It was Straiff who forced my hand. Straiff was scared.

"If you don't kill that boy...." I remember clearly the sound of his voice rising quickly to a high pitch and he blinked rapidly as he began to threaten me, yes me.

"If you don't get rid of him Krey the deal's off ."

"Mr. Straiff," I responded in my usual, well-modulated tones, "I would desire you to control yourself, such vehemence is singularly unattractive."

"May you rot Krey!" Straiff's thin, aged face was tight with anger. "You should have made sure your incompetent heavies did their job properly. I hope you stretched them out for this."

I smiled distantly but made no comment.

"If Verdor contacted that boy and he blabs," continued

Straiff ominously, "the Crimmer Council will be down here like a ton of bricks."

"If he is foolish enough to talk, no one will listen to him. His PLA rating reads 'unstable' remember." I soothed.

"If we're lucky those Cellarville militants will have ripped him to shreds." Straiff was moody but appeased.

However when I next contacted Straiff I had ill tidings to report and this time Straiff refused to be calmed.

"Eric Tor!" He screamed. "Who the Hell is Eric Tor?"

"Some smalltime Pretanox criminal." I respond dismis¬sively.

"What in the name of Stevie Gerrard is going on?" Straiff raved on and on in this unpleasant vein for some few moments, interjecting his soliloquy with colourful metaphors normally confined to the gutter suckers of Cellarville. Eventually I interrupted. I was angry; my voice was icy but tightly controlled.

"Your eloquence astounds me but I feel that this incredibly insignificant occurrence hardly necessitates such unhelpful, although edifying, aggression."

"Did you say insignificant? I don't call it insignifi cant when some crook breaks into the daced precinct holdings and steals the daced interbeam recordings out of that daced neosphere right under our daced noses!" Straiff's voice rose to such a high pitch at the end of this tirade that it is questionable whether a dog could have heard it.

"My men," I explained patiently, "destroyed the tapes there is nothing on them."

"Don't you dare preach to me about your brainless employees."

Yes they were brainless; I had to concede that point. Straiff however would not be placated and yes, I'm afraid I was driven by cold anger spawned in some degree by the knowledge that such impercipient, unintelligent individuals such as these could eviscerate my immaculate plans. I manifested my annoyance in the ferocity of my attack.

Chapter 6: The Storm Breaks

Today Jak visits Sten. Eric has placed his ailing brother in the care of a friend, an old doctor. He has been revived from his catatonic state and although there is no other noticeable improvement as far as Jak can determine, the doctor assures him that all Sten needs is therapy, loving attention and lots of time.

"Like a young seedling," explains the doctor in his whimsical way, "he needs nurturing carefully and he will blossom into a fine beautiful plant ...er... figuratively speaking of course." The old man begins to chuckle and Jak looks at him sideways.

"Could you tell me what's happened to him Sir," Ventures Jak, "I did speak to the nurse earlier but she doesn't seem to know much about it."

"I don't tell her anything," The doctor shakes his head and, leaning towards Jak, continues in a conspiratorial whisper, "She's a witch you know." Jak smiles politely but it doesn't seem to him that Sten could possibly be in the best of hands, still Eric had endorsed the doctors credentials.

"He may talk a little crazy but he's the best medicine man this side of the Torstar." Remembering this warm commendation Jak assumes a more receptive attitude as the doctor continues.

"You see this puncture mark here?" He indicates a tiny hole behind Sten's ear which is still infl amed. "He has been injected with cantrotonic acid," he shakes his head in deep melancholy, "nasty stuff, not the sort of thing I would use." He looks at Jak intently from large myopic eyes as if to make sure he fully understands this reassurance. "The cantrotonic acid has dissolved his neuron passages. There's nothing there." He tapped his own head at this juncture, looking very wild and disheveled. In other circumstances Jak would have laughed, even now he can feel laughter brimming up inside and wonders at himself.

"It is terrible but don't worry he'll learn everything again, he's young and strong it won't take too long. You've no doubt heard of reoccurring offenders being erased in prison? Well cantrotonic acid is the stuff they use." He leans towards Jak again. "My wife's there you know."

"Where?"

"In prison, she steals you know, can't help herself." He stands back enjoying Jak's astonishment.

The faint sound of a distant alarm bell infiltrates the quiet of the sick room.

"Hark!" Cries the doctor. "Something's amiss."

Jak's heart takes a sudden lunge, recent events infusing a kind of paranoia into his mind. He races from the room and along the corridor into the reception area of the private medicare center. An ensign is studying an information map of the whole of subterranean Clancy town. On the board an amber light is flashing insistently.

"If it goes to red we'll have to evacuate the whole area." she comments enthusiastically.

Jak isn't familiar enough with the layout to pinpoint the exact location of the hazard alarm.

"Where's that place?" He covers the beacon with his finger.

"I'm not sure," she hesitates, "it could be Lazo's or the Tor emporium."

"Dace! I knew it." Jak slams his fist into the screen, it shatters and he hears, like a distant sound, the fragments tinkling as they fall to the floor. Jak stares as blood begins to drip slowly from his hand. The girl stares too, then starts to back away.

"Hey calm down man, it's over the other side of town. We aren't gonna come to no harm." Her voice trails off as he raises horrified eyes to her face, but Jak isn't seeing her. No, he is seeing images of all the people who had been harmed these past few days. His friends, people he'd made contact with.

The doctor ambles into the foyer and the ensign runs to cower behind him. He lifts his arms protectively and demands to know what is going on.

"I've met you before haven't I boy?" He asks in a puzzled voice. "Now I'm sure I've seen you somewhere quite recently."

Jak pulls out two currency cells from his wallet.

"I'll be back," he promises, and after pressing them into the doctor's hand he heads for the door. The elderly doctor shakes his head sadly; "there's something not quite right with that boy."

As Jak approaches the Tor residence astride one of Eric's peltavor fleet, the lack of interest in the incident surprises him. Any fire had already been extinguished and overhead extractors were sucking greedily at the fumes. It is evident to Jak that some kind of explosion has ripped through the building. He gazes spellbound by the surreal contortions of the metal and synthetics emerging from the smoke. Jak halts at a distance. Two men are lifting an injured party into a van but otherwise all is quiet. That, he supposes, is the mark of a town largely populated by criminals. The whole place might be razed to the ground but no one interfered with any one else's business.

"Jak! Is that you Jak?"

Jak turns and peers out of the side viewer.

"Leela!" There was a kind of swooning relief as Jak looks through the viewer at her beautiful white face.

He emerges from the peltavor and stands on the pedestrian walk before her, gazing down at her in silence. Leela's face is ashen and strained yet also calm. Her warm brown eyes filled with unshed tears.

“Thank goodness Eric’s at the store ship. He’ll be cut he comes back to this.” Jak murmurs eventually. Leela begins to cry softly then and Jak draws her awkwardly to him. She buries her face in his shoulder and the gentle weeping accelerates until the sobs wrack her body. Jak doesn’t quite know what to say or do so he resorts to stroking her hair in what he hopes to be a comforting manner. Gradually the misery abates sufficiently for her to speak.

“Eric is dead.” She says it so quietly, her voice is muffled by his shirt, that Jak thinks he can’t possibly have heard correctly. Eric, dead? He draws her gently away from him and searches her tear stained face.

“How do you know? Was he with you?”

She sniffs and shakes her head.

“Then what’s happened? What’s happened Leela?” He enfolds her cold hands in his own. She bows her head and her tears fall warm on his fingers.

“Look, we can’t talk here is there somewhere we can go?”

She makes a visible effort to regain control. “There’s Lazo’s.” She whispers.

“No it’s too close. Do you know of anywhere else?” She nods and leads him along the walk.

The Heylar is quiet but with evidence that come evening a light flashing, beat pulsating, over crowded metamorphosis will occur. A tired musician practices a mournful melody on a zither. The soulful notes ripple across an empty dance floor. Jak selects a table away from the entrance. An adjutant asks them tonelessly if they would like to order. Jak requests a pot of hot, soothing herbal tea for them to share. He looks across the table at Leela. It is she who speaks first.

"You should leave Jak, get away from Ecracon. There is someone evil after you. I don't think they'll stop until they have you."

Jak makes no response but stares at the pattern of the wood grain on the table.

"What have you done to cause all this Jak?"

He shakes his head. He doesn't have any answers. Their pot of tea arrives, Jak pours and they drink without a word. Time passes. Leela pulls out a handkerchief and blows her nose. The subject that is foremost in their minds has not been broached. Jak is loath to speak. His youth and inexperience do not equip him to deal with Leela's grief. Finally she takes a deep breath.

"They blew up the store ship too. I was shopping at Stell's and Yoka came in. She'd heard it on the interbeam shipping channel. It happened early this morning. I was at the leisure park with Kit about that time; Eric was dying and I was playing netball!" As she whispers this last her tears overflow once more. Jak takes her hand across the table but can think of nothing to say. He orders some more brew and when it is delivered he stares into the spicy depths until it is cold.

"What will you do now?" He breaks the silence.

"Go home I think."

"Where's home?"

" The east side forest domes, my mother and father work there as tenders."

"Will you be OK out there?"

"It will be beautiful." She stirs in her seat "I wish I were there now."

"Can you leave straight away? No I suppose there will

be no end of stuff to sort out."

"Prov will see to all that, he's Eric's manager."

"Yes but can you trust him? I don't know the man but maybe he'll try to milk off all the assets or something."

"Look Jak I don't really want to talk about all that. I don't really care at the moment."

"Of course, I'm sorry." Jak bites his lip feeling gauche.

She smiles across at him.

"It's sweet of you but you don't have to worry about me, I'll be fine. What about you, what will you do?"

Jak shrugs. What will he do? He hasn't got a clue. "I'll stick around I suppose, look after Sten."

"You can't do that, those people are still after you. If you stay here they will kill you."

"I know." Jaks voice is toneless. He notices Leela shiver

though it is warm in the café. What is she thinking Jak ponders. Does she blame him? He would like to be able to reassure her, tell her what this is all about, what her husband has died for but Jak doesn't know, he cannot tell her more. When he looks up he sees the questions in her eyes. Is she suspicious of him? He doesn't blame her if she is. It would undoubtedly be best if he did get out. Leave what was left of his friends to get on with their lives without his troubles stalking them.

"I can't leave Sten." He says aloud.

"You have to. I'll take him back to the forest with me." He doesn't really like the idea of relinquishing his responsibility and burdening her. She looks at him with a decisive tilt to her chin.

"It's not just for your sake I'm offering to do this. It's for Sten. He needs taking care of properly and you're in no position to do that," she pauses for a moment, "and it's for me too. Sten is my brother-in-law; he's part of Eric, the only part I have left. Let me take care of him Jak."

"What about your parents, will they mind?"

She smiles, "No, they won't mind." She sees Jak still hesitant and unhappy. "When this is all over, you'll come back, Sten will be on the mend and perhaps be able to return to you and your father in Keltian City."

Jak stares at her, it all seems so distant. He, Sten and Verdor, those carefree times, who could have predicted it would be so transient.

"Thank you Leela," he says, accepting her kindness, "you've been so brave. It's helped me a lot." He squeezes her hand. He cannot express it but her bravery in the face of bereavement had steadied him. Eric's had been a brief but true friendship, the loss of his stalwart presence would be a blow.

They leave the café together. Outside the town is still quiet; it's inhabitants mainly about their nefarious business. As they walk side by side Leela looks up at Jak.

"Jak, where will you go?"

He doesn't answer her and she continues, "Zennan is nice. It's a fully gravitational planet. I've heard they get snowfall there, cold but pretty. Eric has…had a friend, Tanner, who runs cargo ships there. I don't know his schedule but he may have a ship going out soon." He still doesn't respond. They walk across town towards the hospital in sad but companionable silence.

"Where does that man live who Eric sent the interbeam recordings to?" asks Jak abruptly.

"Oh that's Mort, I don't know where he lives but he works in the communications department at Stackstead mine. Jak what are you planning? You shouldn't stay it's too dangerous."

He nods but doesn't reply.

"Leave it Jak, don't get involved, don't you see that's why they killed Eric, because he took the recordings?"

"It's no good saying, 'don't get involved,' I'm already involved, I'm in it up to my neck."

"You're in over your head!" she retorts, "they're too big for you, you're just a boy and they seem to know everything you do."

"Even so I'm still alive."

"Yes but for how long?"

"Maybe I'm lucky."

Her eyes are suddenly bright with tears and she whispers,

"I used to think Eric was lucky."

There is an uneasy hush upon them then until they reach the hospital. Once there they enquire of the doctor if it will be possible to remove Sten from his care. At first he seems confused and unable to focus on what Jak is saying, but then Jak soon realises that it is Leela's curvaceous, long legged presence, her lovely, tragic eyes and her beautiful husky voice as she adds her own urgings to Jak's request, which are distracting the doctor from the problem at hand. Jak stops the proceedings, asks Leela to stay with Sten, Then motions the doctor outside.

"Will it in anyway jeopardize his recovery if we move him?" asks Jak.

The doctor takes off his glasses and rubs them furiously for what seems an age then questions Jak shrewdly,

"Are you his father?"

Jak eyes him warily weighing the possibility of answering untruthfully and thus eliminating the need for lengthy and difficult explanations. Does the doctor's craziness go that far? It seems unlikely.

"No." He answers.

"Well it will do him no harm to be taken to...where did you say, the forest domes was it? I was in a forest dome once. It was a dream mind so I don't suppose it counts. Now what were you saying?" Jak opens his mouth to speak but the doctor, who seems to be in a gregarious frame of mind, continues with barely a pause. "Will you do me a favour?" He demands and Jak acquiesces recklessly. From the depths of his robe, the doctor produces a glass phial and holds it under Jaks nose. "This is very precious to me," he explains, "It is the reduced compound of a Bek lizard I once had. We were very close and I want him to be buried somewhere he'll be comfortable. In the forest where the mist clings to the leaves forming tears to shed on his grave. Will you do that for me lad, please?"

"Yes Sir I'll do it," promises Jak.

"I like you lad you're a nice person." He lays a hand on Jak's shoulder. "Now, take your friend, give him plenty of good nourishing food, make sure he receives the medication I'll prescribe for him, twice a day and sit him under the trees but most importantly have somebody with him, talking to him constantly. I'll order a van out for you and print out instructions for his therapy." He looks at Jak searchingly and says with sudden clarity,"I know you people are in some sort of trouble but you don't have to worry I'll destroy all the records." Jak grips the doctor's hand and shakes it warmly.

They leave with Sten in a hospital van and arrive at forest dome 6 at 8.44. Here, they are welcomed by Leela's previously notified parents. These people are extremely hospitable, asking Jak to stay with them as long as he wants. He avails himself of this offer for one night only and is immensely relieved that, although they are obviously curious about him and inevitably notice his battered appearance and long preoccupied silences, they refrain from probing. He doesn't know what questions they ask their daughter but they leave him alone. They had had a previous acquaintance with Sten and seem quite pleased to take care of him. The next day, before he leaves, Jak walks in the forest with Leela. They discuss briefly the arrangements for a memorial service for Eric and the care of Sten. Then Jak, feeling uncomfortable but compelled by a sense of duty, enquires about the state of her finances. She informs him that she is well provided for, scolds him and tells him not to bring the subject up again. They stroll in silence then, each steeped in their own thoughts. Eventually Leela speaks somewhat tentatively.

"What have you decided Jak? Where will you go?"

"Probably Detagon."

"What on Ecracon for? It's infested with Censites isn't it?"

He looks sideways at her for a moment then explains.

"I'm pretty sure my father was delivering supplies there and he hasn't returned." He shrugs, "I know it's pretty thin but I've got to start somewhere."

"He wouldn't go down on the surface would he?"

"No, the ship locks on to the holdings, then jettisons the supplies."

"But what about before or after or anywhere along the route? Couldn't whatever happened have happened any time?"

"The thing is I don't really know if anything has happened. It's been four, no five days since he was due back…maybe he is back. There's no way I could know is there?"

"So what's your plan?"

"I'll go to Straiff Supplies. My father has a contract with them for the Detagon run."

She lays a hand on his arm. "Jak, don't go there, they might be involved. It might be they who are after you." He shrugs his shoulders uncommunicatively. After all she had wanted to know what he was doing and now he had told her she was forever throwing a rub in the way.

"I'm worried for you Jak," She persists, "you don't know what you're doing, you're just a unicamp boy. If you go up against them you'll just get yourself killed."

"Well maybe I won't die; maybe I'll just kick some butt." Jak refutes carelessly; he knows she is right of course but still his pride is ruffled. He looks down at her concerned face for a moment. "Look it's of no use you trying to dissuade me. I can't just hide like a frightened mouse. Neither can I go to the securitor. I can't ask my friends to help, I would just be putting them in danger. You of all people should know that." He looks at her stricken face and wishes he hadn't referred to Eric in this way. It was cruel. "Anyway," he mumbles awkwardly, "they would probably just hand me over to the precinct, why wouldn't they?" He slackens pace and starts to pull at some leafage beside the path. "Leela, you can't expect me to just forget about my Dad when I know somehow he's in danger and any way…" he smiles ruefully, "I think it's time I flexed some muscle."

She nods unhappily.

"I'll go and see Mort first," he muses, "and find out if he's freed those recordings." He hesitates for a moment before continuing more gently. "If, like you say, they attacked Eric because he took those recordings there must be something on them, at the least a message from my father but maybe some kind of clue to what this is all about."

They were nearing the house and it would soon be time to say goodbye. From her pocket, Leela pulls out an interbeam communicard. She presses it into his hand.

"I looked this out yesterday evening. It will get you through to Tanner, the man who runs the cargo ships to Zennan, just in case you get wise and decide to go."

She reaches up and kisses him on the cheek. "Goodbye Jak, take care of yourself." She is running to the house before he has time to reciprocate this valediction.

He sees Leela's father beside the speed he has promised to lend Jak. "Send her back on auto when you get to where you're going." he says. Jak shakes hands with him, enters the speed and plots a ground course for the tobault mine.

Chapter 8
Down the Mine

"This is dud mate." Mort slides the interbeam disc across to Jak. He is a Sitrian, skinny to the point of emaciation. There is a scorch mark on his cheek and it is apparent that, at some time, he has narrowly escaped destruction by a patrolman's 457. His shaved head is decorated with a number of scalp studs and he is chewing gum with outstanding vigour.

"Do you know what's the matter with it?" prompts Jak.

"Well, the chemical structure of the memory card has been dissolved."

"What might have caused something like that to happen?"

"To hazard a guess I would say someone has tampered with it."

"This place, where it was installed, there was an explosion, maybe a fire.,could that have caused the damage do you think?"

Mort shakes his head then eyes Jak speculatively, "You're a Keltian right?"

"Er....yes."

"Well you shouldn't be walking around looking like one. Me I don't give, but there are others out there who'd rip your teeth out and wear them as a hat band."

Jak thanks him for his timely warning then, as Mort seems quite friendly and helpful despite looking like a deranged psychopath, asks him about something he finds perplexing.

"Do they hurt, those scalp stud things?"

Mort laughs "These? Nah, you just screw them in, hurts the first time like, but after that, no problem."

Thus enlightened, Jak refrains from questioning him further on the matter, feeling that undue curiosity would be impolite,

"I wonder if you could give me some information?" He asks instead.

"Any time."

"I want to go back into Keltian city without going through the portals, is that possible?"

"Oh you're on the PLA blacklist are you?" asks Mort with sympathy.

"Well..."

Mort presses a digit panel and the doors of his workshop slide closed.

"How large a reward do you think they're asking for you Jak?" He asks softly, his black eyes gleaming.

Jak blanches, the now familiar fear gripping his stomach. Accompanying the fear however is an alert stillness spreading like a mantle over him, he is ready to do battle.

"Hey kid you're a fish on a rock. Take some advice, close your mouth and open your eyes." Mort continues. Jak raises one eyebrow wondering what is coming. Mort places his skeletal frame into a seat and gives Jak a view of the underside of his boots, raised carelessly on the counter. "You're crazy you know." Mort shakes his head in disbelief and begins to chuckle, a deep throaty sound. Jak watches him carefully. "You must be new at this game aye mate?" He laughs again and it seems impossible that such resonance can be achieved and emanate from his scrawny frame. He leans forward towards Jak. "Tell me, what were you thinking of talking to a thug like me as though I was your auntie?"

Nettled and embarrassed Jak keeps quiet.

"There's a reward out for you 70 cells, 20 just for information," continues Mort, "Believe me mate if it wasn't for the fact that you were a pal of the late, great Eric Tor I'd have banged you on your brain case the minute you walked into this mine," a sudden fervour of honesty attacks him and he amends reluctantly,

"fact is I would have done it anyway except the securitor would have hauled me off for transportation as soon as look at me."

Jak is beginning to relax a little.

“Tell me something mate,” Mort is reclining as far back as is precariously possible in a gravitational area. ”Did you really waste your Dad and that Doc whatsisname?”

Jak feels nauseous all at once, his face turning a sickly hue. The realization that this is what people are thinking of him really hits home.

“I thought not.” Mort jumps up and circumnavigating

Jak, makes a critical study. “You know, it’s your clothes that give you away. You’ll have to splash out on some gear. What’s your jetpak and suit like?”

“Black, vertice epaulets.”

“Braiding?”

“No braid.”

“Pity, what about the contours, slim line or over blow?”

“Slim line.”

“Slim line’s good. Has your helmet got a filter?”

“No”

“You can borrow mine.”

“Are you sure?”

“Have you got 2 credits?”

"Yes."

"Then I'm sure enough."

Mort seems to be satisfied with Jak's Stratos suit but he urges him again to lose his Keltian cravat and waistcoat, eying them with disfavor and adhering to the conviction that they are way off course. Jak submits to all this but then returns to the question he asked earlier.

"Well kid there is a way but I don't know it." Jak looks his disappointment but Mort seems to have more to say. "Maloa Aloy may take you. It'll be touch and go, she's pretty volatile as far as Keltians go but if you can convince her you're an anarchist with the massacre of numerous Kelti headmen in mind she might mellow sufficiently. Some ready credit cells would go a long way as an incentive. Have you got much cash on you?"

"Perhaps I should withhold that information." suggests Jak.

Mort smiles approvingly, showing a set of sharp incisors.

"Well done mate you're a receptive pupil. Now here is how you contact Maloa." He scribbles on a piece of readout paper and hands it to Jak. "Don't tell her I sent you it might harm your suit. I'd offer you more advice but I don't 'spose you'd take it." Despite this conviction he continues without a pause. "If you have upset some Kelti big shot you're best off staying out of the city. Better still scoot off to some other planet, Zennan's nice this time of year."

"Yes I know." smiles Jak.

"You'll live longer, that's all I'm saying. Now get yourself out of here before my boss comes in and finds me consorting with a murderous criminal such as yourself…go on." He cuts in as Jak attempts to show appreciation for his helpfulness. Jak chucks him the 2 credits and he catches them deftly. "Be careful with that Aloy woman, she's a hell cat."

The expediency of heeding Morts precautionary measures is seen as Jak nears the huge holding area as he leaves the mine. When he had entered earlier it had been filled to capacity with clocking in mine workers, and he had been able to pass through without attracting any notice. Now the auditorium is empty except for a group of four or five, idle Pretanox youths, apparently the large, empty gravitational area is an ideal place to hang out. Jak hears his footfalls loud in the empty stillness. He walks with long strides eyes straight ahead. One of the lads, the tallest, sporting a long black brush coat and a black delta hat with the wide brim pulled low over his forehead, pushes himself off from a pillar. He expectorates significantly before speaking in a voice low with menace.

"Hey Kelti boy are you lost?"

There is a high-pitched giggle from one of his cronies and then each of them peel themselves away from propping up the construction and commence a steady advance toward him. Jak knows he isn't going to reach the exit in time, his pace gradually slows. At first he is running scared, his mouth as dry as a teabag in hell, his heart pounding loud so he thinks he can hear the echo coming back from the walls. Then he really looks at them. There are only five and apart from the leader they don't compare favorably with him in respect to height and weight. Humph, he'd come off the winner with more worthy opponents than this in the past couple of days. The fight was in him, coursing through his veins. He feels like Josh'sheb-bas-she'beth, one of the valiant, mighty men of old. Suddenly he lets out a rebel yell and races across the remaining distance between him and his foe. They converge in a melee of reckless young bodies, writhing, lunging, grasping and lashing out without any thought of science but with an excess of angry enthusiasm.

There is an alarm siren blaring and the screech penetrates the frenzy of aggression. Someone must have picked up the fight on one of the monitors and sounded the alarm. Groggily Jak pulls himself free from an ensemble of tangled limbs. The gang scatters like preyter mice and melt away. On the floor lies the unconscious leader.

Physically, Jak leaves the mine a lot worse off than when he entered it. There is a knife wound across his chest, his ribs feel mangled, his face numb but on his back is a long black brush coat, pulled low over his forehead, a black delta hat with silver stud trim, his, he feels, by right of conquest and in his heart exhilaration of a battle well fought.

Chapter 9: Maloa Aloy

It is 9.63. Cellarville, which had been dull and quiet, hardly inhabited, has come alive. The streets are crisscrossed with holographic lazer rays bearing advertising slogans. Nearly every other building, with pulsating lights, proclaims itself a drinking club or dance hall. There are people everywhere, either in their stratos suits or astride every conceivable surface craft. Some of the clubs are so popular that the clientele are queuing for 20 metres along the street. It is an aspect that wholly commands Jak's gaze as he cruises slowly past. Ahead a turquoise beam dissects the darkness with flickering iridescence, advertising the presence of a club called the Vega moon. Jak makes a cautious approach. The Vega moon simply looks like an air lock welded to the planet surface between a warehouse and an empty gympark. It is obviously not reaching the same dizzying heights of popularity as some of the other establishments.

The sensor panel flickers and the lock eases open. Jak settles the speed on the pad, locks it, takes his new hat and stuffs it in his pocket ready and descends to the club. The throb of the music is penetrating the lower door and smoke is seeping through the inadequate seal. As the door opens Jak's senses reel. Some sort of incense is burning and the room is cloudy with potent fumes. He is already feeling lofty so who knew what anyone occupying the place for any extended period would feel like. A bouncer appears before him, holding out an expectant paw for the entry fee. Jak's eyes are stinging as he gropes for his wallet.

"How much?"

"2 creds." Demands the man gruffly, eyeing Jak with suspicion. Jak pulls the brim of his hat lower over his eyes and moves into the room. A young woman in a décolleté gown bumps into him, hiccoughs and slews away, giggling, onto the sparsely filled dance floor. Jak wonders if he's a snob, he certainly doesn't take to this kind of atmosphere but perhaps that is something to do with a headache, which previously was confined to his frontal lobe but is now sending sharp thrusts across his left eyebrow

"If you're not drinking you can leave," is the hospitable welcome of the bar steward.

"Er….thanks yes I will have a drink." Says Jak obligingly.

"What sort or do you think I'm a telepath?"

"Oh…er..I'll have a babysham…with ice."

"We ain't got no ice smart alec."

"Just babysham will be fine," amends Jak quickly.

"Give me that glass then."

Jak picks up the sticky glass indicated from the counter and hands it to the bar steward who, to Jak's astonishment, precedes to slosh a yellowish beverage into it and slams it down before Jak without further ado.

"That'll be all will it?" says the man discouragingly.

"Er…yes, thanks." Jak turns and scrutinizes the room but it is difficult to see much amid the smoke.

"Excuse me," he enquires to the retreating back of the barman, who turns ponderously. "can you tell me if there's a lady here called Maloa Aloy?"

"Lady!" The man rudely gives a rasping laugh. "That's a good one." He jerks his chin towards the far corner of the room. "She's over there. Don't you try and get out of here without paying for your drinks or you'll be pulverized."

Jak assures him that this is not his intention and eyeing the said drink with disfavor makes his way between the tables.

She is a strange sight as she dances a slow tango with an imaginary partner. She lurches occasionally and the weaving steps have no connection with the music being played. Jak lowers himself into a convenient chair and waits with something like trepidation for her to tire of her perambulations so that he can talk to her. She is older than he expects, he places her in middle age but in daylight she will probably look older. She is on the thin side and worn skin sags loosely on her upper arms and under her chin. As she twirls unsteadily the folds of her red strapless dress flare out, occasionally revealing a glimpse of thin white legs. Her shoulders are dusted with glitter and her eyes outlined heavily in black. Jak, vaguely revolted by this tasteless apparition, wonders how this old bird can hold the key to unauthorized entry into Keltian city. Finally, as Jak begins to fall into a semi-stupor by the constant inhalation of the mist of incense that wafts insidiously about the room, she stops and calls out in raucous Pretanox that if anyone wanted to dance with her they would have to wait while she refreshed herself with a drink. She laughs in a self-congratulatory way at this witty invitation then sinks into a chair with a low moan. She lays her head on the table, which allows her dry reddish hair to soak up a little spilled wine. Jak swallows nervously and makes a courageous advance to her side then sits down at her table.

"Good evening Miss Aloy. I wonder if I might have a few words with you." He asks in polite, careful Pretanox.

"Oooh how posh!" she murmurs without raising her head.

"I've been told you know a way into the city without going through the portals."

"It's a lie, a filthy lie, a crumby, rotten, obscene, revolting,disgusting lie.... A gruesome, detestable, vile, sickening …… her voice drifts off as she presumably runs out of adjectives.

"I can pay you," urges Jak.

She begins to chuckle and lifting her head points a finger at Jak.

"It's a lying lie." She chuckles again. "Hey good descriptive noun thingy that, lying lie, don't you think so?" Her slurred voice pleads with Jak.

"Well, I was hoping it wasn't a lie," responds Jak hope¬fully.

She draws herself up indignantly.

"Are you calling me a liar sonny?" She sinks back down on the table muttering tearfully.

"Why do you have to argue sooo much? You know I hate it when you argue."

"Please Miss Aloy I need your help."

"Oh I just hate that." She affirms scathingly. "Rubbishing self-pity that is. Why don't you help yourself mmm… tell me that?"

To Jak it doesn't seem that the interview is going as well as it might.

"I want to get into the city but I can't go through the portals."

"Why? Are you too fat?" The scream of lusty laughter she gives to this sally ends in a paroxysm of coughing.

"Oh Dace! I hate it when that happens," She wheezes, "you know when you're laughing and then you start coughing? It's awful."

"Mmm, most uncomfortable."

"I hate the way you say that 'Mmm, most uncomfortable.' It's so prissy, so... snotty."

Miss Aloy's hatred of everything was beginning to wear on Jak.

"So you can't help me then?" concludes Jak beginning to rise. She reaches out with sudden alacrity.

"Don't take me up so," she wheedles, "what is it you want? Why don't you just tell me... I hate it when you procrastinate," she adds softly, eyeing him.

"Well." Jak heaves a gusty sigh and tries again, "I want to get into the city but..."

"Stop! I can't talk about it now...not now." She ends on a pleading note "I'm too drunk."

Jak looks his exasperation. She takes a forisvex brooch from off her dress and pins it on Jak's coat.

"Come and visit me tomorrow, when I see that I'll remember the arrangements we've made."

"Where will you be?"

"Dace! Why do you want so many details? You're such a pain."

"Here." Jak hands her a piece of paper and a pencil from

his wallet. "Write down your address and I'll come and see you early in the morning. She takes the proffered items and bends studiously over for what seems to Jak to be an age, her hand childishly concealing the work from his view.

There are a few faint marks on the paper when she finally gives it to him.

"What's this?" He asks wearily.

"Can't you read my hand writing?" She says with mock concern.

"Look," sighs Jak, "you tell me where you live and I'll write it down."

She hunches closer to him. "You're clever aren't you?" She says admiringly, and this seems to be a solution for she quite readily tells him her address. Once this is accomplished, Maloa Aloy returns to the dance floor to execute another remarkable tango and Jak, after paying for his untouched drink, leaves the club relieved to breathe the relatively fresh air of his jetpack but feeling quite certain that the morning will find the address to be nonexistent.

Jak is dog tired, he turns over in his mind the possibility of sleeping at Sten's quarters in Pertor Buildings, he knows the entry code. He starts to punch in the ground course before realizing the inadvisability of this move. He suddenly arrests his fingers in the act of touching the screen as the thought of a precinct monitor stationed there, waiting for just such a mistake on his part, fl ashes through his mind and his stomach tightens. He is not used to curbing his actions and figuring out ahead of time the consequences. Probing down the various paths of possibility, calculating the pros and cons. It is so alien to his character and makes his head ache with effort.

Seventy currency cells is the total of his remaining cash, he has to slot ten of these into the carboconductor. Sixty cells. Will that suffice for Maloa Aloy? In any case it is certain there is nothing to spare for lodgings. He would willingly sleep under the same shop awning as the unknown drunk he had seen on first entering Cellarville but he can't afford to be towed away by a patrolman. In the end he drives out of the city, hides the speed under a rocky outcrop, ties it down with a self tapping anchor shot into the dusty surface, secures himself under a pipeline and settles down for the night hoping he won't be spotted.

There is a general feeling of compassion in the court as they watch Jak snuggling down for the night. It makes Jak incredibly uncomfortable as the palpable pity fills the room.

"This is good." His lawyer leans towards him and whispers happily. At the time, Jak remembered, he hadn't cared a hoot about taking on the persona of a hobo but now illogically it seems like the worst thing he'd done. Earlier he had seen himself crying in front of the whole universe but it had somehow seemed sad and noble. This sleeping under a pipeline though that was just not done. He looks across and sees Senya, Felix and Tess his erstwhile friends, staring at the screen their fastidious faces shocked. Well they would see worse than that Jak had no doubt.

The lawyer is right though; all the mothers out there in the universe have their fingers hovering over the not guilty vote even though they know it won't count until the end of the hearing.

It is morning. Jak wakes surprisingly refreshed despite the thinness of the recycled air in his helmet.

Maloa Aloy lives in a rather up-market area. Jak is taken aback by the neatness of her dwelling. True it is detached and doesn't benefit from the amenities of a complex, still the domed skylight is attractive and the anchorage is far less haphazard than most of the habitations in the outer territories. It looks substantial and safe. Maloa herself, in her daytime guise, is a less absurd figure. Her red hair is tied back in a dignified fashion and she wears an overall of neat grey.

"Why are you so late?" She demands peevishly, her eyes red rimmed and her brows drawn down with ill humour, a residue from last night's excesses.

"I'm not," he begins then seeing her lip rise in preparation for a snarling tirade he acquiesces, "well perhaps a little."

"You people are all the same. I'm totally exhausted. Why can't anyone get anything right these days?"

Jak had noticed it as soon as he descended onto her pad. The execution of his landing was heavy, then when he jumped down his legs jarred painfully. His helmet, which he now holds under his arm feels like it is carved out of rock.

"Hey, I'm not from GHQ." He hastens to correct her.

"Then who are you? Get out of here. I never invited you, I know that."

"Hold on Miss Aloy." Jak finds the brooch and holds it out for inspection.

"So?"

"Well don't you recognize it?"

"Nope."

Jak feels his spirits drop as if the over-grav in the dwelling is pulling him down.

"Surely you remember…?"

"Don't you strike an attitude with me Sonny." Maloa

disparages. "I'm as hard as phoris crystal."

"You had it pinned to the red dress you wore yesterday at the Vega Moon. We had an arrangement to meet."

"Oh I bet we did." She responds nastily. Nevertheless she takes the proffered brooch and studies it.

"I don't remember any arrangement," she adds repressively,but she retains the bauble. "What do you want?"

"I want to get through to the city."

"Who told you I could get you through?"

Jak hesitates. "A mutual friend." He suggests.

"You liar, I haven't got any friends."

"Will you take me through?"

"That depends on how many power cells you have."

"Sixty." Jak says defiantly, he knows it isn't enough.

"Hah!" She laughs derisively. "What a silly boy you've turned out to be. There's not enough power in those to keep this place going for a week." She is turning from him with a dismissive jerk of her shoulder. "Now get out of here."

"I can fix your grav-metre."

"No need I've got someone coming from GHQ any minute."

As she says this, the inter-beam blips. She makes her way with difficulty into her living quarters. Jak, fully aware he's been told to get lost, follows her.

The communication is from Gravity Head Quarters. The adjutant explains coolly that the serviceman has been held up and will not be able to fit her in until tomorrow. Maloa rages ineffectually for some time before cutting the beam connection.

"I thought I told you to get out of here." She looks at Jak but with diminished aggression.

"You need me I think."

Maloa sighs heavily and subsides, "follow me." She says.

It is no idle boast; Jak can indeed fix the grav-metre, as

Maloa looks sullen Jak proposes a deal.

"If I doctor this so you get commercial rates will you take me through to the city?"

Maloa's eyes glitter greedily. "How much more will I get?"

"About one third."

"OK" She holds out her hand. For a moment Jak thinks she wants to shake on the deal but then he realises that its sixty measly credits she wants and he hands them over reluctantly.

It is 1.20 and Jak is at the rendezvous point. Most of the factory is closed for the night. He looks curiously around. The name of the firm, Maldis, gives no clue to their line. The holding yards at the back are open and Jak waits there, patiently at first but then as time passes he keeps looking at his watch restively. At 2.30 he sees through the window a boy sweeping inside. Jak leaves his speed, jets over and taps on the window. The boy looks up nervously, Jak signals reassurance and eventually after much sign language the lad is persuaded to open the air lock,

"Have you seen Maloa Aloy?" He asks as he divests himself of his helmet.

Chapter 10
The First Clue

"Left!" Jak gasps. "When?"

"Just after one."

"Well of all the nerve." Jak paces angrily. The arrangement had been for 1.30.

"Are you Jak?" enquires the boy.

"Yes." Responds Jak eagerly. "Did she leave a message?"

"The skimmer was full. Bekka and Tril both came. She said to tell you to come again tomorrow same time."

Jak sighs "and s'pose it's full tomorrow?" He wonders pessimistically.

The boy shrugs. "I don't know nothing about it. Do you want a cup of tea and a bun seeing as you're here?" He asks with a hospitable smile.

Jak is suddenly made aware of the gnawing emptiness of his stomach. He grins ruefully at his young benefactor "I'm so hungry I could eat an elephant." He proclaims.

"Not without throwing up." Corrects the boy.

They chat companionably on a diversity of youthful topics. Del, the young lad, stares with friendly inquisitiveness at Jak's battered face and asks an amazing amount of questions which Jak parries quite skillfully as he devours a large amount of sticky buns pilfered from the works canteen.

"What do they do here Del?"

"Process sewage."

Jak lowers the bun he's been tucking into.

"Really?" He swallows a morsel with sudden difficulty.

The tricky moment passes quickly. Jak shrugs and continues consuming the sugary cake.

"Do you know anything about Detagon?" he asks later.

"A friend of mine knows someone who works in a bar, Ican't remember its name but this guy is married to a girlwhose ex-boyfriend has been to Detagon." boasts Del.

Jak finds this singularly uninformative.

"Why do you want to know about Detagon?"

"I need some input on the Censite."

"I know something."

"What's that?"

"They're idiots."

They both laugh heartily at this.

“How do you know they’re idiots?” Asks Jak curiously after their mirth has subsided.

Del shrugs. “My Dad says so.” Jak smiles at this childish reasoning, yet he himself is little better educated on the subject. His father, who he believes is wholly open-minded, says the Censites are unworthy and Jak accepts this. After all, the Censites have earned their reputation.

“Flebax!”

“I beg your pardon.”

Jak is in the process of donning his helmet before taking his leave.

“Flebax. That’s the name of the geezer that’s married to the girl who knows the other geezer that’s been to Detagon.”

“Oh.....er...well thanks Del and thanks for the food and stuff .”

“You need to know the name of the bar so you can find this Flebax bloke.”

“Do you know it?”

“I do but I can’t remember it.”

“Aw Del!”

“Well I might remember if you give us a moment.”

Jak plonks himself back down in the chair and Del screws his face up in and attitude of deep thought. After what seems an age to Jak, a couple more of the sticky buns and a zillion unlikely suggestions Del comes up with the goods.

"The Blue Mortal! You see I knew it was in the ol' info banks somewhere."

"Thanks. Thanks for everything you've been a real mate."

"You're more than welcome." Del replies sincerely.

At the hearing Del cries out; "I never knew he was a murderer or a traitor or anything!" the pressure to exculpate himself is heavy upon him but Jak, in all his troubles, feels sad that their brief friendship has ended this way.

The owner of the Blue Mortal has had the unhappy inspiration of coating all his employees with blue Melorene. Jak feels slightly uncomfortable conversing with a blue man dressed only in a loincloth but he perseveres and finds out that there truly is such a man as Del had indicated, who had visited that Godforsaken place, Detagon. Reportedly he had actually been on the planet surface and seen the Censites.

"Odd little man," describes Flebax. "Goes by the name of York, comes here occasionally but hardly ever speaks to anyone. I think he's sick actually. Always very pale and he wears a visor all the time, never takes it off ."

"I don't suppose you know where I can locate him do you?" asks Jak hopefully.

Flebax shakes his head but calls over to a blue woman who seems, to Jak's interested gaze, to be wearing merely a few bits of torn cloth.

"Petro, my love, you know that little man who sometimes

comes and sits over there?" Pointing with his chin to dark corner.

"York?" She bobs her head and smiles at Jak.

"Yeah do you know where he lives?"

"He's got an apartment in Rhetros House I think. Stace'll know." She calls in turn to another woman polishing glasses behind an empty bar,

"Stace, you know that little man, York, sometimes comes in on a Friday?"

"Mmmm… moody guy, wears a visor?"

"The very one. Do you know where he lives?"

"Rhetros House. I delivered a message to him once, he's in one of the downstairs rooms - No. 31. He's an odd one though, acted kind of funny. Some sort of criminal I'd say."

"Or a spy maybe," offers Petro, smiling again at Jak.

"More like some kind of pervert," adds the loin clothed Flebax disgustedly.

Jak cuts into their speculations,

"Can you give me directions to Rhetros House?"

This they are more than willing to do. Indeed they seem inclined to engage him in conversation for as long as he can be compelled to remain. Jak cannot oblige them however. He wants to speak with York before meeting with Maloa later.

Rhetros House is a poorly favoured area and Jak enters with a feeling of slight trepidation remembering that the man he wants to meet is odd, a criminal, perhaps a spy, maybe a pervert and who knows what else. Jak rings the heralder.

York is indeed a small man he smiles at Jak in a mild friendly manner and bows him into his apartment. Jak introduces himself spuriously as Delter Pica.

"Krey has sent you for a copy of the report no doubt?"

Jak is about to repudiate this but changes his mind. This is odd, Krey? He's heard that name somewhere before. He looks around the room appraisingly and is somewhat disconcerted to see a wicked looking lazer picot gun lying handily on the table beside York. Perhaps it wasn't such a good idea to come here.

"Mr. Roke is well I hope?"York is smiling ingratiatingly up at him, the black visor hiding his eyes. Jak lifts his hand in a noncommittal so-so gesture. He hopes his demeanor is disinterested because in fact he is quite stunned. Krey Roke is a member of the Kelti board. A notable political figure, Jak has seen him on the news. What on Ecracon was he doing fraternizing with a down town criminal like York?

Jak struggles to find the right thing to say. Something politically corrupt? Would that fit the circumstances? In the end he decides to remain silent on the premise that if one speaks everyone will see he doesn't know what he's talking about but if one keeps his council everyone will know he is a wise authority.

York is over at his computer, takes a disc and pops it in a case, sealing it into a small white envelope. He hands the package to Jak with another of those syrupy smiles.

"Thanks." murmurs Jak, stuffing the papers into his pocket and turning, eager to vacate the vicinity.

"You've forgotten something." The voice mellifluous, Jak turns back knowing the game is up but trying a last ditch attempt.

"Mr. Roke said…."

Suddenly he is lying face down on the floor his arm twisted so far up his back that he thinks it will break. York's knee is there in the small of his back and the cold point of the gun at his head.

"Who are you?' York demands menacingly. At first Jak says nothing, relying on the success of his earlier decision but then his arm is persuaded even further up his back and seems on the point of snapping. He realises that the truth may after all have its virtues.

"Jak Dane." He gasps. To his surprise he is released. He rolls over slowly and looks into the red eye of the lazer gun. Warily he gets to his feet, trying to massage the agony out of his arm. York's face holds an amused though calculating expression.

"Krey, I believe, would like to speak to you. He would probably like to see you dead but I can't be sure."

In the pocket of his stolen coat is the Pretanox boy's knife lying snuggly in its sheath. Jak is acutely aware of its weight against his leg. He knows he can throw it with pretty fair accuracy and speed but he has only ever done so in the environment of the unicamp academy, not quite the same circumstances as here in a drab, ill-lit room with a lazer pointing at his left eye and a live target facing him. Jak stops rubbing his left arm and allows his right to drop naturally, his hand over the pocket. York is edging across the room toward his computer and Jak sees the interbeam consul beside it, because of the visor he can't tell where the little man is looking but there is a possibility that his attention is divided between his hostage and the task of traversing the cluttered room.

Jak's aim is not as true as he had hoped but he has succeeded in cutting off a portion of York's right ear. The pain and surprise of this unexpected attack distracts York sufficiently enough for Jak to lunge over the back of the couch. A chair somehow finds its way into his grasp on the way. He uses this to clout the little man over the head. The abused item of furniture splinters into fragments and York slides among them to the floor. Jak feeling justifiably pleased with himself; resists the urge to flee immediately and sets about searching the room as quickly as possible. The conviction takes hold of him that he has somehow stumbled right into the enemy camp, surely some clue, some kind of answer will be unearthed. Jak's search becomes increasingly more frantic as he finds nothing. He knows the messenger York was expecting will turn up any time but he is loath to go without even a hint of the information he is sure is there. He tinkers futilely with the computer but as expected the screen withholds its secrets, there is no possibility he will stumble fortuitously upon the correct pass code. He inspects the desk but the drawers are full of old junk and a few bills, none are enticingly locked. The fruitless investigation is coming to an end and the last place to look is the bathroom. Jak rummages unhopefully through the medicine cabinet but there he finds a digital scan key. He holds it up to the light and the numbers revealed show a Keltian city code, a site code, which he doesn't recognize and a block number. Certain that it holds some significance Jak slips it into his pocket. Before he leaves he checks the unconscious York. A quick frisk through his pockets yields nothing but as Jak leans over him he notices that the dark visor has slipped from York's eyes. Through the closed lids he can see a strange light fluctuating behind the skin. He draws back, startled. So York is Censite. It makes Jak's flesh creep. It is the first time he has seen one in real life. What is a Censite doing on Ecracon? Censites cannot leave Detagon and he has never heard of one doing so before. Jak leaves Rhetros House with the strange key in his pocket. He also has a report copy destined for Krey Roke on his person but he has forgotten that for the moment.

"Do you have this report?" asks the administrator.

"We do your honor but we intend to present this evidence later if that is acceptable?"

"As you wish."

"Your honor we again ask permission to call Senator Krey Roke to testify."

"Permission denied"

The Lawyer doesn't look disappointed he knows they will have to call Krey eventually. His motive in asking for Krey is to build up public interest and expectation. He wants the case to stay in the headlines.

The days live coverage has left the 12 nations feeling uncomfortable. First the strange indication that one of their senators is involved in the case, then a Censite living in their midst? Whatever next?

Chapter 12
Krey

Mmm…Yes I do remember being startled out of my usual calm.

"Jak Dane was at York's apartment!" I exclaimed. Yes it did surprise me a little. That the boy had once again avoided my destroying tentacles was sufficiently annoying but that he should turn up at York's apartment that was….well… amusing actually... that is, it would have been amusing if such a magnitude were not at stake. I lay one fine white hand on my favoured crystals but did not pick them up. Dekkor who had been my emissary on this occasion stood unafraid but respectful before me.

"I'm not unduly concerned at this present time," I said coolly, "however the boy undoubtedly knows something or he would not have presented himself at our little friend York's despicable dwelling."

There was no comment from Dekkor or Felice, who had draped her elegant form across an easy chair. I closed my eyes and rested my head back.

"I fear we must venture a reconnaissance to Detagon. I am not entirely jubilant concerning the proceedings on that horrendous planet and though I do not relish such an expedition I am persuaded it is necessary. Dekkor you would like to come?"

Dekkor nodded his agreement.

"And Felice you would no doubt like to accompany me?"

"I would like it excessively, may I come?"

"On the contrary you must remain here. We have a little matter for you to attend."

"You can't mean for me to hunt that ridiculous school boy?"

"Precisely my dear, though I don't think we can say he is entirely ridiculous. You must locate and dispose of him before he causes any trouble."

Yes I do remember it all quite well it must have had rather an unsatisfying impact. My plans are always so meticulous and I can't abide error.

Chapter 13
Back Inside

Jak is now entering the city via the main sewage pipe. When he had realised this was to be the mode of entry he was fairly provoked into passing through the portals and throwing himself upon the mercy of the patrol guard. However now his first revulsion has subsided he agrees to enter the maintenance capsule. Apparently Bek has not availed himself of the opportunity this evening and there is space for him beside Tril in the overcrowded compartment. Maloa seems to be in a sardonic humour.

"I take it you feel you are too elevated for this unique form of travel Mr. Dane?" Jak merely smiles and squeezes into the narrow space beside his peregrinating companions. Upon Tril's gloved hand there rests a minute, hooded,lizard, who reveals obvious symptoms of a cold.

"Do you like my little lizzy?" Tril asks Jak hopefully. "I'm selling her at a bargain price."

"...Er no thanks I'm a little short of spare cash at the

moment." Jak replies, looking at the lizard without reluctance.

"It's probably just as well, I think she might die, she's caught this rotten cold off of some inconsiderate idiot." continues Tril, with gloomy foreboding.

"Oh surely not." Jak is saddened by this melancholy prediction.

"Well, it's better she dies this way than at some soup factory which is what will happen if I can't sell her."

Jak, thinking this is a joke smirks dutifully. Tril is indignant at such callousness and terminates the conversation with a sniff that convinces Jak that he is the inconsiderate idiot who has passed his germs onto the innocent lizard.

They make frequent stops along the line, for Maloa to check the seals.

"It's not so bad once you get used to the idea." Observes Jak brightly.

"We may get stuck in here and they won't get us out until the morning, that's what happened a few months back."

"Did you not get caught then?"

"No but we had to pay through the nose for the privilege."

"Do you sell animals in the city then?" asks Jak, intrigued by a number of packages stacked beside Tril, small scuffling sounds emanating from them.

"Yes but business is going downhill fast. I don't think I'll be able to manage it for much longer. It's largely due to the fact that that WITCH is charging me exorbitant rates."

"This witch is charging you less than she aught Mr. cheerfulness."

"These species," continues Tril, ignoring the interruption, "will all be extinct soon."

"Oh they're protected are they? That's why you smuggle them in?"

"In a way I suppose they are but it won't help. All species have to die out, you know, make room for something else and all that."

Jak is beginning to feel depressed.

"We've reached the end of the road." Shouts Maloa as the capsule suddenly begins to slow. "Thanks for flying the sewage line, please come again."

"When do you pick us up?" Asks Jak, checking his watch before climbing out of the hatch.

"Sorry luvvy it's a one way ticket."

Jak is just about to expostulate when Tril gives him a box of rodents to carry.

"5.45," he reassures Jak, "that is unless we all get caught and locked up in the precinct holdings, which is probably what will happen knowing my luck. Hey don't be late 'cos she won't wait."

Jak hands back the box as they stand amidst a network of pipelines in between the outer and inner membranes at the edge of the city.

“Do you know where site code 623 is?” He asks Tril as they part.

The animal seller looks at him sharply.

“That’s Government Tower.” He states with an air of catastrophe.

“Thanks Trill, I’ll see you later.”

“I doubt it.”

Jak hitches a lift across the city to the shipyard, with an elderly shift worker. It is a risk, the man might be of a suspicious nature but Jak doesn’t have time to be strolling around the walkways all night.

The Straiff Shipping Company is open for night deliveries so Jak enters the offices without diffi culty. Inside the foyer he gives the adjutant his father’s data number and she taps it into the computer. He is just admiring the authenticity of her light golden curls when the screen blips ominously. She turns blank eyes to him.

“I’m sorry Sir this data number has expired.”

“Since when?”

“17-20-24.”

“But that can’t be, there must be some mistake. My father was here in 22 shipping out to Detagon.”

"I'm sorry Sir this data number has expired."

Jak vaults the counter and pushes her aside in order to access the computer.

"Securitor will be alerted automatically in twenty seconds if you do not desist." She informs him dispassionately.

Jak reaches out and grabs her hair, finds the place at the base of her neck and wrenches with all his might.

There is a shower of sparks and the smell of burning synthetics.

"You're a pain in the neck." He tells her as he throws down an attachment of wires.The adjutant blips plaintively then lies motionless. Jak taps up Detagon. The file opens:

Last shipment – 5-22-24.

Craft- Lazortrom.

Contractor- Petaman.

Jak knows this to be incorrect. Verdor had called him from the Trellix outpost on his way to Detagon. His father's ship is Lazortrom.

He taps up Contractor Verdor Dane:

File closed.

He taps up Lazortrom: The ship is filed under Petaman.

He taps up Krey: nothing.

Roke: nothing.

York: nothing.

Censite: nothing.

Census: nothing.

402-623-27, the number on the digital scan key: nothing.

Government Tower: nothing.

He combs his brain for something else to try but he knows no more. This is the total sum of the information he has accumulated. He slams his hands down on the consul in exasperation. With a glance at the defunct adjutant, he hurdles the counter, leaves the building and is out of the shipping complex before he hears the thin reedy sound of the alarm.

Jak has been in the vicinity of Government Tower only once previously. He was a child then, with sticky fingers grasping his mother's hand. They were among the vanguard of the swarming hoards attending the liberty parade of 06. There had been carnival bands and floats, Lazer rays and sparkling light fountains. The headmen had filed past solemnly, careful smiles toning their features. There had been street dances and alfresco banqueting 'til the small hours. He can see the pictures clear as crystal in his mind. The backdrop for these festivities had been the Government Tower, tall and straight advertising the very uprightness of the authorities in the severity of its architecture, Custodian of the People.

"Well," thinks Jak, "what a long, long time ago that was." Now as he looks up at the tower, ghostly in its vacuity, he wonders fearfully where all this is heading.

There is no problem getting into the government zone, the key slides into the security lock like a homing probe and the force field dissipates in shimmering acceptance of the legitimacy of his entry. There are numerous guards patrolling the area, these Jak evades with some difficulty, indeed he is perilously near to being caught three times that he knows of. The lock at the main entrance of the tower, however, rejects the key with an alarming series of bleeps. After a moment of uncontrolled panic, Jak reconnoitres the building and discovers a row of unprepossessing posterns, each with a block number over the lock. Towards the end of the row 402-623-27 looks innocent enough.

"Oh hell!" Thinks Jak tremulously, as the door slides silently open and he steps over the threshold into a spacious lift compartment. "I'm going deeper and deeper." Even so, with the disquieting knowledge of jeopardy, there is a rush of adrenalin, a certain delicious anticipation, and a tingling excitement that makes him feel peculiarly energized.

A light pinpoints the ascent on a panel of names. As the climb ceases the light illuminates the legend: Headman Krey p.d.r. Jak smiles into the semi-darkness. Now, he feels, he is really getting somewhere.

There is nothing that isn't perfectly ordinary in Krey's suite of offices. Jak can't believe this unexpected finale. After an age spent analyzing hideously tedious city files on planning and property tax, a vain, and Jak can't help feeling, ridiculous search behind pictures, in innocuous desks, even under cushions and various other items of furniture, he comes up with nothing, nothing more interesting than a photograph of Headman Krey receiving his appointment mace. His long silvery hair is plaited over one shoulder his features, slightly azoic except for the eyes which glitter with an unreadable intensity. Jak places the picture back on the desk. He experiences an impression of anticlimax followed swiftly by a feeling of foolishness. He curses his optimism in thinking that Krey would leave anything incriminating in his offices then hand over keys making the whole accessible to the dubious York. It was puerile to have considered such a thing. Jak paces through the rooms restlessly, reluctant to leave with nothing gained. Th en as if it had materialized from nowhere Jak finds a door! True the door is contriving to look like part of the décor but even so he is amazed that he never saw it earlier. When Jak thinks carefully about the positioning of the rooms it becomes obvious that, yes, there is indeed a considerable area of ground space unaccounted for. The door of course is locked and the code key is, this time, of no assistance. Jak prods the door and fumes for a little while before having a futile kick at the unyielding entry.

He soon thinks of the window, he crosses the room and looks out. Way down below he can see the quiet street. Best not to look down there! Instead he looks across to where he hopes to see a window. There is no window but he can see a ventilation grill. Will it be big enough for him to squeeze through? There is only one way of finding out. Jak climbs out onto the ledge. It is only when he is out there gripping onto the cornices of the building like a demented free jumper that he starts to lose faith in his climbing abilities. Still he is half way there and it's just as hard to go back as forward. Jak grits his teeth and continues along the ledge, grateful for the ornate architecture of the edifice.

It takes a lot of fiddling to remove the grill. When it's finally off Jak slants it and shoves it through into the secret room, squeezing through himself with some difficulty.

The room below is in almost total darkness, with profound relief Jak drops face first into the room. Half landing on a chair, he is sprawled across the floor in considerable pain and slightly dazed before the possibility of an alarm occurs to him. He waits for a breathless moment for the sirens to wail but the soundless darkness presses down on him, unbroken. Gradually the feeling that he will, imminently be captured leaves him. It takes Jak several, shin scuffing, head knocking moments, furniture looming with almost anthropomorphic truculence in front of him, before he finds the means to shed light on his surroundings. This done he notices that he has activated a security camera. From high in the ceiling, the camera follows his progress with a malevolent eye. Unnerving though it is there doesn't seem to be a lot he can do about this except turn out the lights and proceed in total darkness. This alternative he deems to be impracticable and so chooses to ignore the camera in the hope that he is not edifying the mind of some patrol guard by his nocturnal ramifications. In searching the room he finds a case of unmarked holofi les. He selects one and slots it into the reflector. Sitting back in an easy chair he watches the picture shimmer into life. The file consists of a compilation of homesteads and mansions, eminently tasteful, transcending many of the homes he'd seen advertised on the Zennan holiday channel. He tries a couple of other files to find more of the same. Though Jak is impressed by the excellence of these properties it is something else, another common factor that insinuates itself on his notice. Where is this nirvana? He assumes at first that the locations are on different worlds, scattered across the galaxy, so varied and multifarious yet equal in breathtaking beauty are they. Then intruding on his rapt attention is an oscillating globe at the outskirts of the hologram. A light appears on the globe corresponding to each scene and a coordinate, for the viewer's information. Is it possible all this sublimity is contained in one world? It seems so. Jak probes his mind trying to recall the continental outlines from his unistudies but though there are similar, Plerix and Torretos for instance, he knows they are not right. In the end he decides that the planet must be outside Crimmer jurisdiction but he is not wholly satisfied with this conclusion. Reluctantly he switches off the reflector and the picture fades like a dream. With his mind full of images he continues his search of the room. He next discovers an interspace communications system almost of the proportions of the Kelti terminus system at the continuum institute. Jak gazes at it in awe. It is in operation and receiving pulse signals on a number of frequencies. Puzzled he tries to bring something up on the monitor but even in this inaccessible sanctuary the computer is security coded. All Jak can do is write down the frequencies to check later. It is while he is looking through a batch of scripted files that he discovers something that chills him to the bone. He comes across a folder with his name on it. 'Jak Dane' in bold capitals staring back at him. He opens it with such undisciplined vigour that the papers are broadcast over the floor. He stands gazing at the strewn sheets for a moment, the empty file in his hand. His own picture looks back at him. Abruptly he crouches down and collects the contents together. His PLA is there, as well as an abundance of personal information including addresses and details of friends and acquaintances.

To Jak this signifies immediately that Krey Roke is the enemy! The conviction slots into place so there is no doubt in his mind.

Initially Jak is awed by the hugeness of this revelation as he conscientiously slots the papers back in the file but then, naturally, wrathful indignation overwhelms any former feelings of fear. He hurls the papers across the room and as they settle he is surprised to find in himself an inclination to vandalize Krey's inner sanctum leaving it eventually with an aspect of cataclysm including a number of pithy messages to Krey defacing the walls. Instead, he contents himself with continuing his pursuit of information with a certain destructive abandon. For instance, upon discovering a secured drawer in the desk he wrenches and splinters that item of furniture until he has the offending compartment lying with its contents disheveled, on the floor. The items that he finds to be of the most consuming interest are two perfectly formed spherical phoris crystals. After closely analyzing these gems, tapping them together, holding them up to the light and gazing into their lucid depths at the spiders transfixed within, he deduces that they are indeed authentic and of considerable worth. He therefore appropriates them without compunction. It isn't that he particularly admires these baubles, in fact he finds them slightly repulsive but as he now discovers himself to be in rather pecuniary circumstances he feels that the valuable crystals can be used in that ancient mode of currency, barter. This done and his examination of Krey's secret office completed, Jak is able to leave, much to his relief, through the hidden door which unlocks easily from the inside.

Chapter 14
Krey Roke the Sooner

Yes I was faintly amused at first. I remember watching with a slight smile the movements of my uninvited nocturnal visitor not of course in real time but the following morning. Felice I could tell was wondering at my mocking tolerance but that was before he stole my precious mascots. I know it is whimsical of me to feel so attached but I think my desire to efface his very name from the universe became personal from that moment. As Jak Dane lifted the crystals from the mutilated desk a strange stillness came over me. Felice was holding her breath. Then at the precise moment that he slipped them into his pocket he glanced up at the camera and looking straight at it he offered up a rakish grin, touching his hand to his brow in a derisive salute. I can freely admit that my blood was boiling at that point though of course I didn't allow my anger to show, that would truly have been a weakness. I think Felice may have known, she abruptly switched off the recording.

I dispatched her to visit that delightful sewer rat Maloa Aloy, and she went without any of her usual witticisms for I do believe my eyes were particularly hard, my face taking on that implacable quality and my voice, yes my voice was as soft and cold as a Zennan ice crystal it commanded her and she was afraid. There was no defiance in her eye and no pout on her pretty lips. She would not fail me she promised.

Now having seen all this evidence in my inner sanctum you no doubt are wondering about my intentions. Well look to your history books my friend. Have you never heard of The Sooners? They are quite my most favourite of ancient scoundrels and are, I would have to say, the inspiration for my glorious plan.

Chapter 15
A Heavy Load

It is 10.30 and Jak is on his way to visit Peyto Banner, a man mainly remarkable for his huge mop of hair, every individual strand of which sticks out in a contrary direction so that he looks for all the world as if he has been sucked backwards through a vacuum cleaner and is yet living that's what it looks like to Jak anyhow. Also of interest, particularly to Jak and any other person mainly of the male gender, who occupy a great deal of their time thinking about, riding in or upon, taking apart and rebuilding or just tinkering with mechanical contraptions of conveyance, is his ownership of an expansive warehouse enclosing multitudinous components in various degrees of antiquity and decay. On rare occasions it has been discovered that some items of use actually lurk amongst this fantastic array of curios.

Peyto Banner looks out of his little office window as Jak pulls up on the pad. He doesn't recognize him immediately because of the unfamiliar speed belonging to Leela's father. Otherwise it is unlikely he would have received his young visitor at all. Indeed, he most probably would have hidden under his desk and pretended the warehouse was closed.

"Jak!" He gasps when realization dawns. "What the Dace are you doing here?" He makes his way behind his desk with the obvious belief that this will serve as a barrier in the event of a frenzied attack. "I've been seeing your face on every channel." He looks furtively both ways as if the securitor may even now be in hailing distance.

"Hello," replies Jak. "I can tell you're pleased to see me, very gratifying that."

Peyto is rendered inarticulate. Jak looks steadily at him for a long time he is uneasily aware of the distress he is causing the scrap merchant. It is a taste of power, of control over another because they are afraid. He decides he doesn't like the flavour. He notices that Peyto is eying the inter beam on the desk.

"Don't." Cautions Jak briefly.

"What?" Stammers Peyto, raising his hands as though Jak holds a gun on him. "What? I wasn't doing anything."

Jak smiles grimly. "Have you still got that Remmy seven buried out back?"

Peyto, whose nose is a large bulbous affair, rubs this protrusion with the back of his hand, as if this stimulus will relieve him of the necessity of answering. Jak waits however.

“Ah, well. No… I mean yes...but it’s not for sale.” He eventually responds, haltingly.

“I see.” Jak delves into his pocket and retrieves one phoris crystal and places it provocatively on the desk. Peyto swallows, still shaking his head but his eyes are alight with avarice.

“Come on Peyto you know it makes sense.” Encourages Jak.

“But Jak, it’s virtually sold already. I’ve been working on it for a week for a good friend of mine, I promised him ages ago… A deal’s a deal. I’ve got my reputation.” This plea is not made directly to Jak as Peyto’s eyes never leave the crystal.

“Have you?” says Jak in mock surprise. “Oh well.” He sighs regretfully as he places the temptation to Peyto’s integrity back in his pocket.

“Hold it!” Cries the virtuous merchant. “She’s empty. Even if I did let you have her how would you fuel her?”

“You’d fuel her for me Peyto.”

“You must be joking,” expostulates Peyto indignantly, “the cells will be as much, and more, than the ship’s worth.”

This time Jak places both crystals invitingly on the desk. They lay side by side, glittering in the small light from the window. This is too much.

“It’s a deal.” Peyto scoops up the gems greedily.

"Lead the way Mr. Banner." Giving a mock bow, Jak indicates that he wishes to proceed to the vessel in question. With the crystals now in his possession Peyto becomes more businesslike and some of his previous tension brought about through being in Jak's company ebbs away.

"She's a fine craft," he informs the new owner. "one of the old school. They don't make 'em so good now I don't reckon."

Jak agrees abstractedly.

"You'll need your Jet pack and puller boots," continues the dealer, "my grav metre packed in a week ago. It's a bit chaotic in there but kinda handy so I haven't had it fixed."

"Saves you a packet too no doubt."

"You're dead right it does."

Inside the warehouse is an astatic necropolis for all kinds of machinery. It is eerie to see it all at weightless silent rest. They manoeuvre their way through to the back and the disassembled components ripple gently in the wake of their progress.

The ship is small, not much more than a shuttle really. The lines are sleek but outmoded and there is certain old fashioned flamboyance about her long tapering prow. She has wings too, which date her considerably but Jak holds a longstanding affection for the mercurial little vessel. Her name is Capritor, emblazoned in luminous lettering over her wing. He has often fancied acquiring her, little knowing that, one day, necessity would bring her into his possession.

"Her grav metre works." Announces Peyto proudly as they enter the cramped cockpit. Jak lovingly peruses the console while Payto is desperately trying to remove an article of software from one of the side panels without attracting the young man's attention. He looks up to find amused eyes upon him.

"What on Ecracon are you doing Peyto?" Is Jak's interested enquiry. Peyto looks embarrassed and tries to sidle round in a futile effort to obscure his activities from view. He merely succeeds in adding to his discomfort by striking his head upon the low bulwark.

"I do believe you're trying to appropriate my stuff... you old reprobate. Let's have a look at it."

Crestfallen, Peyto moves awkwardly aside.

"You know how it is Jak." Is his somewhat inadequate explanation. A gleaming piece of neoteric equipment is revealed looking singularly out of place among the prenordelic trappings of the Capritor.

"Ve...ry nice." Jak is impressed.

"My mate commissioned this computer. You'll be robbing me if you keep it."

"Consider yourself well and truly robbed then."

"I thought as much." Sadly Peyto lays down his tools.

As it turns out the only thing that actually works

properly on the Capritor is the grav metre and the auxiliary thrusters. Fair play to Peyto, he has initiated a major overhaul but there is still a lot of work to do.

It is late afternoon and Jak is in the process of soldering a complex array of wires on the under carriage en route to the engines. Hampered no end by the antigrav he is feeling vaguely cheesed off, when all hell breaks loose in the warehouse.

Before he is aware of what is happening a projectile cuts through his shoulder and he can smell his own flesh burning as he starts to spin out of control in the buoyant atmosphere.

He catches a fleeting glimpse of Peyto, fear twisting his face as he crouches underneath the Capritor's wing. Suddenly Jak is twisted into a refracted spiral as another projectile pierces his leg. Tossed, like a torn rag in among the assembly of machinery he sees bubbles of his own blood oscillating before his eyes. The ebb and flow of disturbed equipment obscures his view but behind them he can see the red light of lazers stabbing the warehouse. Gasping in an agony of excruciating pain he adjusts his jetpak thrusters with his good arm until his equilibrium is restored.

His thought clarity distorted by burning pain and also a fair amount of shock and fear, he takes a moment to try and drag himself together. Emerging from the bulk of an ancient accident damaged peltavor an armored soldier menaces his injured prey. It is by mere chance that Jak happens to see him and the sight is enough to activate his tortured body. In a second he is gone weaving in and out of battered wreckage with a skill he didn't know he possessed. The pursuer is joined by three of his cohorts. Jak feels the heat of a narrow miss by his ear. Propelling himself between the shell of a corroded bulk container and a crippled loading shovel he turns off his jetpak and waits. They come nearer, stalking swiftly past the container. As it rocks and brushes against his lacerated shoulder Jak is engulfed in agony but the predatory enemy had passed by and he feels that in this despicable one-sided war he has at least won a round. He adjusts the little two way communicator he and Peyto were using while repairing the ship.

"Peyto!" His urgent appeal is barely audible.

"Jak?"

"Hey," Jak swallows trying to keep the distress out of his voice, "hey are you OK out there?"

"OK?" The reply is hoarse and incredulous. "I'm clinging to the side of your ship like a daced parasite, there's lazer shots coming from every which way and…," here he lowered his voice further, "the place is swarming with some kind of death squad. I suppose you know what this is all about?"

"You suppose wrong," replies Jak softly, "listen is the Remmy holed?"

"What the?…. Look Jak, I couldn't care less I just wanna get outa here."

"Just tell me, is she holed?" Urges Jak weakly.

"I guess not, these lazers will mess up the skin a little that's all."

"OK get inside and ignite the thrusters."

"What! You want me to play at being a target. Forget it, I'm staying right here."

"They'll kill you Peyto, you've got to get inside." Jak listens to the silence. All at once he feels like passing out. "Please Peyto. If you don't we're both going to die."

The zip of the lazers is his only answer.

"Peyto!"

"Right I'm inside, what now?"

"Dace, Peyto I thought you'd kicked it!"

"Aah I didn't know you cared."

"Now where's the grav metre for this place?"

"By the main docking lock. What you planning kid?"

"Good." It is going to be easier than he had at first thought. Check, was he kidding? He gazes down at his mutilated leg, his shoulder feels on fire, he is as weak as a kitten. Even thinking optimistically it's going to be the hardest thing he has ever done.

"Are you there Jak?"

"Yeah." Jak groans as a slight movement on his part inflicts yet more suffering."Yeah, I'm fine." He whispers.

"Take the ship up to the roof, then when you feel the drag boost her and come and pick me up."

"Hey you make sure you graduate properly, I don't want all my stuff crashing down."

Jak smiles grimly but makes no reply.

Apprehensively Jak contemplates leaving the security of the bulk container. There is an open expanse before him, below he can see someone probing inside the hull of a disused securitor shuttle and as he watches another comes and joins the first. There seems to be no way he can traverse the space without being seen. He turns with the intention of finding an alternative route to the bay doors when he sees five more slowly making their way through the machinery. How many more are there? He will have to make a move or be caught trapped in his hiding place. Resuming his watch over the men below, Jak sees one push aside what looks like a lift capsule and up it comes like a gift, oscillating gently as it comes toward him. As it reaches the side of the shovel Jak leaves his niche and catches hold of the capsule as it continues upwards. By dint of extremely cautious use of his thrusters he manages to manoeuvre his way into the capsule through the half open door. Once ensconced within, Jak diverts the capsule's course across the void without drawing fire. As it turns out he is able to traverse the rest of the way to the west side, to the cargo doors, without being seen. Evacuating the tiny craft however is more difficult and Jak manages to aggravate the wound to his shoulder so that it recommences to bleed profusely. Jak's vision is becoming blurred at the edges, he shakes his head as vigorously as possible with the pain exploding in his temples and it clears a little.

He discovers the grav metre above and to the side of the great docking lock. With every movement an effort and the concentration needed making his head throb like a sounding bell, after selecting a fusing tool from the belt he still has tied about his person, Jak gets to work. He fashions a sling from a piece of silicone torque strapping. He loops it round his chest under his arms then tightens the clips beneath a secure maintenance platform beside the lock. Streams of telltale crimson globular emissions float about like a beacon. He double-checks his work on the circuit board. To strain his eyes and bring the intricate array of multicolored wires into focus saps away the last of his energy, his mind is drifting. A picture of Leela floats into his thoughts and he wonders in an abstract way at the dreamy beauty of her face as she smiles at him from behind her mask. Intruding from nowhere comes a nagging doubt. There is something odd but he doesn't have the energy to unravel the problem. She is speaking to him but she is too far away, her voice is muffled. What is she saying? Jak feels distressed and it becomes increasingly important that he hear her words. She is laughing tauntingly at him. Why? Why, Leela? As if in slow motion the lazer she is carrying levels at his head. Almost too late his befuddled brain comes to the realization that he is about to die. His hand is on the gravity activator. The face before him begins to change and clarify, it is not Leela but a stranger with witch's eyes and in those eyes Jak can see murder. His hand comes down hard on the lever. Past controlled leveling at 32 mega units past normal grav at 57 and on to security drive at 74. In an instant Jak feels as if ten men are hanging tenaciously onto his legs. The silicone strapping cuts into his chest as if to sever him in two. With a cry Jak is plunged into black unconsciousness.

"Yes I was angry." Says Peyto from the witness stand. "The floating metal that composed the contents of my warehouse were flung at an accelerated rate to the floor. The cacophony of sound was tremendous as the tortured metal plummeted in a chaotic mass." He is reading his statement from a piece of paper and enjoying the effect.

"I surveyed this tumultuous scene from my elevated position at the controls of the Capritor with a jaundiced eye. My beloved collection, a lifetime's work lay crushed below me and I was not in a good mood. After a few moments I remembered Jak. I'm not what is generally considered to be a hard man and...," Here Peyto looks up and shakes his head, "the sight of Jak hanging there under the maintenance platform turned my insides to water. My heart constricted when I realised the limp bleeding form was indeed the young man. Now I've seen my share of slash and gore movies but I was not even nearly prepared for the horror of the reality I beheld." His eyes are back on his paper. "Never had I seen so much mangled flesh or ebbing lifeblood." He turns slightly and addresses the administrator, which he has not been instructed to do.

"If I've done wrong your honor in helping that lad then wrongs right 'cos it would have been criminal to hand him over."

"He could have at least had proper medical attention had you done so Mr. Banner." Reminds the administrator gently. Peyto mutters to himself inaudibly for a moment then continues reading.

"I confess that before, I had been inclined to save myself and leave Jak, who you remember had just destroyed my livelihood. Now though, after gazing upon him I was compelled but still very unwillingly to take part in the drama. Leaving the Capritor on automatic by the cargo lock I struggled against the over grav and made my way over and climbed the ladder to the metre to shift it back to normal. The whole place groaned with the reduced pressure. Here and there I could see evidence of the war party submerged beneath hundreds of tonnes of metal, it was not a pretty sight. With hitherto unthought of tenderness I cut down what was left of Jak.

The sound of movement from amongst the carnage alerted me. The enemy was still present and quite possibly active. Time was running short. With Jak laying on the limited floor space of the Capritor we passed through the inner and outer doors of the cargo lock. Making our escape with the craft still only on thruster power. I made my way across the stratosphere avoiding the traffic lanes above Cellarville. I was faced with a lack of options; I didn't know what my next move was to be. I should have called secoritor. I should have taken Jak to casualty. I should have handed him over to the Precinct. I should have just jettisoned the boy who wasn't going to live anyway and forget the whole thing. I admit I was afraid, afraid of the people after Jak and afraid of secoritor. Every road I looked down loomed with hazards and I was afraid to take them… I admit that. So discarding each idea as it came to me left me exactly where I started. For three quarters of an hour I drifted uncertainly and eventually decided to take the Capritor to an empty warehouse at the deserted tobault mine. Although this solved nothing it at least afforded a safe haven to wait things out. It was well into evening when Jak came round. I was trying to clean the boy up when he groaned almost inaudibly. At this sign of life I pumped some FT restoratives into his arm but he slipped back into unconsciousness. I continued my vigil into the night half thinking that the best thing would be for the boy to slip away without waking again.

"Thank you Mr. Banner. I would like to take this opportunity to remind voters that they may now call and commence questioning. All questions will be vetted for relevance and a limit of fifteen questions will be selected."

Chapter 16
Outer Space

It is 4.10, Jak is swallowing some protein capsules.

Peyto is eying him with disfavor.

"You're a mess," he says, "you need to get to a doctor."

Jak, half reclining, half propped up against the bulkhead,shakes his head slowly.

"That's ridiculous!" There is a thin trail of exasperation running through Peyto's voice.

"Sorry about your place." Croaks Jak. They are the first words he has spoken.

"So am I." Peyto looks moodily out of the window.

"Peyto?"

"What?"

"Don't turn me in."

"Dace it man if I was going to turn you in I would have already done it wouldn't I?"

Peyto swivels round in the captain's chair and looks at Jak unhappily.

"You'd like to get shot of me I guess?"

Peyto says nothing but he lowers his eyes before the solemn scrutiny. With his good arm Jak pulls at his brush coat where it lies in the corner. When he has brought it to his side with Peyto not helping but watching grimly, he tips the contents of the capacious pockets out onto the floor. Leaning his head back and breathing heavily from this slight exertion he rests for a while. Peyto continues bleakly silent and Jak's inactivity seems to have stretched into sleep.

"Peyto, do me a favour?" he says in a while.

"You've had your quota of favours mate."

"Stick this in the interbeam."

Peyto leans over and takes the proffered communicard from Jak's outstretched hand and looks at its shining face.

"Who's this then, who's Tanner."

"My escape route."

Peyto brightens at this.

"Will you talk for me?" Jak asks.

"The dace I will, I'm too far in this rotten business as it is."

"If he sees this," Jak indicates his battered person,

"might put a carbo adjuster in the works eh? He might also not want to get involved."

"You got a point." Peyto rubs his chin, indecision written large on his face. "I'm not telling him my name."

"Tell him what you like just get me on his cargo ship so I can slip through the net."

"But you're in such a state Jak there's no way you'll make it on your own. I can't just leave him." He mutters this last to himself, and Jak smiles slightly.

"You only have to pay for my space and your conscience is clear."

Peyto looks at him sharply. "You want me to pay your fare too?"

"If you don't I'll be left on your hands."

Peyto closes his eyes and presses his fingers distractedly against his forehead. I don't think he can believe this escapade is costing him so dear. In the end though he produces his credit card with a heavy sigh and slips the communicard into the interbeam.

Tanner's cargo ship leaves the dock at 3.70 in the afternoon. In the belly of the ship tucked between the freight containers is the small craft Capritor, Jak is slumped over in the captain's seat. After helping him there Peyto pumps an anti G and combined multi booster injection into his arm. Jak falls into a stupor his mind and body numb. Peyto leaves.

Peyto notices the cameraman zooming in on him. He

knows the people in the court have turned to look and he can feel the accusing eyes of the twelve nations upon him. He had felt a moments regret when he left Jak. He knew he shouldn't have been able to do it, why couldn't he have worked out what was right and then seen it through? Quickly though he had allowed his better nature to subside. It had been dangerous thinking that would lead nowhere and bring more trouble to his door. If only he'd known then that Jak was tagged. Now it didn't matter what he said or how he tried to make himself look good in his statement he would always come across as a swine.

He remembers checking Jak's wounds one last time. They had shown no sign of festering and he had been happy with that. He had left without a backward glance. As the cargo ship launched, relief had spread through him. He would close this chapter and not dwell on it again but even as he had made this resolution an image of Jak hanging beneath the maintenance platform, his face marred with old bruises, his fair hair lying matted across his white brow, his mangled body, so lifeless, had reared up in front of his eyes. He had known then that he would never forget and now he knew that nobody else would forget either.

It is late. We are 10,000 miles beyond the grid portal. The Capritor is jettisoned as arranged. Jak comes to as the small craft is grabbed from overhead and shot through into the airlock. His mind, fuzzy with the consequences of pain, loss of blood and the effects of the sedatives, tries without much curiosity to fathom what is going on. Then as the Capritor spirals slowly away from the cargo hold he feels interest as his body presses against the harness. His vision, blurred but gradually clearing. He watches the cargo ship receding across the depths of space. It is not until the vessel fades from view that he begins to realise that he is totally alone. His wounds start to throb dully. A thought is protruding constantly to the forefront of his mind. He keeps pushing it back; he knows he doesn't want to face it even though his brain cuts it off before it is there. I know it is the thought of the people beneath the wreckage that bothers him but he is incapable of confronting it at the moment and he subconsciously protects himself.

With an effort he brings his mind and his eyes to bear on the console before him. He goes through the motions of bringing the Capritor under control and the ship's computer informs him tonelessly of his status. He calls up the charts and plots a course to Detagon. Swiveling round in the captain's chair he looks at the contents of his pockets, which still lie where he has strewn them earlier. They are out of his reach. He looks at them hopelessly.

Chapter 17
Krey

I suppose the whole of the twelve nations are in love with Jak Dane by now. Along with millions of others I have been watching the live broadcast. I remember that day too as clearly as the others. Felice was standing by the window, staring out. She never moved. Her back was as taut as a bowstring, her hands clasped in front of her, her mouth pressed into a thin red line. Now that, I can guarantee, was somebody who had very different feelings for that wretched boy.

"He is not dead. I know it. I can feel it!" Her lips had opened imperceptibly to utter these words. She turned slowly and my eyes were instantly drawn to the livid red welt running from the finely arched brow to the corner of her hard mouth. She saw this and her anger raged, white-hot.

"I'll kill him I swear." She repeated the curse over and over, very quietly, her voice never varying in pitch. I smiled as I dragged my eyes away from her deformity. I knew I was in possession of a lethal weapon and like a death probe it was after one thing, Jak Dane!

Later Straiff called.

“I’m out Krey. This deal’s falling to pieces.” His manner was calm and firm but I could see the fear welling in the back of his eyes and in the tiny beads of sweat glinting over his upper lip.

“I think not,” I stated. Straiff stared at me over the in¬terbeam.

“You can’t stop me.” Uncertainty accentuated the thinness of his voice.

“Well we must not waste valuable time dissenting pointlessly. I require three sentinel 50s equipped with skeletal crews.” I demanded, rather cavalierly I admit.

“Why?” Straiff wasn’t trying to conceal his fear now it was blatantly inscribed upon his withered features.

“For precautionary measures only.”

“What’s going on Krey?”

“Is it necessary for you to worry yourself over minor details?”

“Krey! Will you stop playing with me.”

“Please, just be content to ensure the supply of the sentinel craft.” I closed the channel before he could reply.

“Why do you push him so far?” Felice asked. She wasn’t concerned just curious. I turned towards her my eyes dwelling on her damaged cheek until she turned away. I suppose she was aware that I did it purposely to fuel the fire that smoldered just below the surface. Knowing, as I did, perspicaciously that her anger was not directed at me but towards Jak Dane. She would not rest until she had had her revenge on him.

From the box on my desk I extract my mascots. She drew in her breath sharply then laughed.

"Shall we say, from a mutual friend of ours and Jak's?" I answered her unspoken question. "You were quite right my dear, our charming adversary has not breathed his last but he soon will, yes he soon will." I fondled the crystals. "I want Dekkor. Summon him for me."

Later I stood before the holographic star chart.

"Here is where the small craft, Capritor, was disengaged. He is heading for one of these three destinations. This, the Zophir perimeter base, here he can reach the Crimmer council without fear of interference from us. I need not tell you that would be the worst scenario. If he has any knowledge of the recordings this will be his goal. I will take care of this eventuality. Otherwise he will either hide out on Pytek III or, more likely, head for Detagon in some heroic attempt to rescue his father."

"I'll take the Detagon run." Stated Felice quickly, her eyes brittle.

"Precisely my dear; and you Dekkor will cover the possibility of Pytek III. We must not let young Mr. Dane evade us again now must we?"

Chapter 18
Arrival

With frequent stops for rest Jak has somehow managed to conquer the ravages to his body and reclaim the small strip of white paper. Back beside the Ibamex he boots it up and enters the first frequency code. He waits with his eyes half closed while the computer commences its search.

01-20-60-33-19. is the main receiver for the Ferris constellation. The incoming channels are from Zennan, Meccan I and II, Moinxe, Yosha, Detagon, in fact all the inhabited planets in the sector. All these are outgoing on one code, it is vaguely familiar to Jak. He punches it into the computer.

010-99-03-20-20 the Crimmer council report line. Jak stares at the screen. Krey is interrupting reports to the Crimmer council? Eagerly now Jak taps in the final code it is a strange one obviously from another sector 30007-05 a receiver in the first quadrant of the Senn galaxy relaying messages from the planet Cybertag, formally known as Census. Jak has the feeling that he now has all the pieces of the puzzle but he doesn't know how to fit them together. He remembers the planet he had seen on Krey's holofiles. Was that Census then? His mind is already rejecting the idea as he taps into the interstellar library network.

He learns that Census is a lost world, murdered by its own people and left a desolate waste, the aftermath of gammatonic warfare. That's why the Censites are hated so much. They polluted and pillaged their planet, the most beautiful in its time it was said, as anything this side of the Tor star. However upon the screen comes the continental outline he remembers from Krey's office. Cybertag, Census a testimony to the mindless neglect of an entire planet. There are library pictures cataloguing the devastation, the holocaust, the death of a world. Jak watches the history of that terrible time unfold. The war had barely started when the Crimmer intervened, many said too late. The destroying tentacles of radiation had Census in its grip. What was left of the inhabitants were lifted off and exiled to Detagon. The crippled world was left to smolder. Then came a period of fruitless cleanup programs, instigated by the Crimmer council. Billions were spent but the magnitude of the task was too overwhelming. With regret the project was abandoned.

Jak closes his eyes, fatigue dragging at his concentration. Tormenting thoughts are again trying to seize his mind. It is somewhat like a door that now and again swings open to reveal a nightmarish interior. Dark, so infinitely dark that he feels that if he ventures inside he may never return. That instant in time when he grasped the grav metre lever, when his own hand caused the death of others, is stored there replaying over and over so that eventually he will have to face it. He senses his thoughts are on the verge of spiraling away from his control and he covers his face with his hands. Sweat films his taut, fevered body and perhaps mercifully he slides into delirium. The anti G has worn off, the ravages upon his person are taking their toll.

The empty loneliness of deep space, interrupted only by the progress of the Capritor, tiny insignificant speck engulfed, a myriad times, in the magnitude of universal silence.

Two days and two nights merge into timeless obscurity and Jak knows nothing of their passing, submerged beneath waves of burning heat and clammy cold as the fever grips him. Aware only of raging thirst he grapples now and then with the dispenser.

At 46.2 from departure time Jak is roused by the insistent blare of an alarm. Something is wrong but as he tries to focus on the monitor all he can see is the red blaze of a warning message he cannot distinguish. A violent shudder rips through the length of the Capritor as she attempts to enter Detagon atmosphere. There is fire, pain and then blackness.

Chapter 19
Zerrin Remembers

It was one of the darkest nights, a haze veiling the stars. Even the Tor star was extinguished that night. Lying on a flat rock I gazed up at the sky, trying to probe the canopy for its blue fire.

If Pal died… there would be nothing. Just loneliness. Was it an omen that the sky was so black?

Beyond the mist, a light, traveling rapidly, appeared as a faint glow just filtering through, tugging at the subconscious, not registering. My mind was back at the cave and the necessity to return. I rolled over and picked myself up from the rock.

When the explosion came it echoed through the length of the rock strewn valley, rebounding off the cliff face. The tremor under foot was enough to make me stagger. Orange light flickered over the stone columns and a dozen or so metoricks flew screeching overhead. In the return to darkness, as I was still crouching down instinctively, I remembered the rapid transitory light.

There was a body.

From my vantage point high above the wreckage I watched uncertainly. In the faint glow from the smoldering craft no movement was discernible. Yet I hesitated. The thought of food and possibly medical supplies was crowded out by the presence of the body.

Eventually though, there would have to be an approach. Soon other scavengers who, no doubt observing the crash, would come and then there would be nothing left.

Scrambling down a rocky incline I closed in warily.

The body moved.

Debilitating fear arrested all movement and then I backed off, tempted to run but the body held a fascination, a magnetism that was irresistible. He was tall, taller than any Censite. I edged closer for now the body was again inert. It was a terribly wounded and mutilated body that would surely die. Suddenly high up in the craggy mountains across the valley, a maniacal yell rent the silence. A line of torches danced. They were coming.

Immediate departure was imperative yet still I lingered beside the form of the stranger, unable to leave him to the mercy of the outer dwellers. He would die anyway. He was a hated foreigner from the corporate planets, an oppressor and yet...

Flagor, I know, would have spat on the injured face and left. Or maybe even terminated what remained of the despised life force. However I, though hating the oppressors as any Censite would, am not quite that hard.

The body was heavy, a dead weight, the path to the cave was uphill all the way. I was wiry and strong but small, not much above half the weight of the stranger.

Detagon dawn was breaking in the south and the scavenging outer dwellers had been and gone. Many times during the arduous night I had left the body on the path and raced to the cave to check on Pal. Each time with a heart heavy with dread but Pal seemed no worse, his face as white as chalk the little boy slept on in the black cave, now there was the stranger to look after too. I was pretty sure I had made the wrong decision that night but I was too tired to care, I slumped down on the rock floor and slept.

When I think of it all now in my, to me, luxurious surroundings at the house of detention, watching Jak and his monitor it all seems so strange.

Chapter 20
Enmity

Jak wakes to darkness and an uneasy sensation. Is this death then? His body feels like it has died a thousand times each more painful than the last and there is a deep weary sickness at the pit of his stomach. Is he going to die? Above him two bright orbs are gazing down at him. The sense of uneasiness increases. He has seen the glow of Censite eyes before, harsh, pale, unnerving. Yet these eyes are not quite like that, they hold a dark blue fire, an almost violet luminosity. Still weird but not repellent.

"Where am I kid?" his voice is barely audible in the hushed stillness of the cave, there is no response, Jak tries again.

"What's your name boy?" The youngster rises from the crude seat beside Jak and walks across to a steaming pot without answering him. Jak raises his head a little and watches the slight figure by the glowing embers of the fire, the small weary face, the tangle of black unkempt hair stuffed into a round cap of no distinct colour, the narrow hunched shoulders, the ragged shirt and trousers, the bare dirty feet. Dace thinks Jak what a little heathen.

Jak perceives that the urchin is again beside him, the deep blue eyes drilling into his face with an intensity detrimental to his comfort.

"Take it." A low husky voice demands in a strange lilting accent.

Jak takes a look at the gruel and as he does a strong odour wafts into his nostrils, his stomach churns. He leans back shaking his head. Impatience and bitterness and yes a blaze of anger swiftly shadow the small face and the bowl is still held determinedly before him. He doesn't refuse a second time though there is no sign of gratification on the hard little face that looks scornfully into his.

Chapter 21
Krey

I can imagine the scene at Detagon as Felice described it to me.

The streets of Gedd the Detagon holding city were narrow and empty. A cold wind pressing in from the east whipped the rubbish into the vacant doorways. A woman gazed out of a broken window into the dusty road her eyes as cold and bleak as the deserted dwellings all around.

"We will wait here until we can proceed under cover of darkness." She spoke quietly to the two men accompanying her without turning her face from the forbidding aspect before her.

A caped figure emerged from the shadows of an adjacent alley and the woman stepped back from the window but continued to watch. The man took a few stumbling steps into the street his cloak flapping crazily. His voice reached them carried on the wind, a muted unintelligible tongue as he moaned some dirge to himself. A sharp gust whipped up a cloud of dust at the hood shrouding his face. As the dark material slipped away the watchers caught a glimpse of his disease ravaged features.

"I hope you remembered to take the vaccination my dear." I said to her when she reported to me.

Six days passed before any word filtered through to them. I can imagine those interminable days. Felice ceasing to believe that her prey was within her grasp. The rest, terrified from the instant they saw the first plague victim, allowing their fear to accelerate as the days wore on. She begged me, she actually begged me to let her withdraw. I just smiled and stressed the virtue of patience. That was easy for me she said bitterly, installed in the luxury of Zophir how contemptible was my spurious patience, while she fretted in the squalor of Gedd. Really she could be quite amusing sometimes.

Then on the sixth day information came through that parts of the Capritor had been sold in the market place. Felice forgot her concerns and became the huntress once more. They left under cover of darkness with one guide to lead the way across the barren, empty outlands. They were relieved, all of them, to vacate the city where death hung heavily in the air. They could feel it weighing down like a shrouding mist.

Chapter 22
The Child

Jak is appalled when he sees the child. The existence of the small boy is news to him. He had lain for hours wondering and worrying and there was no other sound in the cave. The older boy had gone; the one that looks at him with smoldering hatred burning up his eyes. Jak thought he was alone. Restless and uneasily aware that he has been incapacitated for many days while he knows not what plot proceeds against him, he drags himself up off the couch and begins to explore.

Then he finds the child of about six or seven maybe older as Cencites are a genetically small race, wrapped in rags up on a ledge where it is warmest. The deathly pallor, the emaciation of the young face induces him to believe that the young child is dead. Then the long eyelashes flutter slightly where they lay on the ashen cheeks. Jak gives a sigh of relief, the discovery of a dead child not being on his list of favourite things. However the first horror returns as he realises the child is as near as can be to that undesirable state. From the inside lining of his belt he extracts his personal survival kit, which consists of a long row of brightly coloured tablets. Mostly they are nutrients but there is also is a 65lu positive and five anti lex capsules. He dissolves two tablets in a minute amount of water heated over the dying embers. Then he stands over the child gently moistening the pale lips every few moments with the liquid. In little more than an hour the boy is breathing more easily and even beginning to look like a living thing. Jak begins to have a feeling of elation greater than any he has yet experienced. 'Saviour of life.' He muses over the title it sounds good - it feels better. After continuing his vigil for a while Jak's energy begins to flag and he realises that even the sustaining power of his philanthropy cannot keep him standing beside the child for much longer. So while his reserves are not entirely diminished he decides to move the child to his own couch. It is while he is in the process of accomplishing this by dint of dragging the crude crib across the floor, that the other youngster returns.

In less time than seems humanly possible he flies from the mouth of the cave and a tight ball of fury, catapults himself into Jak's midriff sending him sprawling against the jagged wall of the cave. Jak watches with a sinking feeling of inevitability as the youth picks himself up off the floor with what appears to be a heavy metal pole in his hands. But instead of assaulting Jak with this weapon he leaps toward the crib and lifting the bundle of rags holds it close hissing some foreign words at Jak that need no translation and backs warily towards the entrance of the dwelling, the bar gripped firmly in one hand against an evidently expected attack. Jak winces from the looks of fear, hatred and anger that are being thrown at him, and then they are gone.

They will not go far Jak decides. True, the cave holds nothing of value and little of use but it probably represents all their possessions. They will be back. He stands at the mouth of the cave gazing at the hostile landscape, so barren and lifeless. Jak calls out and listens to his voice echo and re-echo among the cold rocks. He holds out the strip of capsules and waves it to and fro.

"These can save him." He yells. There is no response ,just a lone metorick flying up with a squawk into the cloudy sky.

"Look I'll not hurt anyone." For some reason the necessity of saying this makes him feel indescribably weary.

"Come on." he tries once more and maybe there is a little anger in his voice, "these capsules will make him better."

Still nothing, the place seems empty but for the silent cliffs. Jak puts the tablets back into his belt and retreats into the cave. He will rest then go and look for them.

Chapter 23
Zerrin

It is strange to see myself through Jak's eyes, to follow his gaze as he looks out over the rocks. Yes that is just where I was, he was looking straight at me but his eyes moved on.

I rocked Pal gently, huddled beneath the protection of a rocky outcrop. I loved the child so and I found that I was trembling uncontrollably. What had I thought the stranger was doing? I had heard such tales about the cruelty of the inhabitants of the corporate planets that I knew not what to expect. When he was weak and hardly able to move I had felt pity and hatred and bitterness but no danger. Yet now suddenly I was terribly afraid. What should I do? I knew that he had the medicine that had instigated such a wonderful change in Pal and I must get it at all costs, I had heard from Mentel, the old one, that someone was coming across the desert, from the city. Trouble was brewing. I had meant to warn the injured stranger but now I must steal the medicine and leave without telling him.

It was much later and the sun was kissing the top of Temphis crag, caressing its face with a warm, golden touch. He lay at full stretch on the couch his eyes closed. I crept stealthily over the pitted floor. I turned the bar, cold and smooth against my skin. For a second I saw his head shattered and dead against the dark folds of the couch. I rolled the bar slowly in my palms and stared down at his face, the fair hair brushed across his forehead, the smooth creamy skin that had never tasted the sun, the wounds old and new that marred the perfect symmetry of his features. Oh, curse the Crimmer! I couldn't kill him. I searched his person with my eyes and discovered his belt with the evidence of an opening along the upper edge. I shifted the weight of the bar to one hand and with my heart pounding painfully ran my fingertips along the edge. Suddenly my wrist was caught in a vice like grip. I screamed and my eyes flew to his face. We remained thus for a long moment our eyes locked. Then I let out a long breath before launching into the attack but he was ready for me and held his grip on my wrist. Ignoring the sharp blows from my feet and elbows, knees and free fist he twisted me round and raising himself from the couch he took up some cloth to bind my flailing limbs. I couldn't believe he was so much stronger than I given his terrible injuries, my fear of him increased. Then he picked me up with his good arm and tossed me onto the bed. I struggled for a while then lay still, both of us breathing heavily. He stared down at me and I stared back, it seemed like forever.

"OK you vicious little brat," he said finally smiling affably down at me, "what have you done with the kid?" I closed my eyes for a moment, trying to shut out his contemptuous look.

"Listen brat," he spoke again, slowly taking the strip of pills from his belt and running them through his fingers, "if he dies you'll have none to blame but yourself; is that what you want?" I knew he was right of course, maybe I had known all along that he never meant to harm Pal, I don't know. At that moment I still felt a kind of hatred towards him. I had tried to care for Pal, I had tried to save him and now the stranger with his wonder pills would be the one. But I soon realised my stupidity. Pal was going to survive. Relief swept through me, washing over baser feelings. I closed my eyes again and oh no! Tears were stinging at the back of my eyelids.

"Come on boy don't wimp out on me, just tell me where you left the kid."

All my feelings of anger came flooding back, this guy really brought out the worst in me. I jerked my elbow and it just brushed him as he dodged back. Yes he was getting to know me. I was a nasty little Censite.

"Why you ungrateful little swine." He advanced again, menacingly.

"I've left him under an outcrop of rock," I countered quickly, "if you'll untie me I'll fetch him."

"Untie you, you must be joking. I'll wring your rotten little neck first."

We eyed each other with fomenting hostility. Finally he spoke.

"Well, where is he?"

"Over there, to the right of that scrub. There is an overhanging rock…" He was gone before I could finish. I lay back, staring at the cold rocks above, breathing deeply, allowing the irritation to slowly seep away. So he didn't think much of me and I couldn't stand him. Still Pal needed him. He was good for Pal.

Good for Pal and bad for me? How could that be?

Chapter 24
Uneasy Truce

Jak feels pretty rough. He's just had a fight with a girl, not that he'd known she was a girl when he had started. Actually he hadn't thrown any punches come to think of it but still it didn't feel very good.

"How was I supposed to know she's a girl?" He mutters to himself as he walks over the dusty stones. "She looks like seven kinds of hell."

Back in the cave he is ministering to the child in his role as noble benefactor but it doesn't feel quite so good this time and that is her fault, because she is crouched over there in the corner with her hands and feet tied, a dark brooding expression on her face, tear stains on her cheeks and for crying out loud, a trickle of blood at the corner of her mouth. Had he done that?

He comes unnoticed beside her and she stiffens as she becomes aware of him standing there. He lowers himself from his great height and sits beside her.

"I'll untie you if you promise to be good."

She says nothing and he begins to fiddle with the ropes eying her warily.

"I will have to leave you soon, you'll be glad to know. I have to reach the holding city."

"You will die if you go to Gedd." Her lilting voice is blunt.

"Maybe." He replies grimly.

"There is no maybe about it. If you get there without the outlanders killing you then the city dwellers will do it. If they don't kill you then the plague will do it."

"Why don't you write a poem about it?"

"You should wait for your friends they will be here late tomorrow soon after darkness."

He stiffens. There is a sudden intense silence that seems to reach out and enfold every living thing inside the cave and then spread out across the barren rocks. Then the minute sounds of the outlands come pressing back louder than before: The incessant drip of the seepage at the back of the cave, the staccato tapping of the cricketicks, the mournful cry of a lone weltermeek, high up on the opposite crag and their own shallow breathing. For an age he stares out of the cave and she waits for him to speak. Eventually he turns his eyes to her.

"My friends you say? How do you know?" He notices his voice sounds grim and harsh. She must have noticed the same hard quality for her reply is timid.

“Well some people, I don’t know who, not Censites....”

“How do you know?”

“The old one, he...”

“Aah! Some havey cavey vision then!”

“No. No,” she is indignant, “Mentel, an old man who lives up on the Bettel crag, saw their dust coming across the wilderness.”

“Damnation,” mutters Jak softly as he turns his eyes once more to the landscape,“you say they’re not Censites how do you know?”

“The rate at which they’re traveling, there’s nothing that fast in this place.”

Jak nods, frowning.“You will have to come with me.”

The girl eyes him steadily. “Where are you going?”

“To Gedd.”

She shakes her head slowly. “Then I will not come, Pal and I will go up there.” She tilts her chin towards the opposite crags, “to the mountains.”

“Yes that would probably be best.”

“It would be best if you came with us.”

Jak laughs harshly, shaking his head.“I would be no protection for you.”

Quickly anger rises up and flashes into her eyes.“I meant better for you!” She corrects him.

"O!" Jak laughs softly this time catching her meaning. She looks at him quickly and surprises the humour in his eyes.

"You mustn't go to the city." She urges impulsively.

"Why not?"

"Hell, I can think of a million reasons."

"Go on."

"There are ways across the wilderness but you will never find them, you need to know where there is food and water, I would say you would be dead within two days maybe only one."

"Mmm." Jak is unimpressed with her negative presumptions of his capabilities.

"The outlanders, in fact any Censite would kill you as soon as look at you."

"You didn't." He reminds her.

She looks a little uncomfortable and continues with her rendition of the horrors in store for him if he unwisely attempts to cross the desert.

"There are the monten sands, the rayel pits, and the limmex which are found all across the wilderness. Then on the far side, the sphill forest and the ketick gorge. Plus there are storms and bico winds that can hit you at any time day or night."

"So no one can get across?"

"No one, except a Censite of course."

"That's utter rubbish."

"Go then, see if I care."

They look hard at each other.

"Come on lets be friends." Offers Jak awkwardly.

"No." She says sadly, "The likes of you and I can never be friends."

"Please yourself ." Replies Jak stiffly, unused to having his overtures of friendship spurned.

"Well," he continues briskly, "we better get going, for now we'll head for the mountains."

There is a certain amount of triumph in the tilt of her chin.

"Only until I've persuaded you to lead me across the desert," he adds confidently.

"Not in a million years."

It takes only a few minutes to gather together the few meagre possessions of use within the cave. He is appalled really as he watches her choose a threadbare blanket and says perhaps not very tactfully,

"How on earth can you live in these abysmal conditions?"

She stares at him very hard for a moment, then decides to ignore him and he shrugs his shoulders.

They head up a barely discernible path that edges its way across the cliff face. The going is painfully slow. The girl is agile enough considering she is carrying the little boy in a makeshift rucksack on her back his thin legs are dangling almost to her knees as she springs from rock to rock, sometimes easing the weight of the bundle with her hands and at others needing them to pull herself up the steep ascent. Jak on the other hand is slow and ponderous, at times barely able to make headway. The girl waits for him frequently and finally while helping him over a rocky out crop she notices that his wound has opened and is bleeding slowly but steadily.

"We should rest a while." She suggests. Jak slumps against the outcrop his face as white as goat's milk. He does not answer, but lowers himself gingerly onto the dusty ledge. They sit facing into the wind as it blows unhindered across the desert, allowing its cool fingers to caress their heated faces. Not speaking, just staring out into the aching distance until their eyes hurt with the hugeness of the expanse. Jak drags his eyes away from the panorama and focuses on the foreground, asking the girl where the cave they have left behind lay.

"There," she points, "below that black fissure where that scraggy tree shows above the rock."

Jak searches the taupe basin below. "Dace! We've only come a few hundred metres." He reckons in tired disbelief.

"No it's further than it seems." She assures him.

His eyes return to a less gloomy contemplation of the horizon.

“So Gedd is out there beyond the desert?” He asks.

“Yes.”

“Have you ever been there?”

“We lived there when I was a child.” Jak looks sideways at her, ‘when she was a child’? She still looked a child to him.

“Who's we?”

“ My mother, father, older brother, me and Pal.” Her

voice is changed, husky with sadness.

Jak wonders if he should perhaps not trespass further but she seems not to resent his questions.

“Why did you leave?”

“Because of the plague but it was too late.”

Jak looks with concern at the small figure beside him, but the gleaming eyes are dry as they stare into infinity.

“How long ago was this?”

“We left Gedd about a year ago and they died within two months.”

Again Jak looks compassionately at her but she seems to want nothing from him.

"The plague, it still rages in the city?"

"Yes, soon there will be no one left."

"But I don't understand, are the Crimmer unable to find a cure? Why don't they lift off uncontaminated survivors?"

There is a strange look on the face that turns to him.

"The Crimmer hates us." She says harshly.

"That's not true. The Crimmer have always acted fairly. They rescued the Censites before." Jak realises that he has blundered onto dangerous ground. Her face is hard now with anger.

"I'm sorry." He says regretfully, "I don't know a lot about it."

She relaxes a little and seems about to make a comment but her eyes narrow suddenly.

"Look!" She points to the middle distance.

The pit of Jak's stomach tightens as he sees the dust cloud, tiny but ominous.

"How long do you think it will take them to reach here?" He asks.

"I don't know, they are moving so fast." She shakes her head, "maybe tomorrow morning it's hard to say."

"Well we'd better get moving." He rises slowly to his feet. Her face is questioning but he motions her ahead. There is an urgency about him that conveys itself to her and she heads off quickly as they once again begin the tortuous climb.

By the time the sun is kissing the top of the ridge, anointing the bare landscape with orange fire, they have scrambled onto a smoothish plateau. At this altitude the wind is rushing in from the desert, whipping at them, pushing desperately as if to urge them on. Jak turns into the current, leaning slightly forward to hold his place, his coat flying out behind him. The girl turns her eyes from him to follow his gaze but they have lost sight of the dust cloud. Jak wonders uneasily how close they are.

"I know a good place to camp." The wind snatches her words and he hears them as if from a long way off. He nods. They cross the plateau and make their way through a channel into a shallow valley, the wind pressing at their backs. The sun is soon gone and without it a penetrating chill begins to creep through Jak's flesh and right down to his bones so that they seem to creak as they struggle over the rough terrain, the dreadful wind tearing down the valley channel and straight through the figures in its path. At the end stands a buttress of rock stretching up into the twilight sky, silhouetted against dark orange and turquoise, the aftermath of the sunset, as if it were a huge angry fist. As they round the tall column abruptly the roar of the wind ceases and they hover there reluctant to emerge from shelter.

"Over there." The girl whispers. He looks ahead and sees the strangled boughs of a rock cypress twisting contorted shadows over the entrance of a narrow canyon.

"It's a good place." She pursues as if his silence were a denunciation. Jak glances down at her, the hairs on the back of his neck begin to bristle and his heart skips a beat as he looks into eyes where the glow is enhanced by the heavy darkness. He doesn't speak, surprised by the thrill of apprehension that runs up and down his spine.

"Jak!" She is perturbed by the strange quiet.

"Lead on." Jak bestirs himself and hopes she doesn't notice the shaken quality of his voice.

As they start forward to the darker shadows of the canyon, a horrendous racket assaults his ears. A flock of metoricks who were roosting unnoticed in the boughs of the lonely rock cypress, disturbed by their approach, fly up into the night sky with such screeching and squawking they make Jak's ears ring. They stumble through the debris of the tree's tortured life in the high rocky region, then turn to watch as the birds settle back to their favoured perch with much indignant flapping and shrieking.

"You're right,' Jak says in admiration, "it's an excellent hide out. There is a way out the back?"

"Yes."

"Damnation!" Jak looks down to find four bright orbs hanging, as though disembodied in the darkness.

"What's wrong?"

"Nothing." Says Jak sheepishly, "I see our little friend is awake."

"Ah yes." She laughs lightly, happily. "Come on Pal let's go we're frightening the big man."

The child speaks to the girl softly in a strange tongue and Jak stands uncomfortably for a moment, then follows them into the deeper darkness of the canyon.

"Shall I light a fire?" The girl asks him.

"Better not, I daresay they will have heat sensors." Jak, starting to feel an uncomfortable responsibility for the safety of these two young Censites, shudders to think of his unknown enemies. He pulls his coat tightly around him "Dace! It's cold though."

"We should huddle together for warmth." She suggests prosaically. She sits down with her back propped against a boulder and hugs the child close. Jak looks at them both for a moment and, deciding not to feel awkward, takes off his dustcoat and spreads it over the three of them.

"Hang on." The girl apparently remembers the threadbare blanket she had salvaged from the cave. She reaches into the rucksack and pulls it out. Then, putting the rucksack behind Jak's head, she spreads the blanket over them. They huddle together with the shared warmth of Pal lying across them. After a while they stop shivering and Jak feels the girl beside him slowly relax and drift off into slumber. He stares into the darkness for a while, thinking of his enemies somewhere out there in the desert, perhaps sleeping in a makeshift camp or maybe continuing relentlessly through the night. Then he too falls into an uncomfortable doze.

Chapter 25
Dodging

Jak wakes to a minute sound, the skitter of a pebble on the canyon wall. He gives the shoulder resting against his a gentle shake and they are up and running soundlessly towards the entrance of the canyon before they even know what is happening. There are shadows moving along the path behind them. In his imagination Jak can feel the breath of the pursuers on his neck. As they near the mouth he sees the rock cypress outlined against the night sky, he sees the great black wings rise an instant before the alarm echoes off the walls. The din is even louder than he expected it to be, now that it reveals their presence rather than the intruders. He is in no condition to outrun the hunters. He can hear an unconscionable number of feet pounding along behind them, hurried by the siren call of the metoricks. The girl, with Pal over one shoulder is breathing hard behind him urging him on. They are heading south away from the buttress and up further into the mountains. It seems to Jak as though they must be captured; the whole range seems to be full of shadows. Ahead Jak sees two, rearing up to the left of the path, whether they have spied their prey Jak knows not but he instinctively veers to the right and into nothingness. The girl reaches out to grab his coat and is thus unbalanced and pulled over into the darkness of a ravine.

They crash through several layers of canopied vegetation where ancient trees had lived and died, been washed down the ravine in torrents during storms and wedged above the streambed. Overgrown with toppal creepers and coolie weed they break the fall of the descending fugitives and as if by a miracle Jak finds himself relatively unhurt, lying in the shallow waters at the bottom of the ravine. He is the first to recover and he pulls his ill-treated frame upright. The icy water runs in rivulets down his legs as he casts about looking for the other two. There is a deep, deep blackness down here and Jak can see nothing.

"Hey…girl." He realises he doesn't know her name. "Pal, are you all right?" He hisses into the darkness.

"Whoa did that hurt!"

He hears the rustle of leaves above him and then sees the expected violet glow of her eyes peering down at him.

"Are you OK?" He asks.

Something comes round and thwacks against his ear.

"Ouch! Watch it!" He hisses.

"Sssh." She hisses back. "Sorry I couldn't see you."

Jak's ear is again clipped by another vagrant boot.

"Ouch!"

"I'ts Pal will you take him? Quick he's heavy." This request is made on a smothered gurgle of laughter.

"Ssss …you'll have the whole herd down on us." He reaches up to receive the child. "I don't know. I've survived miraculously the clutches of powerful unknown enemies, the wreckage of exploding space craft, a gravity defying leap into a bottomless pit only to be trampled to death by a couple of skinny brats."

"Ssh!" Admonishes the girl.

Jak deposits the clinging child onto the riverbank. "Wait there mate." He charges the child and splashing back toward mid stream smacks into a couple more dangling legs.

"Come on then get your butt down here."

"Where are you?"

"Standing here with your rotten foot in my face." There is a choke of laughter and then a pile of flailing limbs land on top of him. He staggers for a moment before toppling over into the shallows. There is a gasp as the girl comes into contact with the cold grip of the water then the sounds of smothered laughter.

"Sssh," warns Jak cupping water in his hand and splashing her, "they'll hear us."

"I can't stop." She gasps.

"Great pilton!" He gropes around in the darkness

until he finds her, then clamps his hand over where he judges her mouth to be. He helps her to her feet and they make their way to the bank. There the girl lies face down and laughs herself out, her face buried in the grass. Jak's wound hurts like the devil and he becomes aware of a fresh pain in his upper arm but he grins indulgently and looks at Pal.

"Don't worry she'll get over it."

Pal just gazes up at where the voice comes from, then back at his sister, astonished.

" I'm freezing!" Exclaims the girl after a while.

" Have you quite finished?"

" Mmmm." She sighed, "I haven't laughed for such a long time I'd forgotten it was so nice."

" Come on lets get warm." They huddle together as previously.

" Your wound?" She remembers. "Is it all right?"

" It'll do."

They shiver in silence for a long while. Cold and excitement making sleep illusive, Pal alone slumbers. Jak shifts his arm to accommodate her narrow shoulder a chuckle bubbles up and escapes from his lips.

"What's funny now?"

"Oh just things." He was thinking of the things he would normally have been doing of an evening like this. What a bizarre contrast, and suddenly dancing the blang with Senya or Tess seems a bit tame. Jak sighs gustily.

"What's your name?" He asks.

" Zerrin."

" Why don't you ever comb your hair?"

She doesn't answer so he shrugs "Just curious." He explains.

"You're weird you know." She mumbles.

"I'm weird! That's a good one. You should catch a look at yourself in the mirror one day."

"But it is strange." She insists ignoring his rude comments. "We were in such a dire situation, things are so…so desperate yet you laugh and behave as though it where a joke. Don't you think that's odd?"

"Yes, yes I do but if you remember it was you who was laughing your head off a minute ago."

"Yes I know," admits the girl, (he knows her name but still thinks of her as 'the girl'). "But I wouldn't normally behave like that."

"Well don't worry about it."

"I wasn't worried about it; I just think it's odd that's all."

"You're probably right." Jak is loosing interest and thinking about going to sleep.

"Do you think it was hysterical?"

"No I don't!"

"Well I do; it was a kind of reaction."

"Whatever." Jak's voice is deliberately bored.

"Yes but what do you think."

"Look brat, maybe you were hysterical I don't know. I was not. Now can we get some sleep?"

This seems to discourage her sufficiently but after a short silence she broaches a new topic.

"Do you think they will catch us?" She asks solemnly.

"No."

"What do you mean 'No.' you can't just say 'No' like that."

"Why not? You asked me what I thought and I said 'No'."

"Yes but to just say 'No' like that, you can't possibly have any idea what is going to happen."

"OK yes then. Is that better?"

"Who are they?" The girl perseveres.

"I don't know; somebody from Ecracon 3."

"So how many people are there on Ecrecon 3?"

"Millions."

"Oh right then that really narrows it down!"

Jak makes no response and as the silence draws out he feels optimistically that he will be allowed some slumber.

"What have you done Jak, are you a criminal?"

Now Jak is wide awake and feeling very uncomfortable. The recent past that lay not quite dormant he did not want to wake. Already he feels the familiar panicky tightening in the pit of his stomach.

"Why do you keep asking such damn silly questions?" His voice is sharp. "Shut up and go to sleep."

"But I like to have a…conversation."

"This isn't conversation, it's arguing."

"Well it must be the arguing I like then."

"I bet it is. It's just my luck to get saddled with a brat who wants to argue with me all the time."

" Well I haven't spoken to anyone until you came, except Mentel the old one, for… let me see… it would be coming on for forty days and I can never understand what he's saying 'cos he's got no teeth."

Though Jak chuckles drowsily at this he thinks it's pretty poignant. The girl apparently feels it too.

"And before that there was only Pal," she finishes sadly and is silent.

It is morning. Shafts of sunlight bore through the leafy

canopy like soft lazers. Jak stirs slowly then stops as his stiffened body protests.

"Ouch." He groans softly and relaxes back onto the mossy grass. He looks at the girl beside him, whose head lay in a pool of sunshine. He looks at the glossy black tangle of hair, the curve of the throat and chin, the fringe of thick eye lashes. Zerrin's eyes open suddenly as if aware of his scrutiny and with the sight of those bright orbs comes a vivid memory of the events of the night.

"Great Pilton!" He exclaims jumping up, aches and pains forgotten. "Last night those filthy swine who chased us all over this rotten mountain, they were your lot."

She looks hurt for a moment then turns pale.

"The Uluru." She whispers.

"So…," replies Jak, squatting down beside her as she sits up, "that's bad I take it?"

She laughs on a bitter note.

"I don't know why you bother to ask me, we must have been born under the same unlucky star, you and me."

"Then why don't we just kill ourselves?" Jak eyes her with disapproval.

She flushes, gets up and stands with her back to him.

"If you had lived like I…," she begins.

"Oh stop whining."

Instantly she turns and lashes out at him with the back of her hand. Caught unaware and off balance he takes the slap across his face. Slowly he rights himself and ascends, looking down at her from his great height. There is fear in her eyes but her chin is up defiantly.

"You've got the devil's own temper." He observes coldly.

"And you have the devil's tongue." She counters.

Jak shrugs and looks away.

"I'm going to wash." She states looking around for the backpack.

"Here." Jak picks it up from where it had fallen half in the stream and throws it at her. She grabs it to her chest and her face takes on a look of indignation as the icy water seeps through the front of her tunic. Jak grins as she casts him a furious look before turning and pushing her way through some bushes and out of sight.

Jak rubs his stinging cheek thoughtfully.

Chapter 26
Felice

Felice lowered herself onto a rock; her pampered body was stiff and aching from sleeping under the stars. She hated this place. All the sand in the hellish planet was either in her hair or inside the collar of her jacket. They had reached the mountainous region, the men were arguing heatedly. She knew without a doubt they would have to leave the overlanders and continue the journey on foot but she would allow her men to snipe pointlessly at each other for a while longer before she put a stop to their pathetic nonsense. The mountains loomed in front of her; she stared up into the sunlit peaks, somewhere up there, Jak was running. She ran her finger along her cheek. It had become a habit with her to trace the path of her wound and feel the raised scar tissue beneath her forefinger. Every time she completed the ritual she thought of her quarry, wondering what it would be like when the time came, remembering that other time when victory had been so close. She saw again his mangled body with death written in his dark pain filled eyes. She remembered again the astonishing look of welcome that had reached out to her across the battlefield and made her hesitate just that instant too long.

“Captain Damak!”

She dragged her thoughts back, her blank eyes taking on their accustomed look of impatient scorn.

“What do you want, wretch?”

“Shall I make a camp or do you wish to go further?”

She stared for a moment into his hard gleaming eyes.

“How dare you speak to me without my permission?”

He ought to be aware of his inferiority but there was no sign of it in his demeanor, his charged gaze went boldly over her and his lip curled as if he had found something in her dark soul. Suddenly she felt the chill of the evening on the back of her neck. She averted her gaze and looked back at the mountain. She should strike him but instead she ordered hollowly.

“No, we’ll continue for a while.” She quickly turned to her own men, easily stimulating anger and authority. “Stop arguing you idiots and get all this stuff together.”

She turned back and caught the edge of his smile.

“What’s your name, wretch?”

“Your’s is a pretty name, Felice, I like it.” He began. Stunned by his insolent manner she took a step backward and he caught her arm as she stumbled a little on the treacherous ground.

“Get your filthy plague infested hands off me.” She hissed and saw his eyes snap, as brittle as ice for a moment then he laughed softly.

"Gelff is the name." He called after her as she stormed up the incline.

Hours later Gelff touched a crumpled bed in a cave.

"This is a good a place as any." He commented.

Felice averted her eyes.

"Get that stuff in here you idiots." She shouted harshly at the men outside. They eased awkwardly under the low entry, one after the other, the huge baggage packs snagging against the rocky opening. "Don't just stand there, get out of the light."

Gelff, smiling at her sarcasm, pulled together the charred remains of the cold campfire.

"I'd say the residents left in a bit of a hurry." He observed as he lifted a half filled pan of water, ashes floating on the top, out of the way.

"Who asked you?" Felice was sulky.

"Excuse me; it's only that I think your friend was here."

Felice brightened and she touched her cheek.

"He's no friend of mine."

She slept wonderfully that night. She had taken the bed, though her fastidious nose wrinkled in distaste but her body balked at another night in the inadequate camping hammocks. She dreamt of nothing, but woke with the smell of victory in her nostrils. In reality it was the scent of the breakfast the Censite was cooking. She stretched luxuriously and opened her eyes to find him standing over her.

"Get your filthy creepy eyes off of me," is what she wanted to say, but for some reason the words never left her lips and instead she eased herself off the bed. She was in a good mood today she would let it pass.

Outside the squad slept. She kicked them awake.

"Today we kill the little rat." She announced to the morning. She caught the Censite's amused eyes and laughed.

"It's true Gelff, I can feel it." She stared up at the craggy peaks and her voice was soft.

"Eat up, then we'd best get going. They headed off up the mountain sometime yesterday I'd say. I checked out their tracks earlier but they're not going fast."

"They?"

"He's got someone with him." He beckoned her to follow him. He crouched down in a slightly hollow area a little way from the dwelling. "See?"

"Are you waiting for applause? I don't see anything." She stood aloof above him looking bored, her eyes drifting as always to the mountain, to Jak.

"Get down here and take a look then." He pulled at her hand. She wrenched away but after a moment bobbed down beside him, taking a closer look.

"Here." He pointed to a place where the soil was scuffed. "Pretty big guy, your friend."

"He's just a kid."

Gelff shrugged,"And here, these prints are much smaller, a youngster or maybe a smallish woman."

Later that day they stood at the brink of the ravine looking down at the trees and the thick web of coolie weed. Gelff turned, his eyes following the course of the river.

"It will be easy from now on." He said.

Felice was looking down into the ravine. He noticed the way she touched the scarred cheek and her dead eyes, he always thought of them as dead without the Censite glow, took on a faraway look. It made him smile. He didn't mention to her the other tracks.

The Uluru.

Chapter 27 Capture

Jak leans back against the stubby trunk of a rock cypress. They have been resting for a while. The girl watches him stonily as he tries to adjust the bandaging around his waist. She hasn't spoken to him much since their row of the morning. He figures her resentment is fueled by the fascination of the little boy for his new associate. He has seen her following them with jealous eyes. Even now he sees Pal watching him with a worried look of concern as he proceeds to unravel the bloodstained cloth.

"Ya coali methi sed?" he asks Jak softly.

"He doesn't understand you." Zerrin tells him gruffly.

"What did he say?"Jak asks letting his hands fall wearily to his side.

"Nothing."

Much to Jak's surprise Pal continues in the Kelti tongue.

"Why don't you help him?" bewildered Pal looks from Zerrin to Jak.

"I'm going to," she looks annoyed and throws down the water bag she'd been drinking from. "you should be more careful who you make friends with… he...," she gestures towards Jak's pallid face, "is not a nice man."

"I like him."

"Well you're stupid."

Pal turns back to Jak laying a small hand on his arm.

"I like him 'cos he's big and his hair is white."

"Big people aren't better, they're clumsy and they get in the way."

She is beside Jak, unwinding the bandage, her face close to his while she talks, at this last comment he catches her eye and she looks quickly down at her work. Pal's fascinated eyes are wide as the angry wound is revealed. The annoyance drains from the girls face as she gently lifts the dressing. Taking some yellowish cream from a small earthenware pot she lays it thickly onto the wound. He can feel her cool careful fingers on his inflamed skin. He closes his eyes for a moment then as he opens them again he just catches a glint of something way back up river, catching the last rays of the sun.

"They're coming." He states tonelessly.

She turns and after a moment she too sees the glint of sun on metal.

"You're in a mess Jak and in no fit state to go haring round the countryside like this."

smiles weakly. "I don't think 'haring' is quite the right word to describe what I'm doing. You and Pal had better hare off by yourselves."

"I think we'll carry on haring along with you." She says stubbornly.

"No, I'm serious you should go, I'll be OK." Why hadn't he told them to leave before, he should have done. He wishes he had.

"I don't think Pal would countenance me leaving you." She says dryly.

"If we keep running they will eventually catch us you know."

"OK so we fight then." She seems quite pleased at this prospect. Jak is not so sure.

"Fine warriors we make." He laughs mirthlessly.

"I can fight anyone." Her chin is up in that half proud half defiant gesture he'd seen before.

"No doubt you're right." He cannot deny her violent nature. "However I don't feel up to it at the moment and I don't think Pal here quite makes the grade."

"What then?" She asks.

"We'll cut back and nick their overlanders."

Zerrin smiles slowly, she likes the idea. "Let's go then." She says eagerly.

Jak stares over her shoulder. "I don't think we're going anywhere we want to go just now." He breathes softly.

She turns swiftly, behind her stands a slight middle-aged man with a long dagger. He speaks to her in their tongue. She replies briefly, shaking her head. He speaks again more sharply this time and she begins to retreat slowly until she backs up against Jak who is now standing with the aid of two Censites in ragged uniforms, there are others Jak notes, many others standing in a wide circle watching proceedings.

"Who are they?" Jak asks urgently. He receives a cuff about the head from the guard who is tying up his wrists.

"Uluru." Whispers Zerrin under her breath.

Jak wishes that he had fought like the times before. His instinct had always been to fight no matter what the odds but this time he had thought the enemy way up the river. These Censites had jumped them so swiftly and silently there had been no time to fight. Still Jak wishes he had, instead of just standing here meekly having his hands tied.

"What do they want with us?" He asks Zerrin.

She speaks again to the man who seems to be their leader. There is a short dialogue then the man lashes out and knocks her to the ground. She picks herself up more quickly than seems possible with her hands tied behind her back, snarls some words at him and spits on the floor at his feet. The man laughs and grabs her by the hair, growls something at her then shoves her away.

He speaks to his men and they roughly shepherd their captives along the river route.

"I think they are annoyed about the things I took from

the wreckage."

"You took things from the wreckage?"

"Yes I sold them to a trader from Gedd. They want to know where the money is."

"Did you tell them?"

"No I said I'd traded for food and that we'd eaten it."

"Have we eaten that much food?"

"No."

"Did they believe you?"

"No."

"Will they let us go if you tell them where the money is?"

"I doubt it."

Just then Jak hears the sound of his name mentioned

by the men trudging along in front of them. Zerrin

hears too and strains her ears to catch what they are saying.

After a moment she turns to Jak.

"They know who you are and they think they might be able to get a ransom for you from the Fedek. What on

Census would the Fedek want with you?"

Jak shrugs. "Everyone loves me I guess…who are the Fedek? "

"Sssh." She strains forward again. One of the men looks back and on seeing her so close, shoves her, causing her to stumble. Pal starts to cry. She mutters something softly to him, and they march on in silence.

They have been trudging along for some time when Pal whose hands are not tied tugs on Jak's sleeve. Jak looks down at him and the boy jerks his chin to indicate something he has seen ahead and to the left. Jak strains his eyes to see into the darkness. There! He sees it too, a shadowy movement among some scrubby trees. 'It must be the others from Ecrecon 3' thinks Jak. If there is going to be some kind of ruckus there could be a timely escape for them.

"When I give the sign we'll run for it." Says Jak under his breath.

"What's the sign?"

"You'll know." Replies Jak, after a moments thought. He waits until they are almost level with the trees where he saw the movement then he lowers his head and makes a charge at the nearest guard just as the lazer lights split the air. He and the Censite man go rolling along the ground as the sounds of confusion erupt all around them. Groggily Jak picks himself up realizing he has struck his head against the stony ground. The guard also has risen and seems inclined to engage with him.

Jak kicks up and catches him in the chest, sending him reeling. Jak turns and peers through the smoke of battle looking for Zerrin. She is between two men being dragged away to the shelter of some rocks. Even while enduring this rough treatment and trying to protect her little brother he realises her eyes are upon him.

"Run!" She calls. "Run!" Her voice comes to him small amongst the chaos of the battle sounds galvanising him to action. He scrambles away back up an incline and behind a large boulder. To his amazement nobody seems to have seen him. He looks for the guard and sees him fall. Many others fall and Jak notes an Ecronite lying on top of his 37 lazer.

From his vantage point he can see the ebb and flow of the battle. One would think that the superior fire power of the Kelti fighters would make them the obvious victors. After some moments a woman comes into the light of a small conflagration amongst the supplies. To Jak's astonishment it is that woman, the one he thought had died beneath tonnes of scrap metal, had died by his own hand. With an illogical sense of relief he sees her. At first he thinks she comes into the glow of the fire as the conqueror but she is soon followed by two of her team, their arms raised, and behind them a man a Censite holding the sophisticated weaponry of the corporate planets. From this distance Jak can see rage in every line of her body. She hurls words of abuse at the Censites in general and especially to the man who has captured her. 'Treachery' and 'duplicity' are words that drift up to Jak behind the rock.

At this stage in proceedings the Censites begin to

argue viciously. Of course Jak can't understand their tongue but he gathers that some want to kill these new captives and others feel they should be kept alive and held for ransom. The leader taking a captured lazer to the main dissenter concludes the argument and this seems to resolve any difficulties the others may have had. Meanwhile Jak probes the darkness for Zerrin and Pal thinking there may be a chance to rescue them during this animated discussion. He finds them only when they are brought roughly into the dying light of the battle fires. The prisoners are then rounded up and they start off once again along the river track. As soon as they are out of sight Jak makes his way quickly down to the carnage. The Ecronite he had marked earlier still lies at the edge of a steep drop. Jak eases the man's dead weight off the weapon and picks it up examining its workings. Unfortunately for Jak the Ecronite is not quite finished. Jak feels hands gripping feebly at his ankle he shakes them off easily enough but he is unbalanced and tumbles headlong over the edge. He doesn't fall far but hits a ledge and then begins to slither and roll down a shale slide. It takes him a while to scramble back up the slope he picks up the gun along the way and angles across coming out onto the path beyond the battle site. He follows the path but by this time the others are too far ahead and he can hear no sound of their progress.

The pale glow of dawn is lighting his surroundings before he hears them ahead of him. They are making their way down to the base of a large buttress, as he climbs over the brow of a rise he sees the snake of torches wending its way down into the basin. He doesn't hang around to be silhouetted against the brightening sky but scuttles down quickly, whilst concentrating on this manoeuvre he loses sight of them and when he searches the base of the buttress there is nothing to see. They seem to have disappeared in those few short seconds. Jak runs the rest of the way into the hollow of the basin and then walks along the base of the cliff until he comes across a fissure, hidden from him before by the early morning shadows. Peering inside he sees the flicker of receding torches on the walls of a narrow tunnel. He follows at a circumspect distance and the tunnel soon opens out into a large cavern. Stalactites hang like glistening daggers from the domed roof almost blocking the entrance of the cave.

When he looks in cautiously upon the inhabitants he sees them discarding their weaponry in a heap. A large fire burns invitingly in a central grate and most of the men hover near this heat source, warming themselves luxuriously. Zerrin is nowhere in sight but he can see Pal seated a little back from the fire looking worried and frightened. The leader has thrown himself upon a large settle and already in his hand is a huge goblet of ruby red liquid from which he drinks copiously. A woman enters from an inner room dressed in brightly coloured flowing robes. She holds in her hand a large flagon from which she fills the cups held out to her by the men. There is a lot of rowdy talk going on. The woman laughs flirtatiously with one man and another who has been glowering at them grabs her by the hair and they enter into a heated discussion. A group of women come in with trays of food, which are lain upon a rough wooden table, torches are lit and the women and men commence eating. The leader retains his seat by the fire and food is brought to him. Jak searches the women's faces to see if he can find Zerrin but in vain. Just as he is about to move forward his weapon raised, another group of women cross the threshold from the inner compartment. One is in custody between two keepers. She is clothed in a long white dress and her hair is thick and gleaming in the flickering light of the fire, falling in long tresses almost to her waist. Jak takes all this in before he realises the woman is Zerrin. She is brought before the leader and he looks her over in approval while she glares at him and struggles pointlessly with the ropes that bind her wrists. The man says something to her and she hisses a reply before spitting on the ground at his feet. He roars with laughter and then while they are still laughing Pal springs from his chair in the shadows and hurls his slight frame at the man seated on the settle. Pal's attack has little effect but the man's wine is spilled down the front of his tunic. A tense hush spreads through the room, a man's inebriated hilarity, which lingers behind the others is stifled abruptly. The incensed leader reaches for his dagger, Zerrin screams and in walks Jak the lazer levelled unwaveringly at the leader.

"OK easy now." His quiet words drop like stones into the pool of silence. Fortunately enough Pal runs eagerly to him before the Censite leader has time to grab him. His voice sounds a little cracked as he speaks again.

"Let the girl go!"

No one moves and Jak's eyes never leave the leader's face there is a look he doesn't like in the man's eye. He lets off a blast from the lazer and a front leg of the man's chair disintegrates in a lick of flames. The man is left sitting at a crazy angle his hands raised. There is a long moment when nothing happens and Jak wonders irrelevantly if the chair will collapse entirely. The leader gives a slight inclination of his head and Zerrin is released. She runs to him and the Censite band seem to converge a little closer he knows they will jump him any minute. He fires a warning shot at them and turns to run towards the tunnel.

"Have you got a plan?" Asks Zerrin hurriedly.

It is only when he hits his head on one of the stalactites at the entrance of the tunnel that Jak's plan reveals itself. They run into the tunnel and with the roar of the angry Censites in his ears Jak turns and fires at the long needles of rock until they crash in a heap of dust and rubble blocking the aperture. The three of them run and stumble through the darkness of the tunnel and out through the crack into the bright morning sun.

"We'll have to run, there'll be a back way out or they'll move the rubble fairly rapidly." Urges Jak.

"Jak…"

But there is no time for speech and Jak grabs her hand, lifts Pal and heads for the ridge but the girl is tugging at his arm.

"This way." She says, pulling at him.

"How do you know…?"

"I used to live here. Now come on."

They run round the buttress and down into a gully, at the foot of the dry channel is a small opening where storm waters obviously tumble through. Zerrin bunches up the folds of her gown and drops through the hole, after a second there is a hollow splash from below. Pal and Jak look at each other uncertainly for a moment then they hear the sound of hot pursuit coming from the other side of the buttress and Pal quickly follows his sister. Jak squeezes through into the black pit with difficulty and finally plunges into the freezing water, as his head breaks up through the surface and he gasps for air he hears Pals plaintive voice.

"Zerrin!"

Jak looks around as his eyes become accustomed to the semi-darkness but the girl is nowhere to be seen. He signals Pal to keep quiet and then dives frantically under the icy waters, his eyes open he can see nothing in the misty darkness. He pulls himself down; down into the murky depths and in his desperate flailing he at last feels his hand catch at her hair. He grasps her under her shoulders she is a dead weight as, on his last breath he kicks strongly for the surface.

Pal helps him to pull her out. Jak realises that it is the heaviness of her waterlogged robes that pulled her down as she tried to swim for the ledge. She lies now as white as death on the ledge. As Jak drags in a great lungful of air he sees her eyelids flutter and he never heard a more pleasant sound than her retching up the water that chokes her. Jak heaves his weary limbs out of the water and they lie in a sodden heap for a moment. Pal shedding a few tears of relief, Zerrin alternately spluttering and dragging sobbing breaths into her air starved lungs and Jak feeling too tired to move.

Soon though they must move, Jak rouses the others.

"Come on let's get out of here."

"This way." Gasps Zerrin staggering to her feet. They enter a narrow crack in the rock face, which opens out into a low tunnel. Jak can feel his head brushing the craggy roof and crouches lower. It becomes pitch black as they move further into the mountain.

"I hope you know where you're going." Says Jak feeling the darkness pressing upon him almost like a tangible thing holding him back.

"Don't worry we'll be fine now." Assures the girl.

At length the tunnel opens out into a dry cave, the entrance overgrown with creepers, yet letting in a few warm rays of early morning sunshine.

"Shall we wait here 'til night fall?" asks Zerrin.

"No, we need to get back to the overlanders. Do you know what happened to our friends from Ecracon?"

"No." She shakes her head.

"They were imprisoned in one of the back caves." Replies Pal.

"Well on the off chance they've also escaped we'll make our way as quickly as we can to your place then to the crash site, I reckon that's where they'll have left them."

"Are you up to it Jak?" She asks.

"I feel great. How about you?"

She nods. He wants to ask her something, it's been plaguing his mind ever since she'd said she used to live at the Uluru hideout. He reaches out and grabs her arm as she turns to leave.

"Were you…?" He stops; it is difficult to articulate the question now he has started.

"Was I what?" Her chin has come up and her tone is belligerent as if she knows what he is thinking.

"That guy back there."

"Karrif I suppose you mean."

"Well?" He hesitates. She knows his name. "He seemed a bit keen on you back there."

She regards him stonily.

"Even when they first came upon us I thought, you know, there was something."

"What, you mean when he was smacking me in the mouth?" Her face has a shut down, hard look and Jak feels he has made a mistake questioning her. He wishes he had kept his questions to himself.

Pal is looking from one to the other aware of the sudden tension that has sprung up between them.

"Karrif is a bad man." He says finally. Zerrin drops a hand to his shoulder.

"You're dead right Pal." She says bracingly. "Come on lets hit the road." As she turns to go she stops and looks up at him. "Thanks a lot Jak." She says bitterly and Jak feels sorrow and regret as he stares at her straight, stiff back for a moment before following them out of the cave into the sunlight.

You should have said sorry Jak," His lawyer whispers.

"If they were voting tonight you wouldn't get any of the female ballot. I hope you make up for it." Jak thinks back. Had he made up for it? He sits there casting back until the court adjutant taps him on the shoulder.

"Hey you could have said sorry man." He accuses Jak as he leads him to his quarters.

Chapter 28
Overlander

It is coming on to evening when they reach the dwelling. Zerrin unearths some tins of food.

"What on Ecracon is it?" Asks Jak as he sticks a fork in.

"Some kind of moully beans I think. Hey if they aren't good enough for you I'll eat them." Says Zerrin moodily.

"They're way past their sell by date." Says Pal eyeing one of the tins. Zerrin snatches away the tin and shoves a plate of dark brown beans at him.

"Try to be a little more grateful." She sighs at them righteously as she sits down.

"They smell really bad Sis'." Grumbles Pal as he moves them about on his plate.

"Well I like them." She states determinedly as she shoves in a couple of spoonfuls.

"Is that why you left them here?" asks Jak.

A dimple shows at the corner of her mouth though she says nothing.

They eat all the beans and they at least assuage their hunger.

"We can't stay here." Jak says as the others look like they're settling down for the night. Zerrin lowers the blanket she is holding.

"You think they'll be coming?"

Jak thinks of the woman, how she has survived and tenaciously followed him here to Detagon.

"Yes I do."

Without further questions Zerrin prepares for departure.

"Do you think you should come?" Asks Jak reluctantly. "You might be safer up in the mountains. They're not actually after you."

Zerrin's shoulders suddenly droop and she stands not saying anything her eyes lowered.

"But Jak, we want to come with you." Says Pal without reticence. Zerrin lays a quieting hand on his shoulder.

"Jak doesn't want to have to worry about us." She says finally looking fully at Jak for the first time since their discussion in the tunnel cave.

"The reason I say go to the mountain is because I am worried about you. You don't want to get hurt in a fight that's not your own."

"Surely that's for us to decide?" She asks quietly, then abruptly, 'but you're right we'll go to the mountains."

"Zerrin what about...?" Starts Pal but she quiets him with a sharp look.

"What about what?" asks Jak, looking from one to the other.

"Nothing." Replies Zerrin. Jak looks at Pal questioningly.

"Er.. Nothing." Affirms Pal with less assurance, shootinga glance at his sister.

"O. K." says Jak on a long breath. He thinks it is something to do with Karrif but he's reluctant to ask any questions on that score.

"What about getting across the desert, can I do it without a guide?"

"No. You need us." Says Pal triumphantly. Zerrin says nothing "He needs us Zerry." Says Pal entreatingly to her.

"Are you willing to come?" Jak adds his own gentle persuasion.

"OK." She says lamely after a moment looking down at Pal but throwing Jak a quick glance from under her eyelashes.

"Let's go then." Suggests Jak and they head out.

Jak sees the wreckage first. It gives him a strange jolt to see the broken Capritor. The little craft from which he had survived was just a tangle of metal. He looks down at Zerrin.

"How did you manage to drag me all the way to your place?" he asks in amazement.

"Oh I'm pretty strong." She murmurs but her mind doesn't seem to be on those past events she points to the edge of the clearing.

"There they are." She makes to go down.

"Wait." Cautions Jak the overlanders are out in the open, shadowy bulks in the half-light. "You stay here and I'll mosey round, see if all's right and tight."

He moves off but turns back to see their bright orbs staring after him. "If you hear anything just get the hell outta here."

"Yeah right." Answers Zerrin.

"I mean it, you run, you hear?"

"Yes I'm listening."

"Yeah but you're not paying attention are you? No." mutters Jak as he makes his way over the scattered boulders. He hears her voice reach out after him.

"Keep out of the skyline Jak."

"Yes you idiot keep out of the skyline." He says to himself.

He makes a thorough reconnoitre in a wide circle around the wreckage site but all seems clear. He calls out a low halloo as he circumnavigates to his starting point.

“Well you’re back.” States Zerrin needlessly.

They scramble down to the overlanders Pal in the lead.

“Wow.” His appreciation is obvious.

“Wait!” Shouts Jak again; arresting Pals hand in the act

of reaching to touch one of the motors. Pal looks at

him enquiringly as he steps back. Jak reaches down,

picks up a small stone and tosses it at the overlander it

hits the front visor and rattles down onto the footrest.

Pal and Zerrin both look curiously at Jak.

“Do you feel better now?” Asks Zerrin and he shrugs.

“No need to take chances. I thought there might be an

electrical security field that’s all.

“Can I touch it now?” asks Pal.

“Sure go ahead.” Jak moves forward also to have a closer look at the land vehicle.

“Nice motor.” He nods approvingly. “Look its got triple g sparkers and flange boosters.”

“Look at this Jak,” says Pal, “are they automatic rough

terrain suspension adjusters?"

"Yeah pretty neat and these, look, motion sensors."

"What's this?"

"Don't touch it!" Jak warns the boy sharply, he examines

the box. "Oh it's OK it's a water compartment."

The brother and sister look at each other.

"You're a bit jumpy aren't you Jak?" suggests Zerrin.

"There's every need young lady, every need." He responds piously.

"Hey Jak this has got down hill descent." Pal is once again busy admiring the overlander.

Zerrin swings herself up to sit on the pilot seat.

"Wait!" Says Jak and checks under it. "OK go ahead."

He sees the edge of her amused smile. "It's better to be safe than sorry." He moralizes.

"What's this?" She asks him.

"Well," He leans his arm along the steering mechanism and looks at the attachment she indicates, preparing to air his knowledge. "Oh....well...that's a navigation unit."

A tense hush envelops them.

"You don't need us then." Says Zerrin softly her eyes

lowered. The heavy silence lingers for a moment after her statement.

"It's broken." Replies Jak.

Zerrin's eyes fly up to his. "Are you sure?" She says at last.

"Positive. Now let's get going. We'll take one bike and some spare fuel cells from the other two." He makes his way to one of the other overlanders. "I'll just check and make sure the slot is not alarmed." He inspects the cell slot briefly. "No we're fine." He extracts four fuel cells. Meticulously he checks the fuel slot on the final bike and extracts the cells.

"Now they may have spare cells on them." He refers to possible pursuers. "So we'll just…" he searches amongst the wreckage and pulls out a twisted splinter of metal, he jabs this into the tires of the other bikes excepting one spare which he takes and clips along with the spare already on the chosen overlander.

"Right is that everything?" He asks them rhetorically. "What about food?" He looks in the box panniers and brings out some packages he stuffs them quickly into their own bags.

"Mmm whoozles." He says inspecting a packet that escapes to the ground and tosses it to Pal.

"Right are we ready?" He asks again. He looks at Zerrin's sleeveless dress. "You'll be freezing." He says taking off his dust coat and throwing it at her. "And this," he unwinds his cravat, "tie this round your hair."

He notices how her fingers linger on the luxurious silky fabric before she ties it round her glossy braids.

Jak climbs into the pilot seat and Zerrin and Pal squeeze behind him.

"We're away." Says Jak as he pushes the ignition. Suddenly there is a wailing scream. Zerrin and Pal cover their ears and Jak repeatedly kicks the alarm he has missed with the heel of his boot until it is smashed in and the dreadful siren is hushed.

"You missed that one." Zerrin's words drop into the intense quiet that follows.

"Mmm OK we'd better scoot on out of here." Says Jak and he re-ignites the engines.

Off they go full throttle skimming over the bumpy ground. Zerrin leans forward and calls into Jak's ear.

"Carry on towards the west until you can see a tall pinnacle sticking up out of the ridge then you need to turn north west and head for the last peak, that will bring us to the first waterhole." Jak nods as he catches her words before the wind takes them. He waits until she is sitting back with Pal before he flicks on the navigator and checks his bearings.

It is well into the night before Jak decides to stop. Sleep beckons and cannot be ignored. The other two are dozing already in the back and he wonders if they will be more comfortable squashed in their seats or on the desert floor. He longs to stretch out his limbs. As he is looking in at them Zerrin opens her eyes.

"Do you want to kip in there or out here?" He asks her softly.

"It'll be cold out." She answers.

"I want to lay flat." Replies Jak on a yawn.

"You'll be cold." She insists.

"We could huddle." He wanders round the back of the overlander as she climbs stiffly out. "Hey look here's a tent of some kind folded into the back hatch." He presses a button and then jumps out of the way as with a loud hiss a fair sized tent erupts from the box and rapidly unfolds and extends. When it has finished morphing he unzips the entrance. Inside is a comfortable looking airbed.

"Well would you look at that."

Zerrin peeps in too.

"You Keltis sure know how to look after yourselves." Is her dry comment but she seems pleased enough to go inside out of the chill night air.

"Hey, Jak?" Zerrin is standing by a small, inflated sink protruding from the wall of the tent. She winds a knob and a thin trickle of water oozes from the narrow gauge hose. "I hope you brought your toothbrush."

"As a matter of fact I did. Don't waste the water." Jak cautions as he watches her.

She flops down on the bed and as the bounces diminish she laughs delightedly.

“This is better than I’ve slept in for…ever.”

“Let’s get some shut eye then. I’ll fetch Pal.”

When he returns carrying the little boy she is fast asleep. She has removed his dust coat so they can share it and he looks down at her for some time in the faint glow of the camp light; lying there in the long white dress with her dark hair spread out in a soft tangle on the fabric of the airbed. He stays there until the child starts to feel heavy in his arms then he lays him gently beside his sister and squeezes himself onto the remaining few inches, spreading the coat over them.

Chapter 29
Bico Wind

It is morning; the light from the sun, shining through the yellowy beige fabric of the tent casts a bright glow into Jak's sleepy eyes. Pal is still snoozing but Zerrin is up and out. Jak washes at the little sink then wanders outside yawning and stretching, looking about for the girl. He sees her standing on a hillock looking out to the horizon and climbs up to stand beside her.

"Morning squirt." He salutes and looks down at her frowning face. "What's the matter aren't you an early morning person?"

"Well I'm a bit worried about that." She points eastwards and Jak looks at the sun rising, rapidly being eclipsed by a bank of glowering clouds, an unhappy mix of orange and sullen dark grey.

"Looks like a storm brewing." He observes.

"Mmmm and we are right in the path if there's a bico wind." Suddenly she steps down from the raised earth. "We've got to get going." She begins to run back to the tent. Jak wants to ask her what the significance of a bico wind is but she is becoming increasingly urgent.

In a few minutes they are ready to go. Jak presses the button on the back of the overlander and the tent, rather amazingly folds and compacts itself into the box.

"Did you get Pal out?" asks Jak. He looks down at the tousle haired, sleepy eyed boy. "You are so lucky." He reminds him. The child smiles up at him and takes hold of his hand. Zerrin smiles briefly too but her eyes quickly stray back to the storm clouds.

"We can try and race it," she says, "but if we see any kind of shelter, big boulder or something we'd better stop." She doesn't look very happy and Jak lays a hand on her shoulder.

"We'll be alright." He says gently, she gives him a quick flicker of a smile but her eyes tell him he doesn't know what he's talking about. Immediately they are on the bike and racing away northwards.

The brooding sky has become increasingly dark. The wind begins to race in sharp gusts making it progressively more difficult to drive the overlander. The stinging sand whips their faces. As the roaring wind abruptly becomes icy cold Zerrin leans a white face over his shoulder.

"We must find shelter quickly!" She cries. He barely hears her above the howl of the storm and roar of the bike engines. Jak becomes aware of another sound joining the cacophony. A penetrating screeching whine faint at first but becoming rapidly ever more imperious. Zerrin hears it too for she clutches his shoulder so hard it hurts.

“Stop!” She yells in his ear.

Jak wrenches on the brakes and the rear wheels slide in the loose sand. Immediately Zerrin tumbles out even as the vehicle slithers to a halt. She drags Pal out with one hand and pulls Jak’s arm with the other. The scream rises high above the roar of the wind.

“What is it?” Asks Jak gritting his teeth against the high-pitched intensity of the sound and fear of the unknown.

“A bico wind.” She says breathlessly tearing off the coat of his that she is wearing and stuffing it into the space between the seats and the steering rack.

“It’s not enough.” Desperation wrings her voice and drains her face as she looks up at Jak.

“Wait.” He says, her obvious terror increasingly unnerving him yet galvanising him into action. He wrenches out the air hose to the tent compartment then forcing the lid with the heel of his boot, he drags out the voluminous folds of the tent. Zerrin’s relief is apparent as she and Pal help him to pack the tough fabric in the gap and under the footrest. They huddle together then in the shelter afforded by the overlander. Jak hardly has time to wonder what will come to pass next when the piercing, unearthly wail reaches a crescendo then fragments into individual screams. They are instantly engulfed in a barrage of needle sharp lances. Some of this armoury dashes onto the exposed flank of the bike. One spike pierces through the tent cloth at eyelevel beside Jak’s head.

"Your leg!" Screams Zerrin her voice mingling with the sound of the sleek spear like missiles as they race past. He jerks in that exposed member just as razor sharp splinter embeds itself into the sand exactly where his foot had been a second before. A moment later they are staring after the thick volley as it disappears into the flying clouds of sand listening, in the comparatively lesser noise of the storm, to its receding whine.

"What on earth was that?" Jak leans forward and pulls the gleaming barb from the sand.

"Ice." He says wonderingly, already it is beginning to melt.

"Sometimes when there's a storm over the Dorliegh ranges this happens." Her voice is trembling slightly and she still has to speak loudly over the sound of the storm. Jak pulls out the tent from where it is wedged and casts it over them making a relatively sand free air pocket. They listen for a moment in the shrouding darkness to the muffled howl of the wind.

"How long will this last?"

"I don't know." Says Zerrin.

"Sometimes they last for days." Offers Pal.

"Let's hope not eh." He reaches into one of the pockets of his discarded coat and finds a torch. "You're totally covered in sand." He says as he catches sight of Pals face in the feeble glow. He turns the light onto Zerrin then flicks it away as he notices her surreptitiously wiping away some tears mingling with the sand on her cheeks.

"You're mucky too!" Says Pal delightedly as he takes the torch from Jak's unresisting hand and shines the beam full into his eyes. Jak blinks and Zerrin laughs shakily.

"Don't do that Pal, you'll blind him."

Pal switches off the torch and they again sit in dark¬ness.

"So tell me about the bico winds." Suggests Jak

"There's a long ravine up in the Dorleigh ranges," commences Zerrin sniffing a little, "I've been up there once it's really very beautiful. The sides of the walls arch over almost like a huge tunnel and the water dripping down during the thaw freezes up again making long icicles that hang down into the valley. It was late afternoon when I was there and the sun was shining low through the ice daggers. They were glittering like diamonds it was the most breathtaking thing I've ever seen but when there's a storm over the mountains the wind comes racing through the channel breaking off the icicles and carrying them along like....well like today."

"Lethal. Mind you I wouldn't have missed it."

"What do you mean?" There is a trace of astonishment in Zerrin's voice.

"Hey, cool stuff like that doesn't happen every day, nobody else I've known has seen it 'cepting you two and I shall always remember it knowing I, Jak Dane was here, in the desert on Detagon in the middle of a bico wind."

"But it was so dangerous.'

"Nobody was hurt."

"But we could have been."

"But we weren't. See you've got to think positive."

"Humph." Is Zerrin's only comment to this piece of philosophy and Jak wonders what she is thinking about as he listens to the mournful whistle of the wind outside.

Suddenly there is the sound of great dollops of rain on the canvas.

"Hey it's raining!" Announces Zerrin.

"Are you glad about that?" Asks Jak curiously.

"Sure thing, if the wind dies down."

"And why's that?"

"We can wash off this stinking sand otherwise we've got to have it cleaving to our skin and rubbing us raw 'till we reach the waterhole tomorrow."

"Hell yes I hope it rains torrents." Says Jak with feeling as he makes to get up and eliminate the possibility of this fate.

"Wait for the wind to drop." Advises Zerrin.

They linger for a while as the precipitation gathers

momentum and Jak worries it will stop before the wind does but Zerrin's confidence is well founded and soon

they are able to discard the protective tent cloths and run out into the pouring rain. Zerrin stands with her face uplifted and lets the water pelt down and over her splashing on her eyelids and quickly washing away the tear clogged dirt from her cheeks, Jak sees the rivulets running down her rain drenched skin. Pal capers about splashing up muddy water and hindering any benefits the rain might give to his cleanliness. As soon as they are thoroughly soaked the rain slows to a patter before stopping altogether. As if by a miracle the clouds are whisked away and the sun beams forth. They spread out the tent to dry and inspect the damage caused by the ice daggers. The areas that were fully exposed to the onslaught are cut to ribbons.

"I don't know if this will ever be any good again." Says Jak regretfully.

"We can patch it up I've got some silver tape." Says Zerrin. "We'll wait until it's dried out a bit."

"Shall we have some eats? Are you hungry Pal?" He reaches down and ruffles the boy's wet hair.

Chapter 30
Eric Testifies

Yes well it was all very well for Jak Dane having a splendid time, running around the desert with some gorgeous Censite princess or whatever, watching the rivulets on her smooth wet skin or what have you, I always knew that lad was a bit of a dark horse. But I was stuck out on Plyten II with the bugs. I'll tell you what happened. We went off, my men and I to do our usual kind of business you know, well we were just scooting off on our way to Lexon when all hell breaks loose on board. First number two and then number three engines blow up in our faces, the whole kit and caboodle is falling apart round our ears so we have no choice but to jump ship in our escape pods and we have no choice but to land on Lexon which is the worst part of the whole deal. Nobody ever goes to that god-forsaken place only once a year at harvest time and this was spring! Our distress beacon was transmitting of course but we all know why that wouldn't do us any good. Any how I switched it off as soon as I thought of it 'cos when you're in my line of business as you know your honour and somebody's trying to kill you the last thing you want is a distress signal beaming out your location. So any way there we were. It was dark when we arrived.

“Where abouts are we?” I says to my navigator. There he is S B Proctor as fine a man as you're ever likely to meet.

“Lexon, south west sector.”

“Good grief, what the hell are we doing here?” Well your Honour you can imagine my annoyance I wasn't blaming the lad you understand.

“Nearest place within our range Sir.” He says, as if that made it any better.

There were five of us that had survived. Two of my men were killed when the ship went down. Curse his eyes but I got.....

“Excuse me Mr Tor,” interrupts the administrator, “I hope you were not about to tamper with the integrity of continuity that we strive to maintain in these cases. I must remind you that your testimony is for the benefit of the public please refrain from commenting on future events.”

“I apologise to your Honour and to the voters but it just makes my blood boil to think of that swine.”

As I say there were five of us, it is dark and we know that mainly giant reemer silk worms inhabit the planet. That's not what's worrying us it's the rotike spiders that prey on the worms we're concerned about. Now I'm not a timid man your Honour but those spiders now, I shudder to think of them. They're as big as your hand you know. Any ways we start up a fire thinking that'll keep 'em off. However seeing as my men, and I'll admit myself, aren't all that well educated we didn't know that it's light that attracts them. Sure enough in a few minutes they were swarming all over us. Yuck it was the most hideous thing, I almost died of disgust. Even now your Honour I sometimes want to kill myself when I think of that time when those things came scuttling out of the darkness. Anyways we soon got the hell outta that particular sector.

There were other things to concern me now, more important things. Now I'm not the kind of bloke to be always thinking negatively but I was worried about my Leela and young Sten and at that particular time I was worried about Jak Dane not knowing of course that he would fairly soon be dallying with some Censite filly. Any way that's neither here nor there, I was worried about him and I was uneasy about our own prospects; no one we would welcome was going to come for us and the harvesters wouldn't arrive for half a year. How long could we survive on our few rations and the slimy tasteless meat of the

Reemer worms? Well your Honour I think that's about it up to this point. I wouldn't want to carry on with my recital and mess with your continuity what have you's so I'll just bow out for now if that meets with your Honours approval?

"Very well, thank you Mr Tor. I believe we now need to call a...Mr Mort before we continue with the narration. Is that correct Stabbard?"

"Er...yes Mort Shaltag your honour." "Proceed."

Chapter 31
The Tape

"Well it was a couple of days after I'd been visited by that young chap, or should I say the defendant your honour? Anyway Jak Dane, he goes and leaves the recordings on my desk see and while I was doing the late shift and as bored as hell as you can imagine, my eye lights on the damn things. After a bit I got to wondering whether there were any traces I could build on. I didn't have anything else to do so I thought why not give it a shot.

It took me a couple of hours to program in possible prognosis using the shadow imprints and I just left it running until the next night. The computer had selected four possibilities and had been working on them simultaneously all day. I had used a little persuasion on my colleague to leave the computer running without interference and then I had to wrangle for the next night shift, which surprised my boss 'cos he's run away with the idea I don't like doing the night shift but hey why wouldn't I? By the time I clocked in three of the prognosis were discarded and by the hazy images I could tell there were five individual messages that had come through to the Dane household that day. Elements of old messages kept popping up in distorting patches but the computer was gradually sifting them out.

I knew it would be the final message that was important so I halted the process and cut out the earlier ones. This final section was about two points long and I switched on the audio for a while listening to the garbled sounds. By about dawn the picture was clearing and the process accelerating. I was starting to get quite keen; I had known it was possible to rebuild an inter message from traces on the head but I'd never actually done it before. The fact that the content of this message had caused the deaths of an unknown number of people did cross my mind and added a bit of spice to the enterprise.

I was pretty disappointed when the computer indicated that the task was complete. The picture was more or less the quality of an early teleware transmission, the eyes of the man on the screen were great black holes and his mouth was a wide gash across his face. The audio was scrambled, sounding hollow and tinny. I wasn't very impressed. I tinkered with the dials, adjusting endlessly, trying to synchronise the sounds but I kept coming up with just this garbled rubbish. Then I saw this ancient icon in the corner of the screen I didn't recognise it and had dismissed it as being a gap in the sequence but then suddenly I thought maybe it was one of those old translation devices. I went to work on it and eventually got the translation Censite to Keltian.

"I don't recall seeing the disc offered as evidence, there is some irregularity here."

"I destroyed the disc."

"Ah."

"It worried me that it was in my possession. I would have given it to Jak Dane but I couldn't contact him and after I'd thought about it for some time I decided I'd better get rid of it."

"Can you give us some indication of its contents?"

"Sure can, it was some kind of ransom demands from a terrorist Censite cell. They had Verdor Dane hostage and stipulated access to the Crimmer council. They said their transmissions had been blocked and the message was coming through an old telewave beacon the code was 12-17-14-92-03. Then there was a message from the hostage to his son telling him to contact the Crimmer council with the information. The message was incomplete it had obviously been discovered and interrupted. Any way I made a copy and sat thinking about it for the rest of the night then in the morning I crushed the disc and threw it in the waste bin then I deleted the file from my computer and destroyed the disc head. I contacted Leela Tor and asked her if she knew how I could contact Jak Dane but she said he was gone she didn't know where. There didn't seem like anything more I could do so that was that."

"Why didn't you divulge the information to the securitor?" asked the Administrator.

"It did cross my mind but on reflection didn't seem the wisest course for me to take. I was under no obligation."

"No moral obligation Mr. Shaltag?"

Chapter 32
The Waterhole

Jak has tried quite hard to return the tent to its compartment. He started out in quite a positive frame of mind, however the reams of fabric seem to have extended somehow and no matter how neatly he tries to fold it it still ends up an untidy great bundle. Now as they head towards the waterhole it is stacked up behind the rear seat and tied down with bits of bungy rope. It is dark before they reach the waterhole they are chilled from travelling in damp clothes. The tent doesn't work anymore and they have to spend an infuriating hour trying to prop it up with sticks and rope.

"Let's light a fire." Says Jak, "That'll cheer us up."

"Is it safe do you think?" Asks Zerrin worriedly.

"Well we'll light it in amongst these rocks so it can't be seen and the smoke will be dissipated through the leaves of that gnarled old tree. I reckon we'll be alright."

"OK you're the boss I'll see if I can rustle up some grub." She disappears into the darkness.

"Be careful." He calls after her. "See if you can collect up some wood young man." He addresses Pal who dashes off with alacrity. Jak draws together some dry seedpods from under the tree and with some gentle blowing and careful arrangement of twigs he soon has a little blaze going. He then helps Pal and they soon have a nice pile of wood to last them.

"How are you feeling now?" he asks the little boy. He had been taking one of Jak's precious tablets daily for the past four days. There are only two left.

"Mmm pretty good." Pal squats down and stretches his fingers out to the warm flames.

"What do you reckon she'll rustle up?" Asks Jak, aware of hunger pains for the first time.

Pal shrugs "Who knows, we ate rat once."

"Mmm sounds tasty." Jokes Jak but then he wonders if it is true and they were reduced to eating that unhealthy rodent.

"Did you really eat rat?" He asks after a while.

"Yes." Answers Pal nonchalantly.

"What did it taste like?"

"It was kinda tough but it tasted OK."

Just then Zerrin emerges from the darkness into the little pool of light cast by the fire. In her hand she carries a long heavy kimmick lizard, its green and gold scales gleaming in the flames. She lays this on a rock and Jak notices she is carrying something else carefully in the folds of her skirt.

“Hey good news.” She announces, “ I’ve found a looly hog.”

Jak glances at Pal to see how he receives this information. He looks pleased but then he had eaten rat and pronounced it fair. He turns his eyes back to Zerrin in time to see her toss the contents of her skirt onto the rock, take another smaller stone in her hand and deal the prickly creature a blow to its head. She then takes a knife from the rucksack, quickly severs that member and then holds the hog by its diminutive tail to let the blood run away into the sand. It seems amazing to Jak that a young and pretty girl should be indulging in such activities. He watches, fascinated as she then takes the knife to the already departed lizard.

“Er would you like me to….” He feels compelled to ask but as she looks up and he meets her scornful eyes his words run out.

“Have you ever done it before?”

“No.”

“Well then don’t be so stupid.”

“She likes doing it.” Chimes in Pal helpfully.

Zerrin throws him an annoyed look then addresses Jak.

“I’m sorry if it offends you. I’d have done it out in the dark if I’d known it was going to turn your precious stomach.”

Jak shoots a look of appeal across to Pal who shrugs eloquently then watches her mutilate the lizard with angry strokes. She brings it to the fire after washing it with water from the pool.

"I think Jak could have done a better job of it than that." Says Pal eyeing the hacked flesh with disfavour.

Jak doesn't say anything. He notices that her lashes are wet.

"We can have some coffee." She says in a moment, quite brightly, as she lances the lizard through with a twig and rests it carefully on two stones either side of the fire.

"I didn't know we had coffee." says Jak in glad tones.

"See, you're not the only one who can nick stuff from other people's supplies."

Jak thinks sheepishly of the whoosles they ate for lunch. Meanwhile Zerrin has unpacked a sack from under the seat. Jak and Pal watch in amazed delight as she produces coffee, sossa bread, butter, beans, a small can of milk and two small cooking pots.

They are just relaxing after a sumptuous repast and are about to have their coffee when they are alerted by the sounds of an approach. Jak and Zerrin exchange startled glances.

"Sounds like only one." Whispers Jak.

Zerrin listens. "Pretend you're asleep." She says. She lays a hand on the knife but Jak stops her.

"I'll take it." He says gripping her wrist. He can tell she is reluctant but there is no time to argue. He helps them quickly hide their remaining food.

"The bike!" Gasps Zerrin.

"Too late," Says Jak quickly wrapping himself in his coat and depositing himself in a suitably slumbersome position. Zerrin sees an old bottle left by a previous camper lying unbroken in the sand and tosses it to him. Just as the stranger comes into view over the rocks Jak closes his eyes, the bottle suggestively in his hand.

It seems to Jak that Zerrin and the stranger talk for hours. He can tell that she offers him coffee and maybe some bread. Of course Jak doesn't understand a word they say but he listens carefully to their measured tones alert for any form of aggression. His body is tense but he tries to breathe regularly and heavily as any drunken sot sleeping off his excesses would.

Finally the stranger leaves and after waiting for what he considers a sufficient interval he throws off his covers. Zerrin holds a finger to her lips indicating they should wait a little longer, after a while Jak trots up the path to make sure he has actually gone.

"What do you reckon?" He asks Zerrin on his return.

"I don't know, I'm pretty sure he was just a traveller who happened to be passing and smelled our coff ee."

"Happened to be passing?" Says Jak sceptically.

"Well people do travel around, we are after all."

"Mmm, what did you think Pal?"

"He was just a geezer." Is Pals confident answer.

"I bet he thought it was odd you sitting in the middle of the desert in that get up." Jak says to Zerrin looking over her as she stands in the firelight. She looks down at her dress and there is a small smile on her lips as she thinks of some remembered comment.

"Did he come on to you?" The impertinent question is gone from his lips before he even thinks of asking it, she receives it badly. Her face flushes up and her eyes flash daggers at him.

"You must think me some kind of floozy." She says bitterly. "You'll be glad to know nobody has ever made me feel as cheap as you do Jak."

Jak knows he aught to apologise but he just stares at her in dismayed silence across the fire.

"He was just some old geezer Jak." placates Pal looking worriedly from one to the other.

"Did he seem interested in the bike?" Jak says finally,turning away from her fiery look.

Zerrin seems disinclined to communicate so Pal leaps inexpertly into the breach.

"He looked at the bike more times than he looked at Zerrin." He offers. The empty supply sack comes flying through the air and buffets Pal softly in the face. Jak starts to grin and there is a chuckle from Pal, and soon Zerrin joins in and they laugh the tension away. Later as they lie in the make shift tent he reaches over the sleeping boy and touches her hand briefly.

"Sorry." He murmurs. She doesn't answer and he doesn't know whether she is asleep or not.

When he wakes in the morning he can hear sounds of laughter and splashing, the others are up and swimming in the pool. Jak throws off the covers and makes his way out into the early morning rays. He stands there blinking for a moment as the sun glitters off the ripples on the water. He sees their silhouettes as they frolic and spray each other.

"Come on in," invites Zerrin as she catches sight of him, "it's wonderful."

Their enthusiasm is contagious, Jak runs and takes a flying leap off the rock, dive-bombing and sending up great swathes of spray over them to their obvious delight. The chill water comes as a bit of a shock so soon after waking and Jak swims vigorously to get the blood pumping and dissipate the coldness.

"Race?" Challenges Zerrin and she strikes out across the pool with a six beat patter.

"Cheat!" laughs Jak and dashes after her. Overtaking her to reach the other side and cling to the dripping wall, breathing heavily. She is soon beside him splashing water into his eyes.

"Hey!" He seizes her wrists and holds them gripped in one hand, "You're swimming better today."

"Better than what?" She pants treading water and keeping afloat with difficulty as her hands are imprisoned.

"Better than the other day, was it the day before yesterday? You know when I dragged you up from the murky depths. You swam like a brick then."

"Mmmm very funny." She smiles but she looks reflective, in this more serious atmosphere Jak thinks of the times over the past few days when they have saved each others lives, what a strange uneasy relationship they have forged together.

"Why are you here Jak?" She asks quietly as he releases her.

"I'll tell you over breakfast." They swim back across the lake more slowly now. Jak spends a little while trying to teach Pal how to duck dive so she can dress in private then, a little damp but refreshed, they sit down for breakfast. The previous night Zerrin had caked the prickly hog with mud found at the edge of the pool and buried it under the ashes of the fire. This morning they eat succulent meat and the last of the bread.

Chapter 33
Cat Out Of The Bag

"That was delicious." applauds Jak licking his fingers.

"You said you would tell me why you're here." Reminds Zerrin determinedly as she takes the coffee pot off the coals and pours it out.

"Everybody so far who knows anything about this has died." Warns Jak, moodily staring into the fire.

"You haven't."

"Yes well I'm 'tenacious of life' as they say."

"Yes but why are you here at Detagon, that's what beats me?" persists Zerrin.

"He came to save us." suggests Pal only half joking.

"I'm looking for my Father." Replies Jak, with a kind of hopelessness in his voice. He thinks of all the days that have gone by since he had last heard from Verdor.

"You think he's here?" Zerrin looks her bewilderment.

"Every sixty days for the past five years he has delivered

food to the holdings in Gedd, he's a haulier for Straiff shipping."

With this explanation a palpable coolness impresses itself upon Jak and he looks up from his contemplation of a fire whose warmth appears diminished. He glances at Zerrin and arrests an unreadable expression on her face.

"What?" asks Jak surprised and a little unnerved by her glowering look. "Is something the matter?"

"Is something the matter? " She repeats in a strangled voice. Swiftly and startlingly she launches herself at him. Jak caught completely unaware does little to protect himself from the onslaught and allows a volley of blows from her small hard fists to rain down on his chest.

Pal is pulling at her from behind. "Zerrin stop it." He cries in distress.

Recovering from his surprise at her unexpected return to her previous violent hostility Jak grips her shoulders and forces her away from him.

"What the hell's wrong with you?" He glares down at her.

Immediately her face crumples and she begins to weep, covering her face with her hands. Jak leaves her and rises to his feet. He looks at Pal.

"Do you know what's up with her?"

Pal looks very unhappy. "It's the food." He says and walks a little way off to sit on a rock.

For a moment Jak thinks he is talking about the hog they have just eaten.

"I feel fine." He says and then realises instantly that he has it wrong. "Why are you looking at me like I just crawled out from under a rock?"

"The food brought the plague." States Pal.

"Yes, your father has killed millions of people." Zerrin flings at him from behind her hands.

As the realization of what she is suggesting sinks in Jak feels like all his blood has rushed suddenly to his heart his knees begin to buckle and he sits down heavily on the rock behind him. His mind repulses her statement. He looks from one to the other and feels them pulling away from him in spirit as though they were, in reality, running from him.

"You're wrong." He whispers and there are tears stinging the back of his eyes.

"No, you're wrong." Answers Zerrin, quietly now and she looks at him pityingly. "You think your father's some wonderful guy who's worth saving but he's not."

Jak strides over and drags her to her feet.

"You don't know what you're talking about." He says angrily his face only inches from hers.

"I do. The plague came in the food. That's what the founders say." Her voice falters a little.

"And who are the founders." He demands.

"The administration, they told us, and they know what they're talking about."

"How dare you accuse my father on the say so of this so-called 'administration' they're a pack of idiots."

"My father was on the administration. He believed the plague was in the food and I believe it."

"Well I don't." Says Jak and then hesitates, letting go his grip on her. "And even if it was, my father had nothing to do with it he's just the contractor that hauls the food."

Zerrin looks into his eyes and her own hold a hard brittle light. "You may be right." She says and she turns from him. "But he still brought the plague whether he knew it or not."

There is a barrier rising up between them again, Jak feels it, so real he can almost reach out and touch it. Zerrin turns her back on him and stands staring into the water. Jak looks at Pal but he too is on the other side. Jak walks slowly over to the campfire and begins to stow their gear.

"We can sort this out." He says suddenly stopping with the tent half folded at his feet. Zerrin and Pal both look at him from bleak unpromising faces. Their family, Jak knows, was wiped out by the plague and now weirdly and frighteningly the responsibility seems to be settling somewhere in his vicinity.

"Look," he continues doggedly, "if my father is here, which I believe he is, his ship, The Lazortrom will still be docked at the holding yards. There is a lab on board where all the products are tested before dispatch so we can check out the records."

"If all the food is checked that means your father knew what he was doing." states Zerrin hollowly her face very white.

"True." Admits Jak, "However I too need to know what's going on so I'm going to Gedd to find out are you still willing to come?"

Zerrin hesitates.

"If you come I don't want any of this hatred stuff going on. Either come with me and stick by me or go back."

"Fair enough," says Zerrin, "I need to think." She walks up to Pal and takes his hand then they stroll off together along the edge of the pool. Jak watches them for a moment. There is no doubt in his mind that Verdor had nothing to do with the plague. But a keener sense of urgency assails him and he feels as though they've been dallying. He must get to Gedd and find his father and discover what is going on.

He stashes the rest of the gear and then looks up to see how the girl and her brother are getting on. They are still down by the shore talking earnestly. Jak takes the water containers down to fill them and they move off at his approach. When he gets back to the overlander he takes the provisions and divides them. He thinks the others will be heading back, he feels regret. Strange, he only threw in his lot with them a few days ago and yet he knows he will miss them; that their going will be a wrench.

As he stands staring at the meagre fare a small warm hand is place in his. He looks down at Pal.

"We've decided to come with you." Says the little boy. He explains their decision. "It's not your fault the people died."

"Thanks Pal." Replies Jak, strangely grateful for this dispensation. He looks to see if Zerrin feels the same way. She is stowing the water bottles on the back of the bike.

"Are you waiting for my pledge of allegiance?" She asks dryly.

"I don't want you to come without it." Says Jak seriously.

"Here." She comes round to stand before him. For a crazy moment he thinks she is going to kneel, he doesn't know why this possibility enters his head and he feels pretty sheepish when he looks down at the hand she is holding out. He stares blankly at the discs she has in her palm.

"I took them out of your pocket."

Jak remembers them now, the report he had taken from the Censite, York at Rhetros house. He apprehends that giving them back is a token of her alliance with him. He takes the discs realizing that they could be a major piece of the puzzle and he had forgotten all about them.

“Sorry I took them.” She says with difficulty.

“I’m glad you did I’d forgotten I had them. Do you know what they are?”

She indicates some Censite writing on the disc case. “It says they are reports.”

“Let’s have a look at them then.”

“How can we?”

“The navigation unit is a simple computer it will interface with these.”

“You said it was broken.”

Jak shrugs. “Let’s see shall we.” He slots the first disc in. “Here, take a look I can’t understand it.”

He slides out of the way and she takes the pilot seat. He watches her face as she reads, she doesn’t seem surprised at what she finds but she is not happy about it either.

“What does it say?” He asks after a while.

She shakes her head. “It’s a general report. It details how many people have died of plague this quarter, crime figures, food status, and weather patterns; there are reams of it. Where on earth did you get it Jak? It’s a quarterly from the administration to the Crimmer Council. Fat lot of notice they would take of any reports from us.”

"Let's try the other one." suggests Jak. She nods and he exchanges the discs.

"What on earth...?" She reads avidly a frown of bewilderment on her face. "This is another report for the same quarter but it's going on about health care and education, changes to the welfare system, it's a load of rubbish, as if we were a corporate planet....and look at this..., it's detailing preparations for the Jubilee year, that's nonsense nobody believes in the Jubilee."

"Jubilee?" Invites Jak.

"Yes." Zerrin's face is not really bitter only very sad. "When our people were taken from Census in '86 the treaty was that we would return from exile in a hundred years."

When she had said 'taken from Census' it had been on the tip of Jak's tongue to suggest rescued as a more appropriate word but now as she mentions the end of the hundred years some pieces in the puzzle suddenly seem to slot into place.

"And this hundred years is over in 4086?" he calculates.

"Yes," says Zerrin, "two years from now and we ought to be back on our own soil but it's not going to happen."

"Well the Crimmer believes it is." Says Jak with surety and when she looks her fiery look at him he taps the screen. "These are the reports they've been getting. As far as the Crimmer is concerned everything is all hunky dory here on Detagon and on line for the Jubilee year."

For a moment the fire in Zerrin's eyes glows with a glad warm light, turning the irises a deep violet but then the colour quickly dims and Jak sees them awash with tears.

"It's not going to happen." She says despondently. "The plague….there is only a few hundred thousand of us left. You saw the figures, in the last quarter forty three thousand died and the number rises each quarter we won't last another two years."

They both turn on the same thought to look at Pal who is listening avidly. Zerrin lays a hand on his narrow shoulder and Jak wonders if he understands what is being said.

"Zerrin, we won't die of plague will we?" The boy answers Jak's unspoken question, the child had understood perfectly. Zerrin throws Jak a quick entreating look.

"Of course not." says Jak hastily. Pal doesn't seem to take any account of this spurious reassurance and continues to look earnestly into his sister's face.

"No I don't think so." She says slowly.

"Have I got the plague?" He asks her.

"No, it was something else, some bug you caught from that racoon you were playing with and Jak's pills made you better."

"OK." Says Pal. "But you think we will catch it soon?"

"No I don't think so." She says again. Neither of them looks very convinced.

Jak brings an end to the conversation by saying harshly that they had better get a move on.

Zerrin and Pal both look at him and he feels very uncomfortable. He would like to tell them that he,Jak Dane, was going to sort everything out but what the hell could he do? That's what they would say and how would he answer them? Instead he motions them sternly to get in the overlander. They obey him but not with any alacrity or sign of the solidarity that had grown up between them before they had discovered he was the son of the man who had brought the plague to their world.

Chapter 34
The Rayel Pit

It is because Jak was mulling over the pieces of the puzzle that later, midway through the morning, he drove into the Rayel pit. As the overlander bounces down towards the bottom of the pit Jak is dislodged from his seat and thrown clear. As he spits out the dirt he has somehow managed to ingest whilst careering along on his face he hears the cries of the other two. Looking down through the dust he sees the overlander just beginning to sink into some thick grey mud. Even as he quickly assimilates the situation he notices that bubbles are very gradually rising to the surface and popping on contact with the air giving off a highly offensive odour that stings his nostrils as he breathes. He pulls up the fabric of his shirt to cover his nose as he bounds down the slope. Zerrin is climbing over the top of the bike and turning to help Pal. To his dismay Jak sees Pals strap pulled across at an angle and the little boy trying desperately to release the mechanism. Zerrin is leaning over now and tugging ineffectually at the stiff strip of webbing. As soon as Jak slides to a halt before the bubbling mire he can feel heat escaping into the atmosphere. The stench is unbearable as Jak leans over, puts his arm around her waist and pulls Zerrin bodily from the sinking bike. With a knife unsheathed and ready he slices through the strap that traps Pal and pulls him out just as the ooze envelopes the footrest. Jak catches him up and hands him to Zerrin who waits on the bank with outstretched arms. The bike is sinking fast, Jak knows he must jump now from the half submerged bulk but he turns to retrieve the water bags knowing they won't get far without them. While he is lifting them onto his shoulder the boiling mud spills over onto the seat where he is standing immediately he realises that the soles of his shoes together with the fabric of the seat cover are melting. As they turn viscous and Jak feels the heat burning his feet he begins to slide. For an instant he sees the mud coming up to meet him then Zerrin is holding his arm and steadying him. She is standing perched precariously one foot on each wing mirror. As Jak steps up onto the back of the seat and launches himself alongside her onto the bank he can't for the life of him see how they both didn't end up in the stinking acid sludge. As he hits the ground at the edge of the pit he realises agonisingly that the caustic mud has eaten through his boots and has now started on the soles of his feet. Frantically he cuts through the laces and wrenches them off. Zerrin and Pal are watching the last of the bike slip beneath the slime.

"I loved that bike." Says Zerrin regretfully. She heaves a great sigh.

"Well, now what?" She says balefully as she stares at the place where the bike had been.

"Let's get out of this stinking hole." Groans Jak. At the sound of his voice she turns, knowing, that something else is wrong.

"I don't know if it's the smell down here that's making me nauseous or the sight of that." Jak indicates his injured feet. Zerrin is already beside him inspecting, her eyes dismayed.

In some places the burns are deep and open where Jak had pulled off his socks and the damaged skin came off along with the material in others blisters are already beginning to form.

"This is bad." She states apprehensively.

"I think I'm going to be sick!" Chimes in Pal his voice distressed.

"It's the toxic fumes; we've got to get out of this pit." She starts to rip up the seam of her dress.

"Here." Jak gives her the knife.

She cuts a wide strip. She slaps the dust from it.

"It's not clean." She worries. She leans to place it on the damaged skin and hesitates.

"I don't want to put it on because it's not sterilized."

"Well there's plenty of dirt on there already so just slap it on so's we can make our way up the slope." He smiles encouragingly at her, "Well don't precisely 'slap it on' go easy on me even if I am a damn Kelti."

She takes a deep breath and then proceeds to lay the

cloth gently onto his foot and carefully bind it round. Jak looks at Pals white sickly face.

“Pal go on up to the top and breathe some fresh air.”

He says.

“I’m scared of the limmex.” He whispers shamefacedly to his sister.

“Make a pile of rocks and if you see one wait for it to come near before you start pitching.” She advises, not taking her eyes from her work. Pal hesitates.

“You don’t have to go you can wait for us but if you need to throw up make it over there.”

“What’s a limmex?” asks Jak.

“Wildcat.”

“Are there many round here?”

“Fair few.”

“Are they very dangerous?”

“Yeah….Pal, don’t go up wait for us.”

Soon Zerrin has bound up Jak’s feet as best she can. Jak tries to get up with her help but decides to shuffle to the top backwards instead.

“Go on up. He says to her as she attempts to drag him.

“Look out for the Limmex!”

What now? They are resting back from the brink of the

Rayel pit. As Jak looks at the thick yellow smoke rising from the hole he can't believe he never noticed it ahead of him but drove straight over the edge like a fool.

"You can't walk can you Jak?" Asks Zerrin quietly.

"I feel better, not so sick now. I'll give it another go." He looks at his bound feet for a moment. "I think I'd better try getting my boots back on, who wants to volunteer to go down and get them?"

Zerrin produces the shoes. "They're not much cop." She says ruefully.

Jak looks at the boots and sees the soles are completely disintegrated.

"Say we cut some bits of leather from the duster coat and bind them onto these? That'll work I reckon." Jak produces the knife and Zerrin takes off the coat and gives it to him. Jak tries to ignore the look of mingled pity and hopelessness on her face. He himself is feeling pretty panicky and he keeps trying to submerge the reaction as it rises to the surface. He takes the coat and turns his eyes resolutely from her. She must have realised her revealed emotions weren't helping because she speaks and her voice is brighter rather than heavy with impending doom.

"I think it will work, I'll see if there is any twine in the sack." Jak realises then that she had had the forethought to grab the rucksack as she abandoned the sinking overlander, bright kid.

"No twine," she says, "we'll have to cut leather strips."

“I’d give a lot for some heavy duty scissors right now.” Jak holds up a rough square.

“Here I’ll have a go.” Says Zerrin and she commences, slicing away at the coat. Jak recalls that neither she nor Pal has uttered a word of blame. What an idiot he was for driving into the pit. He starts to ease on the remains of his boots. There is sweat on his brow but he accomplishes the feat without too much groaning. Zerrin folds up the squares of leather and presses them gently onto his feet.

“How does that feel?” She inquires.

“Not bad, not bad at all, let’s tie them on.”

She binds the long irregular strips she has cut round and round the boots and makeshift soles and then ties a crude knot.”

“Very pretty.” She admires her handy work.

“Right lets give it a go.” Says Jak with a deep breath. Pal comes forward to help and with the young girl and little boy hovering protectively round him he rises and takes a few shuffling steps. Zerrin comes up close and offers her shoulder; he leans heavily on her and takes a few more hobbling pain racked paces.

“Pal, see if you can find a stick.” Orders Zerrin staggering a little under Jak’s weight.

“I don’t think I’m going far like this.” Admits Jak.

“Gedd is only fifty odd miles away.” Says Zerrin ruefully.

"Mmm pity we haven't still got the bike."

"It wasn't your fault Jak."

"Who's was it then?"

"OK it was your fault," amends Zerrin, "but it could have happened to anyone."

Pal arrives back. "No stick," he says, "sorry."

"Right well here's what I suggest we do," says Zerrin, "me and Pal will trundle off to Gedd and see if we can get Flagor to bring us back with his car.

"Flagor?" Questions Jak.

"Flagor?" Says Pal at the same time in accents of astonishment.

"Yes Flagor." Repeats Zerrin. "If he doesn't want to help I'll steal his car and drive it myself."

Pal sniggers and Jak is not sure if it's at the idea of Flagor helping or Zerrin driving.

"Can you make it to those rocks?" She asks Jak. For answer he starts to limp in the direction of her pointing finger. It is only a hundred or so feet to the meagre shade afforded by the few boulders. There is nothing else to choose from and the desert stretches out emptily in all directions. Jak feels he is fortunate to be near to even this small relief from the hot sun. It takes an age to get over there with Zerrin and Pal helping as much as they can. When Jak is ensconced beneath a slight overhang Zerrin spends a bit of time trying to rig up what's left of the coat to supplement the shade of the rock.

"You aught to take it Zerrin," Protests Jak, "you'll need it come the night."

"I'm going to keep on walking if I can."

"Walking through the night? Won't that be too dangerous?"

"I'll be fine, I know the way." Zerrin reassures him as she puts the finishing touches to the low shelter.

"Do you think Pal should stay here?" She asks Jak and he wonders what will be safest for the little boy.

"Yes he can stay and snooze under the shelter; I think that would be best." He decides. He watches her reach into her pocket and pull out the pills he had given her for Pal. There is a look of quandary on her face. Finally she gives them to Jak there are three half tablets left.

"You should take them Jak they'll stop infection setting in."

He looks long at her, he knows that she knows he won't take them. Pal is not out of danger yet and if he stops taking the half pill they had been giving him each day he could suffer a relapse.

Zerrin takes the few rations that are in the rucksack and gives them to Jak along with one of the water bottles.

"I'll find something along the way." She says as he looks his reluctance to take the little bundle.

"Pal, you stay here and look after Jak, fight off the limmex if they come OK." She ruffles his hair. Jak holds his hand out for her to shake and she grips it for quite a long time.

“Take care of yourself.” He says quietly.

“I’ll see you tomorrow night or maybe the next day.” She says and turns abruptly to strike out northwards across the wilderness. The other water bottle is slung across her shoulders with the rucksack. Jak wonders irrelevantly what was in it that she had taken it.

“Well,” says Jak finally as her small figure disappears in the heat haze, “who’s this Flagor then?”

Pal gives him a clear green eyed look.

“He’s a pretty neat guy.”

“You like him then?”

“Yeah, I reckon.” Pal answers, unconsciously imitating Jak’s accent. He moves off to gather a pile of small stones to ward of the menace of the Limmex.

“Keep in the shade as much as you can.” Advises Jak drowsily. His feet are stinging and throbbing something chronic and he wonders if he should attempt to remove his boots but the heat and the sound of flies buzzing in the hot air lulls him into a doze.

Chapter 35
Flagor Remembers:

She never told me he was a Keltian; she just said some friend of hers was in trouble, stuck out past the Ketick gorge half way across the wilderness. Of course I said I would help. I would have done it for old times sake. Anyway when Zerrin came to our quarters in the plague free zone I was at once shocked and a little displeased to see her.

“Hi Zerrin dressing down I see.” Was my greeting. She was wearing some kind of evening gown which had once been white but was now stained by desert travel it was ragged and torn round the hem with great chunks missing. She was dirty and tired and looked a mess but it was the same sweet face and glowing violet eyes. I regretted my cool welcome. She was sad and worried.

“How have you been?” I asked.

“Oh fine.” She was noncommittal. “I need your help, are you busy?”

I knew what she meant, was I politically active at the moment? I was but I wasn’t about to communicate any details.

“How can I help? I have access to plenty of plague free supplies; you can take as much as you need.”

She shook her head. “I have a friend who is injured about half a days ride across the dust bowl Pal is with him. Will you come with medical supplies and bring him in?”

“Sure, who is he?”

She looked uncomfortable. “Just a friend.” She said evasively.

I lead her through the meeting hall to the rooms out the back.

“Cass will be pleased to see you.” I said. It was an understatement, at the sight of Zerrin, Cass dropped the cutlery she was drying and came forward with a cry of welcome. There was kissing and hugging enough for a wedding or a funeral. I was surprised really, though Cass was never one to hide her feelings. I would have waited until after Zerrin had washed half the desert out of her hair and the other half from her clothes and person.

“Where have you been girl?” She said finally after a few tears had been shed.

“Oh across the desert.”

“I can see that. I mean where have you been this past year we’ve seen nothing of you.”

Zerrin shot me a quick look from under her lashes and I knew she was still angry about the whole Karrif thing. Never mind I would soon bring her round.

"Where's little Pal?" asked Cass.

"He's back in the desert." Zerrin's voice faltered and Cass was all motherly concern.

"Look at us idiots keeping you standing and talking when it's as plain as day your too tired to move. Here come on through and I'll run you a hot bath and then while your soaking I'll prepare you something to eat." As she ushered Zerrin through to the washroom, she looked her questions at me but I just shrugged and smiled I knew I could trust my sister to get everything I needed to know out of Zerrin.

However she hadn't found out he was a Keltian had she.

I left Jeffers and Keenan in charge of the project and drove out with Zerrin later that evening. Zerrin sat beside me clean and fresh, more like the old Zerrin I used to know. I wanted to wait until the next day but she would have none of it, said she was worried about leaving Pal in the wilderness any longer than was necessary. I thought she must trust this guy to leave Pal with him. We didn't say much on the way out, I had to concentrate because of the tricky driving conditions and Zerrin was unforthcoming so I left her to her moodiness.

Midway through the night under the light of a pale moon we reached the small pile of rocks she had spoken about.

They were both asleep under a feebly rigged shelter. Pal stirred as we came up but the stranger didn't move. As soon as I saw this tall fellow with his light hair I knew he wasn't one of us. She was kneeling down beside him one arm around her sleepy little bother and the other stretched out to the injured man, feeling his brow for signs of fever. She hesitated a moment looking at his ragged footwear.

"Who is he Zerrin?" I asked her quietly. She stood up in front of me perhaps a little defiantly and when she spoke I could tell she was worried what I would think.

"I saved him from a crashed space vessel over by the Yenna gorge."

It struck me then that he was Kelti and my anger blazed hot against her.

"Would that be the ship with a Kelti plate?" I asked keeping tight control, other wise I might have hit her.

"Yes he is from the corporate planets but he's saved Pals life and so I must help him."

"Well I am not taking this guy anywhere. I can't believe you're asking me, Flagor Yan, to help a Keltian, what's wrong with you Zerrin? You've lost your marbles out there in the hills."

"How dare you of all people?"

"Just stop OK, you could have come back in any time but you chose not to, so don't try offl oading your problems on to me."

She stood there glowering at me and breathing heavily but I reckon I had her beat.

"Let's not talk about it now." She said eventually and she turned, still holding Pals hand, back to the stranger. I walked away and watched the proceedings from a distance I couldn't stand to be near him.

"How have you been Pal?" She asked her brother.

"Pretty good. A limmex came and I pelted him 'til he went." He said nonchalantly. She dropped a kiss on his forehead and whispered something I didn't hear.

She started, very carefully, to remove the guy's boots and I realised it was his feet that were injured. The stranger roused himself and spoke to her. Fresh anger smote me as I heard them speaking in the Kelti tongue,even Pal joined in. I rose and strode forward.

"What the hell are you doing? Why have you taught Pal to speak that foul language?"

"Just shut up Flagor." She said. I couldn't really believe her cheek so I didn't say anything more just then; I had to make up my mind what I was going to do.

By then Zerrin had removed the boots. His feet were in a mess but there didn't seem to be any infection.

"He seems OK." said Zerrin, surprise and relief mingling in her voice.

"I gave him these when he was in a fever and didn't know what he was doing." Said Pal holding out a small hand in which a red half pill nestled.

"Pal!" gasped Zerrin. Her voice was filled with mixed emotions and I couldn't tell which was predominant.

Anger, pride, fear, relief, I didn't know which.

"Are you feeling alright?" She asked looking searchingly into Pal's face and brushing his dark hair from his brow.

"Yes sis I'm fine. What about Jak?"

She turned back to the foreigner, Jak. "He seems pretty good." She said.

Suddenly I realised the stranger was looking at me. In the dim moonlight his eyes were like great holes in his face. To tell the truth it gave my flesh a creepy feeling.

He spoke to Zerrin and she answered him. I had refused to learn the corporate languages on principle but how I wished I knew what they were saying. I realised it put me at a distinct disadvantage.

A minute later and she was helping him to his feet and heading towards my vehicle.

"Just hold hard." I said. "What do you think you're doing?"

"Well I was hoping we could take him back to your house." She said boldly.

"Of all the barefaced…" I went to intercept them. I grabbed the Kelti's arm and he pulled away from us staggering a little. He said something to Zerrin, she didn't answer and we stood there the three of us with Pal looking on. It was a bit of an impasse I suppose.

"I'll take him." I said to her at last. "But I'm warning you, if I can use him, I will."

"That I can readily believe." She said with bitter sarcasm.

So that's how it was. That's how I, Flagor Yan, happened to have Kelti scum in my house and I wondered if I would live to rue the day.

Chapter 36 Flagor's House

Jak wakes up and finds that Zerrin is back, he doesn't know how long it has been but it is night time. He is glad to see her and recalls the last time he had woken from delirium to find her bright eyes, looking into his.

"We shouldn't keep meeting like this." He says to her.

"How have you been Jak?" She asks him.

"Out of it pretty much but I reckon Pal looked after me just fine." He reaches up with an effort and lays a hand on Pal's shoulder.

"I fought off the Limmex pretty good didn't I Jak?" Is Pals excited input.

"Sure you did." Jak says to Pal, then to himself, "do I remember that? I think I do." He was feeling pathetically weak again though the throbbing and pain in his feet was much less than it had been.

"I'm going to take your boots off now Jak I hope it doesn't hurt too much." Warns Zerrin softly.

Suddenly there is a stranger in the picture; his voice is loud and grating on Jak's ears as he talks to Zerrin.

She answers him sharply and continues to ease Jak's boots off . The pain is pretty intense for a moment and Jak closes his eyes. When he opens them he sees Pal showing Zerrin a half pill left in his hand. As he realises what the little boy has done he feels a strong emotion tugging inside his chest and it occupies him for some few moments. After a while he looks for the stranger and sees him glowering at him his cold blue eyes fiery in the half light. 'He looks like he would like to murder me,' thinks Jak.

"Let's get you to the car." Says Zerrin.

"Where are we going?" He asks her.

"To Gedd, that's where you want to go isn't it?"

Then, abruptly, in front of them is the Censite, talking aggressively and laying his hand roughly on Jak's arm.

"Is this guy a friend of yours?"Wonders Jak as he shakes him off .

Zerrin doesn't answer him but stands stiffly staring at the angry man. Seemingly it is soon sorted however for they make their way to the vehicle. Zerrin installs Jak in the front which elicits another growled protest from the Censite.

Jak dozes fitfully throughout the journey to Gedd. In the early hours of the morning he is assisted by Zerrin and another woman across a long room lined with benches, ahead of him walks the man, not helping but Jak realises that he is entering this mans house and like it or not he is beholden to him.The woman who is on his other arm is talking non-stop to Zerrin and sometimes throwing a comment to Pal or the stony faced man. Zerrin answers her briefly sometimes and Pal, though sleepy, talks openly to her though Jak notices his voice is guarded when he speaks on the odd occasion to the man.

Then Jak is ushered to a narrow bed in a small bare room. As soon as his head hits the pillow he is asleep and knows nothing of the contretemps that he feels sure are being enacted under this roof.

It is well into the afternoon when he wakes up. Sunshine is making a grid on the floor as it shines through the panes of a small window. There is another narrow crib in the room but it doesn't look like it has been slept in. On the floor is a pile of tousled rugs where some one has obviously spent the night on the floor, Pal perhaps? Jak realises he feels quite refreshed and well. He thinks about Pal giving him those tablets and shakes his head slowly. He turns his attention to his injured feet and sees they have been freshly bandaged. When did that happen? Was it last night or this morning? Who had done it, Zerrin?

Leaning propped against the un-plastered wall are two walking sticks. Jak throws back the covers and extends his legs gingerly to the wooden floorboards. On a narrow table under the window is a pitcher of water and a bowl, some soap and shaving tackle, Jak tries out the crutches and sets to with the soap and water. Out of the small window he can see into an alley and across from this dwelling an empty warehouse, the roller doors skew wiff and broken. There are other haphazard buildings flanking the alley in either direction most looking temporary in construction and uninhabited. Zerrin had said this was the plague free zone; well there weren't many people about.

After washing Jak makes his way to the bedroom door,it opens out onto a corridor. From a door at the end he can hear the low murmur of voices. There is a shabby carpet running along the hallway and on the walls a few faded pictures. Jak makes his way along to the end door and pushes it open with his stick.

"It's not white its goldish, like ripe ...." Zerrin's voice drifts into silence as she sees him standing in the doorway and he notices her cheeks look pink and healthy today.

"Morning Zerrin." He says and turns to nod at the other woman. They are sitting drinking coffee at a wooden kitchen table covered with a yellow and white checked cloth. The woman rises and holds out her hand.

"You must be Jak." She says.

"Oh...ahem." Zerrin rises quickly and spills a little of her drink on the bright cloth. "Sorry ...er this is Cass, Jak, she's Flagor's sister and this is Jak." She finishes her awkward introduction lamely and sits down again. Jak pulls up a chair.

"Would you like some coffee?" Cass asks as she rises.

"Yes please." He has to smile at the strangeness of this polite conversation. He looks at Pal eating some kind of cereal and his mouth waters he realises he hasn't eaten since yesterday morning.

"How's Pal today?" He asks the little boy. Pal smiles at him through a mouthful of food and the milk dribbles onto his chin.

"Would you like something to eat Jak?" Asks the hospitable Cass.

"That would be fantastic Cass if it's not too much trouble." She looks at him with her pale green-blue eyes.

"No trouble at all." She says.

"Oh and thanks for the shirt, is it Flagor's?"

"Mmmm."

"Well thanks."

"Zerrin has washed yours and it's flapping on the line this very minute."

Jak looks at Zerrin and smiles, it doesn't feel comfortable to say these polite, shallow thank yous to her he had a feeling she would bite his head off if he tried.

"So you're Keltian," states Cass, as she places a cup and bowl in front of him, "I've never met an alien before, your eyes, they are just so weird." Jak looks surprised at this lapse from etiquette but Cass has no trace of malice on her face so he smiles.

"To me, your eyes seem pretty weird too but I'm getting used to them now."

She nods and sits down beside him.

"So what is it like living on Ecracon 3?"

Jak looks back, for a startling moment he can't remember. He shakes his head.

"That was a long time ago." He says vaguely and begins munching on a spoonful of cereal.

"Do you have a girlfriend on Ecracon?"

"Cass really!" protests Zerrin.

Cass ignores her completely. "Well, do you?" She persists.

Jak thinks for a moment, had Senya been his girlfriend? He couldn't remember what she was like; he hadn't actually known anything about her.

"I think her name is Leela." Pipes up Pal from his cereal bowl. When he looks up three pairs of eyes are looking sharply at him.

"Well." He explains defensively. "When Jak was talking crazy, before I gave him the tablets, He said that name. I remember 'cos I thought it sounded like a nice name." Pal turns his attention back to his food but the ladies turn to Jak who looks first at Cass' raised eyebrows then at Zerrin, she looks quickly down at the coffee stain on the table.

Jak clears his throat and then wonders why he feels the need to explain. He is saved from doing so at the entrance of Flagor along with two other men. There is silence in a room suddenly small and brimming over with people and an air of hostility. Flagor in particular eyes Jak angrily. At first Jak thinks it is because he is sitting in the mans kitchen talking to the girls, then he sees Flagor's eyes on the shirt but that seems a little too trivial. Maybe Flagor always looks annoyed with those cold, blue, blazing eyes. He speaks sharply to his sister and she answers him below her breath as she moves off to put the kettle on. He then says something to Zerrin and her chin comes up. Flagor's two companions stand in the doorway staring at Jak. One of them looks at Jak's borrowed shirt; there is a laugh in his voice as he makes some comment to his host. Flagor growls at him and Jak hears Pals whispered explanation.

"He says Flagor's shirt is too small for you and Flagor doesn't like it."

"That's enough Pal." Zerrin warns.

Then begins a lengthy conversation between the men and Zerrin. Jak divides his attention between finishing his breakfast and listening to the tenor of their voices.

"What are they saying?" He asks Pal.

Pal shoots a look at his sister and seeing her fully occupied, whispers low to Jak.

"They're asking her all sorts of questions about you."

"And?"

"She's just telling them about your ship and how you saved me and the thing with Karrif."

Jak had heard Zerrin mention Karrif, he had noticed the bitter twist in her voice and the way her eyes had raked Flagor with accusation as she spoke. That angry young man had laid a placating hand on her shoulder, which she had shrugged off, to his evident annoyance.

A worrying thought floods Jak's mind and he wonders why he hadn't cautioned Zerrin about it, not that he'd had a chance to speak to her alone since they left the desert.

"She hasn't mentioned..."

He feels a foot strike his leg under the table. He looks down at Pals upturned face innocently waiting for his question. Jak looks across at Zerrin but she's busy talking to Flagor. As he looks at her she turns on him a fleeting, warning glance.

"What?" Whispers Pal.

"How I stupidly drove the overlander into the Rayel pit in broad daylight?"

Pal smiles "I'm afraid she has Jak."

Jak looks up to find all of them are staring at him. One of Flagor's companions reaches a hand across the table.

"My name is Keenan." He says in perfect Kelti. "This is Jeffers." The other man, Jeffers, doesn't offer his hand instead he rests it on a weapon shoved into his waistband. Jak hadn't noticed they were armed before.

"What are you doing here?" asks Keenan.

"My craft crashed here."

Jeff ers fist comes crashing down on the table and he leans over, his face aggressively close to Jaks.

"What were you doing in our airspace?" He shouts at Jak, his accent heavy.

Jak wipes a speck of spittle from his face and Flagor sniggers.

"That's my business." Says Jak quietly to Keenan.

"True," says Keenan reasonably, "but it is also our business."

"Is it against the law to come here?"

"No but people don't normally visit. It's unusual you see; your coming to this quadrant and it's made us very curious."

"Well there you go." Says Jak, "It's a funny old life isn't it? Full of unanswered questions."

Keenan's eyes are hard as he turns and speaks to Flagor. There is a short dialogue between them, Jeff ers says something with his hand on his gun and Flagor seems to agree with him but Keenan shakes his head and turns back with another question for Jak.

"There are some people after you; do you know who they are?"

An idea germinates in Jak's mind and he tests it out.

"Yes I do." He says. Zerrin looks at him sharply and Keenan leans forward a little.

"Who are they?"

"Crimmer Marshals."

"Why, what are you wanted for?"

"There you go again." Says Jak cheerfully, judging that if he gives out information too readily it will be treated with suspicion.

"Just answer the questions Jak, we wouldn't want to hurt you… would we Jeffers?"

On the contrary Jeffers seems quite ardently to want to enter into violent conflict with Jak.

"What was the question, I don't remember?" Says Jak sweetly.

"Why are there Crimmer Marshals after you?"

"OK I'll tell you: Murder, arson, theft."

"I don't believe it," growls Jeffers dismissively, "he looks much too…civilized."

Keenan looks coolly at Jak for a long moment before turning and speaking to Flagor who, apparently, gives them some orders, for they leave soon after. Cass turns as they are going with a tray of steaming coff ee cups. She makes some exasperated comments before tipping two of the drinks into the sink the rest she brings to the table. Flagor takes one, all the time eyeing Jak aggressively. He makes a muttered comment to Zerrin, ruffles Pals hair and after making a signifi cant gesture towards the weapon in his belt, he takes a final long look at Jak. Then he motions his sister to follow him into the hallway. Zerrin is looking at Jak in exasperation.

"Why did you tell them that you idiot? They've gone to check the news archives." She hisses urgently.

"But I am wanted for those things." Says Jak quietly. "Not by the Crimmer Marshals but by Ecracon secoritor police."

A hush settles down on the little kitchen and both Pal and Zerrin stare at Jak in astonishment. Cass comes back and there is no time for further explanation. Jak shakes his head briefly at Zerrin as he sees the look of consternation in her eyes.

"Well jolly old Flagor wants me to find out what I can from you Jak so if you don't mind I'll just ask a few obligatory questions." Says Cass breezily

"Fire away." Says Jak admiring her openness. She sits down and turns on him a confiding look.

"Now about Leela…" There is a laugh in her voice.

Jak groans. "There's nothing about Leela." He says.

"Oh well that's good." She looks significantly at Zerrin who makes a half-hearted face at her. Jak can tell she is still thinking about more important things.

"I'm going out." She announces suddenly.

"I'll come with you." says Jak.

"You can't." Counters Zerrin.

"I can do what I damned well like."

"But Flagor?" She says uncertainly. He hopes he looks his contempt at this comment.

"Can I come?" Injects Pal.

"No you can't, you stay here with Cass and don't go outside the house." She turns back to Jak. "You'll be recognised." She tries a diff erent tack.

"Nobody knows me."

"I mean recognised as an alien."

"That's OK." says Cass. "You'll both have to wear masks anyway if you go out of the plague free zone."

"Right, masks it is then." says Jak.

"And a hooded cape to cover your hair." Says Cass

"Why, it's just the colour of ripe…."

Zerrin glares at her.

"Masks!" Says Jak rudely to Cass and she runs off with a chuckle to find the required items.

Zerrin turns quickly to him.

"Jak you didn't murder……?"

"Sh…," he interrupts and glances down the corridor after Cass. He looks down at Zerrin "Of course I didn't." He pauses for a moment. What about in Peyto's warehouse? Maybe somebody had died there, was that murder or self-defence? Jak shakes his head he doesn't like to think about that time. Zerrin is looking at him earnestly. Cass is coming back along the hallway the masks dangling from her hand and a dark cloak thrown over her arm.

Jak shakes his head at Zerrin. "No I didn't." He repeats quickly.

Cass eyes them knowingly before giving Zerrin the masks and Jak the cloak. He tries it on for size. Cass clicks her tongue and shakes her head as she looks at the length.

"Flagor won't like it when he sees how short it is for you." She says.

They encounter Flagor at the street door and Jak does notice him looking at the hem of the cloak as he steps aside to let Jak pass by on his crutches, but he doesn't say anything.

Jak puts his mask on and waits in the windy street for Zerrin. She comes out pretty soon with a frown on her face.

"What did he say?" asks Jak.

"I can't hear you Jak you've got your mask on."

Jak lifts his mask, feeling a bit silly and repeats his question.

"Oh…nothing." Is Zerrin's non-committal answer. Jak sees she is not going to communicate with him on this score.

"Aren't you going to wear your mask?"

"Not 'till we leave the plague free zone, you should keep yours on though."

After a few more steps she stops and turns to Jak who leans on his crutches and inclines his ear to her.

"I still don't understand why you told them you are a murderer." She says. "Why did you do that?"

"I had to have a reason for coming to this sector and I thought a fugitive might find refuge here. I think they would rather I was a murderer than Verdor Danes son."

"But Jak, if there is anything in the archives about it they'll know who you are."

This was undeniably true of course and causes Jak pause for a moment.

"Oh I don't suppose there will be anything there." He says hopefully.

"I had a notion you hadn't thought it out properly when you said it."

"I don't think I'll go back to Flagor's house anyway." Says Jak as he hobbles forward. "I don't feel like I'm very popular there."

"Cass likes you."

"Yes but Flagor is not too happy with me being there."

Zerrin laughs a little. "He wouldn't sleep in the same house with you last night. He went over to Keenan's

"Precisely; and when the time comes when I want to beat the hide off him, I'll feel uncomfortable if I'm living in his house and eating his food, you know what I mean?"

She looks at him sideways. "He still brought you in from the desert."

"That's true and I will take that into account even though I know he only did it for you."

"Jak I think you should know he said he'll use you if he can."

"'Use me' what do you mean?"

"Well I don't know for sure but he's a member of some political activist group. One never knows what plans they might have."

A thought strikes Jak. "Do you think this group might have my Father?" There is a thread of excitement in his voice. Zerrin looks scared as if she wishes she had not spoken.

"I wonder…?" continues Jak.

"Jak, I shouldn't have said anything, it was wrong of me." There is a pleading note in her voice as if she wants him not to act on her words.

"Do you feel like a traitor?" Asks Jak with interest. She doesn't answer this but sends him a very fi erce, daggerlike, look.

"'Your eyes are like poniards'" He quotes.

Chapter 37
Lazertrom

By now they have reached the end of the street, Zerrin pauses and for the first time Jak takes proper note of his surroundings. The street in which they stand is dusty and unpaved, there seems to be endless gusts of wind blowing through the architectural corridor.

"Is it always this windy?" He asks Zerrin.

"Always."

He turns his attention to the houses, mostly empty, broken windows, unpainted, uncared for, no gardens, no curtains, no comforts. It has the look of a post apocalyptic town but even before it couldn't have been much.

"Not very pretty is it?" She says hollowly.

"Don't take offence but why isn't it better? The Censites have been here for a hundred years haven't they?"

"I don't know." Her voice is so small he can hardly hear it and he notices there are unshed tears almost quenching the luminosity of her eyes.

"I'm sorry." Says Jak awkwardly. "I just don't understand that's all."

"It's OK Jak, it's not your fault." She is already walking ahead of him and he shuffles quickly after her, remembering his difficulties she slows to match his pace.

"Where are the holding bays?" Asks Jak.

She looks at him sharply. "You said you were coming with me."

"I don't know where you're going but I'm going to the holding yards."

"Well you don't know where you're going either then 'cos I'm not telling you where the holding yards are."

"Look Zerrin, if the Lazortrom is here I'm going to get aboard and find out from the records if the food my father delivered here was contaminated. There's a lab on board and the records will be there. I need to fi nd out." A slight constriction enters his voice. He stops, drops one of his crutches to lay a hand on her arm. He looks at her earnestly for a moment then says "Don't you want to know?"

Suddenly her answer seems very important. Her eyes are lowered as she studies her foot making scuff marks in the dust.

"Yes." she says briefly. She bends and picks up his crutch so he doesn't see her face for a moment. When she finally raises her eyes to his she is smiling encouragingly.

"Let's go then." He smiles back at her.

"We'd better fix our masks properly, we may meet some plague victims, don't touch anything if you can help it."

Jak adjusts the mouthpiece of his mask and realises they have seen no one so far, maybe a shadow or two behind a dusty windowpane but absolutely no sign of life in the streets.

"Is it always as quiet as this?"

"It never used to be. Now if I were you I'd fi x my mask and not take it off until we get back here." She advises, snapping her own breathing apparatus into place.

Jak complies and this effectively terminates all vocal communication between them. Zerrin signals for him to follow her and they make their way through endless twisting streets. There are more people about the place now and Jak, with his face partly covered, only catches a glimpse now and then of a plague-scarred face but it is enough horror to turn his stomach to water. He knows his father would never have knowingly brought plague to this dreadful place but he desperately hopes he didn't play an innocent part.

Eventually they come to another quiet and deserted street. Zerrin stops and takes off her mask, dragging in great gulps of air as if her breathing has been restricted all this while. She leans limply against a crumbling lathe and plaster wall.

"I'd forgotten how dreadful it is here." She says to Jak,

the traumatised look lingering in her eyes. Jak removes his mask but keeps the hood pulled forward over his face.

"Was it safe to walk through there? I mean would the people not attack us?"

"We haven't got anything they want. If we had taken the vehicle then maybe they would have hijacked us."

"How long…I mean…?."

"How long do they last after contracting the plague? About four or five months, that's all."

"Come." says Jak taking her hand for a moment before having to relinquish it to manipulate his crutches. "Let's get to the ship."

"How are your feet?"

"They're fine." Actually they are hurting like hell but it seems more than inappropriate to mention it after the suffering they have just seen.

As they turn to walk along the dusty, windy road Jak sees the ship ahead of them rising huge, gleaming and incongruous above the roofs of the decaying primitive city. He hadn't seen her before as his head was bowed low to avoid notice but now she bursts upon him in her full glory. Zerrin too is admiring the ship and he believes, noticing the contrast between his and her worlds.

The holding yards also seem deserted. They hover in the protective shadow of an empty, rusting grain silo and wait to detect any movement. Jak looks up and up at the Lazortrom, she seems unmanned, there are no lights, everything is quiet and still. Around the lower porthole windows Jak notices evidence of explosives being used to blow the triple polectrum panels. Th ere is no way primitive plastic explosives will penetrate any of the outer hull but the Censites had obviously tried quite desperately to breach the secure shell. The belly of the ship is open. He and Zerrin skirt round the edge of the docking bay and come up to the ship from the rear. There is nobody inside the huge cargo hold. Jak knows the ship and makes his way unerringly to the interior hatch. It is locked and here again there are signs that a forced entry has been attempted. There are scorch marks around the lock and lacerations in the outer metal skin. Jak reaches up and presses a button in the roof canopy over the hatch. Down slides a screen and keypad, Jak taps in an eight digit cryptogram, the screen flickers into life and he enters the password. Next there is a three dimensional Peterson code to remember. Th e hatch slides silently back.

"Come on." says Jak to Zerrin who has been watching the cargo doors for any interruptions. She crosses the threshold without a word and stands gazing at the glossy interior. Jak remembers how pleased she was with the tent pack on the overlander. The hatch slides too behind them and Jak directs their steps towards the elevator. As they ascend towards the workshop level, Jak notices her look of wonder and the way she grips the handrail.

"Have you never been in an elevator before?" He asks astonished.

"No actually." She says seeming pleased with the experience. "Of course I've heard of them but I've never been inside one."

They come out on the workshop level. There is a high domed central hall with portals leading off the circular gallery into the various offices. It is eerily quiet in the empty ship.

Jak leads the way to the lab, Zerrin follows closely behind, gazing wide-eyed at her surroundings. Inside he sits down at the computer bank. Zerrin wanders around fiddling with the instruments.

"Don't touch that!" Jak says as he notices her going for the oscillator.

"Why not is it booby trapped?"

"No but it is dangerous so just leave it alone, leave it all alone, so's I can concentrate on this."

She sits down in the swivel chair beside him and after watching his fingers on the touch screen for a while she gets bored and commences swivelling.

"Here it is!" Pronounces Jak.

Zerrin stops playing with the chair and leans forward over his shoulder.

"It says on the 32.24.81 this signature was found in the wheat flour."

"Do you think it's the plague?"

"Uhuh the timing's right."

“Was it rejected?”

Jak clicks onto the trail. “Yes look here are the forms signed by....” He looks twice at the name. “Petaman, that’s strange, what was he doing on my Dad’s ship.” He touches a few more boxes. “And there it is 56672 that’s the same batch number; the wheat flour was loaded anyway!”

He turns and looks at Zerrin, her face has a crumpled look and her cheeks are pale.

Jak turns back to the computer he doesn’t understand why Petaman’s name is on the form. He opens another program and finds the date of departure that he saw on the load of contaminated flour.

“Look! Petaman was piloting the Lazortrom when the flour was delivered.” Jak feels elated. “We must have been on holiday or something and they used the Lazortrom out of schedule.”

He looks back at Zerrin his heart full of relief, thinkingfoolishly that his discovery will have the same relevance for her.

“I’m glad for you Jak.” She says quietly he can see she is in earnest but her eyes are the saddest he has ever encountered. He tries to set aside his own feelings of release and focus again on the plight of the Censites.

“Why would anybody do this? It can’t be a mistake can it?”

Zerrin is staring at the computer screen but her thoughts are obviously elsewhere.

"The Jubilee!" Cries Jak suddenly. "When is it? What is supposed to happen?"

Zerrin gives a start at the strident note in his voice as it breaks the hushed quiet of the Lab then her face turns paler still as her eyes leave his and look over his shoulder.

There is the sound of a loud report, Jak sees Zerrin's eyes widen and a red trickle of blood appears from behind the hairline above her left temple. She sags back into the swivel chair and the light dims in her eyes as the lids droop shut. Jak is up and has lifted her in his arms without looking to see where the shot came from.

"Jak Dane!" Shouts a voice he recognises. "What the hell are you doing here?"

Jak dabs ineffectually at the blood on Zerrin's pale brow. He realises he is trembling with relief as he sees that though it bleeds profusely it is little more than a graze where the bullet has seared her scalp.

"Nuttle you idiot! What on Ecracon do you think you're doing? You might have killed her."

"I didn't know she was with you Sir. I thought the Censites had breached the hull and were taking the ship."

"Can't you see she is just a young girl?"

"No Sir, I could tell she was a Censite and that was all I was thinking about."

"Go over to sick bay and bring back a stretcher."

"One thing, you didn't leave the hatch open did you."

"No, of course not."

When Nuttle returns with the stretcher and as they wheel Zerrin through to sick bay Jak for the first time asks about his father. He is a little shocked that he hasn't asked before but then things were so out of kilter and he was worrying about Zerrin and everything.

"What's happened to Mr Dane is he aboard? Is he alive?"

"Last time I saw him he was alive."

"What happened here Nuttle? Tell me about it."

"Well we had docked as usual and the crew were in the cargo hold unloading the supplies. There was only Jimmin and me still aboard, we were cleaning the galley at that particular time. Then I hear the Boss' voice over the tanoy telling me to batten down the hatches immediately, which I do. Then I goes up to the fl ight deck and watches the monitors. Down in the hold there's all these armed Censites. Now you must know that normally we don't have no truck with anybody here we just offload without seeing anyone but somehow the perimeter field was breached. I don't know how it could have happened and I sees all these scum surrounding the boss and the crew. Suddenly there's shots fi red and I see Linnick go down then Froom. Then the Censites round the others up and take them off somewheres."

"Did you try and find out what happened to them."

"No Sir I stayed put like the Boss said. For hours I had to keep hid 'cos they were trying to get in. Th ey were grinding away at the viewers and shooting at the hatches and everything. Then Jimmin decides he's going to go and look for the others. He went out but he never came back."

"What about radio contact? Did you send a distress signal?"

"Yeah I been trying that every day but I think the damned thing's broke."

"And did you happen to see whereabouts they were heading when they took Dad and the crew hostage?"

"Well no it was like this you see…"

"You were hiding?"

"Well yes by then I was hiding I'd just seen them shooting down Linnink and Froom. I wouldn't be any use to anybody dead now would I?"

"No, no use at all." Says Jak, perhaps a little sarcastically.

By this time Jak has dressed Zerrin's wound he brushes the damp hair from her face and leans close, listeningto her steady breathing."

"She seems OK but why doesn't she wake up?" He mutters worriedly to himself.

"She'll be fine." Says Nuttle uncomfortably, "If I'd known she was a friend of yours, of course I'd never have shot her but I thought she was one of them there Censites."

"You've said that already Nuttle and she is a Censite, a damn fine one."

"Yeah, but Sir, their eyes, don't you think they're the weirdest thing?"

Jak looks at Nuttle for a moment.

"I'm just off to check the beamer." He says. "If she shows signs of waking give me a buzz." Jak takes a communicator off the wall by the door and shoves it in his pocket.

Nuttle looks extremely unhappy with the idea of being left alone with Zerrin and seems about to protest.

"Stay put." Orders Jak then seeing a wheeler leaning folded against the wall he discards his crutches and sits in the chair with a sigh of relief.

"What happened to you Sir?" Says Nuttle, probably in the hope of keeping him by.

"Oh I fell into an acid pit." Says Jak breezily as he wheels out into the corridor.

When he reaches the flight deck it is in darkness. At least Nuttle had the sense to obscure the viewers. Jak switches on the dimmer light and makes his way between the consoles to the radio terminal. He soon sees there is nothing wrong with it only that the signal is being jammed. He remembers the interspace communication system he had discovered in Krey

Roke's hidden sanctum, was that what it was doing? Selectively jamming signals?

He thinks about it for a moment then he fi nds himself worrying about Zerrin. If she wakes up with only Nuttle there she would be frightened. He quickly makes his way down in the lift and trundles along to sick bay. As the door slides open the first thing he sees is Zerrin crouched in the corner a heavy piece of metal apparatus in her hand, the bandage on her head twisting off and falling over her eye.

"What the…?" He turns his attention to Nuttle; he is standing with his gun levelled at Zerrin and a red welt across his forehead. "I thought I told you to call me if she stirred."

He wheels over to Zerrin and tugs gently on the bar. She is reluctant to release it and in the end he has to yank it out of her resistant grasp.

"Come on Zerrin." He says soothingly, "It's OK, everything's fine."

She shoots him one of her withering looks and he realises how inappropriate his chosen words are.

"OK ,so everything's not fine but I'm trying to sort it out."

She strokes the gleaming wheel of his chair as she rises in one lithe movement "Cool." She says and he doesn't know if she's talking about his sorting capabilities or the wheeler, he thinks it is probably the wheeler. He realises Nuttle is still holding the gun on her.

“Put the gun away Nuttle.” He orders in a voice nicely timbered between boredom and exasperation.

“Who’s this bozo?” Asks Zerrin hitching a leg onto the stretcher and gingerly fingering the loose bandage round her temple.

“Leave that alone.” Says Jak rising to fix it for her.

“Bossy.” She says petulantly. When Jak has finished rearranging the dressing he introduces her to the Lazortrom cook.

“This is Nuttle, ship’s cook.”

“Howdy Nutty.” Says Zerrin cheerfully.

“And this is Zerr.....For crying out loud Nuttle I told you to put that damn gun away haven’t you done enough damage?”

“The name is Nuttle, Miss.” growls the cook, finally shoving his weapon reluctantly into his belt.

“OK Nuttlemiss, whatever.”

“I’m starving.” Says Jak on inspiration. “Can’t you rustle us up some of those special thin thingummies you make with syrup all over them Nuttle?”

“That would be crepes Sir and yes I can make you some with pleasure.”

“Never make an enemy of the chef my dear. Don’t you know that?” Says Jak quizzically as Nuttle leaves.

“The guy shot me Jak! You can’t expect me to love him.”

"Never mind, I'll share some of my syrupy things with you."

"Have you found out what's going on here?" Asks Zerrin after sliding off the stretcher and wandering around the room picking things up and looking at them curiously.

"Well it looks like some guys came along while they were unloading the supplies and took my father, along with five of the crew."

"How long ago was this?"

"Must have been 21...no 22 days ago."

Zerrin slides her eyes away from his. There is silence between them for a while.

"I would know wouldn't I, if he were dead?" He can hear his voice a little lower pitched than usual as he asks her this question.

She shakes her head. She isn't looking at him but staring unblinkingly at a wall chart.

"I can't say Jak, I don't know if you would be able to tell or not." She walks over to him and lays a hand on his arm. "I guess they wanted him alive seeing as they took him hostage." After a few moments he feels her grip tighten.

"What?"

"You remember when the Uluru took us and we heard them talking? They knew who you were remember?

And they were saying they would ransom you to the Fedek."

"Yes, I remember. So you reckon the Fedek must have my father? Who are they?"

"Political activists, terrorists."

"So, would they kidnap the crew of the Lazortrom for publicity?"

"Yes, to try and draw the Crimmer's attention to the plight of the Censites, they would."

"Well they're not going to do that, Krey Roke has got all transmissions from Detagon jammed. I don't think the Crimmer knows anything about what's going on here, you remember the double reports I got from York? They are intercepting each quarterly report from the Crimmer delegate or maybe York is the delegate and forwarding one with rosy statistics. You know you read it to me."

Zerrin is staring at him, not knowing to whom he is referring but following the gist of his conclusions. "So why....?"

"The Jubilee." Cuts in Jak excitedly. "What's supposed to happen at the Jubilee?"

"We go back to our land, like it says in the Bible; in the Jubilee year everyone returns to their inheritance, and we are supposed to get to go back to Census."

"But there won't be anybody to go back." Concludes Jak sinking down into the wheeler. "All Censites die of plague before the Jubilee. The Crimmer does nothing about it 'cos they don't know anything about it and in a few more years Krey Roke gets to be governor or whatever of paradise and starts selling off chunks of it to developers."

"What are you talking about Jak? How do you know all this? Are you guessing? Who's Krey Roke?"

"He's the Bad Guy and I know all this because I broke into his offices at government tower in Kelti Town. I've seen the plans. He's even got pictures of the damned mansions he's going to build there."

Chapter 38 Krey

So…,Jak Dane knew and then the whole of the twelve nations knew. Strangely I didn't mind. The game was up anyway and I didn't mind the whole world becoming acquainted with my excellent plan. It had been perfect and if it had been confounded by mischance, I was not culpable. Still I do feel some regrets. Felice for instance had become involved with some Censite fellow. I remember quite vividly the day she contacted me after she had escaped from the Uluru tribesmen. It was nothing in her actual words but I detected a subtle difference in the timbre of her voice. Of course I immediately proceeded to investigate and I flatter myself that within but a few moments I had already used her weakness against her.

"My dear how long it is since I have had the felicity of hearing your dulcet tones." Was my greeting.

"I've been long enough on this despicable dust bowl, come and rescue me." She said, this was so unlike her that I immediately became suspicious.

“What about Jak Dane?” I purred. “Have you dispatched the impudent boy?”

“I don’t care about Jak Dane I just want to leave here.”

“Aha some other emotion has entered your heart to replace the hatred you feel for your young antagonist. Now that is exceedingly piquant.”

“Krey please?” I detected a hint of desperation in her voice and I suppose I am willing to admit at this point I should have heeded her plea. Instead I asked her to relate the occurrences of the past few days, which she did accurately enough and I was able to supplement her narrative with my own impressions of the nuances of their relationship as I have previously disclosed in my memoirs. I gathered this information from the subtle

intonation of her voice. I know her so well you see and I believe my interpretation to be tolerably correct.

“And where are you now my love?”

“I am proceeding to Gedd. The overlanders are restored I still have one man and the confounded Censite, Gelff, he is like a parasite; I can’t seem to shake him off .

“But he did so heroically rescue you from the Uluru my dear you do owe him some small allegiance.”

“He’s leeching scum and I can’t stand the foul stench of this place a day longer. Can’t you get me out of here Krey?”

“I will send reinforcements my love. Now be a good

girl and run along to Gedd, remove that odious boy from floundering in my wake."

So that was that, so to speak.

I wonder what she is doing now.

But enough repining I must make sure all my default arrangements are in good order, which of course they are, immaculate as always.

Chapter 39
Plans

Zerrin is watching him as he demolishes the last of the syrupy pancakes and wipes the butter off his chin.

"How can you eat so much?" She wonders.

"It's recovery food. I'm convalescing and I need all these proteins and things to get me back on my feet."

"You're a greedy pig more like."

"That too!" He scrapes the final sticky residue up onto his spoon and tucks it away. "Right that just about does it....

Now," he says waving the spoon at her, "do you think

your friend Flagor is involved with these Fedek guys?"

"I wouldn't call him my friend." Zerrin looks out of

moody eyes at Jak.

"He likes you well enough." States Jak.

"Don't start that again Jak, please."

Jak licks the back of his spoon. What does she mean 'don't start that again.' He wasn't starting anything. He lets it pass.

"What about Flagor and the Fedek, any connections there?"

"They are affiliated with the same political group."

"I reckon he knows something about my father." Says Jak speculatively.

"He wouldn't get involved in something like that."

"How do you know?"

"I've known him since we were children."

"People change."

"Do they?" She looks at him and Jak can tell she is assessing, quite seriously his banal comment.

"Hell yes; look you at me. A few weeks ago I was just an idiot kid scratching around, doing nothing to speak of and now here I am, intending to save a whole race of people."

"Are you Jak? That's sweet of you." He can't tell for sure if that is sarcasm he can hear in her voice.

"When I've found my father," he says more soberly, "I'm taking this ship to the Crimmer and telling them what's going on here."

She shakes her head sadly. “You have so much faith in the Crimmer Council, I have none at all. If you find your father which I really hope and believe you will and you escape from here alive do you think this Krey Roke will let you take the Lazortrom out of this sector?”

“He can just try and stop me.”

“He will.”

“Yeah I know he will, but he won’t be able to.”

“And if you reach the Crimmer do you really think they’ll listen to you? You said the securitor police are after you for murder, arson and theft. I think they’ll just clap you in irons.”

“They may not listen to me but they’ll listen to my father, He is a volunteer spectator for the social department.”

“I don’t know what that means.” She says after staring at him for a moment the look of scepticism lessening perceptively.

“It means they’ll listen if we can get him there.”

He watches a flicker of hope intensify the violet colour of her eyes and he knows a moment’s fearful concern that he has cruelly ignited false expectations.

“Let’s find him.” She says a little thrill of excitement running through her voice.

“Hold hard, how are we going to go about it?”

“I’ll ask Flagor.”

"What just up and say 'Hey Flagor where's this Kelti guy you've kidnapped?'"

"Not quite that but I'll ask him if he knows anything

about it?"

"And you think he'll tell you."

"Yes I think so."

"Well why didn't you ask him before then?"

Zerrin looks down at her feet and starts to trace the square pattern on the tiles.

"I didn't know if you were telling the truth."

"'You didn't know I was telling the truth?" Jak's indignation is tinged with surprise.

"And anyway," she rushes on quickly, "I didn't know whether they might want to kill you, Verdor Danes son, they still believe he brought the plague here."

"Fair enough, but this other thing. I've always told you the truth Zerrin."

"What about the navigator on the overlander?" She flashes back at him.

Jak is nonplussed for a moment but he soon recovers.

"That was different and you know it."

"Yes you're right," she says largely, "I shouldn't have used it against you."

“OK let’s head back to Flagor.”

“You can’t come.” says Zerrin with finality.

“Look Zerrin I’m sick of this ‘you can’t come’ business you tried it back at the house, don’t try and tell me where I can go and where I can’t.”

“But they may have found out who you are, why don’t you stay here. I’ll get the info and come back.”

“Yeah right and what about if your precious Flagor turns nasty?”

“He won’t and I can take care of myself anyway.”

“I’m not so sure about that, anyway I’m coming so stop making such a hooha about it.”

“OK, so come, see if I care. You’d better tell your friend Nuttlemiss we’re leaving.”

Jak calls through to the kitchen.

Now he has made such a fuss about going with her Jak thinks worriedly about the long haul back through the streets on his sore throbbing feet.

“Do you think we could risk taking the wheeler?” He wonders.

Zerrin looks thoughtfully at the contraption.

“If we throw a rug over it to cover the mechanism and I push you.” She nods, “I reckon with just the wheels showing it would look much like an ordinary wheelchair and I’ve seen one or two of those in the plague district.”

Zerrin runs along to the sleeping quarters after receiving directions from Jak, to find a suitable covering for the wheeler. Nuttle comes in from the kitchen a jug of iced fruit drink in one hand and a bunch of glasses in the other.

"Where is the Censite?" He asks suspiciously as soon as he sees she is missing.

He doesn't like the idea of Jak venturing back out into the city either and agues with him on the point until the return of Zerrin with a plain neutral coloured blanket.

"This'll do the trick." She says and throws it over the wheeler.

Jak lowers himself in with relief thinking about the easy trip back to Flagor's abode.

"Now, where are the weapons kept Nuttle?"

Nuttle leads them to a gun case near the flight deck, he opens it with extreme reluctance due to the presence of Zerrin and Jak looks in with no idea which to choose.

"I'd take a lazer 47 if I were you boss." Suggests Nuttle seeing his dilemma.

"And that would be?"

Nuttle unclips a small silvery blue gun and hands it to Jak.

"It feels pretty wrong taking this." Says Jak as he tucks it away in a fold in the blanket.

Both Nuttle and Zerrin look at him in surprise.

"I don't want to kill anybody." He explains.

"Just wound them then," says Nuttle,"but make it good and wounded."

"I thought you were into all this Jak." Says Zerrin, surprise still lingering in her voice. Jak looks at her thinking about the old days, which were in fact only a couple of weeks ago when he was just another unicamp student who had only ever picked up a weapon in compulsory target training and yet Zerrin seemed to think of him as a battle scarred veteran.

"You'd better take one too." He suggests to her.

"Sir!" Protests Nuttle and moves his large body in front of the open closet protectively. Zerrin, without any hesitation, reaches in under his arm and picks out a 220 marksman and then again for a box of ammunition.

"You gotta be quicker than that." She says to Nuttle.

They head back through the quiet streets as they near the plague free zone and as Zerrin takes off her mask Jak suggests a plan of campaign.

"I'll wait across the alley in one of the vacant lots," says Jak, "you go on in and find out if they've discovered my identity, see if you can detect an increase in hostilities."

She nods and turns to go.

"Wait, what about this?" His finger brushes her forehead near the plaster.

"Oh…er I'll take it off now, it's done bleeding."

"Be careful you don't want to start it off again, here let me do it." He carefully removes the dressing.

"How does it look, does it notice?"

Jak arranges her fringe over the wound. "I don't know." He says worriedly thinking about Cass's knowing eyes.

"It'll be OK." She bobs down and scrutinises the reflection of her forehead in the shiny metal of the wheeler. She rearranges some locks of hair before rising and turning to go.

"Wait, you'd better take this." He holds out to her the chosen weapon, she hesitates.

"I'm not likely to want to shoot my friends Jak."

"Earlier you insisted Flagor wasn't your friend." Jak reminds her.

"True." she admits but she still hesitates before taking the weapon and concealing it in the folds of her dress.

"This is no good," she says, "they'll know something's wrong."

Jak looks at her and can see the validity of this statement; she looks very awkward and is obviously concealing something.

"Here tuck it in your waistband at the back." Says Jak taking the gun from her and turning her round. He slips it into the stiff material of her belt and it nestles in the small of her back. “Now let your hair down.” She pulls out a couple of long clips and her soft curls tumble down past her waistline.

“That should do it.” Says Jak admiringly.

“What about if I lean forward?” She attempts this manoeuvre and her hair slips aside revealing the cold deadliness of the marksman.

“Can’t you stay upright?”

“I could but I’d look like a damned retard.” She says dryly.

“You could say you’ve hurt your back.” She just looks at him and he casts about for some other solution.

“OK why don’t you wear the cloak?” This seems like such a sensible suggestion that Jak

couldn’t understand why he didn’t think of it before. She agrees readily to this answer but recommends they wait until they are right by the house before Jak divests himself of this item.

Jak waits in the empty lot staring at the house from the only remaining dusty window of a tumbled down apartment. He is worried about Zerrin and indeed Pal but there is nothing he can do except wait for her signal. It seems an age to him before he sees her at the kitchen door and he knows it is safe to go across. He leaves the wheeler and only then realises he has forgotten the crutches as he hobbles painfully towards Flagor’s house. As he enters he looks first at Zerrin sitting very upright in a chair and then at Flagor. Keenan and Jeffers are not there and Jak wonders if that means they haven't returned from their fact-finding mission yet. Flagor growls something at him and Cass interprets.

"Hello Jak, how are you? Flagor wants to know where his crutches are."

"Why? Does he need them?" Asks Jak wondering why the guy is so attached to the dashed things.

"Where have you been Jak?" asks Pal leaving a plate of sandwiches at the table and running up to him to slip a sticky hand into his.

"Have you been eating ever since I left?" Marvels Jak.

"Where did you go? I wish you'd taken me with you."

"Oh just looking around the place."

"Zerrin's hurt her back." Pal informs him.

Jak's eyes fly to hers and he sees half hidden amusement in their depths. He notices that the cloak is gone and imagines that of course Cass would have solicitously removed it from Zerrin's shoulders as soon as she entered the house and Zerrin, caught off guard, would have been unable to protest. A bubble of laughter rises in Jak's chest but he holds it in as he sees Flagor watching them with jealous eyes.

"Zerrin, ask Flagor if he's heard of Verdor Dane."

Zerrin looks a little startled at this up front approach but after a momentary hesitation she turns to Flagor and lays the question before him. He turns wary eyes to Jak but does not speak. Now there is a knock on the door, Flagor leaves the kitchen and is back in a few moments with Keenan. They are in earnest confabulation as they enter the kitchen. Meanwhile Jak has shot Zerrin a questioning look to which she responds with a brief nod.

"Hello Cass, Zerrin, Pal, ah Jak, how are you feeling this afternoon any better?" Asks Keenan attentively. Jak feels mistrustful at this suavity but responds in kind.

"I'm pretty well thankyou, a little footsore but otherwise good."

"Flagor tells me you've been out and about. What did you think of our fi city?"

Jak is not sure how he ought to respond to this.

"How about you? Were you able to verify my story?"

"No Jak we weren't but maybe your little misdemeanours were of too little consequence to be reported to the twelve nations and reach our pitiful outpost. After all the fact that over five thousand people died of plague last month on this planet wasn't mentioned either so that doesn't signify." For the first time there is the familiar bitterness of the Censites in Keenan's voice.

"5326 people." Jak says quietly. Keenan stares at him with a very puzzled look in his light grey eyes.

"Who are you Jak? What are you doing here?"

"I'm looking for a man called Verdor Dane. Have you heard of him?" States Jak boldly.

Keenan takes a few paces round the room and then kicks out the chair opposite Jak and sits down.

"Yes, he's here." He says.

Jak finds it difficult to hide his excitement.

"I want to see him." He says.

"Now why would you want to do that? Are you going to pay his ransom?"

"Are you holding him hostage?"

"Not I Jak, but I know who is."

"The Fedek?"

"How do you know these things Jak?" Keenan's eyes flicker to Zerrin's concerned face.

"Karrif told me."

Keenan's eyes narrow, condensing the emitted light so that it is bright and hard.

"Now why would he do that?" He says softly.

"Maybe like you, he thought I was here to pay the ransom. Perhaps he reckoned on upping the price and taking his cut."

"Mmm that sounds like Karrif." Speculates Keenan relaxing a little.

Cass, ministering as ever, sets a cup of coffee by his elbow. With a nod of thanks he lifts it to his lips then lowers it again without tasting the contents.

"So how come you know Verdor Dane and why do you want to see him?"

Jak toys with revealing his identity to Keenan, after all he seems like a decent chap, maybe he will help him. On the other hand he might be eaten up with righteous indignation at the son of a guy he thinks murdered his people. The latter seems more likely to Jak but what can he offer instead? He has taken so long debating his response whilst gazing unseeingly over Keenan's shoulder that Keenan breaks in eventually with a discomforted clearing of the throat.

"You're right, it's none of my business, I'm just curious that's all."

"I can arrange a meeting for you with a Fedek member I'm acquainted with?" Proposes Cass.

"Yes….yes," agrees Jak looking at Cass with a feeling of relief, "please if you can, that would be great."

"You watch yourself with those guys Jak they can be right nutters." Cautions Keenan. He turns and apparently relays the conversation to Flagor. It seems strange to Jak that Flagor appears to be in charge, Keenan seems a much more sensible candidate for leadership.

"He's not tough enough." Says Cass in his ear.

"You're not…? " Jak has a sudden uncomfortable thought that she can read his mind, there was some such rumours about the Censites but he doesn't like to annunciate it in front of them.

“Reading your mind?” Suggests Cass and abruptly the slight smile leaves her face and she commences staring at Jak with her bright orbs opened wide and locked onto his.

“Stop being stupid Cass.” Says Zerrin crossly.

Cass rocks back on her heels and laughs lightly. Zerrin looks scornfully at Jak.

“We’re not that weird you idiot.” She says and Jak realises that he has hurt her, perhaps by his too eager susceptibility.

It looks like Zerrin has been able to dispose of her weapon as she walks away from him now with freer movements. He notices that she has rewound her hair.

The now accustomed sound of Flagor’s angry voice raised in dissent, breaks in on Jak’s thoughts and they all turn to look at him. His even features are marred by a heavy scowl. Keenan is apparently trying to dissuade him from some course of action. His hand is on Flagor’s arm. Zerrin joins in the debate and her voice becomes quite heated. Flagor turns to her and Jak doesn’t like the insolent tone of his voice. Zerrin’s cheeks are flushed and a look comes into her eyes that Jak knows only too well. He rises quickly from his chair and hears it crashing behind him but he is too late. Zerrin launches herself at Flagor and he backs off before her onslaught. Jak is there, dragging her off before Flagor is able to react. Keenan stands by, too astonished to move at first but then he turns and says a few words in a condemnatory tone to his friend who is rubbing a bruised chin. Flagor's eyes are blazing as he drops a comment loaded with spite in Zerrin's direction. She stiffens and Jak has to keep a firm grip on her shoulders. Cass is actually laughing and obviously thoroughly enjoying the scene. Pal looks worried and comes forward to take Zerrin's hand.

Jak can tell that reaction has set in and Flagor is starting to feel bad, he calls something in a softer voice to Zerrin and she hunches her shoulder a little as she replies. However the tension in the kitchen is dissipating.

Zerrin has pulled away from Jak and is now at the kitchen sink preparing some kind of vegetable, Cass is with her and they are talking in low tones. Under normal circumstances Jak would have gone out for a walk with Pal so that this bizarre unit could talk out their differences in private but for some reason he stays put. Maybe it's because he mistrusts Flagor's apparent repentance. Thank goodness Zerrin had earlier disposed of the gun he had given her, would she have used it in her rage on Flagor? Although Jak wouldn't have been that sorry to see the back of this unpleasant young man the game would have been up and what kind of consequences would there have been for Zerrin? She was too volatile by half. He suddenly feels very much aware of the responsibility he has developed towards her and Pal along with a feeling of accountability for handing out guns to all and sundry. 'She didn't shoot anybody Jak.' He acquits himself. 'Yes but she might have done she's so uncontrolled and you gave her a gun you idiot.' As he shakes off these morbid preoccupations he finds the ever-hospitable Cass standing before him with a cup of coff ee.

"Don't worry," she says, "it's one of those love, hate things."

Jak is quite prepared to believe in the hate side of it but the other? No he couldn't accept that. However she had turned to Flagor for help when she was desperate but wasn't that solely for him, Jak? Why was she living alone with her little brother in the outlands? She said her parents had taken her out there because of the plague. She hadn't come to Flagor when Pal was ailing but then she couldn't have made it across the desert carrying a critically ill child without some form of transport could she? What about Karrif, he came into this somewhere? He must ask somebody a few questions, Cass maybe? He thinks of Cass' knowing inquisitive eyes and decides against it.

Chapter 40
The Fedek

"Let's go for a walk Zerrin." He says rather abruptly.

She looks at him. "I'm helping Cass with the dinner." She says a little uncertainly.

"Can I come?" Asks Pal eagerly.

"Sure you can young'un." Says Jak ruffling Pals hair. He raises his eyes to Zerrin expectantly. She doesn't look too sure and Cass gives her a little shove.

"Go ahead I can finish up here."

Other than Cass, Jak gets the feeling there is a distinct air of disapproval in the room and he suspects he has probably transgressed some social rule here. Both Keenan and Flagor have something to say to Zerrin on the subject as she wipes her hands slowly and with unnecessary thoroughness on a piece of towelling. She speaks to them at some length and then takes Pal's hand and makes for the door Jak grasps that this is his exit cue and follows her. He apprehends that her eagerness to accompany him originated with their censure and not any predilection for his society. Before they had spoken she herself had shown a disinclination for an evening stroll with him. Now she is pounding off ahead dragging Pal and he can almost see the anger emanating from her small person. Rather than struggle on after her on his painful pins he sits down on a crumbling wall not far from the house. He notices Flagor's resentful face at the lighted kitchen window. The man can see nothing in the gathering darkness and yet he stands there looking out, discovering nothing while revealing much of himself.

Sitting alone on the wall Jak's thoughts turn to his father. The incredible relief of knowing he is alive! So far he had spent little time dwelling on the wonder of it. What would he say to the Fedek member he would meet tomorrow? He suddenly worries that he has no idea, no plan of action. What would be the good of him ending up in the same predicament as his father? A fine reunion that would be.

A shaft of mellow light widens on the pavement in front of the house, the door swings open and Flagor stands for a moment silhouetted against the golden backdrop of the kitchen. As Flagor turns to close the door Jak flops silently over the back of the wall and watches from the shadows as Flagor first looks up the street in the direction Zerrin had taken a few moments earlier and then turns staring into the darkness as if sensing Jak's watching eyes. Jak ducks down while this investigation is made then as the footsteps start to recede northwards, responds to a sudden impulse and makes his way as quickly as he can to the building where he had earlier housed the wheeler he is about to dart soundlessly after Flagor when a hand is placed on his arm he looks round to find Zerrin's bright violet eyes upon him.

"What are…?" She terminates her whispered question as Jak raises a finger to his lips and points down the street at Flagor's rapidly retreating figure.

"I'm coming with you." She breathes, her lips close to his ear.

"OK hop on the back."

Pal is standing there silently waiting for instructions. Jak moves to direct the child back to the house but Zerrin restrains him.

"They'll think it odd." She warns. Jak looks in her direction and for a moment thinks she has disappeared until he realises she's put on some dark glasses to cover the bright gleam of her eyes.

Immediately Jak grabs Pal and plops him on his lap. He can't really believe he is going on a dangerous mission in a wheelchair with a young woman behind him and a little boy sitting on his knees, what a ridiculous situation.

Now they are heading noiselessly down the street at a fair speed after Flagor and Jak wonders apprehensively if they are heading unprotected into the plague ridden area until he remembers that Flagor is also unmasked. They follow their quarry along a maze of back streets and eventually he stops before a large decayed house that had obviously seen better days. The blinds are all drawn but streaks of light along the edges give evidence of bright illumination within. Flagor knocks gently on the door and turns facing outwards into the street while he waits. Jak drapes a corner of his coat over Pal's face to shield his eyes and eases the wheeler further back into the shadows. Flagor has not long to wait before a small grate towards the top of the door slides open and he is asked a gruff question, his answer is apparently conveyed to the inner recesses and this time he has to linger at some length on the cold blustery street. Eventually, though, the door opens and Flagor is drawn inside.

"OK Pal, will you be alright to wait over here in the shelter of this porch?" Whispers Jak.

Pal, only too pleased to have been let in on the action so far, resigns himself quickly to this exclusion. Jak wants to order Zerrin into the safety of the porch too but he needs her to listen, if possible, to any conversation they might be fortunate enough to overhear. They leave Pal with an admonition not to come near the house whatever he might hear. To go back to Cass in the eventuality that they do not return and thus make him more frightened than he would otherwise have been. They wheel slowly up to the house and linger hopefully beneath each window. The front rooms are empty, there are no windows or doors along the side alley but at the back they find some steps leading up onto a narrow veranda. Discarding the wheeler and hiding it behind a rusty tank they stealthily mount the steps. As they reach the dilapidated old boards the sound of voices drifts out into the night air. Jak presses his nose against the window where a narrow strip is left between the blind and the frame; he can see a slithered section of the room. Inside there is a man, middle aged with a fine mane of silver black hair and beaming amber eyes. A beard streaked with grey flows regally and his whole demeanour is calm and charismatic. Standing facing the man is Flagor his back to the window, there are other men in the room but Jak doesn't notice them his eyes are drawn back to the one holding centre stage. Zerrin's hand is tugging at his shoulder as she waits impatiently for her turn. Jak moves aside, she looks for an instant and then turns briefly to Jak.

"The man in the chair is Norton Lueger he is the head of Fedek." She whispers.

"Can you hear what they're saying?"

"Shhh." She stands on the windowsill so she is nearer the top louvre, which is open a crack. She balances there her face intent.

"They are talking of your father," she breathes after a moment her voice taut with excitement.,"I think they have him at the old Stanner buildings."

"Let's go then." Says Jak half turning in his impatience to depart.

"Wait!" After a moment she jumps lightly from the sill, supporting herself with a hand on his shoulder. "They are leaving." Her eye is back at the crack. "I think they're intending to pick you up Jak."

"The rotten swine." Hisses Jak his thoughts on the treachery of Flagor.

A voice cold with menace cuts into their whispered conversation. A perimeter guard, they have not thought of, is standing behind them at the head of the stairs. Jak realises much too late that his weapon is still snugly wrapped in the blanket on the wheeler.

"Turn round slowly." Zerrin murmurs, translating the order of the guard. Jak feels her pressing something into his hand, it is her dark glasses. As unobtrusively as possible he puts them on before turning to face their captor. The man is holding a large 58 rifle, levelled at Jak and he motions with his head for them to proceed to the door.

"Lomax!" He calls out to someone inside. The door is opened and they are hustled through. Quite a dialogue ensues and it is apparent that the two men have been left alone to guard the house and are finding it difficult to make a decision as to what to do with their intruders. Eventually the first guard gets out a communicator and punches in a number with his thumb, all the while his weapon never wavers, Lomax too has a gun trained on them.

There is a brief discussion wherein the Fedek guard keeps his eyes on his captives while replying curtly to the person on the other end of the line. Norton Lueger who has just left? Wonders Jak. A brief nod terminates the conversation and the man advances towards them, reaches behind Jak and opens a door then with the butt of his rifle he swipes at Jak's head knocking him back through the opening. Dizzily he realises that Zerrin has been thrown in on top of him and the door slammed shut. They listen to the sound of a key grating in the lock and then a bolt is drawn across. There is the scrape of a chair on bare boards and a creak as someone makes himself comfortable.

"Well that's just great." Groans Jak as he gingerly probes his bruised head and strives for a more comfortable position. Zerrin tries to shift her weight off of him but they seem to be in a room no bigger that a cupboard and the space gives little scope for movement. Stacked up beside Jak are tubs of paint and a whole heap of brooms and other store cupboard paraphernalia. He eases round until he is leaning up against these and Zerrin stifles a bubble of inappropriate laughter as she removes an elbow wedged up under Jak's rib cage.

"What are you laughing at you little fool?"

She doesn't answer him but puts her hand over her mouth and he can feel her shoulders shaking in silent mirth. Jak, not able to see the funny side at this precise moment, waits in faint astonishment for her to finish. After a few moments she is composed and in the dim light from under the door Jak sees her wiping her eyes.

"What a nutter."

"Jak." She says seriously. "We know where your father is now."

"Yeah and a fat lot of good I am to him here." He reaches up and pulls futilely at the door handle, more out of exasperation than anything else. There is the thud of a rifle butt on the door as the guard reminds them of his presence and warns against any attempt at escape.

“Don’t do that Jak. Do you want to bring them in here on us?”

“No there’s not enough room for anyone else in here.” He shifts position yet again.

“Can’t you just keep still?”

“Can you just move your arm a little? That’s right, thanks.” He passes his arm along her shoulders. “Well this is cosy don’t you think?”

She doesn’t answer and he realises that she is actually embarrassed and a little confused by their close proximity. He smiles to himself in the darkness.

“Jak, who’s Sten?” She asks after a few moments silence.

Jak feels his heart go cold. The exploits of the past days had kept his mind fully occupied but her words bring to the surface that dreadful fear he had experienced when he first found Sten lying on the storeroom floor in neosphere 19. It seems so long ago he wonders with a sick feeling in the pit of his stomach how Sten has fared since he last looked into those vacant eyes at the forest domes. Was he healing?

“How do you know about Sten?” He asks her. He can tell that his voice is brusque and hollow.

“Pal told me.” Suddenly she jerks upright. “Pal! Oh No!

What will he do? Will he be alright?"

Jak his mind wrenched from thoughts of Sten remembers Pal. Out in the cold and dark in a strange city. What would the poor little kid do?

"We told him to go back to the house didn't we? Do you think he'll find the way?"

"I don't know, I hope so, oh Jak, why did we bring him here?"

"It seemed the right thing to do at the time. He'll be OK, he's a smart kid."

"Yes he is smart." She leans back against Jak's shoulder. "Oh I hope he's alright." The words are twisted from her in a desolate half whisper.

"Don't be too anxious, he'll be sensible." His lips brush her hair, he feels awful himself and doubly bad for her. What a reckless thing to do, bring an eight year old with them and leave him out on his own in the middle of the night. Realising that her thoughts must be running along the same lines and that self recriminations will not make it any easier to bear he attempts to divert her thoughts. He gives her shoulder a squeeze;

"So tell me what did Pal say about Sten?"

"Oh..er...He said you asked about a guy named Sten all the time. He told me a lot of the stuff you said when you were fevered in the desert."

"Did he?" Jak remembers Pal mentioning Leela. "Well Sten's a good friend of mine but he's pretty ill at the moment." Jak realises, as his voice cracks that he'd better not talk about that and tries another subject.

"What was all that back at the house before we left."

"Oh nothing, well...er they just thought you were interested in me and they didn't like it. It's OK I soon disabused their minds on that score."

"What did you say?"

"I said you viewed me as a weird, violent, demented kid from an inferior race."

Jak is unsure how to repudiate this statement realising the underlying accuracy and yet…

"But I am interested in you Zerrin." He says gently.

"Yes but not like they were thinking…anyway I don't want to talk about it."

There is an awkward silence and Jak apprehends that in his bungling endeavours to make her feel better he has stumbled on yet another uncomfortable theme. He supposes he had better not ask her about Karrif, another subject he is keenly interested in.

From outside they hear the scrape of the chair and muffled voices. Suddenly Zerrin stiffens and grips Jak's hand.

"Pal!" She hisses and frantically starts to bang on the door, there is a growled comment from outside and the crash of the rifle butt.

“What on earth are you doing?” Cries Jak trying to steady her.

“Pal’s out there, Oh why has he come inside?” There is a sob of fear in her voice, she bangs the door again and Jak grasps that she is trying to distract the attention of the guard.

“Wait.” He says to her and holds her back.

“They’ll kill him.” She gasps frenziedly.

“No they won’t hurt him; to them he’s just a small boy.”

Zerrin calms down a little and they wait in tense silence. Immediately there is the sound of yelling and a shot is fired. There is more shouting from closer at hand and the thudding sound of something heavy falling against wood. The bolt of the cupboard door is drawn laboriously back and then after a few seconds the scraping of the key in the lock is heard.

The door swings wide and as they blink their eyes in the glare of the hall light they see Pal standing there, a huge grin across his face.

“Hurry we don’t have much time.” His utterance drops into the stunned silence and bestirs them. Instantly they are up and into the corridor. The guard, who is somehow locked outside takes a shot at them and the whine of the bullet hastens their exit.

“This way.” Cries Jak as they run past another door, which splinters under the impact of a heavy boot.

Lomax is kicking it down. They head for the front door and are soon in the chill air of the street.

"You carry on," says Jak "I've got to go back for the wheeler."

"I'll get it." Offers Zerrin. Jak wants to refuse but his feet are killing him. As they hear the sound of Lomax inside the house, booting the door off its hinges and calling to the other man Jak and Pal dodge inside an empty house. Jak casts around in the debris for a place to hide, he sees a hatch in the bare boards and opening it he motions Pal down the rickety stairs to the cellar. Seeing the remains of an old carpet in the pile of rubble and wood he pulls at it and as it comes free relatively easily, he hauls it out and holds it over the hatch as he closes it. Following Pal into the dank underground room he feels confident that their hiding place is concealed.

But what about Zerrin? Noticing where a faint light from the street is coming through a grating, Jak winds his way through some dilapidated old furniture that some long departed hoarder had stored there and standing on a table that seems more solid than the rest, presses his face up against the grid and looks out into the street. He can see no sign of Zerrin but the Fedek guards are wandering about peering into the row of tumbled down houses on either side of the road. As they near him Jak looks round for Pal he sees his bright eyes gazing up at him from the level of the table top.

"OK mate let's get under the table." He says to the boy as he clambers down.

“I saved you!” Exclaims Pal in a burst of suppressed excitement. Jak realises that he has been dying to tell of his exploits.

“You’re a hero, now get under the table and you can tell me about it later.” He presses down on Pals shoulder and the boy crouches down, there is just enough room for Jak to follow Pal and fold his long limbs into the confined space.

‘That’s the second time tonight.’ He grumbles to himself, then muses that being squashed up with Pal was an entirely different thing than being squashed up with Zerrin. He quickly dismisses the thought or rather it is driven from his mind by the scuff of heavy boots on the floor overhead. Through the gaps in the boards slithers of torchlight lance up and down the cellar, illuminating the ghostly shapes of cobwebby furniture in quick flashes. Jak feels Pals warm hand pressing into his. In tense silence they hold their breath while the footsteps complete a circuit of the room. Suddenly the whole light beam floods the cellar like a spotlight as the torch is thrust through a hole in the floorboards. Jak’s heart pounds but the illumination is withdrawn and the footsteps leave in haste.

He waits for what he feels is a sufficient length of time, crushed under the table and then starts to manoeuvre his stiffened limbs out from the confined space. Halfway he freezes into an impossible contortion as he hears stealthy footfalls creeping across the floor. He holds a finger to his lips and glances back at Pal still in the shadows of the table. As he does so he loses balance and crashes forward into a pile of broken chairs. As the echoes of this horrendous cacophony cease, Jak raises his finger once more to his lips as he finds Pals solemn eyes upon him.

“Is that you Jak?”Comes a hissing whisper from above.

“Yeah.” Jak proceeds to make more splintering sounds as he hauls himself out of the matchwood.

“Good grief! What on earth are you doing?”

He can hear her sliding the carpet away from the hatch. She opens it and pokes her head through the aperture. “You’re making enough noise to bring the whole town down on us you idiot.”

“No, I’m fine thanks.” groans Jak heavily sarcastic. He takes Pal’s proffered hand and using that feeble leverage to finally rid himself of the entangled bits of spindle.

Zerrin comes halfway down the stair and they look at each other for a long moment, Jak is thinking about that cupboard.

“You’ve got a piece of wood sticking out of your hair.” Zerrin informs him with smothered laughter in her voice. Jak feels his head and there is indeed quite a large piece of spindle wedged down the collar of his shirt.

“I wonder how that got there?” Says Jak in mock puzzlement. They start to laugh in earnest then but only for a moment, Jak shushes them quickly.

“Did you find the wheeler?” He enquires.

“Yes, it’s out in the alley.”

"Well let's get going then."

As they get up into the room above Pal tugs at his sister's sleeve.

"I saved you." He says proudly.

"Yes you did. You were amazing but we'll talk about it later."

Jak looks regretfully at the little crestfallen face, barely visible in the half light. Jak can read his disappointment in the way the light in his eyes fluctuates to a dimmer, paler green.

"Don't worry little chap, you'll be able to tell us all about it when we get to my Dad's ship."

The eyes flash up with excitement.

"To the ship? Is that where we are going then?" Asks Zerrin in faint surprise. "What about the Stanner buildings?"

"We'll go to the ship first." Jak lays a hand on Pal's dark head and Zerrin nods, catching his meaning.

Chapter 41
The Stanner Building

Now they are skimming silently through the dark streets, there is nobody about and the deserted roadways lined with decaying houses are eerie and depressing.

"What about masks?" Asks Jak.

"We don't need them at night time when there is nobody about. If we'd been on the east side where most of the plague victims go to live out their last days there would be hundreds of people in the streets but we won't go anywhere near there, it's much too dangerous."

Jak digests this.

"I don't like that Nuttle though," says Zerrin worriedly returning to their earlier conversation.

"Don't you want to leave Pal with him....no, I don't suppose you do." He ruminates on this for a while. "You'd better stay with him." He says eventually, reluctantly.

"Don't you need me then?"

Of course he needs her, dace. "I'll think of something." He says.

"Tell us how you did it then."

They are back now at the Lazortrom and Pal looks up at Jak who is sitting on the edge of the table watching him eating ice-cream.

"It was easy peasy." Says Pal nonchalantly. "I looked through the window and I could see this big old guy with a rifle and I thought 'he looks like the kind of geezer that would want to take a pot shot at a stray limmex cat slinking around his yard.' So I made sure I knew where the keys were, hanging from a clip on his belt and I knocked on the door. Sure enough he was out there like a shot and as he passed me I lifted the keys, ran inside and locked him out. There was another guard I could hear in one room so I locked him in there and then I let you out of the cupboard.... easy."

"Well done mate, you saved the day. Now will you be OK to stay at the ship while we nip out?"

Pal looks under Jak's arm and stares apprehensively at Nuttle. "Are you the guy that shot my sister?"

Nuttle shifts uncomfortably from one foot to the other.

Jak hadn't known she'd told Pal about that

"It's OK" he says "Nuttle won't be here, he's coming with us."

Nuttle looks petrified at this suggestion.

"I ain't coming boss." He pronounces.

"Look Nuttle," Explains Jak. "If my Father sees you in his rescue party he's more likely to forget that you left him to rot for three weeks without lifting a finger."

Nuttle immediately starts to see the sense in Jak's argument but it is clear he is still reluctant to venture outside.

Jak leads him aside. "You don't want to stay here with this little Censite kid do you?" He says in a persuasive low tone. "His sister won't leave him with you, she don't trust you, you see. She swears she'll get even with you for taking a pop at her. So you can either stay here, alone, with them or you can come with me and be a hero. What do you say?"

Nuttle smiles weakly and Jak slaps him on the back. "Good lad, you know it makes sense." He turns to Zerrin. "What do you want to do?" He asks her.

"I'll come...as long as you think Pal will be safe here."

"We'll take him down to the playroom. It'll probably be the first time a kid's ever been in there, these guys don't bring their families along. We'll give him a tray of eatables, show him where the bathroom is and lock the doors we don't want him to pass through. I reckon he'll be well away. In fact," he looks down at his watch, "he'll probably drop off to sleep. If we seal the hatch when we leave nobody can get in or out."

He thinks for a moment before concluding. "I'll give you the codes just in case."

"Boss!" protests Nuttle but is completely ignored as Jak writes down the codes.

"Don't let anyone else get a peek at these and don't leave them lying around anywhere." He holds the slip of paper out to Zerrin and holds her hand a moment as she takes it.

"Just in case I get waylaid." He says quietly to her.

"OK, let's go." Says Nuttle suddenly eager to get going.

"It did make me feel a bit uneasy your honour." He says later in his testimony. "They looked a bit too friendly if you ask me, her being a Censite and all."

Now with Jak back in the wheeler, Zerrin pretending to push and Nuttle's bulky figure shrouded in a blanket they are once again making their way across the city.

'We must look a bit bizarre," says Jak, 'but then again this is a bizarre city so maybe we just fit right in.' They take the long route to the Stanner buildings to avoid the east side. Even so they hear the sounds of revelry from those select streets. Once, there is the sound of a small explosion. Jak and Nuttle are startled.

"They're just having a bit of fun." Says Zerrin dryly. After a few moments she leans forward. "What would you do Jak?" She asks with interest. "If you found out you only had a few months to live?"

"That's a hell of a question." Is his response. " Not one I really want to think about."

"I've thought about it some." She says quietly.

"And not before time you hedonistic delinquent, I hope your philosophising led you to mend your ways." Jak tries for a lighter note.

"I'd get as drunk as a lord....and stay drunk." Nuttle readily gives his opinion.

"That's one way of dealing with it." Says Jak fairly.

"What would you do Jak?" She repeats the question and seems to really want to know Jak's answer.

"I guess I'd make peace with my Maker." He says after a pause.

"Wouldn't that be hypocritical if you'd not lived that way before?"

"I don't call it hypocritical I call it sensible, anyway, I haven't done anything I'm ashamed of."

"Haven't you?" Nuttle marvels.

"No, I guess not." Says Zerrin thoughtfully, accepting his admission of a clear conscience without question. After he makes the statement Jak starts to think back.

"Look can we talk about this some other time it's a bit deep for me just now." He says.

"Sure, but I hope you have made peace with your Maker 'cause you may have to meet fairly soon." says Zerrin, gazing up at the façade of a tall white mansion house.

The Old Stanner buildings in better days would have been some kind of government headquarters. There is a tall perimeter fence made of metal with the black paint flaking off . There is a guard patrolling the line accompanied by a large dog. Most of the building is in darkness although a few lights wink on the ground floor.

“How are we going to get in there?” Asks Nuttle. There is no response to his question as the three of them continue to check out the building from their place in the shadows.

Chapter 42
Flagor Makes A Mistake

They put us all in grave danger when they went into the house on Nean Street. I could have wrung Zerrin's neck. So yes, I was handing over her favourite Kelti boy but I had to get myself noticed by Norton to get into a position to make a difference. All was going well until they broke into that house and the guard contacted Norton as we were on the way back home to pick up Jak Dane.

"So," said Norton musingly as he closed his communicator and looked at me for a lengthy period out of those pale brown, almost orange eyes, "your friends have broken into my mansion. What is it you are after? Explosives? Weapons?"

Of course I didn't know what he was talking about so I just sat there looking like an idiot no doubt.

"I think we had better keep you and your little group under observation."

I knew what he meant by that and I felt a tightening of the chest. We were on the way to my house and not only was Jak Dane there, as I thought at that particular time, but Zerrin, Pal, Cass and Keenan, unaware of imminent danger and I was leading Norton straight there.

"Look here," I said, "I'm only doing my patriotic duty, there is no reason to penalize me or the group."

"I have no idea what your little game is son but I don't intend any compromise to my agenda so I am afraid we will have to bring you in." His eyes were aloof and dismissive as he looked away from me.

"Wait!" I said feeling that everything was slipping beyond my control. "Take me in you don't need the others."

"You are right, I don't need any of you but I do remember the harm caused by your little cell in the Uluru incident last year."

"That was not my fault Sir." I said bitterly, I could not believe he knew about that.

"The female was your operative."

Yes, she had been working alongside me then.

We arrived at the house. I could see by their faces that Keenan and Cass were overawed by a visit from the great Norton Lueger. I could only wish that the circumstance were different. I had actually imagined sometimes coming before them beside him, in prominence and honour and I had pictured their faces. I did see something of that look for an instant before they realised that all was not right.

"Jak Dane?" Said Norton's minion in a peremptory voice. Cass just looked from him to Norton to me an expression of shocked surprise on her face. So, I had surprised her at last.

"He is not here" Said Keenan turning reproachful eyes on me.

Norton was sitting at his ease on the table, one leg thrown over the corner. He had a pair of leather gloves, I remember, that he was slapping onto his thigh.

"Come, my good people." He said quietly. "Hand over the young Keltian and we will forget this little incident. We don't want to drag you off to headquarters for interrogation, or harm you in any way. Just do your duty and you will be honoured."

I was staring at Norton in horrified silence.

"We don't know where he is." Stated Cass and I glanced across at her into eyes filled with accusation. It reminded me of the way Zerrin always looked at me.

"Well my young friends you give me little choice." Said Norton with a portentous sigh. He rose from the table slapped his gloves into one hand and indicated to the men with him to bring us along. I could swear there was a smile on his face.

An armoured vehicle drives up to the main gate and Jak sees that there is actually another guard in a small booth there manning the gates.

"OK, let's slip in behind this truck while the guard is distracted, we'll make for that row of bushes and hare along there to the house."

There is no time for debate Jak, with Zerrin hanging on the back, wheels silently towards the gate; he is actually through the gate before he realises Nuttle is not with them. He looks back and sees him, crouching still, in the shadows. There is no time to do anything but curse him.

Instead of making for the bushes Jak grabs hold of the rear bumper of the truck as it pulls forward into the drive, deftly skimming round to the side out of view of the sentry who is by now climbing back into his booth. When they come up to the front entrance of the mansion and the truck pulls round to a halt, Jak lets go and they scoot off in the opposite direction, trundling across some uneven grass to the shelter of an overgrown shrubbery.

As they hide there they hear a dog barking around the back of the house.

"We've got to get inside before that dog is on us." Whispers Jak.

Zerrin shakes his shoulder and points into the deep shadow at the side of the house. Jak can see nothing in the blackness there. He watches until four soldiers pile out of the truck and go round to the rear doors then he heads straight in the direction Zerrin had pointed. As they come nearer he sees that there is a door there. Zerrin hops off and tries the handle. The door yields under her fingers just as Jak hears the sounds of the dog panting at the far corner. He realises then that he should have left the wheeler behind the shrubbery. Too late for that now, he pulls it after him as he slips in through the door Zerrin is holding open for him. He can hear the dog whining and scratching on the other side of the door and knows it is only a matter of time before the guard pokes his head in to see what's going on. However, as luck would have it, they hear the dog yelp as it receives a kick from its owner and a few words in a tone of reprimand.

Jak leans his head back on the wall with a sigh of relief. Zerrin smiles a little as she sees him encumbered with the wheeler.

"If you laugh…" He threatens her and he can hear the mirth in his own voice. They examine the narrow corridor in which they are standing. There are a few doors leading off from it, Jak tries one of them and seeing it is a disused utility stows the wheeler in there out of the way. As he is coming back out they hear voices so he retreats back into the room drawing Zerrin in after him. They wait there in the darkness with the door slightly ajar until the voices are gone. As Jak makes to return to the corridor Zerrin lays a hand on his arm.

"I saw Cass in that truck."

"What!"

"I know it sounds ridiculous but while we were wheeling along beside the vehicle I looked up and saw her face looking down at me through the window."

"I can hardly credit it you mean she's Fedek?"

" No, I don't think so Jak, she looked frightened, I reckon she's been taken by them."

"But why?" Jak breaks off suddenly and snaps his head back sharply against the wall. "Damn it she was going to try and negotiate an audience for me with the Fedek remember. She must have contacted them and they took her prisoner." He notices her eyes looking up at him in concern. "Don't look at me like that, it is my fault and I'm an idiot, I swore this wouldn't happen again."

"She wanted to do it for you Jak she thinks you're fi ne."

"Yes well everyone who thinks I'm 'fine' and takes it into their head to help me winds up dead."

"Come on Jak, I am 'yet living'. Let's just go and save her then you'll feel more the thing."

Jak lays a finger on her cheek. "You're a game little kid aren't you?" He says softly. She pulls out a weapon from the waistband of her skirt. It looks almost too heavy for her to hold and yet she seems fairly at home with it.

"Let's get to it." She says and Jak sees the glint of her teeth as she smiles up at him.

"Stay behind me." He says to her grimly.

Back in the corridor all is quiet and Jak eases along stealthily. His burnt feet still throb but it is all but forgotten as he prepares to enter the fray.

There is a little light relieving the darkness of the passageway coming from a glass panel at the top of the door. Jak peers cautiously through. A vast hall meets his gaze with a high domed ceiling and two flights of stairs ascending together at both extremities and converging to lead onto an ostentatiously pillared gallery. At the foot of either stair is stationed an armed guard. Jak remembers that they had seen no lights upstairs so what were the men guarding? Instinct dictated that prisoners would not be kept in the plush looking floors above. Rather their place would be below, in the cellars. He feels Zerrin pressing against him trying to get a look through the window. He looks down at her,

"Guards," he whispers, "two."

She raises her gun and looks at him inquiringly. Jak has to admit to himself that he is not prepared to barge in, guns blazing, killing everyone who happens to be in the way… unless it is unavoidable. He shakes his head slightly and looking at the door to the left of the corridor eases the handle until it is ajar. He can see no evidence of occupation so opens the door quickly, his weapon raised and ready. The room is a kitchen, empty except for its gleaming utensils and heavy sideboards. They creep cautiously across between the worktables and on the other side is a half open hatchway for passing food through. Jak pokes his nose over the edge and sees just below him the top of a man's head, he is so close he can see the pink scalp through the dark hair. In an instant he has reversed his weapon and brought the butt end heavily down on the guard's cranium. Instead of crumpling over sideways as Jak had hoped he jumps up and turns unsteadily. While he is still dazed Jak grabs his collar and with a mighty effort using both feet against the wall for leverage, he hauls the man through the hatch. Zerrin is standing ready with a huge frying pan and finishes off what Jak has started.

"You have to hit here," she says to Jak indicating the place on the Fedek guard's head, "and you have to hit hard."

Jak is about to ask how she knows such stuff and then remembers her time with the bandit, Karrif. He feels that that subject is taboo and so instead he pulls off his cravat and winds it tightly round, gagging the unconscious man. Zerrin tests the tautness of the fabric,

"Not bad." She says. "I'll make a hoodlum out of you yet."

"Got any rope?"

She pulls a roll of silver tape out of her pocket and hands it to him.

"Better keep watch by the door." Suggests Jak as he sets to work binding up their prisoner.

"Are you going to save any of that?" queries Zerrin from her post a few minutes later.

Jak cuts the tape with his knife and stands back to survey his handiwork.

"Mmmm he does look a bit over wrapped…, still he won't get away." Jak assures her. "We'd better stow him somewhere just in case someone comes down for a midnight snack." As he speaks he grabs the man under the arms.

"Here." Says Zerrin opening a cupboard door for him. "No wait, this is some kind of lift for bringing up stores from the cellar probably."

"Is it big enough to go down on?" Wonders Jak.

"Yeah if we go one at a time I reckon we could."

"Here give me a hand to chuck this guy under the sink." There is a kind of open sink unit with a curtain pulled across to close it in. They hide the limp body behind this curtain and then Jak goes to inspect the narrow shaft and its mechanism.

"I'll go down first," he whispers, "check out the lay of the land and then whistle up to let you know it's OK."

"Are you going to leave me up here long while you 'check out the lay of the land'?"

"No, I'll call you down straight off, as soon as I see it's safe."

Jak squeezes himself into the confining cage and nods to Zerrin, gradually she lets him down. The lift opens out into what at one time was a large vegetable store,now empty. Jak slips out of the cage and has a quick look round. The door is a loosebox type with the top swing door open, he peeps through. The corridor outside is empty.

"Psst, all clear." Returning to the lift he hisses up to Zerrin.

The lift goes swinging back up the shaft. A few moments pass and he sees feet and legs appear but they sure aren't Zerrin's. Immediately Jak grabs one of the legs and yanks as hard as he can a man slides out with a yell and lands with a heavy thump on his back, his gun goes off but he has not levelled it at Jak and the bullet ricochets harmlessly off the wall. Jak seizes the barrel of the gun, twists it out of the man's loosened fingers and then swings it violently at the side of the guard's head, this time the man is knocked unconscious. He can hear the sound of advancing steps pounding down the cellar passage, instantly Jak is over by the door and swinging the rifle again as a second guard hurtles through the storeroom entrance. His own momentum brings him smash up against the rifle butt and it is the last thing he sees before he is engulfed in darkness. Jak looks down at him but he can detect sounds of many boots running across the kitchen floor above. Jak feels like a rat in a trap. Just before he makes a run for it he sees a bunch of keys hanging from the belt of the second guard he lifts these and notices that the man is already stirring. He makes off quickly along the passageway. At the end there is another small room and as Jak peers round the corner he sees across from him a cell door. Cass is looking at him through the bars.

"Jak!" She cries. He is there in moment trying one of the keys in the lock.

"How did you find us? Where is Zerrin?"

"I lost her. I don't know where she is." Says Jak baldly as he fumbles with the keys. Through the bars Cass lays a hand on his that is feverishly rattling a key in the lock.

"Let me try." She says gently. Jak relinquishes the fob to her and moves at once to a doorway leading to the lower hall, there is the sound of many feet coming down the steps.

"There's going to be a hell of a lot of people on top of us any minute." He says grimly.

He hears a man's voice; it is Flagor. Cass has just let him out of the cell next to hers. Jak wants to shove Flagor back in the cell and lock it behind him but there is no time for recriminations. It seems to Jak their only way out is back up the store shaft and he is about to suggest they take this route while he holds the vanguard but Flagor is holding open yet another door, which leads to a fuel hold. He scuttles over a pile of black chunks and pushes the flap of the chute open an inch and then all the way. Jak follows pulling the door to and scrambling after Cass. Flagor has already heaved himself up and out into the night air, he reaches down for Cass. Jak passes up the gun to Flagor and then laces his fingers for her to stand on, boosting her up and out of the hatch. When he looks up he is looking straight into the barrel of the rifle. His eyes meet Flagor's in a frozen moment then the Censite jerks the gun impatiently and Jak realises he is meant to grab ahold and be pulled up. With the guards at the door he leaps up pulling on the rifle barrel and in an instant he is through the hatch and closing it softly behind him.

Chapter 43
Zerrin Lost

"I'm going back in to find Zerrin and my father." Says Jak holding his hand out for the weapon. Flagor keeps a tight grip on the gun and Jak is just about to try wrenching it from him when Cass lays a hand on his arm.

"Now is not a good time Jak. The whole place is crawling with guards looking for us."

Flagor says a few words to Cass and she looks earnestly at Jak. "He says he knows where there are some explosives. He is suggesting we get them and come back, at least we would have an advantage then." Jak hesitates for an instant looking suspiciously at Flagor. The sound of a dog barking not too far away hastens his decision.

"OK, let's get out of here." They leave the paved area and race across the dew soaked grass. Flagor is out front, then Cass and Jak is a very poor third, shambling along on his ill-used feet.

'Right, I know who the dog is going to pick off.' He thinks wryly to himself. He cannot yet hear the sound of pursuit but there is a certain inevitability about the whole thing. He can no longer see the other two ahead of him in the darkness but he can hear Cass' panting breaths. He is not actually sure where they are heading, his sense of direction shot to pieces by the darkness, the house obviously is behind him but he is sure the gate is round the other side. Suddenly he hears the loud report of a shot, instinctively he crouches down and his lumbering run becomes even more erratic as he weaves a little so as not to present an easy target.

"What on earth are you doing? Get the hell over here." says Cass, unimpressed.

"I was tacking so as not to give a straight bead."

"Well tack on your own time we need to get over this fence." They have come up to a gate, chained and padlocked, but where the rest of the fence is topped with razor wire there is none over the gate. Flagor is already at the top and vaulting down to the other side, he crouches there for a moment and Jak sees his eyes darting to and fro. There is an unpleasant connection in Jak's mind to a wild beast in a friend's picture book that had scared the wits out of him as a small boy. He banishes the thought quickly from his mind but for some reason it makes him feel guilty. He boosts Cass up to the top of the gate and as he does so he can hear the unmistakable sound of dogs galloping across the grass, a kind of snarling panting sound that makes him wish he was in the relative safety on the other side of the boundary. Cass is taking much too long, he gives her an unceremonious shove and she teeters at the top of the railing before tumbling over.

"Sorry." He breathes as he clambers up, one dog snapping and jumping at his heels the other content to wait snarling in case he should fall. Just as he is straddling the top bar a spot light transfixes him with its vivid shaft. A number of shots ring out a staccato death knell and Jak hurls himself over into the void left by the blinding brightness of the beam. He hits the far side with Cass and Flagor beneath him, breaking his fall. There is a yelp of pain from Flagor but the probing light has found them and they simultaneously rise from their tangled heap and scatter towards the buildings adjacent and the shelter of the gloomy pathways in between. Jak finds himself separated again from the other two but he can hear their pounding feet on the old stone ways. He rushes as fast as he can along a nightmarish warren of dark twisting alleys. The sound of the dogs fade into the distance but still he runs and suddenly he sees an arm snake out of the black shadow in front of him and grab hold of his arm.

It is Cass; she pulls him into the porch of one of the endlessly empty houses.

"Are you alright?" He asks her a little breathlessly, he has a sharp stitch in his side from running with his muscles so tensed. She nods.

"And Flagor, is he with you?"

"Yes he's inside. You broke his finger when you fell on us." Again there is that strange hint of amusement when she talks of the misfortune of her brother that makes Jak raise an eyebrow questioningly at her.

"I guess I'm no more popular than I was before then?" He says.

"You came and rescued us didn't you? I guess that makes you my hero." She says mockingly as she motions him inside.

At a table sits Flagor a lighted piece of candle weakly illuminating him with its feeble glow. He is attempting to bind up the damaged finger using a thin twig as a splint. His sister goes to his aid while Jak is left to stand uncomfortably by, watching the painful proceedings with a guilty sense of culpability. Eventually he steps forward,

"I read in a book once that you should give your pain a shape. Tell him to imagine his pain." He suggests helpfully. Cass looks at him for a moment without saying any thing.

"Go on it might work."

"Jak he doesn't have to imagine his pain you broke his damn finger, he can feel the pain."

"Yes I know that but he's got to give his pain a shape in his imagination and then draw a red line around it." He sees her looking at him as though he has lost his reason and he wonders himself what he is babbling about but he perseveres with a kind of suicidal stubbornness. "Then he imagines it gradually getting smaller and smaller."

"It's your brain that's getting smaller and smaller Jak." Replies Cass, sarcastically.

"And then when the shape gets so small it disappears the pain disappears too." His voice trails off at this point. "They reckon it works." He finishes lamely.

"There aint no way I'm telling him that psychobabble he don't like you as it is and he's still got your gun." Jak realises that this is true and remedies that situation while Flagor is still preoccupied.

"So how did you end up as prisoners of the Fedek?"

"Well Flagor was doing a little job for them." Here she gives the bandage and extra twist with perhaps not as much sisterly care as he could have desired and he lets out a sharp gasp of pain. She takes no notice as she continues to talk to Jak.

"They start not to trust him, I can't think why," her voice positively drips with sarcasm, "and they come crashing into our place and take us all because we're affiliated with him. Well I can tell you this is the last time I affiliate with him, the idiot."

"Keenan was there when I left was he taken too?"

"Mmm yes he's there." Cass' voice takes on a softer note that Jak doesn't fail to notice, though he makes no comment.

Cass now finishes her tender ministrations on her brother and Jak sees Flagor staring balefully at him.

"Ask him where these explosives are, I can't stand to think of Zerrin in there any longer than I can help." Cass looks long at him and then translates to Flagor who, looking very aggressive, stands up so suddenly his chair clatters back on the bare boards of the deserted room, spitting words at Jak.

"He says it's your fault Zerrin is there, you took her." She steps back with her arms folded as if to watch proceedings and intervene if necessary. Jak wonders at the perversity that makes her translate every word that is said instead of making judicious cuts. Whatever it is she hopes to see, she is destined for disappointment because Jak, after the first moment, forces his anger down. He knows that in this instance Flagor is right. He had taken Zerrin to the Stanner buildings, even relied on her help to find and free his father. Flagor is looking scornfully at him and Jak manfully resists an impulse to knock his teeth out. The important thing is to get to the explosives and then back to the Fedek as quickly as they can before anything can happen to Zerrin. At this last thought his mind balks at possibilities he doesn't want to think about…can't think about or he will not be able to maintain a steady mind for the task ahead.

Flagor is now leading them back to the mansion house in Nean Street. The gun in Jak's hand is not exactly trained on Flagor but the suggestion is there, relations between the two young men are not improving. Every time Flagor speaks he is directing taunts and fury at Jak. After the first couple of times Jak, with a warning look, forbids Cass to interpret and they continue in silence for a while. Then Jak remembers some thing he had wanted to know.

"Cass what's all this about Karrif and Zerrin?"

It is Cass' turn to look uncomfortable, in fact Jak realises it is the first time he has seen her so. Flagor stops in his tracks when he hears mention of Karrif's name and he says something sharply to his sister. There is a strange note of fear mingled with pleading and regret in his voice as he apparently orders her not to speak on the subject to Jak. She turns back to Jak.

"We better not talk about that." She says but there is something in the look of her eyes that makes Jak thinks he will ask her again, another time when Flagor is not by.

They trudge along the streets for a few moments more and then Cass, who had been walking in front of him drops back.

"Where is Pal?" She asks. This brings Jak up short; he doesn't trust her enough to tell her about the ship.

"Back at the house?" He suggests.

"Where did you leave him?" Asks Cass obviously surprised at his lack of certainty.

"At Nean Street across from the Fedek mansion. Zerrin told him to make for home if anything happened." Though it is the truth there are great chunks of the story missing and Cass detects the omissions straight away.

"Surely Zerrin checked before you left Nean Street?"

"I'm sure she did, we weren't together all the time."This seems to satisfy her in one area but now she is worrying about Pal.

"Perhaps I'd better go back to the house and check."

"You can't go there, it's the first place the Fedek will look for you."

"But what about Pal?"

"He's probably asleep somewhere. They won't be in the least bit interested in him he's just a kid."

Cass has to make do with this assurance though she is far from content. Jak has something else to think about, talk of Pal reminds him of Nuttle, where was he right now?

"I was outside guarding the perimeter fence. I heard the shots but I didn't know what was going on so I just waited. It was blinkin' freezing I remember that." Nuttle told the administrator.

Jak watches from the shadows as Flagor approaches the house in Nean Street. He goes straight up to the front door and Jak covers him. He will tell Lomax that Norton has ordered him to wait at the house and as long as they have not been in communication with Norton they will allow him inside. Th at's what Flagor reckons anyway, though Jak is not so sure. Jak never asked what he would do once he had entered, fi guring that was up to Flagor. Now he can see the grating open and Flagor in dialogue with someone on the inside.

It is more than twenty minutes from Flagor entering the building until he comes to a window and signals. Cass and Jak are getting a mite fidgety as they stare worriedly at the empty front façade until the signal is given.

Inside everything is quiet. There are signs of more damage to the house besides the lingering evidence of Jak and Zerrin's previous contretemps with the Fedek guards. Flagor nods his head towards the cupboard as they crunch over broken glass and Jak realises that Lomax and his fellow sentry are now occupying that familiar space.

'Is Zerrin alright?' Jak asks himself for the hundredth time.

Flagor is leading them into a room with shelves lining the one wall, on these shelves are stacked a number of weapons and some primitive explosives. Flagor is helping himself to whatever takes his fancy, Cass is standing by, an unreadable expression on her face but as she does not join her brother in denuding the shelf Jak assumes she is not entirely comfortable with the proceedings. He himself has never really been into weaponry but he does know what he wants and he takes a few grenades, a wadge of plastic explosives along with a detonator and some fuse wire.

"What's your brother up to?" He asks Cass, as they both watch Flagor stuffing a battery of gear into a sack.

"I think he's intending to start a war." replies Cass. Jak responds with a perfunctory smile, but then realises by her face that she is serious. Flagor turns to his sister and speaks to her a few sharp sentences. She in turn clings to his arm as he makes to leave and pleads with him for a few seconds. He shakes her off impatiently and heads back along the passage to the back door.

"What's going on?" Asks Jak.

"We've got to hurry." She says worriedly. "He wants us to make a start and he's gone for reinforcements."

"I don't know why but that makes me very nervous." Says Jak striding to the door.

When they get outside Flagor has already disappeared.

"Come," says Jak after looking briefly up and down the street, "let's get our people out before Flagor brings in the cavalry and we get caught in the crossfire.

Back outside the Stanner buildings, they have hurried desperately across the city to get there ahead of Flagor because Jak doesn't know for sure what his intentions are and Cass' attitude does not instil any confifidence in him, they meet up with Nuttle.

"This is Nuttle, there's no time to explain." Is Jak's brief introduction.

"He had a different girl with him this time your Honour another one of those bright eyed sirens. I half reckon they had him bewitched between them.... you know with their.... Ways." Said Nuttle later to the administrator.

"What happened to you Nuttle I missed you in there?" Jak continues his voice loaded with gentle mockery.

"I was guarding your escape route Sir."

"Well come along for the ride this time." Suggests Jak

handing Nuttle two of the hand grenades. Nuttle takes them reluctantly.

“Let’s go.” Is Jak’s motivational speech as he leads them towards the house, first skirting the fence until he finds the gate where they had lately made their exit. Over they go and this time it seems as though the canine sentries have been taken along with the search party which is, presumably, still out looking for them. All is quiet around the buildings as they lope across the grass, Cass beside Jak and Nuttle breathing heavily at the rear. As they reach the house, at the same point they left it earlier that night, Jak whispers low to Nuttle.

“Go round the front of the house and in five chuck a grenade in through the front door, you’re the decoy alright?”

“I suppose you mean the bait.” Grumbles Nuttle as he looks nervously along the side of the building. “And after I’ve thrown the grenade what then?”

“You’ll see a patch of overgrown shrubbery, run along and hide in there, we’ll meet up with you in a few minutes……hopefully.” He breathes the last after Nuttle has started to move off .

“Where does he come from?” Whispers Cass.

“I’ll tell you later.” Says Jak as he motions her to follow as he skirts around the building

‘Do you have any idea where Keenan is or where they would have taken Zerrin?” Asks Jak.

"I'm not one hundred percent sure but I think they took Keenan across the inner hall, maybe there are some identical cells over the other side."

"That's what I was thinking." Agrees Jak.

Chapter 44
Verdor Dane Feat. Jak to the Rescue

I had been in the cell for weeks. Nothing had happened since the day they had brought me in to make the final recording. I was worried they were sending it to my son Jak. I had deviated from the speech they had prepared for me and they had beaten me but since then nothing, just a regular deposit of food and water every day at the same time. My worry was that this would be discontinued but I tried not to think of such things. Instead I thought about my son, what would he do if he received the message? I had hoped he would contact the Crimmer Council, but it was long since I had given up that expectation for if he had done so the troops would have been here, wouldn't they?

Then there had been some kind of commotion. It was on the night of the 23rd day. The sound of gunfire had woken me from fitful sleep. I had heard running and shouting in the rooms above and across the hall.

Soon afterwards I received a companion in my cell.

She stared at me for a long time from her corner of the chamber, her bright violet orbs unwavering as she searched my face. I said nothing, feeling that if I kept quiet she would eventually communicate. I waited a long time. In turn I examined her; she was youngish seventeen or eighteen. Censites are genetically a small race and she was very slight. I could just about discern in the dim light from the passage outside a thoughtful piquant face. Though I have no real love for the Censites as a whole she gave a favourable impression.

"Did you know?" She said suddenly, her voice strangely deep with intensity. I didn't answer her for a moment wondering if I ought to know to what she was alluding.

"Know what?" I said fi.

"That contaminated food was being delivered by your ship, the Lazortrom."

So who was this girl? Surely not another Fedek agent sent to further inquisit me.

"I have explained already that I knew nothing about it." I said a trifle wearily. "Look I feel....terrible and yes, guilty too that my ship was used but I really couldn't have known." To be truthful I was tired of shouldering the blame and though I had felt accountable at the beginning and in a way understood their bitterness, each time they spoke of it I became less receptive.

She looked at me for a long time and I don't think she noticed that trace of insincerity that I had detected in myself.

"He never believed you did it." Her voice had softened and I thought quite sadly that she must be another one besotted with Norton Lueger.

“My dear I assure you he does believe it and his hatred of any race not Censite completely blinds him to the facts.”

“I was talking of your son Mr Dane.”

I cannot begin to describe my feelings when she spoke those words. I knew one thing; Jak must have been there for her to have met him.

“So, Jak is here.” I said quietly.

“Yes.” She said and her eyes drifted to the little window at the top of the wall.

“You are expecting him then.” I spoke my thought as it occurred to me.

She nodded. “Aren’t you?” There was an inflection of surprise in her voice.

As I looked at her in silence my first feelings of elation began to subside and the fear for my son that I had carried with me for many weeks began to crystallize into a painful constriction around the region of my heart. That organ began to beat very fast and hard as I thought of the danger to him in his being on Detagon. In fact, if the girl’s convictions were founded, the danger of entering the Fedek stronghold. Even as I longed to see him I wished him a thousand miles away.

She must have been aware of my inner agitation for she came over to me and to my surprise slipped a small, warm hand into mine.

"Don't worry Mr Dane, he will come and what is more he will get us out of here." There was so much confidence in her voice that it bewildered me a little. She had a slightly different picture of my son at that time than I had. In my mind's eye I could see his face as I had seen it countless times. Laughing inordinately at some chance occurrence that had tickled his humour or again talking enthusiastically and recklessly about some wild project. Yes he had a lot of charm and I thought him wonderful in a nepotic kind of way. Well intentioned, yes, energetic schoolboy, yes, some kind of heroic saviour, No. I'm afraid I did not see him that way.

I squeezed her hand and smiled down at her, not wanting to erode her simple faith by any of my more down to earth reflections.

"I beg your pardon but in that case you don't know him as well as I do." She said earnestly with a disconcerting perspicacity as to the direction of my thoughts. Then she looked confused and a little embarrassed as the presumptuousness of her comment dawned on her.

"Sorry." She said. "It's been a difficult day."

"Tell me." I questioned her. "What has my boy been up to?"

"He didn't kill anyone." She said defensively. "At least I don't think he did."

Now this suggestion startled me for a moment. "It never crossed my mind that he had." I said slowly.

"Well don't let it."

"Mmmm."

"He saved my life three times. Once when I was drowning in the cavern he swam down to the bottom and pulled me up, before that he rescued me from the Uluru and then when I was in the Rayel pit.... and Pal, he saved Pal too."

It must have occurred to her then that she was defending him to me for she turned her eyes away and there was a hint of disappointment in their luminous depths, her hand moved in mine as if she would withdraw it. For some reason I felt very sorry that I had disappointed her and I suppose a little guilty that my attitude had made her feel the necessity of defending my own son to me. I held on to her hand before she could slip it away.

"Who's Pal?" I asked.

"My little brother."

Again the idea of Jak having dealings with a small child was foreign to me but this time I kept my surprise hidden.

"Tell me about it?" I encouraged her and prepared myself to be pleasantly surprised by the disclosure of these new depths in Jak's character.

We were still engrossed in her narrative when an explosion was heard in the upper regions of the house.

"Here he is." Said the girl jumping up. Her body was taut

with suppressed excitement. 'Well you've made quite an impression on this little girl my son.' I remember thinking to myself before another detonation rocked the little cell and we were thrown to the floor amid flying bits of rubble and dust. I looked up and saw that the cell door, loosed from its locking mechanism by the blast, was slowly swinging open. Then from a large aperture blown in the outer wall at ground level, came a figure emerging from the dust of the explosion, dropping down into the passage, a rifle to his shoulder panning the area. It was Jak, my son. For the first time he appeared to me in the same guise as the Censite girl saw him.

"Sorry, used too much explosives." He grinned at me and I recognised him as the same old Jak. Before I had time to say anything he laid his hand on my shoulder.

"We'd better get outta here don't you reckon?"

It occurred to me that the girl had stayed back in the shadows and was watching, not putting herself forward and I wondered why, given that it was as plain as day that Jak's eyes had sought her first when he had stepped through the blast hole.

Jak links hands to boost his father up through the hole,"Are you feeling OK?" He asks him. To Jak he looks perhaps a little thinner but otherwise fit and healthy.

"I'm fine." Says Verdor. It is in fact the first words he has spoken and Jak feels a wave of relief as he hears the longed for tones, steady and strong. As far as Jak can tell his father seems unaffected by his ordeal, though that would be impossible wouldn't it?

He disappears over the rim of the hole and Jak sees Cass peering down.

"Don't forget Keenan." She says. Jak turns and sees Zerrin standing quietly beside him.

"I'll go." Zerrin makes as if to go but Jak detains her, his hand on her arm, he is about to speak but hears the sound of approaching footsteps descending the stairs.

"Get out of here." He says hurriedly. I'll get Keenan." He lifts her easily and she reaches up to take Verdor's outstretched hands. Jak stumbles across the rubble to the door of the other cell. Keenan's shadowy face is looking out at him through bars, gleaming dully in the first morning light.

"There are no keys." Says Jak. "If you stand back I'll give the lock a few rounds." Keenan retreats to the corner and after glancing quickly at the door through which he expects, any second, to see Fedek guards, he shoots at the lock. As he is inexperienced in such matters he is pleasantly surprised to see the door swinging free. Keenan is out and beside him just as a guard appears from the hallway. The guard has a gash on his temple and blood is running in a dark trickle down to his collar.

"Are you alright?" Jak asks him impulsively. He is aware of Keenan's quizzical regard. Jak looks quickly back at the guard, he is unarmed and leaning heavily against the doorjamb.

"Just sit down here," says Jak, "someone will be with you presently." He picks up a chair tumbled onto its side and rights it for the dazed man, then he turns to Keenan.

"Come on what are you waiting for let's get going."

They scramble up through the opening and are halfway across the dewy grass before Jak remembers.

"Nuttle!" He pulls to a halt and Zerrin, who is just in front, stops too. The others, who are a little way in front, continue on unaware.

"You carry on, I've got to go back for Nuttle." Says Jak. She looks like she's going to offer to come with him but Jak forestalls this by giving her a little push in the direction of the perimeter fence. Without a word she starts to run after the others but before he turns back to the house Jak sees her turn and run backwards a few steps, looking at him, then she swings back, running full tilt and is soon lost in the shadows of dawn.

Jak makes his way cautiously to the front of the house, there are sounds of commotion coming from inside the buildings but as yet nobody appears to be outside. Jak darts across the drive towards the heap of shrubbery.

"Nuttle!" He hisses as he comes up. He sees Nuttle's shadowy bulk rise up from among the greenery, the vegetation falling away from him like the clothes of Guallic, the forest gimp.

"Let's go." Says Jak turning swiftly, as he does so he notices the armoured truck is back outside the front steps. He sidles over towards it.

"What you doing boss?" Nuttle's whispered protest drifts; muffled through the morning mists.

"Just getting us a lift out of here." Upon this utterance he drops low and runs, crouching, up to the back of the truck. Round at the driver's side door he stands up. To his dismay there is a man sitting inside. Jak can't for the life of him think why he's sitting in there with all the kafuffle going on inside the house, until he sees he is wearing a pair of headphones and is lost in listening to whatever is his chosen beat. The man looks at him with equal surprise before making a lunge for his weapon, stowed on the passenger seat. There is no backing out now so Jak wrenches open the door and grabs the man by the scruff of his neck, dragging him bodily out of the truck. There ensues a pretty desperate struggle as Jak tries to wrestle the gun away from the driver. After a frantic tussle Jak finally succeeds in knocking the man senseless but only after receiving several severe blows to various parts of his anatomy. He lies for a moment breathing heavily in the dust, tasting blood and dirt in his mouth and he sees Nuttle's heavy boots in his line of vision.

"What are you doing just standing there?" Gasps Jak much chagrined. "You could've given me a hand."

"I thought you were enjoying it Sir, you know.... practicing all your skills and whatnot."

"Give us a hand up in any case." Says Jak lifting up a bruised and bloodied hand.

"I thought you wouldn't like it if I intervened," Nuttle

is still busy trying to exculpate himself, "I thought, you know, that you would think it was ungentlemanly….. two against one and all."

"And you think I feel like a gentleman writhing in the dirt with some Censite thug trying to bite me ear off ?"

"Hadn't we better get going?"Suggests Nuttle quickly, helping Jak to his feet.

Jak decides to drive for there is no telling what the vagaries of Nuttle's mind might preclude him from doing. As he sits in the driver's seat staring at the control panel he can't for a moment think how to start the vehicle, there doesn't seem to be an ignition button or a touch pad. While he is engaging, a number of guards come tumbling out of the front door in various stages of confusion, some still choking with the fumes and dust of the explosion not yet eradicated from their lungs. They are not immediately interested in the truck but as soon as Jak discovers the keys and starts the vehicle jerkily into motion their attention is redirected. Jak can hear the shouts as he speeds down the drive. Half way down, round a slight bend, he suddenly perceives the necessity to swerve violently as the gate sentry is picked out in the headlights sauntering down the lane, apparently on his way to find out what the commotion is all about. The sentry in turn jumps quite spectacularly into a clump of greenery. Jak realises with a grim smile that the image will be forever printed on his mind, highlighted as it was by the rosy blushed backdrop of a Detagon sun rising.

"Wa-hey." Shouts Nuttle delightedly as he looks back. "That's gotta hurt." Then he cries out, panic stricken, as something else catches his eye. Jak looks across and sees a man standing in the middle of the lawn, legs wide apart in the knee-high grass as he balances himself. On his shoulder is a heavy tubular object.

"Where on Detagon…? exclaims Jak as he slams on the brakes at the same instant he sees the rocket ignite. The trajectory of the launch, calculated as it was on the forward motion of the truck passes hair raisingly close over the bonnet. Instantly Jak screeches away and they see the rocket explode on impact with one of the houses across the road. The barriers ahead pose no problem as Jak ploughs through. The gate is dragged sparking on the road for a couple of hundred metres before it slides off into an alleyway.

Jak follows the road round the perimeter fence until he sees Keenan highlighted on the top rail of the side gate. The vulnerability of their position is impressed upon Jak as they all stand immobilized in the beam of the headlights an instant before Jak flicks them off . Keenan in particular is frighteningly exposed as he balances precariously. Two seconds later Keenan's arm is tugged as if he were a puppet yanked unceremoniously by inexpert hands. Jak sees him fall and the others rush to assist.

Jak jumps out of the truck under a hail of bullets and swings open the back doors. It seems to him that the others are moving in slow motion and he sees his father go down and then Cass. Like a nightmare he sees Zerrin scream as she pulls at Cass's inert form. The bullets are still twanging off the bars of the fence. As Jak helps Zerrin pull Cass to the shelter of the truck he sees blood welling up from a wound in her shoulder. He turns and puts an arm around Verdor as he struggles to rise on a useless leg. He leans him against the truck and sees Zerrin slipping off to help Keenan who is lying prone still in the dust, the early morning sun tingeing his white face with a ghastly orange fire, Jak grabs her arm.

"Stay here." He says quietly and although she cannot possibly have heard him above the noise of the gunfire and Cass's distraught sobs, she holds back and Jak, crouching low, emerges from the safety afforded by the bulk of the truck. He wonders if Keenan is still alive as he feels the tug of a bullet in the sleeve of his coat. The short distance seems to extend forever as Jak throws himself forward and comes skidding up to Keenan's side. To his surprise he sees the Censites eyes, glowing dimly, looking into his.

"I think I'm done for." He whispers weakly. Jak looks down horrified at the spreading crimson stain, ghastly on the white fabric of Keenan's shirt. The young Censite grips Jak's hand as a spasm of pain contorts his face.

"You'd better get going." He breathes; his voice barely audible.

"I've not come all this way for nothing." Growls Jak, and rising, he half carries half drags the young man and they stagger back towards the truck. The only thing he notices apart from the bullets whining past him is Zerrin's eyes reaching out to him across the intervening space, willing him to make it.

"Get us out of here." He shouts to Nuttle as they stumble into the back of the truck. Zerrin and Verdor pull them in as the truck jerks forward.

"Where to Boss?" Calls Nuttle over his shoulder.

"To the ship." Orders Jak.

As they listen to the last of the shots ricocheting off of the armour plating, Jak looks around, sickened by the havoc before his eyes. His father has blood dripping from a wound in his upper thigh and it runs thickly along the runnels in the floor of the truck. As he removes his belt in preparation for use as a tourniquet Jak looks across at Cass leaning weakly against the panels, the wound at her shoulder scarlet against the whiteness of her face. Her eyes are closed and her head rocks gently with the motion of the truck. Jak is almost afraid to look at Keenan. When he does look down he sees Zerrin's eyes gazing beseechingly up at him. She has her arm under Keenan's shoulders as he lies flat out on the floor. In her other hand is a scrap of material, which she is holding against the dreadful wound just under Keenan's ribs. Already the makeshift wad is soaked.

"I don't know what to do." She whispers in a frightened voice to Jak, her eyes swimming with tears.

"We'll be back at the ship soon." He says to her quietly, matching her low tones, then loudly, harshly to Nuttle. "Step on it Nuttle."

With the tourniquet around Verdor's leg as tight as he can get it Jak secures the knot.

"How are you doing Dad?" Jak realises that this is the question he had asked his father earlier and it is the only thing he has said to him, which seems strange. Verdor opens his eyes and looks into Jak's. He smiles.

"Hey this father-son bonding thing we've got going here is fun; we should do it more often." His voice is low but Jak catches his words over the sound of the engine and he lays his hand on Verdor's shoulder. He smiles back but he feels pretty choked.

"I'm sorry Dad." He says.

"What for?"

"Oh I don't know, thing's have just gone really badly."

Verdor grips his hand. "You're doing just fine." He says softly and after looking at Jak for a long moment with what seems to Jak a kind of contented glow in his eyes, he allows his lids to droop and close.

Jak half stands, balancing against the side of the truck and stepping carefully over Cass' legs he leans his head through the little window leading into the cab. He looks at the road and the dwellings sliding away passed the windows.

"Are you going the right way?" He asks worriedly.

"I think so Boss."

Jak has a sinking feeling as he searches for some kind of landmark but he recognises nothing. The whole city of Gedd looks the same to him, just streets and streets of empty tumbled down buildings. He is just about to call Zerrin to find out where they are, when they drive out from behind a large warehouse and there is the Lazortrom looming ahead of them, the early rays of sunlight glinting off of the silver polectrum outer hull. Jak feels such relief that he tousles Nuttle's bristly head.

Chapter 45 Foiled

It is only a matter of moments before they are driving into the cargo bay. Jak slides open the door of the truck.

"Sit tight for a minute." He says to Zerrin. "I'll bring out a stretcher, how's he doing?"

"He's alive." She says briefly but Jak notices she is shaking her head while she says it. He turns and runs the few steps to the hatch, punching in the codes with fingers not wholly steady. As the doors start to slide open he feels cold steel at the back of his neck.

First of all he thinks of the woman, Felice, as he raises his hands.

"Thank you Jak." Says a heavily accented voice that he recognizes. It is Jeffers, Flagor's equally unfriendly cohort.

Jak turns slowly and sees Flagor standing there beside Jeffers. Jak's eyes leave Flagor's swaggering countenance and swiftly turn to the truck. There are about half a dozen armed Censites positioned with their weapons menacing the occupants. He sees Zerrin standing by the sliding door her eyes blank with astonishment. After a few seconds of stunned silence a sharp, angry string of words bursts from her lips. One of the armed hoodlums advances nearer and holds his gun close to her head. Jak takes a step and finds his own head similarly threatened by Jeffers.

Zerrin seems to know her assailant for she speaks to him by name before knocking his rifle contemptuously aside. After a few moments of dialogue the aggressors start to help carry the wounded up into the ship. Jak leads the way to the sick bay, all the while conscious of Jeffer's gun barrel pointing unwaveringly at the back of his neck.

There is a strange hush over the company as they traipse along the plush corridors of the Lazortrom. The Censites gaze around at luxuriously appointed interiors but they are never too distracted, their guns are at the ready. The thing that is worrying Jak the most is whether they know who the tall man with the wounded leg is. If they know, what will they do to his father?

Inside the hospital wing Jak all at once finds himself incredibly grateful to his captors. One of the men, Destril is obviously somewhat experienced in the medical field for he is immediately ministering over Keenan, his erstwhile comrade. Jak knows that without this man they would never have been able to treat the injuries. As Jak opens the instrument cabinet and looks for various items named by Destril he hears the murmur of the Censites as they discuss matters amongst themselves. He would like dearly to know what they are saying.

"What do they want?" He asks Zerrin in the only chance he gets to speak to her.

"The ship." She says briefly.

Jak wonders if her thoughts are running along the same lines as his own, are any of their captors harbouring the virus? Before he has a chance to articulate his concern one of the Censites, Norfax, speaks to him, Jak sees with an icy feeling of dread that he is standing over Verdor.

"Who is this man?" He demands and Jak relaxes just a fraction.

"He's one of the crew." He says, quickly looking at Nuttle to make sure he is following proceedings.

"His name is Plithen, he is the navigator."

He realises he is giving out too much information and stops abruptly. Flagor is looking at him unblinkingly. Norfax touches the material of Verdor's jacket.

"You have not seen the Captain of this ship, Verdor Dane?" He says quite loudly looking up piercingly at Jak.

Verdor's eyes open for a brief flickering moment but his lids slide wearily closed again without any incriminating sounds leaving his lips. Jak searches his mind. Are there any pictures of his father aboard this ship? He doesn't think so. What about registration shots on the computers? He can't remember. There is bound to be something there.

"You!" says Norfax turning to Nuttle after speaking briefly with Flagor, "can you start the ignition sequence?"

Nuttle stares blankly at him for a moment. "Oh start her up." He says eventually smiling weakly. "Er, no, I'm just the cook."

Norfax spins round to Jak and there is anger in the blaze of his eyes. "What about you Jak? Can you get this ship off the ground?"

"No." Says Jak without hesitation. Norfax's eyes snap.

"Then the navigator will have to do it." So saying he starts to pull Verdor savagely off the cot. Verdor cries out as his wounded leg slips off the mattress and he crumples to the floor, fresh blood showing on the fabric of his trousers.

"OK, OK." Cries Jak. "I may be able to help you." He starts forward to see to his father when suddenly there is a great rushing fire in his brain. Darkness closes in from the edges of his vision and the images around him start to race away as he sinks to the floor.

It is later now and Jak slowly comes to. At first he thinks he is alone but then a cool hand is laid on his brow and he can feel gentle fingers stroking away the hair from his temples. He knows that touch. He closes his eyes for a moment longer but then he is fully awake. He turns his head sharply enough to cause a jagged spike of pain to shoot along the lines of his skull, he winces and then looks fully at Zerrin who is leaning closely beside him.

"What happened?" He asks her hoarsely through parched lips.

She smiles. "Jeffers's brain went awol when you made out you couldn't start up the Lazortrom. I don't know, I guess he thought he'd make sure you couldn't."

"What an idiot."

"They're all up in the flight deck now fiddling with things."

"They'll never get her going. I hope they don't discover anything about Dad up there. How is he?"

"He's sleeping, He'll be fine; Destril has patched him up. I can't believe he's joined Flagor in this crazy scheme."

"What is their plan?"

"I'm not sure. Maybe it doesn't go any further than taking this ship. I'm guessing they'll be down here for you soon." Her voice trembles a little and an errant tear spills over her lashes. Jak lifts his hand and wipes it away with his thumb.

"It's been a tough few days." His voice is thick with empathy. There is silence between them for a few moments and then Jak reluctantly drags himself off the bed. They are in a small quarantine room off the sick bay.

"How's about Pal? Where is the little tyke?"

"I left him in the playroom, he's sound asleep."

"Do they know he's there?"

She nods "I had to tell them so I could go and check on him."

Jak fiddles with the door.

"We're locked in." Says Zerrin unnecessarily. "I made them let me stay with you."

He turns and looks at her.

"How did you do that?"

She laughs. "I don't know, by nagging continuously, with my voice pitched at a high decibel level until they surrendered."

"You know, I feel quite sorry for them." He comes and sits back down on the bed. "How's Keenan?" He asks quietly, it's the question that has been on his mind but is reluctant to ask.

"He is,.... stable." Zerrin's voice is suspended for an instant and it looks like she will cry but she brings herself under control. "Cass is sitting with him."

"Are they an item?" asks Jak.

Zerrin shrugs. "I don't know, maybe. She never said anything."

"Maybe she'll pull him through."

"Yes, maybe, I hope so." Zerrin pulls out a tissue and blows her nose. "It will be difficult for them you know if they are... you know...together."

Jak raises an eyebrow at her.

"They're different and people won't like it."

"What are you talking about?" asks Jak, confused but unaccountably feeling a little hard flint of anger sparking somewhere.

"He's a Pennelite haven't you noticed how his hair is so straight? All of us Wantages have curly hair and his eyes are kind of elongated, he's different from us."

Jak looks at her in puzzlement noticing a new hard look about her chin and eyes.

"That's nonsense." He say's shortly.

"Unfortunately, in this world, it's not nonsense Jak."

"Are you seriously telling me you think it's wrong because she's got curly hair and his is straight?"

"I didn't say I thought it was wrong, I am just intensely aware that other people would hate it. They will hound them Jak, don't try to make out you don't know that."

Jak is staring at her trying to read her eyes. "And that would weigh with you?" He asks her eventually, very quietly.

She looks up at him gravely for a moment and then she bows her head. "I don't know. Maybe eventually he would wish he'd never done it." She whispers. Jak looks down for a long time at the top of her head and feels a strange tug of compassion in the region of his chest. He lifts his hand and lays it, just for an instant, on her glossy curls. Suddenly the door is sliding open and Flagor stands there in the aperture glowering at them scornfully.

He says something to Zerrin that makes the delicate colour in her cheeks deepen. She says nothing and Jak feels an almost irrepressible desire to close with Flagor in a bout of fisticuffs, however there is the slight problem of the 57 rifle in the Censite's hands and the two other guys looking on menacingly over his shoulder. These things help Jak to see reason and when Flagor indicates aggressively with his weapon Jak follows him readily enough. Zerrin goes with them as far as the sickbay.

Jak looks round to see how the inmates are faring but Flagor is impatient and Jak is only able to note that his father seems to be sleeping peacefully before being ushered into the corridor. He is quite aware on the journey to the flight deck that Flagor introduces many unnecessary prods and nudges with the point of his rifle to encourage his captive along.

Norfax is in the Captain's chair when they arrive.

"Ah… Jak, sorry about that little confusion earlier." He says quite affably, his eyes flickering to Jeffers who is standing uncomfortably by. Jak notices a small strip of plaster above his left eye and feels a certain amount of satisfaction that the lout didn't get away with his idiocy without any recrimination.

Norfax rises from the pilot seat and offers it politely to Jak.

"Please, make yourself comfortable."

Jak eyes him steadily for a moment.

“How do you know none of your men are incubators of the plague?”

“We will be on this ship for some days we will know by then.” Norfax speaks quite matter of factly and Jak supposes that is because he has lived some time with the prospect of plague but to Jak the experience is a novel one and he feels his collar somewhat constrictive.

Norfax smiles grimly. “Quite so.” He says to Jak.

“What will you do if....?” Jak finds his voice petering out.

“Well I guess this ship will become some sort of shrine.” Says Norfax, he looks around the flight deck as though the idea appeals to him.

Jak feels impelled to explain to Norfax the horrendous possibilities that he seems to have missed.

“But what about..?...no wait.” He says as he sees a sudden blaze of impatience in the Censites eyes. “Just imagine this scenario. You regrettably succumb to, the...er debilitating effects, or shall we forget politeness and just say death and somebody else who’s not very bright,” here Jak waves his hand in Flagor’s direction,“takes charge and decides to land the ship on one of the corporate planets.”

“That’s not going to happen Jak. There is no plague on this ship. Now fire her up and let’s get out of here.”

“No.”

"What the Hell?" Rage suffuses Norfax's eyes with a red tinge and he raises his gun. Jak looks down the barrel, only inches from his face but he knows, in all conscience, he cannot take the ship out of Detagon if there is a risk of plague. Here he has some kind of tenuous control even in his death but if the ship were let loose in the solar system there would be no containment.

"Here's the deal." He says swallowing with difficulty, his eyes mesmerized by the depths of the gun shaft. "Destril takes blood samples from every one and if we are all clear I'll take her out."

Without letting the gun waver, Norfax picks up the communicator. The bleeps as he punches in Destril's number sound inordinately loud in the hushed stillness of the flight deck.

Norfax carries out the dialogue in Keltian for Jak's benefit.

"How long to take blood samples from all of us and test them, Destril?"

"I've already had a bash."

"Say again."

"I've already started. I've taken mine and Neshett's and all the pr....patients. We're clear."

"OK, well I'll start sending the other's down." His eyes never leave Jak's. "Seems like Destril's in agreement with you Jak."

"What will you do if someone is found to be contagious?"

"Well I think that's my business, you let me worry about it eh Jak." Norfax's eyes are still angry and Jak decides he'd better not push it any further.

"How's about some breakfast?" He says to the roomful of tense Censites. "Shall we get Nuttle to rustle us up some grub? He's a pretty fine chef." Jak detects a slight change in the air, a lessening of pressure, eagerness, as the overwrought men think about their breakfast.

"Is that a yes?" Asks Jak rising from his seat. Norfax has a few words with Flagor. Jak is conducted back down to sickbay by three armed guards; it seems they want to keep him under close guard until he can get the ship underway.

He is received with cries of welcome from a refreshed Pal as he enters the sickroom. Ignoring the guards the little boy runs to Jak and slips a warm hand into his. Jak looks down into eyes blazing with excitement.

"Is it true we are going into outer space?' Asks Pal eagerly.

"News travels fast." Says Jak ruefully.

"But is it true?"

"Well it looks like a distinct possibility." He glances up and catches Zerrin's eyes, questioningly upon him.

"They're taking blood samples first just to make sure we're all in the clear." He looks back down at Pal. "Three hours and then..." He mimics the take off with his hand and Pal smiles.

He sees that Zerrin is beside his fathers bed and that Verdor is sitting up watching his son curiously. Jak walks over with Pal in tow to the foot of the bed.

"How you doing Dad?" He asks.

"Not bad." Says Verdor wincing as he shifts his feet to make a space for Jak.

"Don't do that." Cries Jak. "You're not supposed to be moving about like a blinking whatever. I could've pulled up a chair."

"No matter. How about you Jak, how are you coping? Zerrin here has been telling me some of your exploits."

"Well if you two have been slagging me off between you I think I'll go and visit Keenan instead." Jak belies this threat by lowering himself into the space on the edge of the bed.

There is a gap in the conversation here and Jak fills it in by pretending to punch Pal on the nose.

"I didn't know you got on with children Jak." Mentions Verdor smiling quizzically.

Jak gives a snort. "You mean Pal? He's no child; he's a little squirming zephwort." He holds Pal's head trapped under his arm and the little boy laughingly wriggles free. Jak tousles his already crazy hair.

"Hush now." He says his voice deep with mock sternness. "Don't you know you're not supposed to make all that kind of racket in the sickroom?" He turns to Zerrin remembering suddenly.

"Where is Keenan by the way?"

"They've wheeled him through to the quarantine room where it's quieter."

"How's he coming, any change?"

Zerrin nods her head slowly. "It's early days I suppose but Destril reckons he'll pull through."

Jak instantly thinks of their earlier conversation and disconcerts Zerrin by staring at her with contemplatative eyes for far too long without saying anything.

It is later now, Jak has been asleep on the vacant cot next to his father's, the wearing effects of a sleepless night gradually expunging the excitement and peril and ushering in dreamless rest. At the foot of his bed he sees that Zerrin too has succumbed, her wild curls rippling around her head. He wonders for a moment as he looks at her why she is there, had she been watching over him? Or had they been talking in a desultory manner before they drifted off? He can't remember. He looks across at Verdor, he too is sleeping soundly. He eases out from under the covers and going to her, lifts her easily in his arms and lays her in the warm place he has just vacated. She doesn't really stir just nestles her head comfortably on the pillow. He pulls up the covers and lays them gently over her. Looking up he is startled to find Verdor eyeing him, one eyebrow raised.

"I thought you were asleep." Jak whispers quickly.

"Evidently." Is Verdor's brief comment.

Jak gazes back down at Zerrin. "She's a good kid." He says and there is a troubled note in his voice.

"Jak," says Verdor as his son makes his way around the bed and sits down on the chair beside him, "do you know what you're doing?"

Jak stares at him for a while before his eyes slide away and he takes a deep breath.

"Sure." He answers exhaling slowly. "If I have any choice in the matter I'm going to head out to the Zophir outpost. I think we can get a clear signal to the Crimmer from there and let them know what's going on."

Verdor eyes him with interest, letting the fact that his son had wilfully misunderstood his question slide.

"Do you know what's going on then?" He asks somewhat surprised.

"I reckon, don't you?"

Verdor shakes his head. "All I know is that there's plague on this planet and for some reason the Censites think I'm to blame. They think I brought the virus here in the flour but viruses don't travel that way as far as I know and anyway, everything was checked, I don't see how it could have gotten through.

Jak detects the note of dread in his father's voice as it rises a little at the end of this sentence. Zerrin stirs and Verdor lowers his voice again. "Everything was double checked." He repeats.

"Petaman stole the Lazortrom in 24.81, that time we

were at Leager Lin. He brought the contaminated shipment in."

Verdor stares at his hands lying clenched on the counterpane. "Impossible." He says at length."…. Unless he had cooperation from Straiff Shipping." He looks at Jak, "Are you saying Straiff is implicated?"

Jak is about to explain further in the affirmative when the door slides open and Norfax is standing there.

"Ah Jak, are you plotting?" He asks mildly.

Jak is about to disclose the subject of their discussion but then realises the unwisdom of stirring things up in that quarter. Instead he answers with a question.

"Are the tests completed?"

"Yes finally, you'll be glad to know everyone is in the clear."

"Do you mind if I have a look at the results?"

Norfax raises his eyebrows.

"I never knew you were a doctor too Jak, you just keep on surprising me."

Jak knows well enough the inadequacy of his analysis of the test results however he feels a certain amount of trust in Destril and at least if he looks at the papers and speaks to the doctor he can get a feel for their accuracy. Anyway it is all he can do short of refusing to initiate take off. He wonders coldly for a moment if that is exactly what he ought to do.

He looks hard at Norfax. That strange white gleam comes into the Censite's eyes, Jak has seen it before up on the flight deck, it is only for an instant before Norfax lowers his eyes and the look is concealed, but it is enough to set the hair on the back of Jak's neck bristling.

"You know," says Norfax conversationally, "if you refuse to fly this bird I'll just have to kill all your friends."

There is a long silence while Jak stares at Norfax and Norfax raises his eyes and stares back. Just then Destril enters the room, a lingering expression of relief on his face, which does more than anything else can, to reassure Jak. In his hand is a sheaf of printouts that he holds out. Jak takes them and notices grimly that his hand is shaking, he is fairly sure that everyone else sees it too and he quickly straightens the corners of the sheaf. As far as he can tell everything is in order.

"Let us escort our young friend up to the flight deck shall we?" Suggests Norfax in his usual mild way.

As they leave Jak shoots a quick look at his father. Verdor smiles his encouragement and Jak feels a restoration of his customary bravado.

They are heading along the corridor and Jak finds Destril by his side.

"Tell me Destril, how long is the incubation period? You know….if there was a mistake, how long before there were any noticeable symptoms?"

"In four days you would start to see high fever and

irrational behaviour and in six or seven days white patches appear on the skin. Don't worry Jak there is no mistake we are all in the clear."

Jak looks down into Destril's round solemn face and believes him.

"There is something I don't quite understand." Says Jak, pausing for a moment and lowering his voice. "How could the virus have been in the flour? I don't know a great deal about such things but I thought viruses were airborne or transmitted by contact."

"Yes, this plague is transmitted that way but the flour was contaminated with elemental braucite, which weakened the immune system of those using the flour and made them susceptible to the reptilian disease indoela. It is rampant here on Detagon but previously posed no danger to us. Once the immune system is weakened however the virus can take hold. It was after that happened that indoela mutated into this deadly respiratory illness." Destril's explanations drift into silence and Jak, thinking about the cold-blooded calculations that have gone into this dastardly plot, lays a hand very briefly on Destril's shoulder.

They continue on to the flight deck in silence. Jak sits in the Captains chair, suddenly nervous about flying the huge craft. He has actually never piloted the ship before but has been present when the Lazortrom has departed on other occasions. He knows the sequence off by heart but is aware that doesn't make him a pilot. He runs his hand over the control panel and takes a deep breath.

"You do know what you're doing of course?" Says Norfax into his ear.

Jak swallows. "Where are we heading?" He asks.

"Just get us out of this sector, I'll give you coordinates when we're out there."

This is just the kind of free hand Jak wants but never thought he would receive. Quickly he plots a default course for the Zophir outpost. He sees Norfax looking at the figures with understanding but he doesn't say a word to Jak about it. There is a short exchange between him and Flagor as Jak initiates lift off .

Chapter 46 Take Off

A tense excitement fills the flight deck as the distant pulsating thrum of the engine is heard. However when Jak gives the instructions for disengaging the docking apparatus, an urgent alarm signal floods the deck with high discordant sound. Jak feels cold metal at his temple.

"What the hell are you doing?" Norfax has that white-hot look in his eyes.

"The dock seals won't release." Says Jak, quick alarm in his voice as the Censites, en mass, press in upon him menacingly. "Your people must have messed with them trying to breach the security."

Norfax's hand snakes out and he hits the manual override.

"Just get her out of here." He says his voice loaded with menace.

"I think you'll find that a very perilous exercise." Says Jak, ignoring the steering column as it slides up from the consol. He feels the hard pressure against his temple increase and then it relaxes. Norfax gives a sharp command to Flagor who leaves immediately.

"Send someone out to look at them? It's probably no big deal." Suggests Jak. Nobody answers him. Destril attempts a few words with Norfax but the latter has his eyes straight ahead and does not respond. There is that slightly maniacal glint lingering in them and Jak feels moisture dampen his palms. The sound of the doors sliding open breaks the silence that ensues with a soft hydraulic sigh.

Zerrin looks dazedly across the room at him. She has that soft ambient look of someone just awakened from deep sleep. Flagor thrusts her into the room and she staggers a little. Jak watches as Norfax reaches out and draws her to him the barrel of his gun nestling against her cheek. She is close enough for Jak to see the tendrils of hair that frame her face clinging damply to her forehead, he turns his eyes towards the console and grips the column with both hands.

"Better buckle up." He says briefly as he reaches for the tanoy and warns the ship at large to secure themselves, he waits as long as he dares and then slams on the throttle. He speculates quite detachedly whether one quick jerk would be better than gradually increased pressure. Either way the huge ship was going to buck around something crazy. Jak wonders what is wrong with Norfax that he is prepared to risk everything in this extravagantly insane gesture rather than send someone out to check on the docking arms. He wants to suggest again that he will volunteer to climb the shaft but Norfax's eyes are boring into him and the gun is pushed so hard into Zerrin's cheek that her face is forced sideways.

"Buckle up." He orders Norfax harshly and the Censite leader moves reluctantly to a vacant seat, he pulls Zerrin down onto his lap and buckles them both in, his eyes never leaving Jak's face. As soon as they are set Jak gives a hard jerk on the column and the ship screams like a living thing as she lists heavily towards the docking station. Jak cuts the thrusters and levels her back down before firing once again on all cylinders. The tortured metal gives a final shriek before tearing away from the docking arms. The release sends the ship lurching upwards almost on its side.

Alarms flash red all across the control panels and the sound of sirens add to the cacophony of fearful shouts on the flight deck. Jak wrestles with the steering,trying to bring the huge vessel back under control. She veers wildly to starboard taking out a row of empty warehouses then rears upwards again and finally steadies into a normal flight path. Jak uncurls white fingers from the column and switches off the manual override. The synthesized voice of the computer speaks soothingly of systems returning to normal and Jak leans back in the pilot's chair.

"Is that what was supposed to happen?" Asks Norfax, his voice relaxing to its familiar mild tones.

Jak smiles, a grin of released tension and relief.

He stays in command of the ship until they pass out of the Detagon atmosphere then he is ushered, along with Zerrin, back to the hospital area.

His Father, still strapped in from take off, looks at him quizzically,

"Was that you driving son?" He asks Jak who nods sheepishly. "Remind me when we get out of all this not to enroll you as a pilot."

"You're still alive aren't you?" Says Jak placidly as he unbuckles the straps. Pal comes bouncing up,

"Did you fly the ship Jak?" He asks blinking, wide eyed.

"Yup, did you enjoy the take off ?'

"Yeah, it was awesome."

"See," says Jak. "Here's someone who appreciates my talents."

"Apart from the take off, how did it go up there?" Asks Verdor.

"I'm not sure, I plotted a course for Zophir and Norfax watched me, he seemed to know what I was doing but he didn't intervene so I guess it went well." He catches sight of an untouched sandwich on the bedside cabinet. "Do you mind?" He asks perfunctorily as he lifts it and prepares to take a huge bite.

"I tell you what, why don't you help yourself?" Suggests Verdor sarcastically. "What about you dear? Are you hungry?" He asks Zerrin with pointed politeness.

"It's OK, I'll just eat this crumb that's left on the plate." She says.

Jak looks at the limp crust in his fingers, which is all that is left of the sandwich and offers it gravely to her.

"You eat it." She laughs. "You're obviously very hungry, here have the crumb too."

Into this scene of nonsense comes Cass, rubbing her head.

"Whoever's flying this damn tub should be shot." She complains.

"Er,.. That would be me."

"Well you undoubtedly will be shot at some point." She says optimistically.

"How's Keenan?" Asks Jak more soberly.

"He's doing good." Responds Cass after a moment's hesitation. "Come and see for yourself, he'd like a visitor…even you."

Jak follows Cass across the ward, he looks at Zerrin but she doesn't follow. They find Keenan his face very white and dark smudges under his eyes.

"You look terrible old bud." Says Jak very quietly. Keenan's eyes remain closed but Jak sees a faint smile suggest itself on his lips.

"I think he's going to be OK." He says looking earnestly at Cass. He hopes it doesn't sound like a platitude because he believes it. She nods.

"I think so too." She agrees. She briefly lays a hand on his arm, he thinks it's in acknowledgement of his good intentions, and walks round to the other side of the bed to sit down on a chair. She glances up and catches Jak's look.

"What's the matter?" She asks.

"I just noticed your hair is curly."

"And what's in that to make you look like a thundercloud?" She responds with her disconcertingly direct gaze.

"Nothing" Jak mumbles feeling foolish. There is silence for a moment, as Cass' knowing face looks unusually puzzled.

"There is something I want to ask you." Says Jak by way of changing the subject.

"What's all this about Karrif?" After he has asked the question he feels unaccountably that he hasn't changed the subject at all somehow.

Cass smiles at him and her look of bright insight returns. "Oh right, well a long time ago when Zerrin was young and very foolish. She and Flagor were a bit of a thing..... She thought he was some kind of hero I suppose." Her voice takes on a sadness he hasn't heard before as she looks through him into the past. "You know, he behaved very badly, I haven't liked him that much since then." Jak sees to his dismay that her eyes have the increased brightness of gathering tears. Before they spill over though, she blinks them away.

"Anyway," she clears her throat a little as though to get rid of some constriction," he took her on a mission to try and recruit Karrif to the Fedek. It was a disaster. Karrif had...has no interest in politics but as soon as he saw Zerrin he wanted her. He called Flagor in and said he would free him and the other emissaries if he had her." Cass begins to pleat the sheet that has been clutched in her fingers, when she speaks again her voice is shallow, hard as though a softer tone will not stand up to the emotion she feels. "So anyway in the interests of saving Censites everywhere he sent back to the camp and had her delivered. He told her she had to stay. His excuse was that she would be able to turn Karrif to the cause, seeing as he thought so much of her."

"She went freely?" Jak asks and as she stares at him blankly he modifies his question "Was Flagor able to persuade her to stay?"

Cass gives him a wintery smile "There wasn't any choice Jak. Zerrin was Karrif's prisoner from that point. Flagor, my beloved brother, handed her over on a plate."

"What about her family."

"They were pretty much estranged at that point. They didn't like her affiliation with Flagor and the Fedek. They knew she'd disappeared and they searched for her but we never let on where she was."

"And then?" Prompted Jak.

"I don't know any details, as you can imagine, it's not something either Zerrin or Flagor likes to talk about. I didn't see her again until after she escaped."

"She escaped then." Muses Jak softly..

"She was there for almost six months but I'm sure he never touched her. She was only just sixteen when she went there and Karrif told Flagor that he wouldn't go near her unless she came to him willingly. I guess he lost patience."

"What do you mean?" Jak asks sharply. His soul rebels from hearing more and yet again, his every fibre it seems, listens attentively to Cass' story. In the pit of his stomach he has a sickish feeling that he ought to tell Cass he doesn't want to invade Zerrin's privacy any further but he sits there just the same, his ears and eyes wide open, looking intently at Cass' face before him.

"That scar on his face, she did it and there is another under his ribs."

Slowly a smile spreads over Jak's face. He reaches out and grasps Cass' hand briefly.

"Thanks."

"Don't let on we've been talking her over, she would hate it." Warns Cass. Jak smiles to himself, as if he would be foolhardy enough to let her know.

Yes and now the whole of the twelve nations knew it. He looks down at the papers in front of him but he can feel the heat of her eyes blazing across the auditorium at him.

"I think we've changed course." Verdor is standing, supported by a crutch beside the viewer, staring out at the endless star spangled night.

"How can you tell?" Jak asks his father.

"If you kept your eyes open son you'd know as well as I

do that the Kesil constellation, which has been ahead of us all the way, is sliding down and out to the side."

Jak peers intently at the trillion tiny pinpricks. He nods but he can see nothing different in the ribbons and swathes of the galaxies hanging in space like grapes on the vine of the universe.

"Isn't it just because we've slowed down?" Suggests Jak tentatively. Verdor looks at him for a moment then he smiles.

"I'm glad you've shown such potential lately otherwise I'd be seriously worried about you." He hobbles away from the viewer toward the coffee dispenser. Jak stays for a moment staring vainly out.

"What do you think they're up to?" He muses. Verdor is beside him again spilling hot coffee over his fingers and making the appropriate exclamations. He looks out once more into the void. "Look." He points an instructive finger. "They are holding this course now. I think they do have a particular destination in mind."

"Any idea where that might be?"

"If we continue on this heading we'll arrive at Zennan in six or seven days."

"Why would they want to go there, it's just a holiday planet isn't it?"

"Perhaps they feel they deserve a holiday."

Jak shakes his head unimpressed with his father's ponderous levity. He feels certain this new twist is not for the better.

"Is the Doc anywhere?" He asks the room at large.

"Is he in with Keenan?" Suggests Zerrin looking up from a desultory game of cards with Pal.

Jak strides across to the anteroom and pokes his head round the door.

"Got a minute Doc?" He asks as he sees Destril leaning over Keenan. Destril doesn't look up but nods. "I'll be right with you." He says and Jak sees he is changing the dressing on Keenan's wound.

"No rush." Assures Jak and wanders back out a little sheepish at his mal apropository but he has a really strong feeling that something bad is going to happen.

"Zerrin." He hails her as he walks up to the little table scattered with cards and she looks up at him enquiringly. "We've changed course and are heading for the corporate planets, any idea what that could mean?"

He notices that her face pales a little and a fear that she immediately dismisses comes briefly into her eyes. She shakes her head and looking across the table at Pal she collects up the cards. "Here." She says. "Take these and go and ask Aunt Cass how you play Knock Off ."

"What's that?"

"That's what I'm saying to you. Go and ask Cass, she'll show you how to play it."

They both watch him as he trots off .

"So what are you thinking?" Asks Jak looking down at her curly head.

She lifts her eyes to his, a frown insinuating itself between her brows.

"I don't know, what are you thinking?"

"I think something bad is going to happen. What were you afraid of when I first told you we were heading towards the corporate planets? You thought of something and then you whisked it away. What was it?"

The look of distress returns.

"I just suddenly thought maybe they were planning some terrorist attack."

"So why did you dismiss it?"

She looked up at him for some few seconds considering her reply.

"I think…only because I don't want to believe it."

"Have these guys perpetrated any terrorist activity before?"

"Yes they drove a truck of explosives at the administrative buildings five months ago."

Jak closes his eyes for a moment.

"I'll have a word with Destril, see if he knows anything." Jak makes to go then turns back and lays a hand on her arm. "Might be best not to mention it to the others, we could be wrong." As he looks at her face he can tell she doesn't think there is much chance of that.

Destril is just coming out of Keenan's room as Jak reaches it and he drives the Doctor back through the door.

"A word with you Doc." He says, his voice urgent. There is a faint shadow of fear in the Doctor's eyes as Jak bears down purposefully on him.

"What is it Jak? What's the matter?"

"Do you know where we are going?"

Destril looks uncomfortable. "I can tell we have changed course and from some talk I believe we are heading for Zennan." He says.

"Why?"

"I don't know and I don't believe you should be threatening me in this way."

"I'm not threatening you." Jak takes a step back in confirmation of his words. "It's just that I've a bad feeling. Is there any way you can find out their plans?"

Destril gives him a piercing look "What makes you think I would tell you if I was able to discover anything?" He asks; his voice soft yet heavy with significant meaning.

Jak shrugs. "I just don't really believe you are with that pack of nutters."

Destril looks steadily at him. "I am with them, Jak." He affirms and Jak feels a sharp disappointment.

"However." He continues quickly as Jak stares at him reproachfully. "I don't hold with terrorism." He reaches into his pocket. "I found this in the IT stores; do you know what it is?" He holds out a tiny disk, Jak takes it and rolls it in his fingers.

"It's a spy patch. How did you know?"

"I watch TV." He reclaims the disk and looks earnestly at Jak. "If I can unite it with the main computer can you link up from here?"

"Yes of course, but it will only tell us for sure if they are heading for Zennan won't it?"

"Jak." Says Destril reprovingly. "You haven't watched Portal Swings or you would know we can pick up all intercom messages with this. If we listen in we'll hear something of their plans."

"OK when will you do it?"

"Tonight, when there are only a few people on deck."

Back with his father and Zerrin Jak feels a little better but not wholly satisfied that they will actually be accomplishing a great deal.

"Of course it's only information; we won't actually be able to do anything." He concludes moodily.

"Can't we hack into the systems once you have a portal into the main computer?" asks Zerrin excitedly.

Jak looks down at her "And what film did you get that from?"

She looks sheepish.

"Didn't they have any firewalls in Portal Swings?" Jak asks her.

"Well yes they did but the hackers got through quite easily."

Jak smiles in a very superior way. "Well I'm sorry to disappoint you but I'm not a computer nerd and I've never hacked into anything." He raises an eyebrow at her. "Have you?"

No, Zerrin had never used a computer.

"I'm pretty good." Says Verdor "But I've never broken through a firewall."

"I have though."

They turn to see Nuttle's shiny round face animated by an unaccustomed look of eagerness.

"Excuse me?" Says Jak in an unintentionally repressive voice

"When I was a teenager I was a member of the Hack Patch." He looks round with expectant portentousness. "A computer fraud gang." He explains, as he encounters their blank looks.

"Yeah, but you aint a kid no more by a long shot. Things have moved along old buddy."

"Well I guess I know more about the business then any of you folks." Says Nuttle petulantly.

"He should have his shot." Decides Verdor with finality.

"But Dad," complains Jak drawing him a little to one side, "if an attempt on the firewall is made and detected the game is up. They'll know we've made a portal and be down on us."

"That's true, but we'll have a shot at regaining control of this ship and preventing, who knows what kind of terrorist attack on Zennan."

"That's the point, we don't know what kind and if Nuttle goes blundering in we won't get a chance to find out."

"Give him some credit Jak."

"No!" Hisses Jak feeling desperate. "I gave him credit before. I thought he would watch my back and..," he looks up, draws his father further away and lowers his voice to an urgent whisper, "found him snivelling in the bushes when it was over."

"That wasn't his field of expertise, this is."

"His field of expertise is cooking." Says Jak too loudly.

The others are all looking at him. Can he see reproach in their eyes? Certainly Nuttle looks pretty peeved.

"Jak, I'm surprised at you, you are just a unicamp student and look what you've accomplished." Reminds Verdor his voice nicely pitched between reprimand and cajolery.

"Yeah and now I'm a superhero who's got us all stuck as prisoners on this ship and can't do anything about it." As soon as it is said Jak feels like an idiot. "Oh hell." He ends sheepishly. "Now I really do feel like I'm in an episode of Portal Swings."

Verdor squeezes his arm. "We've all been having a

tough time." He turns from Jak and starts to speak with Nuttle.

Jak doesn't listen but sits down on the bed feeling as though he's been well and truly fobbed off .

"Jak." Zerrin is beside him her voice a little timid as she speaks and Jak realises he's been staring straight through her for the past couple of minutes, probably as though he wanted to murder her 'cos he sure feels like turning out somebody's lights. He isn't sure who the lucky recipient might be but it certainly isn't Zerrin. He flings himself back on the empty cot and kicks his feet up onto the counterpane.

"Hey relax." Says Zerrin smiling down at him. She waits to see the effect of these mild words and then asks him:

"Do you really not want Nuttle to hack in?"

"No I don't."

"But why? It's a good chance isn't it?"

He turns on his side and looks down at her fingers resting on the white bedclothes.

"Look." He says, "I don't know why but I just have such a bad feeling about it, I know it's not a good idea."

"Because it's not yours?"

Jak's eyes jerk up to hers, he must look fairly annoyed because she takes a step backwards but as her hands slip off the bed he instinctively reaches for her. He doesn't say anything just holds her slim fingers in his for a moment then releases her and swinging his legs off over the other side of the bed, sits up with his back to her. Maybe she is right. Maybe he doesn't like the plan because it isn't his. He thinks about it for a while but now his assurance is undermined. He had been so sure previously that increased peril lay down that road but now she'd messed with his head. He turns to speak to her but she is not there. He sees her over the other side of the room with Cass and Pal. She looks across at him but quickly lowers her eyes and he can't tell what she is thinking.

"By the way." Nuttle is beside him looking down at him with intense hostility. "You told me to hide in the shrubbery, remember?"

Jak can't remember but there is enough uncertainty to make him feel uncomfortable.

"Hey sorry mate." He says with some reluctance. "No hard feelings I hope."

"Humph." is Nuttle's comment as he walks away.

Chapter 47
Flu-like Symtoms.

A little while later the plotting is interrupted by a call on the intercom for Destril. As a token of the trust his confederates feel for him he is only allowed out of the sickbay when specifically wanted by Norfax and then only accompanied by some one or two of his fellows. Jak wonders how he intends to plant the patch; it would seem to be no easier for him than any of them.

All of the prisoners suspend their activities when they hear Norfax's voice demanding the doctor's presence on the flight deck. There is something about his tone, some quality that alerts them all and compels attention. Five minutes later Destril returns, his face very pale and behind him two more Censites carrying a man on a stretcher.

For a few seconds only, they all stare at the incapacitated man. In another instant Jak is standing in front of the Doctor.

"What's wrong with him?" He demands.

"I don't know as yet." Destril answers him but continues

ministrations to his patient. Jak looks at the man's flushed face and fevered, terrified eyes. He reaches out to bar Destril's way.

"Why the hell are you bringing him in here?"

"This is my lab, I must make tests." Says Destril blankly.

"This is a room full of innocent people, get him out of here."

"I'll take him through to Keenan's room."

There is a little cry from Cass and she and Zerrin run from the furthest corner, where all had retreated, along the wall to Keenan's room.

"Get him out in the corridor while we prepare." Says Jak quietly but firmly.

Searching in the cupboard Zerrin discovers a pack of ten respirators. She shows them to a greatly relieved Jak, as she does so the door slides open and Jeffers stands for an instant in the doorway. At precisely the same time he and Jak look down at the filters. Jeffers advances with menace; his gun levelled and relieves Jak of the precious package. As he strides around the room he sees Pal who has somehow placed one of the oversized masks on his face. For a moment Pal and Jeffers look at each other then the Fedek guard snatches the filter from the little boy's face. He adjusts the mask over his own nose and mouth then opens the door to the little side room and says a few words to Destril who comes out of the room shaking his head. Jak is sure he can taste fear in the very air he is breathing. It is in his own mouth and making him gag.

"They are looking for some kind of medicine." Says Zerrin at his elbow. Her voice is strangely pitched. However it is not fear that Jak can trace in her lilting tones but bitter acceptance of the inevitable.

"Anti G." He answers her comment. "I've already looked I can't understand why there is none here." He looks up and catches Nuttle's eye, noting the conscious look on his face before he slinks away out of Jak's line of sight.

Jeffers is crashing around frantically in the cupboards and Destril is trying to restrain him.

"What an idiot." Pronounces Jak dispassionately. "He has no idea what he's looking for, he could be crushing it in his great clumsy fingers for all he knows… that is if there were any which there isn't." He adds.

The hours tick by and they listen to the retching cough emanating endlessly from behind the closed door.

It is the inactivity that gets to Jak, the feeling of total impuancy. There is absolutely nothing he can do. He looks around at the faces of the others. They appear listless as if they don't really care. His father across from him has his eyes closed though he does not sleep. Cass is talking in a low tone to Keenan. Declaring herself Jak wonders, now that there is no chance of recrimination. No, her face looks too mundane for that. On these thoughts he turns his eyes to Zerrin who has chosen the most uncomfortable seat, the floor, and has Pals head resting on her lap. The child is in repose and she is looking down at him tenderly, stroking the hair that flops onto his brow. She looks up at Jak at that precise moment and as she catches his gaze she smiles. Something twists inside Jak but in an instant the feeling is gone and he is left with a gall of bitter anger that things have turned out so unsatisfactorily. The smile fades on Zerrin's lips and her eyes also lose a little of their light. She still looks at him and Jak is about to rise and go to her, to try and make things right, when Cass starts to sneeze. Five times she sneezes and then blows her nose. Everyone stares at her. Her face turns as white as can be at their looks. Keenan lifts his weakened arm and pulls her head onto his shoulder and he holds her there.

'Now that's how you support someone you care about.' Thinks Jak irrelevantly and his eyes seek Zerrin, but she is looking with horror filled eyes at Cass.

"Get the Doctor!" Says Verdor to Jak.

Jak goes but he wonders what good it will do.

So is it really going to end like this? He wonders as he crosses to the antechamber, all of them gradually being picked off by the plague? It seems so offensively pointless.

"How's it looking?" He asks Destril as the doctor removes his mask.

"Well, I've done some tests but I can't say for sure at the moment."

Jak takes this as the mandatory evasiveness incumbent on anyone in the medical profession.

"You'd better take a look at Cass."

"She should be isolated with the other Censite." Says Nuttle querulously. "I demand it."

"She did ought to be." Concurs Jak reluctantly.

"I can't put her in there he's violent with the fever and I can't find any sedatives."

"What's wrong with this place? Why isn't there a proper supply of medicines?" He turns to his father for enlightenment but Verdor shrugs his shoulders.

"The full quota was aboard when we left Freeport."

"There was a half bottle of Meriscine but I used it on Keenan."

"Anyway." Says Jak. "We could duff this guy over and tie him up."

"You're asking me, a doctor, to do that?" Smiles Destril grimly. "Don't worry, I would do it but he has a weapon which he will not relinquish and I haven't even been able to take a blood test because he keeps waving it in my face."

"I still think we should jump him." Says Jak after a moments calculation. "After all, he might do for the Doc and then we would stand no chance." In the sudden hush that follows this statement Jak realises that the look that has come over Destril's face means that they don't stand a chance either way.

"The best we can do is isolate her as much as possible and put her by the extractor so that her exhalations don't circulate."

It is later and Destril, with Jak's help, has rigged up an antiviral spray system, which is gradually filling the sick bay with a strong smelling fog.

"Do you reckon this'll work?" Jak asks as they watch the mist seeping from the nozzles.

"I see no reason why it shouldn't help."

"How long is the incubation period?" Jak queries, watching him closely.

"Five days."

Jak doesn't say it but the conviction that the precautions they are taking are next to useless lays heavily upon him.

Jak hates the feeling of dread, a kind of dismal certainty that hangs over them all like the pall of antiviral mist.

Next Jak speaks to his father.

"We must put paid to this ship reaching Zennan." He says quietly. Verdor looks long at him and Jak watches his face harden.

"You are right." He agrees. "What do you have in mind?"

"If there is some way I could get into the engine room I could cripple her."

Verdor shakes his head. "The door is the only way."

"What about the ventilation shaft?"

"What ventilation shaft."

"You know, where the air comes in."

"The pipes are only twenty mil."

Jak pauses for a moment, reflecting on Zerrin, watching Portal Swings and thinking they could emulate Lt Mekker. Didn't everyone escape through the ventilation?

"What about the door mechanisms couldn't we scramble them?"

"They are designed to seal up like a vault if the switches are tampered with."

A stifled gasp followed by a murmur of exclamations of concern, alert them to further developments and they look across the room. Cass sits by the extractor her face as white as snow, blood streaming from her nose and soaking the wad of tissues in her hand.

Destril goes straight to her, adjusting his mask, the others watch, from a distance.

"Have you experienced nose bleeds before?" Asks the doctor. Cass nods miserably and he exchanges her soiled tissues for fresh ones and tilts her head back gently. Destril says nothing more for a moment and there is a strained silence stretching across the room. Finally it is fractured by Cass' strangled voice, compressed by her unnatural position and the fear that weighs down on them all.

"I always have a nose bleed when I've got a cold." There is such a desperate quality there that Jak feels almost physical pain at her distress and tears sting the back of his eyes. He feels a warm hand slide into his and he knows it is Zerrin's. He wonders how she always knows when to come and console him and then realises that, of course, it is she that seeks comfort. Cass is probably the only female friend she has ever had and though they had been estranged lately they must have been very close at one time.

"Does Flagor know his sister is ill?" He asks.

"I think he does." She replies tonelessly.

Destril approaches and although the thought doesn't take expression, Jak wonders vaguely why the doctor had gotten into the habit of conferring with him, after all it must be as plain as a pikestaff he didn't know his aorta from his pulmonary gland.

"I took a blood sample earlier but I need access to the lab. I've made a request to Norfax but he is not responding. I don't think they intend to let me out of here again."

"Have you told Flagor that Cass is ill?"

"Yes, I impressed upon him the impossibility of seeing her."

"Did he want to?" Asks Zerrin quietly.

Destril nods but then hesitates, remembering. "I don't know, I told him he couldn't before he asked."

Destril's communicator bleeps and he moves a little to one side, out of habit rather than any quest for privacy.

They listen to his side of the conversation:

"Yes, she is in a stable condition but I need to get to the lab,…..no,…..no, I tell you there aren't any here,….I don't know but if I could get to the lab I could fi nd out how serious it is and maybe make some progress,….. OK, …..uhuh,….right,…I'll do that."

At the start his voice had been loaded with frustration but right at the end Jak noticed the lift of excitement.

"That was Flagor enquiring after Cass; he's going to get me into the lab. Watch that light there and when he gets an opportunity he will release the seal. I'll get my things ready."

He turns to go and Jak touches his arm.

"Is he coming down or just releasing the door?"

"He indicated he would do it from the flight deck."

"That seems incredible, is he an idiot? He must know we would all make a run for it."

"It probably hasn't crossed his mind to suspect me of throwing in my lot with you. After all you forget I am Fedek, he probably thinks I'm loyal to the cause."There is a hint of troubled bitterness in Destril's voice.

"What? and he think's that you would slip out without us noticing?"

"It wouldn't matter if you did, I'd be gone and the door resealed."

Jak nods, it seems reasonable. Destril goes to collect his kit and Jak leaves Zerrin to watch the door while he briefs his father.

"I'll mosey out with the Doc and slide off to the engine rooms."

"Who'll go with you?"

"You could come." Says Jak doubtfully.

"No." Verdor declines the invitation, gingerly touching his injured leg. "I'd be a hindrance. What about Nuttle?"

"No, I think if given the chance he'd scarper, I'll take Zerrin she's all I need." And he looks across at her noticing her thin almost frail body, taut as she watches for the door release.

Verdor eyes him thoughtfully. "What will you do, you have no weapons?"

"I have this." He shows Verdor a piece of heavy metal apparatus. He recalls that it is the same piece he had seen Zerrin with that day, oh so long ago, maybe a week or eight days, when she had held Nuttle at bay. It flashes into his mind that he had thought she was dead that day and how he had felt.

Now he is contemplating destroying them all in an effort to stop the spread of the disease to the holiday planet. For what? To save a load of people he didn't know and didn't care about at the expense of those he loved. Did that make any sense?

"What will you do?" Asks Verdor again, breaking across his thoughts.

"I won't blow her up; I'll just try to cripple her."

"Do you realise you put the whole of the sector in jeopardy when you made that decision?" Asks the administrator sternly, as he looks over the top of his glasses at Jak.

"That's irrelevant your honour." Says Jak's lawyer quickly.

"True, strike that comment."

Jak notices how pessimistically Releau shakes his head. Later he rants at Jak. "I know it's irrelevant, I said it was didn't I? The thing is they....", and he waves his hand to indicate the whole of the viewing public, "they will know you were willing to throw over the whole of the twelve nations for your "friends" won't they? It doesn't look good Jak." He shakes his head disapprovingly. "I wonder if I should file for a mistrial?" He mutters almost to himself. Then he looks up at Jak his eyes glaring "That includes me you know, I'm a member of the twelve. Mind you I was away in Koovek at the time." He mellows. "Don't look so peaky maybe they won't notice the implications."

"JAK DANE ENDANGERS THE LIVES OF

MILLIONS TO SAVE LOVER' Jak stares at the headlines the next morning.

When the door is eventually released the first thing Jak sees is the butt end of Flagor's rifle an instant before it hits him between the eyes.

"What were you doing? Where were you going scuttling off to, to save your own skin?" These are the first words he hears when he comes to and it is Nuttle's high-pitched voice that rips through the mists of unconsciousness. He hears the low rumble of Verdor's calming tones as he explains the circumstances. Jak opens his eyes painfully and sees Zerrin standing over him protectively with the metal widget grasped firmly between her hands.

"If you knew the door was going to be opened you should have informed us. What right have you to conceal that kind of information?" Continues Nuttle.

"It's irrelevant isn't it?" Observes Keenan mildly.

"Yeah, perhaps you would have preferred Flagor's rifle butt in your face instead of mine." Says Jak thickly. "I know I would."

Nuttle subsides eventually but not without many clichéd phrases including the words trust, rights and teamwork.

"Do you think we should have mentioned it?" Jak approaches Keenan after things have quieted down and questions him tentatively.

"No." Replies Keenan. "Nuttle would have legged it and we can't leave this room until it's confirmed that whatsit and Cass have the flu and not the plague."

Jak looks down at the injured man sorrowfully, feeling a little awkward at this pathetic display of optimism. Keenan catches his look.

"Look at her. I've seen plague victims and they look worse than that."

They both look at the sick girl. They see her snuffling into a tissue, then, once again the red stain.

"She always gets a nosebleed when she's got a cold." Says Keenan defensively. He leans forward in his cot as if he wants to go to her, which of course in his injured state he can't. Even so Jak lays a hand on his shoulder.

"Wait until the tests come back." He says. And his words sound meaningless and hollow even to himself.

"So what now?" Asks Jak of his father.

"Destril still has the patch."

"Ah, yes the patch."

"I saw his hand go to his pocket just as they were leaving." Says Zerrin. She reaches up to Jak's brow to adjust the dressing and he instinctively flinches away. She looks at him. "I never mentioned it before because I knew you'd be moody about it." She says pointedly.

"Don't be ridiculous." Says Jak scowling at her. "It doesn't look like we've got an option now anyway."

Destril soon returns with his escort. He is deposited roughly into the sick bay and the door slides to, sealing with an ominous sigh. Jak watches it regretfully and then transfers his gaze to contemplate Destril's approach.

"We should get the results within a couple of hours." He says.

"The patch?" Enquires Verdor eagerly.

"The patch is in place but don't you think we should wait for the results?"

"Why? Do you have any reason to believe this is not the plague?" Jak's heart begins to pound as he waits for Destril's reply.

"It's very difficult to say in these early stages…"

"Just tell us." Verdor urges.

"There do seem to be a few anomalies but it's impossible to say anything for sure until the results come through."

Jak can see that the doctor is unwilling to commit himself but hope surges through him and as Zerrin's hand is conveniently near he clasps it briefly.

"There is no point in waiting, whatever the results; it's still only three days before we arrive at Zennan and we've got to stop this ship." States Verdor with finality. There is a murmur of assent but Jak has that niggling feeling when he sees his father beckon Nuttle over.

Nuttle is able to work on the firewall for precisely three

and a half minutes before a hoard of armed guards descends upon them. It is difficult to tell who's who with the breathing apparatus covering their faces but when the front man speaks his voice, though disguised, still emits a certain magnetism edged every now and then with shades of psychosis. His first act is to shatter the sickbay computer with a single blast from his firearm. Then he looks round slowly at them all.

"Do you want to hear the good news or the bad news first?" He asks. The uncomfortable silence stretches out. Thinking the question is rhetorical nobody speaks. But Norfax wants them to play his little game.

"Come on! The good news or the bad?"

"We'll take the good." Says Verdor repressively.

"And who might you be I wonder?" His tone is silky as he walks over to Verdor and looks him over insolently "I think I know." His voice explodes violently on the last word as he brings back the barrel of his gun and strikes Verdor across the side of his temple. Jak takes the inevitable, pointless, retaliatory steps forward only to be brought up short by the guards.

"OK." Continues Norfax affably as he swings back to face the others. "The good news is you're cured. Nobody is going to die of plague, isn't that great?" He waves a printout and hands it to Destril. "Just the common cold, there's no cure for it." He continues with mock regret. "But I'm afraid that is not the bad news." Jak swears their tormentor is smiling behind the mask.

"I thought it would be nice for all those of you, who

have never had the experience." He looks exaggeratedly from Verdor to Jak to Nuttle. "To be incarcerated on an uninhabitable planet and left to die. For those of you who are familiar with this approach to dealing with an annoying problem, don't worry, the tedium will be relieved via the knowledge that you have no food, I'll give you a little water to prolong the lesson." He turns as if to go and then looks back at their horrified faces. "By the way that was the bad news." He reaches his hand into a pocket of his jacket. "And here's something to lighten the last few days of your lives." He holds a phial in his gloved hand and waves it too and fro before their eyes. "All those holiday makers will be making the long trip home with a little extra something for their nation. Mmm what do you think? Good isn't it?" He laughs and the sound is as maniacal as his scheme.

"I don't understand." Says Jak to Destril after they have been hoarded by the guards into a life pod. "Why didn't he just kill us, why go to all this bother?"

"That's because you don't comprehend the psyche of a terrorist. For one thing it wouldn't be theatrical enough and for another you can't feel like a hero to the cause if you just out and execute little kids and women."

"But they're going to kill millions by releasing the plague on Zennan, how do they feel good about that?"

"They will surrender their own souls. They won't have to live with it on their conscience."

Jak can't imagine Flagor surrendering his soul.

“Still…” He continues, questioning Destril.“Why didn’t they dump us on Zennan?”

“I think Norfax was worried we might think of a way of stopping them so he’s got rid of us.”

“But why…?’

“Pack it in Jak.” Cuts in Zerrin her voice taut. “Can’t we just contemplate our demise without your continual jabbering.”

Jak looks down at her.

“Same old Zerrin.” He says gently. “As it happens I don’t want to contemplate my demise, but you’re right I should be thinking of a way of getting us out of this mess.”

“Same old Jak.” She returns softly, and there is a tenderness in her voice that makes Jak’s heart beat a little faster.

“I can’t believe Flagor has countenanced this. You wouldn’t think he’d leave his sister to die like this.”

“Humph.” Is Jak’s only response.

Jak stares out of the porthole across the pitted surface of the rock they have landed on. He has just had a struggle with Nuttle, who wanted to open the hatch and step out into the hostile atmosphere. It ended when the panic stricken cook was struck from behind with a blow from a fire extinguisher in Zerrin’s capable hands. It was starting to get really cold inside the pod.

"We have enough air to last about ten days, as long as the recirculator is efficient." Says Verdor emerging from behind a panel. Jak gazes at his father, they both know there won't be any lasting ten days.

Chapter 48
Eric To The Rescue

Well your Honour, I just think I'll remind your worshipfulness that we were stuck out on the silk planet and I don't think I've explained to you all the details of our daring escape."

"You are quite correct Mr Tor." Agrees the administrator."But keep it brief, if you please, as this omission is spoiling somewhat, the continuity of the narrative."

"Right, continuity your Honour, exactly. Well as I was saying, we were stuck there and for some unknown reason this guy whatsisname that you now have in custody, comes snooping around the silk swathes.

"That would be Disman Sir." Injects the adjutant.

"Yes thank you. Continue Mr Tor."

Eric throws the adjutant a rather threatening look before proceeding.

As I was saying before I was so rudely interrupted, this geezer lands on the planet. Well we just hangs back as you might say until he starts wandering off into the spider infested interior and we nips in and absconds, like we do best your honour with the little ship. It didn't seem like a minute before we were back home checking out the damage that b.... I beg your pardon your Honour.... that rascal had perpetrated on my property. Well I only stayed to pick up the wife and my little Bro. before setting about acquiring the Frigrittac. A mutual acquaintance of mine and Jak's who is in the scrap metal trade.,"

"That would be Peyto Banner Sir." The adjutant starts out bravely, but trails off a little towards the end of his piece of information as he encounters Eric's baleful stare.

Yes Peyto Banner your Honour, He told me after a little gentle persuasion where the boy was headed, it takes a while your Honour, as you know to get all the arrangements coordinated as you might say but we set of to Detagon as soon as we were able. Now when we arrived we were in time to see the Lazortrom leaving its dock in rather a bizarre manner if I might say so your Honour. Well anyway we kept out of reach until we might find out what was in the offing and we trailed the ship. After a bit of space boogieing and wandering about they set on a course for Zennan and we trailed her, keeping just out of range. About two days out of Zennan we see the pod. Heading straight for Lesser Jurra she was and so we sets our sights on picking up the passengers. We take a bead on the Lazortrom and head down for the surface.

"Thank you, Mr Tor that will be all."

"But your Honour I haven't finished yet."

"Yes, you have Mr Tor." Insists the administrator firmly. "We will continue with the help of the Narrator."

Jak hears the drone of an approaching shuttle. He rises from where he has been huddled against the cold. Who is it?

Beside him, Zerrin has also heard the sound and her face brightens as she tilts her head up.

"Flagor." She whispers. Jak stares at her, a suspicion is rekindled and it leaves him feeling much colder than he was before. The sensation lingers so that, even in the excitement as the others become aware of the shuttle overhead and they dare to believe in a rescue, a depression settles upon him.

He sees the shuttle through the porthole and as it lands in a swirl of dust he knows it is not from the Lazortrom.

"It's not Flagor." He says and watches for disappointment to register. Her little face is eager however as she squeezes beside him to look out and her vivid eyes probe the dust cloud expectantly.

"Who then?"

"I have no idea." He says quietly and he is not even looking out but down at the top of her bright head.

Zerrin allows Pal to squeeze in front of her and they watch the appendage snake out across the powdery ground towards the hatch of their pod. As soon as the appendage is attached they are hailed from the shuttle.

Jak recognises the gravelly voice and is stunned.

"Hulloo, this is Eric Tor currently of the Frigrittac.

Who the hell are you?"

Smiling, Jak takes the microphone from its place beside the hatch.

"Hi, Eric how you doing?"

"Jak! You little...what on Ecracon are you doing here?"

"What am I doing here, are you kidding me, what are you doing more like have you been raised from the dead?"

"Oh... that.... I'll tell you all about it. Is it safe to unseal the hatch?"

Jak looks across for confirmation to the doctor, who nods, Nuttle, fully recovered from his previous attempt, is already pulling the levers.

"Yup." Confirms Jak.

"Right... get your butt up here and tell me what the heck is going on."

In the noisy confusion of relief that swells the reception foyer Jak is greeted by Eric, his voice rises above the babble in hearty salutation.

"Jak! You son of a gun you look like the Crimmer troops have been tramping all over you."

"Yeah... something like."

"Introduce me to all your friends."

"First of all we've got to get after the Lazortrom."

"Wa-hey! He's only been on board five minutes and already he's trying to take over. I tell you this boy will go far, mark my words." He is shaking Verdor's hand and calling out to his adjutants instructions for the care of his guests. "Yes take this young man to the medic, he looks in a bad way, my word. Welcome to the Frigrittac, Eric Tor at you service as you might say. Yes and rustle up some victuals for our company, come on now, step to it. How do you do my dear?" He turns from Zerrin to Jak and asks very audibly. "Do they speak Kelti or what?"

"I'll be with you in a minute." He assures Zerrin, He catches her worried look as they are ushered away.

"What on Ecracon were you thinking of lad bringing all these Censites aboard?"

Jak looks sideways at Eric wondering whether to get uppity or not and concludes quite rapidly it would be fairly unreasonable in the circumstances.

"No need to take offence my boy." Says Eric as though reading his thoughts. "They're your friends and I'll treat 'em as such, only I hope we don't have no slitting of throats at midnight or any other such treachery while they are here.|"

"You're quite welcome to set your spies on them."

"Come now Jak no need to get in a mood. I dare say you never thought much of them either till you met up with that little filly."

"I beg your pardon." Says Jak his wrath rising.

"No need, no need, I can quite understand where you're coming from. Now what's all this about the Lazortrom?"

Jak bites back whatever retort wants to come and asks quickly after Sten.

"How's your Bro? Has there been much improvement? I've been wondering how he's getting on." He follows Eric along the corridor, firing question after question at him.

"Sten's fine, we'll talk of that later, didn't you have something important to tell me?"

Although Jak wants to know in more detail about the recuperation of his friend he dutifully turns his attention to the much wider issue of the imminent danger posed by those on his father's ship. He launches into his story as they make their way to the flight deck.

"Right." Says Eric after Jak has brought him up to date, it is his only comment for some few moments. They are already winging it after the hijacked vessel.

"We'll be up with her in eight or so hours, that's twenty six hours before she reaches Zennan airspace."

"Krey Roke you say." These are the first words since the

end of Jak's recital and the subsequent chase initiation and there is a martial glint in Eric's eyes, he broods for a moment and then slaps his knee.

"I've someone for you to meet! Dang if I didn't forget about it in all the excitement."

"I'd better check on the others first." Says Jak, wondering how they are doing and knowing they'll be worried about Norfax and his dastardly plot.

"Oh." Eric looks childishly disappointed at this reception of his treat. "Well, OK then you go ahead and I'll bring my little surprise to you in the dining hall. That's where your friends will be but I suggest you get washed and change your rags first. They'll all be spruced up by now and you don't want to give that little girl a disgust of you by turning up in all your dirt."

"Look, I wish you'd stop talking that kind of nonsense it only serves to embarrass everyone." Says Jak goaded.

"I'm not embarrassed Jak."

"Anyway she's certainly seen me like it before."

"Well it's up to you lad whatever you feel comfortable with."

So Jak decides to take a quick shower and change before reuniting with the others. He looks dubiously at the fancy suit Eric has provided for him but having no alternative dons it anyway.

As soon as he enters the dining area where the others are he realises his mistake. They have not indulged themselves as he has, but have stayed all the time in the dining hall awaiting anxiously his news when he returns. Fortunately, for some reason he still has Flagor's old duster coat flung over his arm. He supposes it must be an excess of love for that acquired garment that made him inadvertently pick it up as he left his quarters but he's jolly glad he did. Even so Zerrin catches sight of him as he enters the room and looks in astonishment at him in his borrowed raiment. He notices she does that depreciating act where she shimmies off into the background and tries to remain unobserved.

He is telling his father and the others the state of affairs as they now stand regarding the Lazortrom, when he hears Eric coughing and ahemming rather loudly at his elbow. He turns and there stands Sten beside the ever lovely Leela. She greets him with many kisses to the cheek and hangs upon his arm while he looks Sten over.

"How's it going old buddy?" He says quietly.

"Just peachy." Answers Sten. His voice is a little slurred Jak notices and when he looks into his eyes he realises his friend doesn't actually recognise him.

Sten smiles. "It's OK I've heard all about you."

"Great Pilton! I'm glad to see you up and about." Says Jak his voice a tad jagged at the edges. He reaches out and shakes hands, shy yet hearty with his old friend who doesn't remember him.

"Here let me introduce you…." He turns, but only finds

Verdor sitting there at the table; Eric, has ushered the others off . “This is my Dad…” Mmm awkward.

Verdor rises from his chair and shakes hands with Sten. “Nice to know you my boy.” He says and Jak envies him his smooth ambivalent greeting.

“Here, let’s have a coffee together.” Says Jak motioning to a waiter.

Verdor puts his hand on Jak’s shoulder.

“I’ll nip off and have a hose down.” He says and smiling farewell to Sten he is gone. Jak doesn’t know whether to be glad or sorry. Leela is the next to take her leave.

“Bye Hon.’” She strokes Sten’s hair smooth across his forehead. “And I’ll see you later.” She turns to Jak and kisses him once more on his cheek.

There is silence. Jak watches Leela leave, undulating her way between the tables, then turns back to Sten who is running fingers through his flattened hair. He grins at Jak.

“This is damned uncomfortable aint it?”

“Too right it is.” Jak says laconically but inside he feels a rush of joy. It is the same old Sten after all. The waiter arrives and they accept coffee from him.

“Why don’t you tell me what you’ve been playing at and why you’re wearing that pig awful suit that belongs to my Bro? I’ve got some gleamers you can borrow.”

Jak looks down ruefully at the suit. “I kinda like it.” He says. “It grows on you.”

"Not if I can help it." Says Sten promptly. "I should get it off before it takes you over."

Jak laughs and takes a sip of hot coffee.

"Tell me from the beginning." Says Sten seriously. "I'd like to know."

So the story comes tumbling out and it is not long before they are laughing together over the more macabre details. The narrative is almost complete and Sten has just been guffawing heartily in the place where Jak tries to sneak out of the sickbay and gets a smash in the face for his pains, Jak is feeling that area tenderly and Sten is wiping the tears of mirth from his eyes.

"So what about the girl?" He asks.

"What girl? I hardly mentioned a girl."

"OK." Says Sten, not prying but looking at Jak with a smile in his eyes.

"Has anyone seen Zerrin or Pal?"

Cass looks up as Jak pokes his head inside one of the smaller salons allocated to the rescued party.

"Er, No she was here earlier but then she flounced off to her room."

"What do you mean flounced?"

"You know she…flounced. She looked all uppity and moody and then she scowled at me and said she was going to sort out her luggage."

"Sort out her luggage?"

"I think it was an attempt at levity."

"Have you argued with her?" Says Jak sternly.

Cass looks hard at him "You're an idiot Jak." She concludes.

After discovering Zerrin's room number Jak makes his way there and stands a long time outside the door before knocking.

"Oh…hi." She says, and gives him a small sweet smile. Her hair is all straggly and wet from the shower and he notices that her eyelashes are matted together. The gentle glow of her violet eyes strikes him afresh. She is dressed in some kind of frock that is too large for her and he thinks she looks very young and vulnerable.

He realises that he has been standing some time without speaking. Her hand goes self-consciously to the borrowed dress.

"Hello." He says.

"Do you want to come in? Pal's here."

"Yeah sure."

He steps inside and looks around the spacious suite.

"So what do you think?" His gesture encompasses the room.

"Mmm it's gorgeous."

"Zerrin…." He turns to her and she looks up at him enquiringly. He doesn't know what it is he was going to say but Pal comes in from the little kitchen at the sound of his voice.

"Jak!" He walks up and shakes hands solemnly. "This ship is bounteous."

"It's a new word." Explains Zerrin and Jak wonders if the look on her face is one of relief. Was she glad they were interrupted before he could say anything?

"Do you want a sandwich?" Asks Pal hospitably and when Jak nods vaguely he drags him in to look at the kitchen. "Look at this stuff ." The little boy points out to him all the appliances and conveniences that Jak has used and taken for granted all his life. He mutters all the appropriate signs of admiration but his heart's not in it and he feels weirdly distracted. Eventually Pal turns to him and takes his hand.

"What's the matter Jak, are you worried about Norfax?"

"No….Well yes." Jak decides to grab the straw; after all he is worried about Norfax. "But it's all under control so there's nothing for either of you to be concerned about."

"What is going to happen to the Lazortrom?" Asks Zerrin.

"We'll be up with her in about six or so hours and then I suppose we'll take her out." He watches her face and wonders if she is thinking about Flagor. She says nothing and he amends his story.

"Eric will probably take prisoners first."

"That means a battle I guess. I hope no one gets hurt I'm sick of wounds and blood and death."

"Whose wounds and blood and death are you particularly thinking about?" Asks Jak trying to inject a note of flippancy into his voice but he looks at her intently feeling that he would really like to know the answer to that question. She just gazes at him with a little frown between her eyes and Jak, feeling gauche, shoves his fists into his pockets.

"Well are you coming to the party tonight?" He asks abruptly. He knows his voice is too loud and his timing is appalling, they've just been talking about death for goodness sake!

She looks at him quizzically. "The fate of the universe is hanging on a thread and they are arranging a party? That seems odd."

"It's a pirate ship my dear, they have a party every night."

"Is it? I didn't know that."

"This is a pirate ship!" Exclaims Pal in thrilled tones. "That's..that's.. bounteous." He hands Jak the limp sandwich he has prepared and some of the innards fall out on the immaculate floor.

"You could have used a plate." Says Zerrin in exasperated tones and she bends down to pick up the pieces.

"It's OK." Says Jak scooping them up and shoving

them back in. “The floors clean.” He catches the look of surprise on Zerrin’s face and wonders why he is being so gross. He takes an exaggerated bite out of the sandwich.

“MmmMmMmmm that is just too good.” He congratulates Pal.

“Can we go to the party Sis?”

“Will it be suitable?” She raises an eyebrow at Jak.

“For the first couple of hours yeah sure.”

“And how long will you stay?”

He grins at her. “I gotta leave at eight that’s when we expect to come up with the Lazortrom.”

Zerrin’s face becomes eager as she thinks about the party. “I would like to go. When I was a little girl…” She leans against the kitchen side and her eyes take on an ambient dreamy look as her thoughts drift away. Jak doesn’t remember seeing that particular look before. “We went to a party in a Marquee. It was before the plague and sure everyone was poor and displaced but things weren’t so bad. The Marquee was lit with lamps and there was this kind of yellow glow everywhere. My Mum and Dad were there and my older brother Torrin. It was sweet, you know, a family party and there were children dancing on a sawdust floor. I had a new dress…” Suddenly her eyes cloud over and Jak sees her look down at her borrowed gown. “Still I guess it won’t be like that and we could do with an early night.” She gives her little brother an apologetic pleading look. Pal turns to Jak.

"Yeah, I need an early night, I'm just a little kid and I've had far too much excitement these past few days." Zerrin clamps her hand over his mouth and laughs nervously.

Jak tousles the lad's hair wondering how he got to be so sharp. "Don't lay it on too thick." He warns.

There is an awkward few moments now while Jak wonders how he can sort this out without seeming officious; he knows how prickly she can be.

In the end he just leaves. "Right, well I better get going. I'll see you two…er… later."

He passes Eric in the corridor.

"Can I have the key to the store?" He asks him.

"Sure lad what department do you want?"

"Er…." Now this is embarrassing. "Umm…the womens section." He says it like it's a question and Eric looks at him narrowly for some time.

"The key." Prompts Jak eventually.

"Of course, right what am I thinking of I'll get it for you."

After some deliberation Jak gives the key to Leela. "Can you let the girls into the store?" He asks her. She doesn't say 'what girls?' in the obtuse fashion of some people he could name. She takes the key with a smile and turns to go. Jak lays hold of her arm. "Do it nice can you, they can be pretty touchy."

Later as he ambles up to the flight deck he ponders why, at a time when they should all be contemplating the possible destruction of the quadrant, they are all spending far too much time thinking about a stupid party. It must be association with Pretanox pirates that did it. It was their kind of mentality.

When he arrives in the ballroom the party is in full swing. His eyes sweep the room taking in the ribbons and balloons that adorn the great arches. There are couples swaying energetically on the dance floor. He would guess there are about 100 people present along with some children. He gives the hall another 360 degrees. He recognizes few faces but on catching sight of Sten he merely nods a salute and moves on. A few minutes more of this pointless search and he starts to get annoyed with himself. What kind of pathetic moron props up the wall at a party, slights his traumatised best friend and thinks about girls when the well-being of millions is at stake. He saunters over to Sten with a scowl on his face.

"Still hobbling mate." Greets Sten. "Are your feet giving you gip?"

"Nah just throbbing a bit." It is a good enough excuse for his petulance.

"Girls not here yet then?"

" Mmm…what girls?"

"Oh come off it Jak! Those gorgeous Censite girls, don't tell me you haven't noticed 'cos that I will not believe."

The hubbub in the room subsides almost imperceptibly and both young men quickly turn to look at the entrance. Eric is standing there enjoying the attention, Leela and Cass on either arm. Leela looks her usual seductive self in some kind of red off the shoulder number and Jak notices that Cass looks extremely pretty in silvery green that reflects the glow of her eyes but his glance flickers past her.

Where is that damn tiresome girl?

Immediately a couple of guys step up and after a few moments chat, one of them leads Cass off to dance.

"I don't suppose poor old Keenan stands a chance now." Observes Sten cynically.

Jak looks at him sharply. "How do you know about that?" He asks.

"Oh Zerrin and I were having a little chat this afternoon. I know all the histories now."

Damn! Thinks Jak. Sten's just the kind of guy girls go for. What with his tall darkness and his recent interesting illness…all those issues lurking there that females love. He glares with hostility at his friend.

Jak turns his attention to the fruit punch.

She is not coming then he thinks blankly. He spoons himself a tall glass of the ruby red liquid. For the second time the noise in the room abates and the music seems to take second place to a hush fallen on those at the entrance. Jak looks up slowly.

There she is on his fathers arm dressed in a robe of floating pale yellow silk. Jak is reminded of a place he's seen as a child, on a fresh dewy morning in a woodland glade, the mossy grass studded with flowers. If he had even a slightly educated acquaintance with flowers he would know he is thinking of primroses and violets. Her eyes meet his across the room and it is strange how muted the sounds and sights of the ballroom have become.

The still, breathless moment is broken by Sten.

"Good grief, I'm gonna get over there and ask her to dance before one of those other creeps snaffles her."

He jostles Jak in his hurry and Jak is left standing alone, his eyes have never moved from her face and as Sten and the other lads hone in he lifts his glass to salute her. She raises her chin a little and smiles at his homage, before she is lead off onto the dance floor.

He stares after her retreating figure. 'Look back at me.' He wills her but she is lost in the crowd of dancers.

Jak is called away soon after this. The Frigrittac is within range a little earlier than expected but by the time he reaches the bridge Eric Tor is there before him with bad news.

"She's not there Jak, we've made numerous sweeps and the damn thing has just disappeared." Eric is fiddling pointlessly with the controls as if some fine tuning will bring up the location of the Lazortrom.

"And yet we caught a glimpse of her earlier." There is

a slight edge of panic in Jak's voice as he thinks of the phial of destruction that has somehow eluded them.

We had better make some kind of systematic search." Suggests Verdor.

Chapter 49
Things Change

"We searched for five days your honour, absolutely nothing."

"It seems incredible to me that in all this time you were unable to contact the authorities Mr Tor."

"Well yes we couldn't believe it either could we Jak?"

"Really Mr Tor we cannot have you attempting to communicate with the accused."

"'The accused' what's wrong with you people? This boy's done nothing wrong. He's been hounded by one of your members I know that, and now you're continuing to harass him when all logical explanations for doing so are gone."

"I would ask you to kindly hold your tongue. You are in danger of being in contempt."

"I'm already in contempt your honour this court is a travesty."

"Remove the witness."

"Where is Krey Roke? That's what I want to know." Says Eric as he leaves the stand.

Krey Roke

My location is no concern of yours my dear fellow. Unlike you I have the forethought to make myself scarce when I find myself 'de trop.' Whilst you, however wily you may think yourself, very conveniently presented yourself to the authorities. Extremely unwise if I might be permitted to say so.

I dare say you've guessed precipitously that it was I who eradicated the universe of that nest of undesirables aboard the Lazortrom. (I thought at the time that I had destroyed them all, however now I believe there were some survivors.) Of course I will admit to being ill informed as to the occupants at that particular time. However now I find I am the Saviour of the twelve nations I must consider whether I enjoy wearing this mantle. It is amusing I grant you. Nevertheless after contemplation I do believe I would rather Jak Dane had been aboard. I know, perverse of me is it not? But you see I care very little for this part of the universe or should I say the inhabitants thereof and I really do not think it would have come as such a dreadful blow had they been destroyed by the indoela virus. Then I could have proceeded with my initial plan, as I really find I am not so enamoured with the compromise of a plan B. Still who would have been available to invest? How long now... You'll excuse me while I proceed with some small calculations.... Five months.... Seventy billion people.....mmm perhaps things are best this way. I will regroup and there will still be plenty of pigeons to pluck, if you will excuse such a crude expression.

Now damnably I find my thoughts reverting to Felice, that capricious beauty! Where has she disappeared to? I have had no communication from her for many weeks. Perhaps I shall toddle off to Detagon first and have a little look for her. No I had much better not. I have a healthy regard for my own safety and how humiliating to be captured in the pursuit of a recalcitrant woman.

"We must get to the Zophir outpost so we can contact the Crimmer Council." Jak's thoughts have reverted to the plight of the Censite people. He knows it is morbid but how many more people had died down on Detagon while they were chasing a ghost ship round the quadrant. "We've seen no reports on the BBc Uni watch, Nothing has happened. There is a limit to how long we can look for her."

"These Guys might have just nipped off somewhere to pluck up courage." Eric is reluctant to give up the chase.

"Well in that case we still must go to Zophir and get a warning off to the Crimmer they can do a better job of searching the quadrant than we can."

Eric looks aff ronted.

"I think we've done a damn fine job."

"Yes of course we have but we are still only one ship, they can send out an army."

"That's true." Concedes Eric. "But have you considered how long it will take us to reach Zophir. Anything could happen during that time."

It is true. Jak feels torn both ways. "Let's talk to Verdor, see what he reckons."

After talking and talking it over and, Jak feels, repeating the same arguments until he wants to blow his brains out, they eventually decide on The Zophir outpost. Relieved and exhausted Jak goes in search of Zerrin, hoping for some balm. He finds her in the garden hall seated at a table with Sten. Cass and Keenan are also there but he doesn't really notice them. He finds it incredibly irritating to find his two friends here.... together.

It seems to him that every time he wants to speak to Zerrin there Sten is, at her elbow, being a damn sight too attentive in his opinion. She turns at his approach with her usual sweet smile. He scowls down at her until the smile fades.

"Why Jak, how are you?" Her voice trembles a little, is she laughing at him?

"Yeah how's it going Bud, found the old bird yet?" This from Sten.

To Jak his comment seems so amazingly flippant that he can only put it down to the fact that Sten's damaged brain is not working properly yet.

"No." He says shortly. "You could always come up on deck and find out how the search is going."

"Bro. won't let me, says it's too stressful for the old fragile workings." Sten taps the side of his head.

"Humph." Is Jak's reply to this. All the eyes around the table look at him in startled reproach.

"I'll go and order some drinks from the booth." Offers Sten looking a little crestfallen. "What would you all like?" After all the orders have been given and Sten walks off to the booth, Zerrin turns on Jak.

"What's wrong with you Jak, how can you be so mean?"

Jak wants to say that trying to save the galaxy is stressing him out but although he feels a little light headed, in a fairly unpleasant kind of way, he is sane enough to know that a self consequential comment like that will make him sound even more of a jerk than he already does. Instead he just shrugs and begins to play with the sugar papers from their previous libations. Zerrin seems prickly and uncomfortable beside him and Jak counts the cups wondering how long they have been here, chatting cosily.

"Where is Pal?" He asks. "It's a big old ship to let a kid run loose you ought to keep him with you." He'd heard of lemmings that did this, just rushed straight for the cliff unable to stop themselves.

"Jak, it's nearly midnight! He's been asleep for three hours."

"So what are you doing up so late?"

"Well, I go to bed exactly when I feel like it." Her voice is low but trembles slightly with the control she's keeping over it. Her eyes are blazing and he stares into them. Here is the cliff edge and he sees the deep blue beckoning him.

"I don't like to see you hanging round with Sten so much."

In the background he can hear Cass' voice coming from a million miles away. "For goodness sake Jak."

Zerrin has jumped up. She doesn't speak straight away but he can hear her breath coming fast, He is aware of the pulse beating in her slender neck and fire in her eyes throwing showers of sparks his way.

"I won't say anything at the moment because it might be something I regret so I'll just say goodnight. Keenan, Cass, make my apologies to Sten." Her eyes never leave Jak and as she turns to go he sees them fill with tears.

"You'd better go after her Jak." Cass' voice is full of laughter. "This is better than watching a soap opera."

"Why did you do that Jak?" Asks Keenan mildly interested.

Jak groans and leans his hot forehead on his hands, pushing his fingers into his tousled hair until it hurts.

"Go on Jak." Urges Cass "Quick or Sten will get there before you."

Jak jerks upright but Sten is still at the counter and Cass' eyes are brimming over with mirth.

"There's something not quite right with you my dear." Observes Keenan appreciatively.

"Jak!" Continues Cass with mock urgency ignoring this affectionate comment.

"It's no good." Says Jak "I'd only make things worse; I'm in a hell of a mood tonight."

"You don't say! Let me congratulate you on hiding it so well."

"Well what's she up to? Has she been spending a lot of time with Sten?"

Cass is about to elucidate when Keenan digs her in the ribs.

"There's nothing going on Jak." Says Keenan, taking pity on him.

"I gotta turn in." Says Jak as Sten comes up with the drinks.

"Hey Jak you old dog you've scared the birds away." Accuses Sten. Jak eyes his friend. Why does he feel like punching him on the nose?

"You never used to be that interested in girls." Grumbles Jak.

"Didn't I?" Sten is astonished. "Must be the old 'messing with the mind' thing…knocked something into place, thank goodness."

Jak sits back down relaxing a little and taking one of the drinks.

“By the way did I tell you we’ve lost the Lazortrom?”

“Yes you said. How come?”

“I have no idea. We had her in our sights then she just slid off the edge of the universe.”

“Maybe the military took her out when she came into Zennan airspace.” Suggests Sten his mouth full of peanuts.

“It is possible but we’ve not heard anything on the BBc bulletin.”

“Mmmm, does seem weird.”

“Anyway we’re off now to the Zophir outpost to contact the Crimmer. All our contact lines are blocked at the moment as you know.”

“We have searched Mr Roke’s offices your Honour there is no sign of the communications network as displayed by the narrator.” Stabbard says portentously and looks knowingly first at the administrator and then around at the audience. His voice so meaningfully suggestive that Jak looks up quickly wondering what is coming.

The administrator sighs and closes the book that is in front of him with a strange kind of fi nality.

“You may submit the new evidence.” He says gravely Jak’s lawyer lunges to his feet.

"Your honour I protest, this was not in the bundle!"

"A request has been made to submit new evidence and upon careful consideration, has been accepted."

"But your Honour, oughtn't I to have been informed."

"You are being informed Mr Releau. Now kindly remain seated and do not disrupt this court."

Jak's Lawyer seats himself reluctantly, he turns to Jak and whispers. "I don't know what they're up to this is highly irregular."

A film of Krey Roke's apartment is now shown to the viewers. The secret inner office now has a very prosaic door leading to it and is furnished as a conference room with no trace of the former illicit activities present. As Jak watches this inane piece of footage the temperature in the auditorium seems to escalate and the wide-open space becomes suddenly airless, he feels uncomfortable and shifts in his seat.

"For goodness sake sit still and act surprised, the cameras are watching you." Hisses his lawyer urgently.

'Act surprised?' Jak is nothing but, even so his eyes flicker to the camera.

"Your Honour without making any assumptions we would like to call Doctor Strivit Hogar to the stand."

"Dr Hogar you are a doctor of psychology is that correct?"

"Yes."

"Would you please explain to the court and the viewers at home your field of expertise."

"Yes. I am an expert on schizophrenia and paranoid delusion."

"And could you explain in simple terms what kind of mental illnesses you would encounter"

"I have seen many cases where a patient would construct in his mind a complex series of events or shall we say an alternate reality..."

Chapter 50
Pal

Zerrin has been crying again. I can tell of course because her eyes are red and puffy but also because she puts on this phoney cheerfulness which I hate; why can't she just be honestly miserable? I would join her and it would be much more comfortable. She is permitted to go to the court hall every day. I am not allowed because I'm underage.... but I don't know why she goes she always comes back crying. I watch it on the screen.

The lady, Mrs Koop who is our warder and is quite nice, showed me how to use the TV and find the right channel. Jak used to be on Channel One but that was when they were using the monitor recordings. Now they've said they are unreliable and can't be admitted as evidence. In fact they're saying they never should have been used because the tag was inserted one day when Jak was at the dentist for the express purpose of monitoring his friendship with Sten Tor, the Pretanox brother of a master criminal and should not be used for any other eventuality. Now does that sound a bit on the off side of on to you? 'Cos it does to me. So now apparently it is just an ordinary court case and won't be judged by the public. Now it's on Channel 57. It's since then that Zerrin's been most upset. Before that, some days she used to come back happy as a lark. She would sing, which was awful and we'd make pancakes in the little kitchen, which was nice. Those were the days when everyone knew Jak fancied her. Other days she'd be angry and then there was all this crying. I bet she's used twelve boxes of those nice soft tissues.

I liked the bits best when I was in them and Mrs Koop showed me how to replay them but I restricted myself to only one replay otherwise it would be a bit weird. I never showed Zerrin how to replay cos I was worried she'd play the soppy embarrassing bits over. Perhaps I ought to tell her now so she can cheer herself up but she probably wouldn't do it, she's funny like that.

They wanted to send me back with Cass and Keenan but Zerrin pleaded for me to stay. Apparently she's a material witness 'cos it was she that was with Jak when he drove the shuttle through the window at the Crimmer headquarters. I wish I'd been there and now I won't even see it on the monitor 'cos they've stopped playing it.

I must say I quite like it here although I do miss going outside but then nobody goes outside in Kelti town all the houses are inside this great big dome thing. It's pretty weird. I heard that Sten and Eric Tor live outside the dome I'd like to go and see them sometime but I haven't seen them in person since we were brought here. In fact I think Eric Tor is in prison now. You see that's another one of those things I don't understand. All of a sudden they're saying Eric Tor is a criminal and he's done this and that but surely they must have already known that before the sessions started.

Anyway now they're saying Jak's a nutter the whole things gone way off beam.

Today they talked about the day of the battle. I got myself some of those frosted ring thingies and cosied down to watch. The judge has got this giant hairball thing. I think it must be a wig 'cos I've never seen anyone with hair like it. He's got this trick of looking over his glasses at Jak so that he's actually looking down his long nose at the top of Jak's head. The long nose of the law I call it.

I don't really like the way Jak is handling it all. From the looks of him he's just closed off . I mean at first he did get raging angry and shouting and stuff but I can see that didn't do any good and when he threw himself at that phoney Doc. Phew! That was like… awesome. I suppose if you've got hoards of people saying you've lost your marbles it must be a bit difficult to act like a sane man. I can tell Jak is finding it very traumatic. When I see him just staring down at the desk like that I'm worried about him.

Anyway today they reckoned that the ships that attacked us at the beacon were not Krey Roke's private forces but were routine patrol troopers. They say they hailed us but we didn't respond. Now I was up on the flight deck at that particular time and I heard this guy saying that if we didn't back off he would blow us to smithereeens. He didn't use those exact words but a lot of high faluting ones that sounded a bit nonsensical to me. Anyhow I got the gist of it. Actually you don't need to speak the same language to know what was going on when a load of battleships start firing on you. It was pretty exciting I can tell you.

The session went much the same as always. Jak was some kind of psycho and everyone else was trying to help him. Poor Jak I don't think he's getting much of a kick out of it.

Then Zerrin came home with her eyes all red and started stroking my hair and sniffing. Then she made some kind of weird bake thing for tea. I couldn't eat it 'cos I reckon she left half the ingredients out and the top was on the black side of crispy. See and that's something else I don't understand she used to be able to cook… so what happened? Surely being upset doesn't suddenly make you incapable of throwing some lunch together does it? Anyway I don't think I can remember a time when Zerrin wasn't worried about something or other and we always ate pretty good; even when it was rat she roasted it to a turn. Oh well time goes by as they say.

"Are we going to go back to Detagon?" I asked her later. OK so it wasn't tactful but hey I gotta know these things. She just stared at me bleakly for a while then looked pathetic and started stroking my hair. Hell I wish we were back on Detagon at least she had a bit more pip then.

OK so yesterday I'd had a bad day and went to bed hungry that's bound to put a man in a bad mood. A man's gotta eat that's what I always say. Well the sessions where just as dire today. They talked about the day Zerrin and Jak flew the shuttle through the window of Bleatermans office in the Crimmer buildings and that's never going to look good for a man you're trying to prove is perfectly sane. But Mrs Koop brought us up a pie she'd made and Zerrin and me made custard. It was fantastic. It reminded me of the day we were at Cass' and Zerrin made the dinner. She made a lovely pie then with custard. I 'spose she was trying to impress Jak at that particular time. But he never noticed it. In fact I think he said no thanks! What an ungrateful bloke! I ate heaps of it though and that's what she ought to remember. He don't appreciate her like I do. I cram in everything she cooks, unless it's burnt of course.

So the trial is over. They are sending Jak to some kind of Nutters home. I don't know what's happened to Mr Dane. He could have told them that everything the monitor showed was real. You don't think they've paid him off do you? I can tell you it was a pretty terrible thing to watch our Jak while they read out the verdict. I wonder how Zerry will take it, she can't cry any more than she has done already. I wonder if they'll let us go and see him. Mind you I don't relish visiting a nut but Zerrin will want to go and I'll support her. What am I on about? Jak's as sane a man as goes around. But maybe all this has turned his brain! That would be hellish. There is good news though? I saw it on the TV that they've sent anti-whatsit down to Detagon. They showed some hospital in Gedd. I don't know where they found it 'cos I'm sure it don't exist. Well it was all sparkling white and new for one thing and there were people queuing for miles to get a jab. I never saw any Geddites queue like that. But I 'spose they must have made them stand to order and if a jab is gonna stop you getting plague you'd sort yourself out wouldn't you? I know I would. Then there was a lot of talk about the Jubilee preparations and it was like, yes, we really are going to get back to Cybertag formerly known as Census. Not that I know a lot about Cybertag formally known as Census but Zerrin does. Surely it will cheer her up. To find out we are going to be repatriated after all.

"Do you believe all the hype?" She smiled half pityingly at me. Yes, that's how she took the announcement that she was going back to her homeland.

"Yes I do." I replied stubbornly and I suppose jutting out my chin like people do when they know what they are saying is about to be disproved. "The Crimmer know all about it now."

"Pal." She sat down on the sofa beside me and took my face in her hands. It's the kind of manhandling I can't abide but one look at her tight face and I stayed put. "Jak put his faith in the Crimmer and look what they've done to him." There was no denying it, she was right there. After we'd eaten, I say 'we' very loosely, 'cos she spent all the time staring down at her plate. I can understand her lack of appetite but I'm afraid I'm too young to be that sensitive; anyway it was another of Mrs Koop's creations, a meat cobbler this time with thick, rich gravy oozing out from under the melt in your mouth topping. Irresistible!

"We've got to get him out of there." She said suddenly.

I said "Ug." With my mouth full. OK, so I don't always sound as intelligent as I am.

"You remember when the Uluru captured us, who rescued us?"

"Jak."

"And when I was drowned in the cavern pool, who saved me?"

"Jak."

"And the Fedek prison?"

"Yeah it was Jak, I think I'm getting the picture sis." Girls can be such retards sometimes.

"And the rayel pits?" She looked at me accusingly as if I'd forgotten it. I didn't like to mention to her that if it hadn't been for Jak we wouldn't have been caught up in all those adventures. Anyway in spirit I agreed with her. However she hadn't finished yet, she had some philosophical stuff up her sleeve.

"If it hadn't been for Jak we would still be mouldering away in that hovel on the side of Lawley mountain. He liberated us."

I didn't like to remind her that we were now locked in the house of detention.

I think she must have sensed my cynicism because she looked at me reproachfully.

"You would have died if he hadn't come, you were so sick."

"And I appreciate it, believe me."

"So why don't you want to go?"

Who said anything about not wanting to go? What was she on about? It was the dishonesty I had a problem with.

"Look Zerrin, why are you selling yourself short. We all three of us stood by each other all the way, and of course I want to rescue him, but why don't you just admit that you're pining away for him and that's why you want to set him free and quit going on about this 'I owe it to him' nonsense."

She looked at me a little shocked.

"I do admire him." She said slowly.

'Admire him' what a load of rot. I just raised an eyebrow at her; there was nothing more I could say.

"You're too young to understand." She said after twiddling with her hair and staring straight through me for a few minutes. What a cheek, fancy lashing out with an insult like that just because I had her in a corner. 'Too young to understand?' Utter rubbish.

Anyway the important thing was that we were going to break Jak out. She could disguise it as duty if she wanted to. I knew why I was doing it.

Chapter 51
Loose Ends

Krey Roke

I wonder if you have guessed? No of course not. How could you possibly deduce that I would show such a dearth of intellect? I must admit that I have astounded myself. I made an unforgivable error. When I saw the direction the trial was taking, I was tempted to return. I had been on my way to Cybertag, No, I must go further back than that for I don't think you completely understand… but yes I think…yes I have revealed that. My goodness, I really have taken a bad knock and I'm afraid it is affecting my lucidity. Ah yes, on my way to Cybertag, yes, feeling that to remain in this quadrant would be foolhardy in the extreme, but the damnable thing is my mind kept returning to Felice and her predilection for the society of the Censite scout. I wanted her back. I'm not sure why, probably just to punish her if I read my own character accurately, but as I say I'm not completely certain. Little did I think that it was a ruse. I was totally unprepared for the Crimmer council to act with such duplicity. Whether it was simply a ruse to capture me, or to deceive the public,

I don't know. I will not waste my time and yours in idle speculation. The fact is I'm incarcerated here with no prospect of imminent release. I wonder where that pestilent fellow, Jak Dane, is at this precise moment. My only consolation is that, he too, is imprisoned as I am.

The CIA (Crimmer Internal Affairs.) agent looks across the table at Jak.

"On behalf of the Crimmer Council I'd like to thank you for your cooperation."

Jak thinks back to the first time his lawyer had introduced him to Cherick. It was the day after Doctor Hogar had been called to the stand. What a dreadful time that had been. The worst part was when Jak had jumped the barrier and lunged himself at the Doctor. Without the rest, that was probably enough to convince the twelve nations that he had a screw loose. Afterwards he'd suffered the most awful night, filled to overflowing with bad dreams and dark premonitions. Then the next day, Cherick had come, accompanied by Verdor who Jak had not seen since the start of the trial. "He's in Hospital." They had kept saying to his enquiries. In fact he'd been worried lately that his father had taken a turn for the worse but there he was, seemingly healthy enough.

So it was going to be one big cover up.

"For the good of the Crimmer Council." Said Cherick.

Jack stared at him beligerently. "Why?"

"Well because we can't have the public running around thinking that its members are criminals it would bring the whole system down.

"And?" Persisted Jak stonily.

"Well you must see that that would be bad for the administration."

"So I've got to pretend to be a mental nutcase to save you embarrassment?"

"You wouldn't have to pretend Jak, just behave normally. They will believe anything we tell them."

"Rubbish." Said Jak uncertainly.

Cherick slapped a newspaper down on the desk. Jak read the headline with a tight knot in his stomach.

IT RUNS IN THE FAMILY …and there was a picture of his mother. She was looking wistfully at the camera, her straw coloured hair blown by the aerolator at forest dome 3. They had gone for a visit when Jak was two years old, of course he didn't remember it but he did remember the photograph. He turned shocked eyes to his father.

"How could you let them do this?" He asked in a whisper. Verdor stared back at his son. His face granite hard and his eyes not quite focusing on Jak's.

"You shouldn't blame your father Jak. We didn't ask his permission. In any case your father is in a slightly awkward position. I mean, nobody would listen to him anyway but if he did decide to kick up, the public would start to believe that he had been involved in the shipping of contaminated foodstuffs to Detagon causing the deaths of millions. Well actually er.., he was involved but, at the moment the public, believe he was a pawn. What though if they saw bank statements revealing large monthly instalments?"

Jak's shoulders sagged a little.

"That would be awful wouldn't it?" Said Cherick sympathetically. He paused for a moment watching Jak's face then continued.

"I tell you something else that would be awful; if your Censite friends were banned from going back to Cybertag at the jubilee, you know, because of their involvement in the storming of the Crimmer Buildings. Imagine their disappointment." He shook his head in a melancholy way.

"But what about the other witnesses?" Asked Jak his voice cracked and harsh, he hardly recognized it as his own.

"Oh, really Jak, I'm surprised at you, and they told me you were a bright boy. Think about it. Eric Tor, a criminal. Mort whatsit, a criminal. Peyto Banner, Maloa Alloy, all criminals Jak, your friends, Censites. Do you get the picture Jak? Nobody will give them any credence. We can say what we like about them.

Jak stared down at his hands on the desktop.

"Why did you let the trial go on for so long? The Monitor showed Krey Roke was implicated from when I broke into his office. He asked after a few moments.

"Oh that would have been easy for us to contain it was only when he attacked you at the outpost that things started to look bad."

"And you'll let me go?" Jak found it hard to believe. "How can you do that? After all the whole of The Twelve know I drove a pod into the Crimmer buildings."

"Details, Jak Details, everything will be arranged you don't have to worry about any of that."

"But…."

"Look Jak you don't really have any choice." Said Cherick gently. "And we will be very generous; you can have anything you want."

"What about Dad?" Jak looked again at his father.

"He'll be fine, reinstated to his former position as a volunteer for the Crimmer he'll have his ship restored to him… everything will be back to normal."

"Your kidding me right?" Jak's anger flashed up again at Cherick's flippant words. He felt a touch on his sleeve; it was his father's hand steadying him. He shifted uncomfortably in his seat but when he spoke again his voice was calm.

"I don't think my father will want to work for Straiff, will you Dad?"

"Straiff is finished but don't worry Mr. Dane we will see you right." Cherick's voice had regained its former sympathetic concern as he adjusted to his mistake. "I assure you there will be lucrative government contracts coming your way. We will look after you both very well if you cooperate with us. Also your friends whether Censite or Pretanox will be dealt with most generously."

"O.K. I'd like to discuss this privately with my father."

"Sure take as long as you need I'll be waiting just outside." Cherick got up to leave but at the door he turned back.

"If you decide not to take us up on our offer we will arrange everything to our satisfaction anyway, you just won't benefit and nor will any of your friends so make it easy on us all will you."

Jak nodded and the agent went out leaving the door slightly ajar.

Jak turned to Verdor strangely reluctant to meet his eye.

"I'm sorry Dad." He apologized and reached out to grip his father's arm. Verdor was looking thinner and more tired than he had realised.

"What for?" Those were the first words he'd spoken since their greeting.

"I don't know…" Jak threw himself back into the chair,

"…being such a git just now for starters."

"Don't feel bad Jak , none of this is your fault."

" How have you been Dad you don't look so good?"

"I'm all right." Verdor lent forward and smiled warmly at his son. "These last couple of days have been a bit traumatic but I'll be fine I'm just glad to see you."

"Dad… where have you been all this time?"

"They've had me under guard. I've known for some time they were worried about the direction the trial was taking."

"It's turned into a right fiasco." Jak rubbed his eyebrow

distractedly.

"Jak you must accept their off er."

"But what about….?" Verdor interruped him by grabbing his hand.

"Accept it Jak don't worry about what's past. This," he picked up the newspaper and waved it towards Jakt "This is nothing compared to what you can get out of them…go for it Jak, make them pay."

Now as Jak looks down at the papers in his hands he realises that they have paid out…on everything he had asked for. He realies he doesn't care about the trial, the humiliation or the injustice of it all. His father is back on track with a government contract to take supplies out to Census and looking more himself every day. Cass, Keenan and Destril are back on Detagon making preparations for the Jubilee. Eric Tor had been pardoned and he, Leela and Sten were back in Clancy town probably up to their old tricks.

Now all he can think about is one thing.

"Where are they?" He asks the agent.

"Who?"

"Zerrin and Pal of course."

"They are at the docking station waiting to be deported."

"What?"

"They were caught at the west portal, something about trying to rescue you from the Jolkat institution. Poor kids thought you were incarcerated down there. If you hurry you'll catch them.

Jak is off in a flash and Cherick has to run after him.

"Hey! You'll need these." Jak hardly stops as the agent hands him more papers. "Those are their release documents." He calls out.

Jak sees Zerrin sitting tiny and forlorn between two securitor guards in the terminal hall. He sees her from right over the other side and wends his way through the crush of people.

About halfway across she looks up and sees him coming. She half rises but the guard lays a restraining hand on her arm. There is something in her eyes that he can't quite fathom and as he approaches he feels he must search their depths. Without looking at the guard Jak hands him the release documents, after a moment he and his colleague melt into the background and Zerrin rises slowly to her feet.

"Where's Pal?" He asks her.

"The guard took him off for some fish and chips." She says staring up at him and after a moment "I wasn't hungry." She finishes lamely.

"Why did you do it?" Jak asks eventually.

"What?" She swallows nervously and her voice is a little breathless.

"Risk everything."

"Everything?" She whispers questioningly.

"Yes, your chance of repatriation."

"I didn't know that's what I was doing." Her usually steady gaze wavers and she drops her eyes to the floor. There is a sweet wrapper there that seems to engage her attention and she begins to nudge at it with her foot.

Jak looks down at the top of her head a faint smile playing about his lips.

"Look at me." He says softly.

She raises her eyes with some difficulty to his face and he notices the delicate tinge of colour rising in her cheeks.

"Why did you do it?" He insists.

“Because I….because you see I….” She falters and he takes her fluttering hand in his.

“I couldn’t bear to think of you in that place Jak.” And as she lifts her eyes briefly to his he sees them swimming with tears. He lifts her hand and brushes her fingers with his lips.

“I’m taking you home Zerrin.” He says.

She doesn’t say anything and he feels a moment of uncertainty. He puts his hand in his pocket and his fingers close round the deeds that lay there. The deeds are for the luxurious house that had caught his eye in Krey Roke’s secret domain, all those weeks ago before he had even met her. He wanted to give it to her but not quite yet.

“Will you come?”

“I do believe I would go anywhere with you Jak Dane.” She says and her voice trembles.

When Pal comes back he is quite surprised to see Jak… but more particularly shocked to see him kissing his sister, quite roughly, in the middle of the terminal…..

The End

Lightning Source UK Ltd.
Milton Keynes UK
24 November 2010

163346UK00001B/1/P

9 781452 024042